SCALPEL

Less than twenty minutes later Dean Lynch started up his car. As he did two security men were breaking open the door into the laboratory. And as Lynch eased his BMW out along the ramps and down to the exit, Mary Dwyer's lifeless eyes stared back at Pat O'Hara, night security officer. 'Jesus Christ,' he muttered as he staggered backwards. 'Jesus Christ. Jim, call the cops! Quickly! Call the cops!

For Dublin's Central Maternity Hospital the nightmare had begun.

The cages were starting to rattle.

Paul Carson is a doctor based in South Dublin where he runs an Asthma and Allergy clinic for children. He has published a number of health books, two children's books and, as well as writing regularly for various medical journals, he is on the editorial board of *Modern Medicine of Ireland*. Dr Carson is married and has two children.

D1494428

SCALPEL

Paul Carson

ARROW

Published in the United Kingdom in 1998 by
Arrow Books

5 7 9 10 8 6 4

Copyright © Paul Carson 1997

First published in the United Kingdom in 1997 by William Heinemann

Arrow Books
Random House UK Ltd
20 Vauxhall Bridge Road, London SW1V 2SA

Random House Australia (Pty) Limited
20 Alfred Street, Milsons Point, Sydney
New South Wales 2061, Australia

Random House New Zealand Limited
18 Poland Road, Glenfield
Auckland 10, New Zealand

Random House South Africa (Pty) Limited
Endulini, 5a Jubilee Road, Parktown 2193, South Africa

Random House UK Limited Reg. No. 954009

A CIP catalogue record for this book
is available from the British Library

Papers used by Random House UK Limited
are natural, recyclable products made from wood grown in
sustainable forests. The manufacturing processes conform to
the environmental regulations of the country of origin

Printed and bound in Great Britain by
Mackays of Chatham PLC, Chatham, Kent

ISBN 0 7493 2447 3

To My Wife Jean

Acknowledgements

Many people helped with this book by checking the various medical and legal details. Others helped by explaining operational procedures within the Garda Siochana, Ireland's largely unarmed police force. My thanks are due to Dr John ('Jack') Harbison, Professor of Forensic Medicine, RCSI, and State Pathologist for the Republic of Ireland; Dr Barry Gaughan, consultant Obstetrician and Gynaecologist at the Rotunda and Beaumount hospitals in Dublin; Professor Tom Matthews, consultant Paediatrician at the Rotunda Hospital and Children's Hospital, Temple Street, Dublin and Mr John Hyland, consultant Surgeon, St Vincent's Hospital, Dublin. Ms Feena Field of the Blackrock Clinic laboratory explained procedures in a hospital laboratory.

Stephen Rae is crime correspondent for the Independent group of newspapers in Ireland and provided much valuable information and insight into Dublin crime and the workings of the Garda Siochana. Ronnie Lynam, Solicitor with Partners at Law, Dun Laoghaire corrected legal inaccuracies. A number of serving members of the Garda Siochana advised on investigative procedures within the force. They wish to remain anonymous, but they know who they are and I am grateful to them for their assistance.

To all, may I offer my sincerest thanks and gratitude for their time, information and extraordinary patience.

Paul Carson
Dublin, September 1996

Prologue

8.45 pm, Monday, 3rd February 1997
Public phone booth, Molesworth Street, Dublin

'Hullo?'

'I want to speak to John.'

Pause. Breathing clearly heard over the line.

'This is John speaking.' Cautious. Wary.

'Hello John. This is Bobby.'

Grunt of recognition.

'Hi there, Bobby boy, how are you?' Oily, greasy. Slick Cockney.

'I'll be in London on Friday twenty-first, arriving at eleven fifteen in the morning.'

'That's nice, Bobby boy.'

'I'd like to place an order for collection that day.'

'It's a good time to buy, Bobby boy. Some things are coming down in price. Want your usual?'

'Yes.'

'That's no problem, Bobby boy.'

'I'll call you as usual.'

'As usual.'

Pause on this end now.

'Can you get me a girl?'

Sharp breath. Clicking of teeth, tut-tutting.

'Oh, that's gonna be difficult, Bobby boy. We had a lotta complaints from the last girl.'

No response.

'You hurt her. You hurt her a lot, Bobby boy. You know that, don't you?'

1

Pause.

Then: 'Can you get me a girl?' Firm, pressing. Cut the crap.

Grunt. More clicking of teeth.

'I'll have to go outside for one, Bobby boy. That means it'll cost you.'

'How much?'

No pause.

'Five hundred. Per night. And if you rough her up that's it for good. Never again. You understand? You make a mess of this one and never again. You understand?'

Angry. Slickness gone.

No pause.

'No problem. I understand.'

'No hard feelings, Bobby boy. Business is business.'

No more tut-tutting. Just business. Terms agreed.

'Call me as usual?'

'I'll call you as usual.'

'See you soon, Bobby boy.'

Click.

He placed the handset down slowly. The frost from his breath misted up the receiver and call box windows. He pulled his overcoat up, tugging tightly on the lapels at the front before walking out into the cold night air. He looked neither left nor right; careful, purposeful strides away from the phone booth. As he made his way back towards the crowded streets he peeled off the protective gloves he had been wearing. The first he pushed into a used McDonald's chip bag he had in one pocket before dropping it into a wastepaper bin. The second he kept for nearly another ten minutes before it too was stuffed into another McDonald's bag and dropped into a different bin.

Like everything he did in life, he was efficient and exact. Clinically precise.

Reporting on the official government enquiry held to investigate the events that follow, one newspaper headline captured the public mood:

'11 DAYS THAT ROCKED A NATION!'

Monday, 10th February 1997, marked the beginning.

Day 1

The foetal heart rate dropped again.

June Morrison, sister in charge of labour ward three, frowned and walked quickly to the monitor screen and pressed a button. The current foetal heart rate cleared and was replaced with the previous three minutes' graph. The rate had been steady, no blips at all. She flicked back to the current rate and gave an inward sigh of relief. The heart rate had climbed back again to normal.

'Is everything okay Sister?'

Morrison turned around and smiled to the young woman lying in the bed behind her.

'Yes, don't worry pet. Everything's going really well. Your baby's doing just fine. How are you feeling?'

Sandra O'Brien placed both hands behind her in the bed and tried to push herself into a more comfortable position. She licked her lips and pulled a face as she tasted again the chalky antacid that had dried there. With a deep sigh she lay back on the mound of pillows and ran her open palms along her heavily pregnant stomach. 'God, I'll be glad when this is all over,' she groaned.

Morrison gave a little laugh. 'We're nowhere near the end. You'll have to hang in there.' She adjusted the CTG belt around Sandra where it had come loose. 'You'll have to keep still or this belt will slip off altogether.'

'Do I have to keep it on all the time?' Sandra moaned.

'I'm afraid so. It gives us a clear picture of how O'Brien

5

junior is progressing and how he is adjusting to his entry into the world.'

And what an entry, she thought to herself as she looked again around the room. There were no fewer than three foetal scanners, one beside the other on a specially assembled rack. Harry O'Brien had insisted on three in case the first or even the second should blow a fuse.

'Mr O'Brien,' Morrison informed him starchly when he'd finally choosen the suite for his baby to be born in, 'never once have we had to replace a foetal monitor during a labour. They are checked regularly to make sure such an event does not happen.' She thought she had been firm, making her position clear. She was staking out her territory. This is my playing field, Mr Big Shot. These are my rules. This is not the boardroom of the O'Brien Corporation.

Harry O'Brien listened politely, taking in every word as she gave him a guided tour of the private room and adjoining delivery suite where his young wife would lie. He fixed Morrison with a rheumy eye and placed an arm across her shoulders.

'Sister, I'm sure you're right. I'm sure there's never been a faulty scanner in this great institution of yours. But Sister, let me tell you one thing I know that you don't.'

She moved away from his over familiar gesture and turned to look at him, face to face. His eyes were now hard, cold.

'We make most of the stuff that you guys rely on in this place and I know the quality of the workmanship in some of our plants. So I'm telling *you*. I want at least two back-ups and I want only new equipment used wherever my wife goes. So you can replace things like that,' he pointed distastefully at a suction machine in the corner of the room, 'and that,' he nodded at the slightly bent IV set fixed to the bedrail.

Morrison had protested long and hard, to O'Brien himself and finally to Luke Conway, the Master of the maternity hospital. Conway and she had been close friends for years and she had watched him progress from junior doctor to registrar and finally, after eight years' extra training in

Canada, to consultant. Conway was possibly the only one in the hospital who knew more than Morrison about labour and the safe delivery of babies. His eventual promotion to Master, medical and administrative head of the hospital, was a fitting tribute to his skills and knowledge.

'Luke,' she complained angrily after O'Brien's visit, 'that bastard's treating this place like one of his corporation power plays. He wants to actually take over ... Jesus, can you believe it? ... he wants to actually take over room three and the delivery suite for a whole month. He says he's going to get the frigging room decorated again and replace every frigging piece of equipment!' She could barely contain her anger. 'I mean, really now Luke, this is going to be a frigging media circus, not a birth.'

Conway sat across the table from her in his office, listening to her anger grow. He brushed a nonexistent piece of fluff off his jacket sleeve and straightened his bow tie when she finished. A tall and graceful man, he exuded confidence and stability, a man at ease with his position in life. He always dressed soberly, usually in a pinstripe suit with crisp white shirt and bow tie. Like most gynaecologists he found traditional long ties interfered with his manipulations during intimate examinations. He reached across and took both Morrison's hands in his own and held them gently. For a moment he said nothing and just stared at the large, strangely rough hands now held in his own. How many babies have been eased into the world by those hands, he thought briefly to himself. He looked up to find Morrison staring at him in surprise.

'June,' he said, not letting her hands go, 'June, every word you say is absolutely true and I'm embarrassed I ever got the hospital into this situation. But you know the background and the current state of the hospital finances.'

Morrison groaned and pulled away. 'Stuff the frigging background and hospital finances,' she muttered.

'It's easy for you to say that,' continued Conway, 'but I have to deal with the situation as it exists. Sandra O'Brien only became pregnant thanks to the success of our developing IVF programme. Harry O'Brien is over the moon. He's been hoping for years to have children after that car crash. You know, as well as I do, how much this pregnancy means to him.' He studied Morrison's face carefully to see how she was taking all this. He didn't want to get on the wrong side of her. The hospital board had chosen her to oversee Sandra O'Brien's antenatal classes and early-labour care. The hospital had a huge financial stake in the safe delivery of Harry O'Brien's baby, two million pounds to be exact.

With no sign of a pregnancy after a year of marriage, Sandra O'Brien had decided to seek medical help. She was found to have blockage in both her fallopian tubes following a severe infection in her early twenties. Despite a number of surgical attempts to correct the problem the chance of a baby by natural methods was remote. So Harry O'Brien intervened in the only way he knew how, with money.

'Give me a child and I'll make sure the O'Brien Corporation marks the event,' he said to Luke Conway one morning after listening to him explain the options on achieving a pregnancy by IVF, in vitro fertilisation. With this procedure Sandra and Harry could have their baby conceived outside the womb in the hospital laboratory and then the embryo transferred back inside her body.

'That's very kind of you, Mr O'Brien,' replied Conway, wondering what exactly he had in mind. 'But we'll not rush into anything just yet. Maybe Sandra should wait another few months before she makes up her mind?'

'How does two million pounds sound? Deliver me a healthy baby and I'll organise two million pounds, no sweat.'

Luke Conway reached for the telephone. 'We'll start tomorrow.'

After three failed attempts a viable embryo was finally created in a Petri dish and successfully transferred to Sandra O'Brien's womb where it took a firm hold on life and began to develop into a normal foetus.

Throughout it all Luke Conway took a special interest in

the pregnancy, going that extra mile to keep the big man happy and protect the hospital's stake. 'There's no one more competent or experienced than June Morrison,' he'd told Harry O'Brien one day as the big man checked on progress and plans. 'We have never ... *never* ... lost a baby under her care in all her years here and, boy, has she dealt with some difficult cases.'

O'Brien had listened carefully, his private medical adviser beside him.

'If she's as good as you say, then book her. Clear all her other work and cancel her holidays. I don't want Sandra going into labour when Morrison's sunning her ass in Tenerife.'

Conway laughed politely at O'Brien's rare attempt at humour.

'Put her on a double-wage bonus and tell her there's an extra grand, in cash, when it's all over.'

Conway pretended to take all this in his stride.

'There'll be no need for such a gesture, Mr O'Brien,' he replied evenly, keeping eye-to-eye contact with O'Brien throughout. 'The staff here do their duty to the best of their abilities no matter whether the patients are public or private, rich or poor. I know that Sister Morrison will take good care of Sandra.'

O'Brien leaned back heavily in his chair and rested both hands on the desk in front of him. His big frame filled the chair. He sighed deeply, then ran a hand through his mass of now grey hair.

'Dr Conway, I don't want Sister Morrison to take good care of my wife and child.' He leaned forward suddenly and almost spat the words out. 'I want her to take *excellent* care of them!' Even Conway was taken aback by his aggression. 'If this hospital wants to get back on some sort of sound financial footing and build that new wing then make sure my wife gets the best of care. And I mean the best, nothing less.'

Conway never revealed the details of this conversation to anyone, certainly not to June Morrison. But she soon found her holiday plans rearranged without explanation and work schedules changed to free up her time. She was moved from position of sister in charge of midwifery for public patients in East Wing and given sole responsibility for Sandra O'Brien's pregnancy, under the overall control of Dr Tom Morgan, Sandra's choice of obstetrician.

When the changes were announced, Morrison knew she had lost the battle with Harry O'Brien.

'Sister,' the voice sounded muffled. 'Sister, can you give me a hand up? My back's killing me.' Sandra O'Brien struggled awkwardly in the bed, trying to get some relief from the increasingly strong ache she was experiencing. Morrison moved behind her, both arms under her armpits, and lifted her into a higher position.

'God, what's happening?' Instinctively Sandra O'Brien's hands clutched her swollen stomach. 'What's going on?'

The movements inside the womb could be clearly seen, like a cat struggling inside a paper bag. It was as if the baby was fighting desperately to force a way out. Morrison quickly placed her own experienced hands over the swelling and felt the activity inside. There was a threshing, an unusual and ominous burst of frenzied activity. She quickly turned to the foetal monitor screen and felt the blood drain from her body. The heart rate had dipped again, this time down to sixty beats per minute, danger level. Just as suddenly as the frenzy inside Sandra O'Brien's womb started, it stopped. Morrison could feel little limbs ease and settle. She watched the screen all the time, urging the baby's heart rate to recover. Slowly but steadily it climbed back upwards. From sixty through seventy to eighty, where it seemed to pause for another agonising minute. Then, within seconds, it was one hundred and thirty and steady. The drama was over. She turned to Sandra to find a look of horror on her face. She smiled as reassuring a smile as she could and brushed a wisp of hair away from the young woman's face.

'Is . . . is everything all right, Sister?'

'Everything's fine, Sandra,' lied Morrison. 'Junior is preparing himself for the next stage.'

'When will Dr Morgan be back?'

Sandra's eyes betrayed her disquiet. Sister Morrison, her expression screamed, I'm sure you're a fine nurse but I'd like Dr Morgan here. Right now.

Morrison made a show of looking at her watch. 'He said he'd check in at twelve to see how things were progressing. We don't really expect you to deliver for a few hours yet. I'll give him a ring. He's in the house somewhere, probably doing his rounds.'

Dr Tom Morgan was something of a media star in Ireland and every woman's dream gynaecologist with his boyish good looks and air of casual confidence. He had a weekly TV slot, a radio phone-in programme and a Sunday newspaper column all dealing with 'women's problems'. It was common knowledge that Tom Morgan was the top fantasy man for every woman, aged sixteen to sixty, in Ireland. He had also been voted 'the man you would most like to get into bed' by the readers of Ireland's only gay magazine.

June Morrison tucked an edge of sheet under Sandra's behind and adjusted the CTG belt again. 'I'll just go and check where he is. Nurse Roche will sit with you until I'm back.' She smiled again. 'Don't worry, Sandra, everything's going to be fine.' She nodded towards the foetal monitor screen. 'Baby's heart rate is bang in the middle of normal. We're right on course for a safe delivery.'

Sandra's face relaxed and then a grimace slowly crossed her beautiful features. 'Oh God,' she moaned. 'Here comes another contraction.'

Morrison made her way quickly to the Sister's Office and closed the door. Out from the adjoining room came other labour-pain groans. For someone so experienced and with so many crises safely overcome in the past she found herself unexpectedly shaky and anxious. She picked up the internal phone and dialled switch.

'Pat, it's June Morrison from labour ward three, North

Wing. Will you page Dr Morgan and ask him to come up immediately.'

An icy hand gripped her heart when she heard the reply.

'Dr Morgan slipped out about half an hour ago. He said he could be contacted on his mobile phone. Do you want me to ring him?'

For the first time in almost fifteen years of midwifery June Morrison noticed her hands trembling. 'No, just give me the number, I'll contact him myself.' She scribbled the number on a pad as it was read out. 'Pat, just one more thing, who's on duty for emergencies?'

A rustle of paper came over the other end of the line. 'Dr Dean Lynch.'

She stared into the receiver for a whole minute before hanging up. Her mouth was dry and she could feel her heart pounding. 'Shit, shit, shit,' she muttered as she dialled.

Somewhere up in the satellite she could hear the digits clicking as the numbers were fed in. Then a mechanical voice interrupted, 'Your call is being diverted, please wait . . . Your call is being diverted, please wait.' There was a short pause, then a ringing tone.

Unexpectedly, a woman's voice answered. 'Hello?'

For a moment Morrison was confused and could hardly put two words together. Finally she burst out, 'Is Dr Tom Morgan there?' She could sense the phone being passed and then the familiar voice.

'Dr Morgan here.'

You bastard, Morgan, she almost screamed. You frigging bastard! But that would all have to come later. He shouldn't have been out of the hospital, and certainly not in the company of the woman whose voice was definitely not that of Mrs Tom Morgan.

Her voice was ice cold with controlled rage. 'Dr Morgan, this is Sister Morrison. I suggest you get back here immediately. We're in trouble with Sandra O'Brien. She may need an urgent section.'

She hung up before he could reply, imagining the panic

at the other end. She picked up the internal phone again and punched in three digits.

'Can I speak to Sister Mullan please? Tell her it's urgent. This is June Morrison in ward three.'

At the other end the phone was laid down and she could hear Mullan's name being called. Then came a shouted reply and the patter of feet hurrying across tiled flooring. The phone was snatched up.

'June? Hi, it's Breda here, what's up?'

'Breda, get a theatre ready for me as soon as you can and warn the duty anaesthetist he may be needed.' There was an urgency to her voice that came across clearly. 'Ring Paddy Holland down in paediatrics and put him on protective notice. Tell him we may have an urgent section for foetal distress.'

'Right.' Breda Mullan had known Morrison long enough to realise she didn't issue such orders lightly. She also knew by the tone of voice that something big was brewing. 'It's as good as done.'

'Just one more thing, Breda. It's the O'Brien girl we're dealing with.'

Morrison just heard the 'Oh my God!' before she replaced the receiver. She looked out the office window onto the streets below and the crawling traffic. It was raining. Umbrellas were being blown inside out in the wind and people were huddling in doorways, newspapers and bags over their heads for shelter. One word kept repeating itself in her mind and she mentally shook herself, as if trying to dislodge it.

Nightmare.

Nightmare, nightmare, nightmare. That's the way this was turning out. A nightmare.

Tom Morgan out whoring with his mistress leaving her with Dean Lynch as back-up. Dean Lynch, the one person in the world she knew would cause trouble if she had to call on him. She prayed she wouldn't need to.

Dr Dean Lynch, consultant obstetrician and gynaecologist, wouldn't exactly stand out in a crowd. Physically short at five foot five inches he at least had enough body weight to save him from looking totally insignificant. His once black hair was now mainly grey and combed severely from front hairline into a duck's tail at the back, accentuating his high forehead and pencil-thin eyebrows. His clothing was quiet to the point of being dull, which in turn matched his manner most of the time. The only noticeable physical feature in Dr Dean Lynch was his eyes. They unsettled those who worked with him, seeming to pierce their very souls. Few held his gaze for long.

He sat at his desk fiddling with paperclips, surveying the scene before him. Outside in a large waiting room sat rows of patients. To his right, about ten feet away at another desk, sat Dr Ali Sharif, his Egyptian registrar, while to his left and slightly closer at another desk, was Dr Donald Armstrong, his house officer. Behind them were three examination cubicles, separated from one another by curtains only. Dean Lynch dealt with most new patients, Dr Sharif with follow-up surgical and minor procedure cases while the house officer acted as general dogsbody, taking blood, filling in laboratory forms and waiting for a call from Lynch when anything of interest came in. Not that Lynch called him often. House officer to Dr Dean Lynch was one of the least sought after positions in the hospital. He examined every patient himself, always without a nurse in attendance despite hospital guidelines advising otherwise, and wrote up all his own lab tests and X-ray requests. He was meticulous in his note taking and almost obsessive in his selection of surgical material. Dr Sharif had long since abandoned attempts to be included in the major surgical cases on Lynch's theatre list. When Dean Lynch held his outpatients' clinic everyone knew better than to disturb him. He presided over these clinics like an overseer in a sweat shop, relishing the human misery that came his way, delighting in the female flesh. He passed all minor problems over to his registrar, concentrating only on the major conditions that might require operative intervention.

Dean Lynch was considered more than anything else a surgeon.

The nursing staff felt he had no bedside manner whatsoever, showing neither interest nor sympathy in the emotional feelings of his patients. June Morrison had once privately commented that the only time she felt Lynch looked happy was when operating. 'I'll swear he just loves to see his patients unconscious,' she'd confided to her colleague Breda Mullan. Morrison always cautioned the other girls who had to work with him. 'Never get on the wrong side of Dr Lynch,' she'd warned. 'Keep him happy, even if you have to frigging well go out of your way and it sticks in your craw. And whatever you do, don't upset him during an operation.' That was her way of protecting the staff in East Wing and at the same time keeping the theatre and maternity work moving smoothly. Despite Lynch's reputation no one could find fault with his work. He was reliable and punctual, careful and controlled. Unexciting and unpleasant, yes, but not unreliable.

'You can show the first patients in,' Lynch ordered without as much as acknowledging the nurse standing at his side. Massaging his throat, he scanned a referral letter from a local doctor and placed it on the edge of his desk. 'That one can go to Dr Sharif.' He picked up the next letter and read it quickly. 'Give him that one too.'

Dr Sharif looked at the nurse and they exchanged knowing glances.

Finally Lynch found one that interested him. 'I'll take this woman, thank you Nurse. Show her into my cubicle and ask her to undress.' He turned to his house officer. 'Donald, there are some reports from yesterday's theatre list in pathology. Would you mind popping down and getting them before we go up to the wards?'

Don Armstrong almost leapt from his seat, disappearing down the corridor past the hospital library, towards the laboratories. Anything was better than the endurance test of Dean Lynch's outpatient clinic.

'Right Nurse,' said Lynch, finally looking up, a thin smile breaking his usually dour expression. 'Let's begin then, shall we?' He slipped his right hand inside his trouser pocket and felt for the penicillin tablets he had placed there earlier. As soon as the nurse had her back to him he popped two into his mouth and swallowed them whole. His throat had been feeling raw for some days now and he had finally forged a prescription in a nonexistent patient's name for some antibiotics. Strangely they were not working as quickly as he had expected.

3

June Morrison returned to Sandra O'Brien and, without even looking at her, did an immediate print out of the foetal heart rate. It had dropped a little again, not dangerously so, but down certainly from a healthy one hundred and thirty beats per minute. She pressed the CTG scan printer and inspected the graph closely for further signs of distress.

'Everything okay?' she asked Nurse Roche, one of the best girls ever to train under her care.

'Yes Sister.' But something in the nurse's eyes warned Morrison that everything was very far from okay. 'Mrs O'Brien's observations are perfect, blood pressure one twenty over seventy, heart rate eighty-four and regular, urine clear and no sign of protein. She's getting regular contractions, three minutely and strong, lots of backache but no liquor draining yet.'

Morrison flicked her eyes very deliberately downwards at a CTG print out she held tightly in her left hand, all the time keeping her back to the pregnant woman who was listening closely to every word. Nurse Roche's expression betrayed alarm.

Morrison turned to Sandra. She couldn't even force a reassuring smile.

'Sandra, I'm going to examine you again to see how far you've progressed. Dr Morgan will be here soon and I want to be able to give him an up-to-date assessment.'

At the mention of Tom Morgan's name Sandra O' Brien

17

looked relieved and relaxed back in the bed. She ran her hands over her stomach again. 'Come on Gordon,' she muttered. 'Let's get a move on.'

Nurse Roche adjusted the pillows behind her. 'Is that what you're going to call the baby?'

Sandra looked up, trying to suppress the pain on her face as another contraction built up. 'Yeah. As soon as the ultrasound scan showed a boy, Harry insisted on calling him Gordon. That was the name of his little boy who died in the accident.'

June Morrison washed her hands thoroughly at the sink before slipping on a pair of sterile surgical gloves. She dipped her first two fingers into a tub of antiseptic examination cream on the bedside locker then gently lifted the white maternity smock that loosely covered Sandra O'Brien's stomach and upper legs.

'Just a gentle feel inside,' she murmured as her fingers entered the young woman's body.

Sandra drew in a deep breath. Nurse Roche took one of her hands and held it tight. 'Squeeze me if you feel any discomfort. It'll all be over in a moment.'

June Morrison's trained fingers explored the cervix, noting how much further it had dilated since the last examination, two hours earlier. It was thinning perfectly and she could feel the distinct soft, bulging sensation of forewaters pressing against her tips. The hard surface of the baby's head bounced slightly as she pressed upwards.

'Cervix eight centimetres dilated, forewaters bulging,' she reported. Nurse Roche recorded this in the labour progress chart. 'Pass me the Kocher forceps.'

Roche placed the chart on the rail at the foot of the bed and turned to open a sterile tray resting on a stainless steel trolley nearby. She picked up a long sealed slim packet, peeled it open and, without touching, dropped an instrument into Morrison's free hand.

Sandra O'Brien started deep breathing exercises, pressing her head back fully against the pillows. She gripped hard onto the bars of the bedhead behind her.

'You won't feel a thing here, Sandra,' Morrison reassured her as she gently slipped the forceps inside with her free hand. 'I'm just going to break the baby's waters.'

Nurse Roche took hold of one of Sandra's hands. 'Grip tightly,' she whispered into her right ear.

Then it happened again.

Sandra's pregnant stomach suddenly began to heave and ripple violently. The baby's threshing limbs punched out, clearly visible as her abdomen seemed to stretch to breaking point. For one, two, maybe three minutes, the heavily pregnant abdomen seethed and buckled with a frenzied activity. June Morrison stared at the foetal monitor screen as the heart rate initially rose slightly to one hundred and forty beats per minute and then steadily and inexorably began a slow decline. Nurse Roche looked on in horror.

'What's happening? For God's sake, what's happening?' Sandra O'Brien started screaming.

Just as Morrison was about to withdraw her examining fingers, Sandra O'Brien's forewaters broke.

'Oh, my God!' screamed Sandra. 'What's going on? For Christ's sake tell me what's going on?'

The heavily stained liquor poured out from inside the young woman's body. Instead of a clear, free flowing issue this was dark green, thick with meconium, a sign of severe foetal distress.

Sandra O'Brien's baby was in imminent danger of dying before he was born.

'Foetal distress!' Morrison's years of experience took over. She reached across to a red alert button situated above the bedhead and pressed it three times in rapid succession. Nurse Roche also moved into automatic pilot, disengaging the brakes holding the castors on the bed wheels and swinging the bed around swiftly and with a remarkable degree of accuracy so that the end pointed towards the door. Ignoring totally O'Brien's frightened pleas for help, Morrison and Roche had the bed through the door frame and into the corridor within seconds.

They rushed along towards a lift which had already risen

to the third floor and opened, and would remain open until the release button inside was engaged. Dublin's Central Maternity Hospital prided itself on its emergency procedures. In recent years they had become automated, tested, and re-tested to the highest level of performance. Once the bed was fully inside the lift, Roche engaged the release mechanism, punched in the code for the theatre level on the North Wing and watched as the doors glided shut in front of them.

Sandra O'Brien stared at June Morrison, a look of terror on her face. 'Is my baby going to be all right?' she sobbed.

Morrison took one of her hands and squeezed it tightly. 'You're baby's going to be just fine, Sandra, it's just that he needs to part company with you sooner than we thought. You're going to need a Caesarean section.'

Sandra O'Brien pulled the sheet up to her lips and bit into it deeply. 'Poor Harry,' she sobbed. 'Poor, poor Harry. He wants this baby so much.'

As another contraction cut in, Sandra O'Brien suddenly pulled June Morrison closer, her nails cutting into the other woman's arm. 'Don't let my baby die,' she pleaded through the pain. 'Don't let my baby die.'

Morrison and Roche glanced at each other, but said nothing.

It was now 11.48 am.

The piercing double alarm signal went off in three separate areas at the same time.

Over a welcome cup of coffee and cigarette in the staff canteen, Dr Don O'Callaghan, consultant anaesthetist, was reading the *Irish Times* and its predictions for the next Ireland versus England soccer match.

'Bugger it,' he muttered as he threw the paper down and rushed to the nearest red phone to dial central information.

Down in the paediatrics section of West Wing, Dr Paddy Holland was inserting an IV line into the scalp of a three-day-old baby when he too heard the emergency signal on his bleep. He grunted with satisfaction as he saw blood flow back along the line, confirming he had struck a vein.

'Strap that IV down securely, would you Nurse?' he murmured, holding the butterfly needle in place all the time lest the struggling baby would dislodge his best effort. As soon as a tape was secured he rushed to the nearest red phone and dialled.

Dean Lynch was writing an X-ray request when the alarm sounded on his bleep. Without stopping he lifted the phone beside him and contacted central information.

For all three men the details were the same, exactly as June Morrison had called them to the nurse in charge of central information when they reached theatre.

A twenty-eight-year-old primagravida, Sandra O'Brien, already in established labour needed an urgent Caesarean section for foetal distress. Her vital signs gave no cause for alarm, the blood pressure holding at one twenty over seventy, pulse rate up to one hundred and ten beats per minute, but this was put down to the panic she was now experiencing with the sudden change of events. Her urine had been consistently clear throughout the pregnancy and labour and she had shown no signs of toxaemia at any stage. There was only mild oedema of the hands and ankles, consistent with the usual fluid retention of many pregnancies.

By contrast her baby was distressed, in definite risk of imminent death. There had been dips in the foetal heart rate over the previous three hours but it had always recovered to normal. The CTG scan had started to show irregularities over the previous forty minutes only. However, at exactly 11.32 am, she had spontaneously ruptured her membranes, with heavy, dark-stained meconium draining. The baby's heart rate had also dipped at that point and was now hovering around sixty to sixty-six beats per minutes. There hadn't been time to clip an electrode to the foetal scalp to measure pH levels.

The consultant obstetrician in charge of this pregnancy and delivery could not be located.

For all three men this was all the information they needed to act on and act quickly. An unborn baby was in danger and only swift intervention would save his life. The speed of that intervention was vital, even a minute's delay might prove fatal.

Don O'Callaghan sprinted from the canteen, passed startled onlookers, and along the corridors that would take him to the theatre where Sandra O'Brien was now stationed. He almost knocked over an elderly nun shuffling along directly in his path and shouted a rushed 'sorry' over his shoulder.

Paddy Holland was in the Emergency Only lift within seconds, punching in the level he required on the dials. He knew if he was in the lift at that point no one could interrupt its steady passage upwards, the security code would not allow it to stop until the exact level requested had been reached.

Dean Lynch cursed all the way as he took the steps from his outpatients two at a time. For the fourth time in as many months he was on his way to the North Wing, the exclusively private section of the hospital and so different from the world he inhabited, East Wing with its grubby theatres, tatty corridors and shoddy paintwork. As Dean Lynch ran, he cursed silently but deeply, anger building up inside with every step.

At the same time as the three men converged on the operating theatre of North Wing a mobile phone clicked into action further down the corridor from the room into which Sandra O'Brien had just been whisked. Theo Dempsey, ex-Irish army sergeant and Harry O'Brien's minder, was beaming his message through the satellite directly to his boss at his North Wicklow mansion.

Big Harry had chosen to stay there while he awaited news of his wife's progress, no longer able to cope with the hospital atmosphere. He hated the smell of disinfectant, the muffled moans of women in labour and the incessant crying of newborn babies. He'd had to spend so much time there at the beginning of the IVF programme that the very sight of the front door made his stomach knot. Harry O'Brien was a man who liked to be in control and was most uneasy in any setting where he had to rely on someone else's judgement. When Sandra had suggested that he wait at home until it was closer to the time the baby was due, Big Harry readily agreed but still despatched Theo Dempsey to keep an eye on all developments, instructing him to make immediate contact when Tom Morgan or June Morrison gave the nod.

Within seconds of Dempsey's call, O'Brien was running through the house and out to his waiting chartered helicopter. The journey from North Wicklow to the improvised helipad in the hospital car park would take only thirty minutes.

Dean Lynch was scrubbing up alongside June Morrison who was going to assist at the operation. While she was at least three inches taller than Lynch and not easily intimidated, Morrison could barely bring herself to look at him.

'I'm sorry to call you, Dr Lynch,' she said through her face mask, trying to make herself heard above the running water and the noise of scrubbing brushes. She knew by the way Lynch had entered the theatre he was livid.

Lynch continued scrubbing, his eyes fixed on the brush as it swept across his nails, first one hand and then the next.

'She's one of Tom Morgan's patients but he wasn't in the house when the crisis arose. That's why we had to page you.'

Lynch still said nothing, not even acknowledging Morrison's presence. He spun around on his heels, still scrubbing, and observed the frantic scene.

Sandra O'Brien was lying on the operating table of Theatre Two, her eyes darting about like a frightened rabbit. All around her was activity.

Don O'Callaghan, the anaesthetist, already had an IV drip inserted into the back of her right hand and was checking his anaesthetic gases. His heavy paunch stretched his shirt to its limits and he had to hoist up his trousers every now and then to keep comfortable. He made a quick note in a chart clipped to the anaesthetic trolley beside the operating table, then took out his endotracheal tubes and sized them. He glanced quickly at Sandra O'Brien and selected one. With a spare syringe he injected air into a narrow tube connected to the endotracheal tube and grunted with satisfaction as the sides expanded. As soon as he had Sandra O'Brien asleep this would be inserted down her throat and into her windpipe, then insufflated so that a tight and full connection existed. That way the anaesthetic gases went straight to the lungs and did not seep around the edges of the tube that drove them there.

Breda Mullan was busying herself for the operation, now only minutes away. Already scrubbed up, she was counting sterile gauze swabs with a nurse assistant so that the number used during surgery would match exactly the number counted back again when everything was over. A different nurse passed by quickly, clutching two packs of blood. She hung them off the same rail that already held the saline IV.

Lynch spun back again and rinsed his hands thoroughly under the running water before knocking off the flow with an elbow. He reached for the sterile towel offered by another nurse without looking at her. As he dried his hands he tried to control his breathing, fighting to contain the rage building up. His throat was feeling especially uncomfortable and he swilled some saliva in his mouth and swallowed to try and lubricate the raw dryness.

'The patient is Sandra O'Brien,' interrupted Morrison again, hoping desperately to get him onside before the operation began. She didn't want him near Sandra O'Brien with the anger she sensed. The rapid breathing, the rage filled eyes and agitated hand movements warned her to tread carefully. She glanced around quickly to see if Tom Morgan had turned up but there was still no sign of him. 'You know the one I mean? Married to Harry O'Brien? O'Brien Corporation?'

Lynch threw the towel at the feet of the nurse who had offered it and took the sterile gloves she now peeled out. He slipped one on, then the other, and turned to look up at Morrison for the first time. She thought her heart would stop as his fierce eyes centred on her own.

'Sister Morrison,' he hissed through his mask, 'I don't give a fuck who she is. Why don't you just shut up and let's do it?' He walked away from the stainless steel wash sinks and stood slightly to the side of the operating table, eyes fixed on the swollen belly of Sandra O'Brien.

June Morrison and the nurse aide exchanged glances as the younger woman offered another set of sterile gloves. Their looks said it all. This was going to be an ordeal for everyone concerned.

It was now 12.06 pm.

Inside his helicopter Harry O'Brien was barking into a mobile phone, trying desperately to make out the faint signal coming back down the line. 'Jesus, Jesus Christ!' he screamed into the mouthpiece. 'What's going on?' But the roll of the chopper blades was too strong and drowned out the reply.

He flicked off the phone and stared ahead, stony faced, as the helicopter pulled off to the east and its descent towards the maternity hospital. If anything happens to this child, I'll kill. I swear I'll kill.

It was now 12.07 pm.

Inside Sandra O'Brien's womb her unborn son was struggling to survive. His heart rate was barely sixty beats a minute, his limbs were weakening. He was getting tired. The threshing movements had stopped and only the foetal monitor showed life still existed. Everyone in Operating Room Two kept checking that monitor and everyone was becoming more and more concerned. Time was running out.

Dean Lynch looked to Don O'Callaghan and nodded he was ready. O'Callaghan, a man nearing retirement and glad of that, nodded back. Lynch looked towards Paddy Holland who was standing by the paediatric resuscitation trolley. To his immediate right stood his senior registrar, a young female doctor with over six years' paediatric intensive care training, and to her right again a paediatric intensive care nurse. Holland acknowledged Lynch's nod. The team was ready.

Lynch turned to Don O'Callaghan. 'Let's do it,' he said.

All eyes focused on him as he stepped up onto a small foot stool beside the operating table to get a higher position. No one else needed such a lift, the stool usually reserved for some of the smaller nurses assisting at operations. As he swabbed and draped, June Morrison noticed his breathing settle, become much slower. His hand movements also relaxed. She looked up in time to see his eyes narrow to slits as he picked up the scalpel in readiness to carve into Sandra O'Brien's pregnant stomach.

The staff of Theatre Two braced themselves.

It was now 12.09 pm.

The blade entered her body in one decisive hand movement. From somewhere deep inside her almost totally anaesthetised brain, Sandra O'Brien screamed. The blade continued its downward sweep, from navel to pubis, opening up her belly and exposing the bulging muscle layers underneath. Dean Lynch felt her buckle with pain underneath the green drapes. Behind his face mask a smile flickered.

Don O'Callaghan noted her chewing on the endotracheal tube, head rocking slightly, and squirted extra pethidine down the IV line. He had barely had enough time to get Sandra O'Brien anaesthetised before Dean Lynch started his one stroke incision. O'Callaghan hated working with Lynch and always tried to keep one step ahead with adequate anaesthesia before the scalpel was used. But today Lynch was in total control, the urgency of the operation taking priority. Feeling the sweat run down his back, O'Callaghan began conferring with his anaesthetic nurse who was already checking Sandra O'Brien's pulse and blood pressure. He slipped a fresh plug of nicotine chewing gum into his mouth. Out of the corner of one eye he kept a close watch on the operation, noting the speed of the surgeon's hand movements.

Within one minute Lynch was through the outer and inner muscle layers and had exposed the thin lining of peritoneum covering the swollen womb beneath. He cut into and divided the peritoneum with a pair of blunt scissors and pushed it out of the way with a gauze swab. Two warm moist cloth packs were used to keep the exposed bowel at bay. Then, with careful but precise strokes of scalpel, he began cutting into the lower segment of Sandra O'Brien's womb.

By now, mercifully, she was totally anaesthetised, her writhing had ceased. With a grunt of satisfaction Lynch noted his scalpel finally paring through the womb muscle and exposing the membranes surrounding the baby inside.

'Suction,' he barked and June Morrison quickly had the stainless steel suction tube ready for the next stage.

It was now 12.16 pm.

Again using blunt scissors, Lynch ruptured the membranes. June Morrison sucked away the liquor that seeped out, careful not to block the operating view with her hand. Lynch dropped the scalpel onto a sterile tray, then turned to manoeuvre the baby inside the womb so that his face appeared through the artificial incision.

'Wrigley's forceps,' he barked again and they were in his hands within seconds. He inserted one blade through the gaping incision so that it slipped behind the baby's head and then, pressing slowly but firmly on the upper part of the womb, Lynch eased Gordon O'Brien's small but perfectly formed head into view and out through the opening.

Carefully and skilfully, he took the baby's head in both hands and started to lift him so that one shoulder, then the next became exposed and born. Within seconds Gordon O'Brien's body was taken from inside his mother and considered fully born into the outside world.

It was now 12.19 pm.

The baby lay for about five seconds in Lynch's gloved hands while his umbilical cord was clamped and cut.

'He's very flat,' grunted Lynch as he handed him over to Paddy Holland. 'Apgar of zero from where I stand.' The apgar score reflected the baby's dangerously poor condition. A healthy newborn baby, crying vigorously and moving all limbs, would ideally have an apgar score of eight to ten.

June Morrison felt her world crumbling as she watched. It looked like they had lost the baby. Her body trembled and shook and she tried to steady herself by gripping tighter on the retractor she was holding.

The blue-grey colour of the baby was a poor sign, as was his total lack of movement and zero respirations.

'Apgar score of one,' shouted Paddy Holland as he listened through a paediatric stethoscope for the baby's heart beat. 'Blue-grey colour, no respiratory effort, no response to stimulation, poor muscle tone.' He looked quickly at the theatre clock. '12.20 pm, heart rate of approximately fifty beats per minute.'

The drama had now switched to the paediatric team. Holding a paediatric laryngoscope in one hand, Paddy Holland inspected the baby's throat and upper windpipe. He took a fine bore plastic suction tube with his free hand and sucked away any mucus and fluid he could see blocking air entry into the lungs. Then, through a small endotracheal tube, he sucked mucus from further down in the windpipe. His registrar stood by with a small face mask connected to an air bag which in turn was connected to an oxygen cylinder. As soon as Holland was happy that nothing was blocking the free passage of air into the baby's lungs, the mask was placed over his face and he was artificially ventilated.

'12.21,' Holland shouted, after a quick glance at the clock again. 'Apgar still one.'

Each detail was being meticulously recorded by the neonatal intensive care nurse. All eyes were fixed on the tiny, lifeless baby, now lying on an open incubator with overhead heater.

Don O'Callaghan, Breda Mullan, June Morrison, the assistant nurse and the rest of the theatre staff were transfixed as they watched Paddy Holland trying to breathe life into him. Only Dean Lynch showed no interest in the battle for survival.

'Sister Morrison,' he snapped, 'would you pay attention to your patient. I'm trying to close her up and I find it extremely hard to work with everyone's attention elsewhere.'

30

Morrison and Mullan turned back quickly and stared into the opening in Sandra O'Brien's body. There was a lot of work to be done to close her up. A lot of layers of tissue, muscle and skin to be pulled and sutured together before her side of the operation was concluded successfully.

'Sister Mullan,' continued Lynch, relishing the tension and discomfort he had placed the nurses in, 'would you reach me a one chromic catgut? I'd like to get home before midnight if you don't mind.' He was obviously enjoying the power trip. Mullan and Morrison exchanged angry glances. They could sense his triumphant glee.

Then a tiny, fleeting whimper was heard. At first it seemed no more than a squeak, the faintest of whispers.

'Apgar up to four,' shouted Paddy Holland. 'Some grimacing, heart rate up to one hundred. Feeble attempts at spontaneous respiration.'

His registrar pushed a small plastic cannula into Gordon O'Brien's elbow vein to establish an IV line. The child winced. Then, almost as if furious with everything that had gone before and the sudden pain he was now feeling, Gordon O'Brien took a few spontaneous breaths and tried to cry. His first attempts were no more than gurgles, grunts at respiration. Then he seemed to draw himself up to his full weight with a deep breath and let out a piercing cry of pain. All activity in the theatre stopped, apart from the movements of Dean Lynch's hands as he sutured tissue together.

'Apgar five at seven minutes,' shouted Holland. 'It's now 12.29 and his apgar is up to five.' There was a collective sigh of relief throughout the theatre. After two or three more convulsive gasps and grunts Gordon O'Brien finally let out a prolonged strong and healthy cry. Two of the nurses clapped with delight and June Morrison felt tears welling up. She blinked furiously to keep her field of vision clear. Breda Mullan gave her a reassuring smile. They both couldn't resist taking a peek at the tiny arms and legs now threshing on the resuscitation trolley. The deathly blue-grey colour had been replaced with a pinkish glow as blood rich in oxygen flowed throughout his body.

'Apgar up to nine or ten,' shouted Holland triumphantly. 'Well done team. We've saved him.'

Only Dean Lynch kept his eyes firmly down, continuing his careful and painstaking closure of each layer of Sandra O'Brien's abdomen.

A figure suddenly appeared beside them, one hand holding a face mask over his mouth. 'What happened? What's going on? Is everything okay?' It was Tom Morgan.

At the sound of his voice Dean Lynch looked up sharply.

'Is she okay, Dean?' asked Morgan nervously.

Lynch turned back momentarily to his suturing. 'Cut,' he snapped and June Morrison snipped the catgut where Lynch had tied a firm knot. He dropped the needle handle onto the floor and kicked it to the far end of the theatre.

'This is the last fucking time I save your ass, Morgan!' he snarled. He turned on his heels and marched out of the theatre, leaving it in pandemonium.

Lynch didn't notice the burly figure of Harry O'Brien hurrying along the corridor towards theatre, nor that of Theo Dempsey, heart pounding with anxiety, following at his boss's heels. The only thing Dean Lynch was aware of was a dreadful pain in his head. His face was white with a barely suppressed fury as he changed out of his operating greens. Within minutes he had left the hospital buildings and was in his car, tyres scattering gravel in its wake as he swung out into Whitfield Square. The car sped along the narrow streets that led away from the hospital complex, finally joining the afternoon traffic along O'Connell Street. Lynch ignored the blaring horns and shaking fists as he cut across, switching lanes without warning. The clock on Trinity College chimed one thirty as he drove past on his way to Nassau Street and out towards Ballsbridge.

As he neared his flat, one of a group in a modern complex just off Baggot Street, Lynch made a conscious effort to control himself, drawing in deep breaths and letting the air out slowly through pursed lips. He slipped quietly into the car park and glided to a halt in the numbered position reserved for flat twenty-three. After double checking the car alarm, he walked as casually as he could across the tarmac and into the building, hoping no one would notice him home so early in the day. Ignoring the open lift, he took the fire escape steps two at a time up to level three and was inside his flat within minutes.

He pulled back a rug that lay across the maple floor in his exercise room and inserted a kitchen knife into an edge that was barely visible between the boards. The board lifted in one short piece. Reaching his hand down into the opening, he groped for a few seconds before retrieving a green plastic bag. Lynch squeezed the bag twice, as if for comfort, before sitting down at the kitchen table and spilling out its contents onto the formica top.

'Fucking bastards,' he muttered as he tapped out white powder from a small clear plastic bag onto a stainless steel spoon. He flicked the top off an ampoule of sterile water before igniting a methylated spirits wick with a lighter. Drawing up the water with a fresh needle and syringe, he gently flushed it back onto the spoon and then heated it over the flame until all the powder dissolved. Then carefully, oh so carefully, he drew the mixture back up into the syringe. He was still cursing and muttering as he pulled a tourniquet across his left upper arm, slapping at the veins. Very slowly he inserted the twenty-three gauge needle into the proudest of the bulging veins and drew back slightly to make sure he had the point in accurately. He grunted with satisfaction as he watched his blood waft back into the syringe. Then he gently pressed down on the plunger and injected. This was the bit he enjoyed most and was careful never to rush in case he felt overwhelmingly sick and vomited. Just slowly and gently, every now and then drawing back to make sure he was still in the vein, Dean Lynch emptied the heroin into his arm. He had this timed to a fine art, finishing just before he felt the full rush to his brain. His mouth, lips and tongue felt heavy and he licked repeatedly to keep them moist. The needle, syringe and plastic bags were carefully dropped into a kitchen drawer, to be dealt with in the morning, before he slumped down on his bed, watching the ceiling and room drift in and out of his vision. He felt relaxed again, contented. Clumsily, he stuck an Elastoplast across the entry point of the needle, fumbling to peel away the adhesive strip.

Dean Lynch was at peace again.

Day 2

The light was on. Lynch was sitting over the side of the bed, gasping for air, suffocating, shaking, knees trembling. One hand wiped his face clear from dripping sweat, the other grasped tightly onto the locker for support. He felt sick and struggled to the bathroom, leaning heavily against the basin, waiting to vomit. But though his insides heaved nothing came that might have eased the waves of nausea. Groping his way around, he found the shower, turned it on and played the spray of water across his face and body, turning it slowly to icy cold to wake himself up.

He sat on the wooden chair in the kitchen staring out at the early morning sky. The nightmares were becoming more frequent, so frequent that he now dreaded the dark and sleep. Daylight usually found him lying on sheets soaked with sweat. He was turning more and more to heroin for comfort and he knew only too well its danger.

Dean Patrick James Lynch had been born on 20th April 1951 in a maternity hospital in Portlawn in the Midlands of Ireland. That was all he knew about himself. The only physical evidence he had of his early existence was a tattered and grubby birth certificate confirming those basic details. There were no photographs of the young Dean Lynch, no letters or postcards to remind him of his childhood. They simply did not exist. The birth certificate was the only confirmation that he had a past, that he had been a child once.

He had grown up with nothing, no material possessions to call his own and he had continued throughout life that way.

Even as an adult, apart from a second hand car that was necessary for work and a few basic pieces of furniture, he owned nothing. Nor did he want anything. Growing up always wearing someone else's hand-me-down clothes, sleeping always in a bed someone else had vacated because they had been moved on elsewhere, struggling to fit into somebody else's cast off shoes, left him with an instinctive feel he would never have anything of his own. Every vest, every shirt, even the threadbare socks that barely kept the cold out during the long Irish winters he knew would one day be taken from him and passed on. And he knew why. He was a nobody.

Like the rest of the children in the orphanages he'd lived in over the years he was part of the flotsam of life in Ireland in the 1950s, abandoned, discarded and avoided because they represented sin, the sin of being born out of wedlock. The staff in charge of the institutions were often a mixture of religious orders and local authority appointees, most of them imbued with the religious fervour of the time. Inadequate state finance often led to harsh, strictly disciplined regimes to save on day-to-day running costs. There was no small change in the orphanage budgets for toys or food treats that might have made the children's lives more pleasant, their lifestyles more endurable. And if the children ever looked for any form of affection, any cuddle, any simple caress, any kind or consoling word to help at a difficult time they were rebuffed, often angrily, occasionally violently.

Dean Lynch was rejected so often he learned not to seek attention, not to expect any comforting embrace. He learned, too, how to avoid the beatings so often handed out for even the most trivial offence. In the orphanage he spent the years between his fifth and sixteenth birthdays becoming a master of self-control, of containment, of self-protection. Even at that early age, Dean Lynch's make-up was different from that of other children. He watched when other children were beaten and learned which of the staff were the most dangerous, the ones with the shortest tempers. He made notes of when they were on duty and avoided them accordingly. It was in this orphanage that Dean Patrick James Lynch's personality was shaped. It was in this orphanage that he learned the art of apparent submission, of expressionless compliance.

And it was in this orphanage that he learned the art of carefully planned revenge.

He looked at his watch. It was 6.30 am. He pressed the replay button on the answering machine on the kitchen counter. 'You have one message, please wait,' spoke the mechanical voice. It was unusual for him to have any messages, unusual for anyone to telephone him at home, ever. But he knew what this message might be and wasn't surprised to hear Luke Conway's voice.

'Eh, Dean, I tried to contact you this afternoon but no one could track you down. Look I heard all about the carry-on in theatre today and I'd appreciate if you would call in on me tomorrow just to go over the events. Shall we say about ten o'clock? Thank you.'

Lynch poured himself a cup of coffee and went back to staring out the window, urging the morning light forward. For the tenth morning in a row he had no appetite for breakfast, the only meal he ever cooked for himself, the one meal he usually enjoyed. The coffee burned his mouth and throat. He swallowed another penicillin tablet.

At exactly the same time, in another part of the city, another pair of eyes was also staring at the daybreak.

Tommy Malone was sitting at the breakfast table in his red-bricked terraced house on Anderson's Quay, the morning papers spread in front of him. The kitchen window looked over the river Liffey with its collection of Guinness barges and container ships moored at the quayside, waiting to be loaded or unloaded. Tommy often spent hours on end watching the grey light break through in the morning, smoking cigarette after cigarette, observing the river traffic struggle awake. Malone's kitchen window had one of the best views of Dublin port and docks, a view that was rarely dull. Every day, just as he sat down to listen to the eight o'clock news on the radio, he would open the window slightly to savour the salt and seaweed smells of the morning air, often mixed with the heady aroma of roasted malt that blew down the river from Guinness's brewery in St James's Gate. But that morning Malone's mind was elsewhere, the river traffic ignored.

He looked again at the headlines. O'BRIEN'S BABY! and THE £2M BABY and HARRY'S BOY and A BOY FOR HARRY! All the morning papers carried Gordon O'Brien's birth as their lead story. Inside, under an 'EXCLUSIVE' banner, the *Daily Post* featured a four-page spread accompanied with photos of Harry O'Brien, his family and home. The *Post* had scooped the other dailies with a well researched and detailed reporting of how the previous day's drama had unfolded. The report even had a minute-by-minute breakdown of the emergency developing and how it was handled, naming the main participants.

Tommy read the *Post* story for the fourth time. Then he folded the other three papers and pushed them aside. He pulled open a drawer in the table and rustled inside, finally producing a pair of scissors. He carefully cut out all the reports about the birth and background details of Harry O'Brien himself, studying the clippings carefully. Reaching inside his shirt pocket he tapped out a cigarette from a pack he kept there. Outside a horn sounded on one of the barges, sending seagulls squawking into the air as if cursing with fright. Oblivious to their raucous screeches Malone leaned back in his chair and lit up an untipped Sweet Afton, watching the hazy blue smoke drift slowly towards the ceiling.

He was hatching a plan.

Thomas (Tommy) John Malone was an ageing and failed criminal. Aged fifty-eight, his once five foot nine frame had lost an inch to advancing years. His fingers were almost chocolate brown from nicotine staining and his eyebrows and eyelashes also showed smoke staining. Lack of money, lack of attention and years of drawing on cheap cigarettes had left him with stained and slightly crooked teeth. To cover this he had let his moustache grow thick and bushy so that it overhanged his upper lip slightly. He did wear decent clothes and kept himself clean and tidy, lessons he'd learned the hard way in gaol where poor personal hygiene could cause trouble in confined, shared cells.

He had grown up in the squalor of one of Dublin's inner-city flat complexes on Steevens Street, only minutes away from Whitfield Square and the Central Maternity Hospital. Tommy Malone had been born there in 1938 and was fifth of the eight children his mother had carried. Like most of the flats' residents he knew nothing else but crime from childhood. From as early as he could remember he had been robbing and stealing, hand bag snatching, smashing car windows and grabbing whatever was on view.

At his mother's knee he was taught that the Gardai were bolloxes, big culchie bastards from the country with big thick heads inside big thick caps. And they all had big red ears to stop their caps falling over their big stupid eyes. His father and uncles and older brothers were all involved in crime, all coming to sorry ends one way or the other, either ending up in gaol or in early graves from the ravages of drugs or criminal vendettas. Malone's father had been a pathetic alcoholic who'd staggered from one bungled robbery to the next and usually into the arms of the law at the end. It wasn't long before the young Tommy Malone came to the attention of those same big thick culchie Gardai he had been taught so much to hate.

By the age of eight he had been before the juvenile courts no fewer than six times for petty theft. By sixteen he had been in and out of juvenile detention centres so often he'd lost count. He spent his twentieth birthday inside Mountjoy gaol on a three-year stretch for armed robbery and was back in again for his twenty-sixth birthday, this time for six years. By the time he was in his thirties Malone had moved into buying and selling drugs for distribution among the many tenements around the inner-city areas. But the Dublin drug scene was in the process of changing dramatically; a number of small time criminals had decided to go big by carving out territories for themselves and now controlled the distribution for the entire area. Police statistics were now confirming what almost everyone in the capital knew, that as much as eighty per cent of all crimes in the Dublin Metropolitan Area was drug related. Official Gardai figures suggested there were approximately seven thousand heroin users in the city, each requiring up to sixty pounds a day to feed their habit. Tommy Malone quickly discovered he was on the outside of this drug business looking in and with no chance of a share in the action.

Over the next few years, he became known as a loser, a hit man with nothing to hit, a gangster without a gang. 'Tommy,' one of his long time buddies had advised him as he reached his fortieth birthday with yet another court appearance looming, 'get outa this, will ye? Yer fuckin' bad news. Ye can' even walk down O'Connell Street withou' the rozzers itchin' to pick ye up just for breathin'. Nobody wants to work with ye. The word's ou', yer a fuckin' loser.'

Malone had no intention of getting out, he knew nothing else. But the next gaol sentence, six months for receiving stolen goods, brought him abruptly to his senses. 'You're a season-ticket holder,' one of the prison guards laughed as Malone was driven from the courthouse after sentencing. It was there that it suddenly hit him. The total waste of his life, almost a third of it spent behind bars and the rest spent on the run from the police. He'd shared a cell with one of the real 'lifers', Harry O'Neill, a small time crook from the border who had shot and killed a Garda while robbing a bank. While a life sentence for most usually meant eight years, O'Neill was in for the rest of his natural life. And that wasn't very long, as Malone learned one day after his cell mate came back from the prison doctor. O'Neill died within a month from cancer, three weeks before Tommy Malone was released back into society. The prison sentence, the gradual dawning of the waste of his life, the knowledge that the guards considered him a 'season-ticket holder', all rocked Malone. Watching Harry O'Neill being carried out on a stretcher from the cell was the final straw. 'There's no way I'm gonna be carried outa this place on a stretcher,' Malone muttered to his new cell mate the day before he was released. 'No fuckin' way.'

Now, he stubbed the butt into a tin ashtray, poured himself another mug of strong tea and rested his chin on his hands. He had split the clippings into three pieces. One read O'BRIEN'S the other BABY, while the third was £2M. He put the three clippings side by side. O'BRIEN'S ... £2M ... BABY. He rearranged them again. This time the £2M was put to the right of the table while O'BRIEN'S and BABY lay in the middle. Next he slid BABY to the left so that the three clippings were spread out across the table in a line. He leaned back in the chair again, lit up another cigarette and gazed out at the dark rain clouds as they swept in across the river.

The weak winter sun had disappeared.

'Have a seat, Dean.' Luke Conway pointed towards a hard-backed chair to the right of his desk.

Sitting only a few feet away and looking distinctly uneasy was Tom Morgan, dressed as usual as if he had walked straight out of the latest Armani catalogue. His navy blue suit was carefully cut to show off his tall, slim frame; his shirt faint pink with a white stripe. His tie was fashionably loose. His curly hair showed just a hint of grey around the temples.

Luke Conway studied both of them for a brief second over his half-moon glasses. There could have been no greater contrast than between the two men on the other side of his wide, leather-topped desk. One was tall and slim and dressed like a male model awaiting a photo call. The other smaller and stockier man looked as if he had thrown on the most ill-fitting, uncoordinated clothes possible to find in an Oxfam shop.

As Master of the hospital Conway had seniority over them. And as Master he was also in charge of discipline within the hospital. Even though Tom Morgan had been on the hospital staff longer than Lynch, they were of equal importance in the hospital hierarchy as consultant obstetricians/gynaecologists.

Conway's first instinct on hearing about the previous day's fiasco had been to suspend both doctors, but he knew such a move would have been splashed across the newspapers.

The emergency birth of Harry O'Brien's baby was the hottest news story of the day, even taken up by outside networks. If word filtered out that two of the consultants involved were almost at each other's throats while the operation was in progress there would have been uproar. Apart from the media having a field day, Conway knew that Harry O'Brien's two million pound donation would have disappeared like the snow in the ditch. And Luke Conway wanted that money so much.

'Dean,' he began, 'I have just had a long discussion here with Tom about yesterday's events in Theatre Two.' He paused and shifted in his chair as if trying to decide the best way of proceeding. 'First of all I want to thank you for the speed with which you responded to the emergency call and the manner in which you delivered that child. I'm quite certain you saved his life.'

Dean Lynch sat impassively, his gaze fixed at some distant spot slightly to the right of Conway's glasses. He might have been meditating for all the expression he showed.

'However,' continued Conway, his voice taking on a sharper tone, 'to abandon an operation half way thr – ' He stopped in mid-sentence as a manilla folder was suddenly pushed onto his desk in front of him.

Lynch had produced it from inside his jacket and made an exaggerated show of opening it, revealing a sheaf of papers stapled together.

'You probably have a copy of this,' he interrupted, his voice slightly raised but carefully controlled. On the other chair Tom Morgan shifted forward.

'This is my contract with the Eastern Health Board. I spent a full hour reading and re-reading it before I came in this morning.' He looked straight at Conway and held his gaze. 'My contract is with the Eastern Health Board and the Eastern Health Board only. I have no contract, let me repeat that, no contract with this hospital whatsoever. I am answerable to the Minister of Health and his appointees on the Eastern Health Board for all matters, and that in particular includes matters of discipline.'

Luke Conway's mouth opened slightly as if he was trying to say something that would allow him to regain the initiative.

'If you care to read your copy you will see that I have agreed to provide specialist obstetrical and gynaecological services to the public patients who choose to attend the Dublin Central Maternity Hospital. Further on you will read that I am specifically precluded from the rights of private practice for as long as I continue to be employed by the Eastern Health Board.' He paused to let these words sink in.

Tom Morgan slunk back into his seat and studied the ground in front of his carefully polished Gucci loafers. Conway slipped off his glasses and leaned forward, taking every word in.

'In other words, Dr Conway,' the words were spat out angrily, the even temper replaced with an icy edge, 'my job is to look after the public patients in this hospital and the public patients only.'

Lynch closed over the manilla folder, stood up and leaned slightly against the desk so that he towered over Conway. He could not conceal his anger, or his contempt.

'Four times in the past four months I have had to perform emergency procedures in the private wing here.' He reached into a side pocket of his jacket and pulled out a small notebook which he flipped open at a marked page. 'I have done two high forceps and one Caesarean section for Dr Tom Morgan and dealt with a retained placenta for Dr Matt Grogan. All of these were their private patients. Where the treating doctors were on these occasions I do not know, nor for that matter do I care.'

He slipped the notebook back in his pocket, picked up the manilla folder, turned slightly as if to go out, then paused.

'I came here this morning out of common courtesy and nothing else. My days of being called before the headmaster are long gone, Dr Conway. If you have a problem with my performance or technical skills then I suggest you take it up with the Minister for Health directly. I'm sure he would be very interested to learn how much of my time is spent looking after the interests of the one or two consultants here who can't even bother to turn up for their private patients.'

He was out the door before Conway could draw enough breath to reply.

The room was silent. Tom Morgan continued to stare at the floor. Finally Luke Conway spoke, his voice clipped, razor sharp.

'Dr Morgan.'

Tom Morgan looked up to find the older man's eyes boring into his own.

'Dr Morgan, if it wasn't for the fact that this hospital can't take any more bad publicity I'd have you run out of here.' He tucked his glasses into his breast pocket. 'But there's more than just yesterday's fiasco I want you to know I'm aware of and prepared to act on if it doesn't stop.'

Tom Morgan's brow furrowed and he pulled at the knot on his tie nervously.

'I know that you have been having sexual relationships with at least two of your patients. For all I know there may be even more. While I can't exactly prove this I can tell you it's more or less common knowledge in the house.'

Morgan twisted awkwardly in his chair but said nothing.

'I'm warning you, Tom Morgan, and I'm warning you this once only. If you bring one whiff of scandal to this hospital or the staff here, I'll open such a can of worms you'll never practice in this city, or any other city, again.'

The subdued figure of Tom Morgan heading back along the hospital corridors was in stark contrast to the beaming and bustling Harry O'Brien as he strode through North Wing clutching enough flowers to open a small shop.

'Good morning, Sister; good morning, Nurse,' he boomed at anyone in uniform. Behind followed Theo Dempsey gripping tightly onto a bottle of champagne and grinning from ear to ear as he watched his boss's antics.

Big Harry had made a point of stopping and thanking anyone and anybody, from kitchen staff to hospital porter to nurse's aide, from the moment he'd entered the hospital. He handed out cigars to expectant fathers, doctors, even the little grey-haired tea lady whose trolley he pretended to hijack. As she tried good humouredly to wrestle it back from him, he pinched her bottom and managed to slip a long-stemmed red rose down the front of her blouse. She crimsoned and clasped a hand over her mouth to stifle a fit of giggling.

June Morrison was just leaving room three when Big Harry spotted her.

'Sister Morrison,' he roared from down the corridor. 'My one and only Sister Morrison.' He rushed forward, a bouquet of twenty red roses clasped in his extended right hand. Before she could speak or resist he had planted a wet and sloppy kiss firmly on her lips. She blushed furiously and tried to regain her composure, aware of the giggles of the younger nurses watching on.

'Mr O'Brien,' she protested but Big Harry moved in again and grasped her in a bear hug.

'Sister Morrison,' he laughed. 'Sister Morrison, I love you to bits. Thank you for looking after my Sandra. Thank you for everything you did yesterday.'

Before Morrison had time to draw breath the big man had slipped past her into the room.

Inside Sandra O'Brien was lying back on a pile of fluffed-up pillows, her long blonde hair trailed to one side. Even without make-up and subdued by painkillers she still looked beautiful. Harry O'Brien paused at the door and just gazed at her, as if he had just seen her for the first time. A nurse sitting to her side made a quiet shushing noise but beckoned the big man in further. He tiptoed slowly towards his wife and laid a gentle kiss on her forehead. Sandra opened her eyes slightly and smiled. They held hands for a short moment but Sandra could sense Harry was itching to get over to his son and she released her grip.

'Don't wake him, I'm warning you,' she whispered, holding onto the thick padded dressings that protected the long operation scar on her stomach. 'We've only just got him back to sleep.'

While Sandra and the nurse watched, Harry O'Brien, one of the wealthiest and most powerful men in Ireland, melted in front of the sight of his newborn baby lying fast asleep inside the same Moses basket he himself had lain as a baby. He stroked a finger hesitantly across the baby's left cheek, pulling back quickly as the tiny face grimaced, then sneezed. As he stared down, tears welled and he was unable to stop one plopping onto the blue babygrow beneath.

'What weight is he?' he whispered over his shoulder. 'Have they weighed him yet?'

'Seven and a half pounds,' Sandra whispered back.

'Oh, that's a good weight,' muttered Big Harry proudly. 'That's a good weight for an O'Brien.'

Through the partly open door Theo Dempsey watched and waited. And as he watched he couldn't help but think back to the bad days and nights he'd sat with Big Harry when he'd gone off the rails.

Harry O'Brien was chairman and majority shareholder in the O'Brien Corporation, one of Ireland's few multinational companies. Founded in the 1940s by his father, O'Brien's Herbal Cures, as it was known then, was one of the first companies to become involved in the developing pharmaceutical industry. Dan O'Brien, Harry's father, began dabbling in a range of herbal remedies and was soon able to produce them in modest quantities for sale to the public. The steady sales persuaded O'Brien Senior to look closely at the possibility of processing and distributing them on a nationwide basis. Never a man to rest on his laurels, he soon began looking for a partner and entered into negotiations with BPP, British Pharmaceutical Products. Selling a thirty per cent share in his company, O'Brien received close to a quarter of a million pounds, a fortune in 1947. The extra cash, the pharmaceutical research and development, and the distribution network that BPP provided ensured O'Brien's Herbal Cures were sitting on the shelves of almost every chemist shop in Britain and Ireland. Dan O'Brien became one of Ireland's first millionaires in 1953 and the family became national celebrities as O'Brien sought to promote an entrepreneurial spirit among Irish businessmen.

Through it all his only son Harry grew up comfortable and secure, occasionally being caught in the media glare of his father's success. But young Harry realised early on in life that he would have to excel personally to match his father's record. And excel he did. While not academically brilliant, Harry O'Brien was a gifted athlete, representing Ireland in both track and field events and collecting gold medals at many European meetings. His progress through boarding school and on to university at Trinity College Dublin appeared effortless but was marked by hard work and extra tuition. Young Harry soon became Big Harry, as his six-foot-three-inch frame filled out, topped off by a mass of dark curly hair. He had an awkward, almost self-conscious look about him but he had a beguiling smile that won the ladies easily. However Dan O'Brien had young Harry well primed to the wiles of women. 'Some of those hoors are only gold diggers, Harry,' he'd warned repeatedly. So while Big Harry's hormones often urged him forward, his father's repeated warnings kept him in check most of the time. That is until he met Eleanor Dixon, a twenty-year-old raven-haired beauty from Cork city. She was studying French and Italian at Trinity while Big Harry was studying her. Eleanor Dixon led Harry O'Brien on a merry chase, refusing all overtures and only agreeing to a visit to the theatre after many months of dogged persistent requests. But Eleanor had as much of an eye for Big Harry as he had for her and romance soon flourished. They married in secret to escape the media and the suffocating attention of both families. Their first child, Mary, was born two years later in Denver, Colorado, where Harry had moved to study business and marketing.

Returning to Ireland in 1982 after the sudden death of his father, Harry bought out his mother and two sisters and became managing director of the business. He also bought back the thirty per cent shareholding from BPP, even though his bankers almost gagged when they learned the price he was asking them to support. Within the first year he had taken over a small electronics company based in the Midlands and turned it round from just breaking even to showing healthy profit by specialising in the manufacture of medical equipment. By the time his next two children were born, Harry O'Brien had changed the company name to the O'Brien Corporation and expanded its range of products.

It seemed as though Harry O'Brien could do nothing wrong, he had the golden touch. But all that ended on 20th December 1991. On a trip back from Dublin to the family residence in North Wicklow, the Lexus Eleanor O'Brien was driving collided head on with a sand truck. She never stood a chance, nor did her three children. That fateful afternoon Harry O'Brien lost his family. Within a month he was fighting for his own life in an exclusive London private clinic, having taken an overdose of drink and tranquillisers. He spent months in recovery and was a shell of his former self when he finally returned to work in the autumn of 1992. There followed eighteen very lonely months as he struggled to keep off the booze and get his life together again. But finally a new beginning came in the alluring shape of Sandra Greene, one of Ireland's top fashion models and twenty years younger than himself. Sandra, a long-haired blonde, had the style and grace of a Greek goddess with a quick wit and infectious laugh. They were introduced at a cocktail party and practically fell into each other's arms. They were married within a month, in February 1994.

As Dempsey watched the new family unit a sense of unease stirred inside him. He stepped back into the corridor, closing the door quietly behind, and sat down on a chair in the corridor. A nurse walked past pushing a perspex open-topped cot in which lay another newborn baby. Behind followed the mother, walking slowly, the bulge of her shrinking womb still obvious underneath her dressing gown. Dempsey smiled and she smiled back. He settled in the chair, picked up a discarded newspaper and began to read. The lead story was all about his boss and the birth of his son. As he read Theo Dempsey's sense of unease increased. He wasn't at all happy so much of Big Harry's personal life was being made so public. He wasn't happy about it at all.

Theo Dempsey's unease matched that of Luke Conway.

'Cancel all incoming calls to me,' he directed his secretary. 'If there are any media queries about the O'Brien baby refer them to Central Information.'

He replaced the phone and gazed at the names of the Masters engraved on the huge brass mount on the wall in front of him. To be head of this hospital was a rare honour indeed. The Central Maternity Hospital had a worldwide reputation for research and development in obstetrics and gynaecology and was often visited by eminent international gynaecologists wishing to see at first hand one of the oldest maternity hospitals in the world.

During the 1790s, a Dr Matthaeus Goldsmith had been so moved by the plight of the expectant mothers he had come across in the inner-city slums he founded a 'Lying-In' hospital, a hospital for pregnant women, seeking to safely deliver them of their offspring and see that they and their children left in as fit and nutritious condition as could be afforded. The first child, one Patrick Michael Joseph O'Leary, was safely delivered on 27th March 1798 and the hospital went from strength to strength from then on. The two hundredth anniversary of the opening of the building was to be celebrated in the following spring and Luke Conway had the responsibility to see the institution up to and past that landmark date.

He was aware that slack discipline had crept into the

hospital over the last few years and now threatened its standards and reputation. So he'd had to swallow his pride and accept the strict government guidelines on new consultant appointments. When the vacant position in the public sector had been advertised in the medical press only one suitably qualified candidate, Dean Lynch, had applied. And Luke Conway had snapped him up before he could change his mind. He was beginning to regret it.

He picked up the *Daily Post* and read again the minute-by-minute breakdown of the previous day's events. Fortunately all the newspaper reports had painted the hospital in a favourable light with not the slightest hint of the conflict that had surrounded the emergency birth.

Luke Conway stood up and walked slowly to the window at the back of his office and looked out. It's time to get this house in order, he thought as he watched the traffic below. It's time to rattle a few cages.

1.45 pm

Dean Lynch's whole body shook.

He sat at the desk in his consulting room, empty apart from himself, the outside corridors quiet during lunch hour. He looked again at his hands and tried to steady their agitated tremble. He could feel drops of sweat forming on his forehead and he wiped the sleeve of his white coat across it. Slowly, unsteadily, he stood up and went back to the mirror above the hand washbasin in the corner. He opened his mouth wide again and shone the light from a pen torch inside and stared wild eyed at the view reflected in the mirror.

There was no mistaking what he saw.

This was the third time in the past half-hour he had inspected his throat and he still could not believe what he had discovered. But it made so much sense. The sore throats, the rawness in his mouth, the lack of improvement from penicillin. He had been self-medicating for what he thought was a straightforward throat infection. But he had a very different type of infection altogether, one that would never clear with antibiotics and one which had disastrous medical implications.

Dean Lynch had oral and pharyngeal thrush.

The first time he looked he could barely make out the white plaques; but as the torch lit up all areas of his mouth and throat there was no mistaking the patches of white, cheesy-looking material formed in wavy layers along the inside of his cheeks and back of throat.

Thrush.

Candida albicans.

Monilia.

The three medical terms for the same type of yeast infection sprang at him and rushed through his brain like express trains, whooshing and hissing, rocking his head from side to side. He sat down again, trying to control his agitation and trembling.

He knew only too well the implications of someone like himself developing thrush. His immune system must be compromised in some way. The part of his body's defence system that fought and controlled infections wasn't working. Thrush infections just did not develop inside the mouth in healthy males. While there might be a few simple and uncomplicated reasons in certain situations, Dean Lynch knew only too well they did not apply in his case.

Dean Lynch knew he had AIDS.

It was just after two o'clock and the afternoon's out-patients would soon be starting.

Outside he could hear the familiar sounds of chairs in the waiting room being moved and the occasional cry from a child accompanying his mother to the clinic.

Think fast, he urged himself, you've always been a fast thinker. Think, think. What are you going to do?

He slipped the lock closed on his office door and quickly washed his hands and face in the basin, eyes avoiding the mirror. He dried himself slowly and deliberately with a hand towel, taking great care to remove all traces of sweat from his brow. Then he straightened his tie, buttoned up his white coat and unlocked the door.

Walking slowly and deliberately past the early arrivals he made his way to the medical library and checked inside. It was empty. He closed the door behind him and propped a chair against it so that anyone trying to come in would first have to push it aside, giving him a few seconds' grace. He quickly scanned the shelves lined with text books of obstetrics and gynaecology, until he came to the section dealing with infectious diseases. He flicked through one or two until he found what he wanted. In one large tome there was a detailed and comprehensive chapter on AIDS. Checking to make sure no one was about to suddenly disturb him, he ripped the pages out, folded them in two and slipped them inside his coat pocket. The textbook was carefully placed back on the shelf, its spine pushed slightly inwards so no one would see the title easily.

Back outside again he made an excuse to be alone. 'Nurse, would you ask Dr Sharif to look after this afternoon's clinic? I'm going up to the wards to check on one of my patients. You can page me if you need me.'

He made his way along the back stairwell to the 'on-call' bedroom where he sat on the edge of the bed, the pages from the textbook spread out in front of him. The 'on-call' bedroom was located in an inaccessible corner of East Wing and was never used during the day. As he read his hands shook. He felt slightly nauseated. The more he read the more his insides churned and heaved. The textbook set out clearly the staging of AIDS, the steps of disease progression.

By his reckoning he was already at stage IVc1, HIV related secondary infections: *oropharyngeal candidiasis.*

There were only two further stages.

As he read details of the symptoms it was like a jigsaw coming together in front of his eyes. The recent night sweats, the bouts of nausea, the unexplained recurring diarrhoea he had put down to eating from unhygienic takeaways.

All these reflected earlier features. He was by now convinced the AIDS virus had totally destroyed his body's defence system. And in his already tormented mind he decided he was dying. He didn't know when, he didn't know how, but he decided there and then he would soon be dead.

He finished reading and stood up slowly, mind racing, heart pounding. He knew what he should do, but equally knew there was no way he would inform Luke Conway of his suspicions. If he went along the orthodox and correct route his whole underlife would be revealed. He would immediately be suspended from working and almost certainly dismissed from the hospital. Next would come a Medical Council enquiry. There was no way he would allow the medical establishment, the very bastards he hated and despised, to look at the darkness under his stone.

No way.

They would have a field day.

No way.

He folded the textbook pages into his pocket again and set off along the corridors of East Wing, face rigid, jaw set in determination.

First find out if you really have AIDS, he told himself, then decide how to handle everything else.

Get the facts.

Find out exactly.

He walked as casually as he could, past a room where three newborn babies cried with hunger while their mothers padded around in slippers, watching as a nurse showed them how to prepare a milk formula feed.

Maybe you won't be positive, he tried to convince himself, maybe this is a simple infection you've picked up from some patient.

Fuck off!

He heard the real Dean Lynch.

Fuck off, you've got it!

He slipped out of the hospital through the basement so that no one would notice.

10 3.00 pm

Tommy Malone had spent most of the morning sitting at the breakfast table, deep in thought. Around his feet screwed up balls of paper lay scattered, all torn from a simple lined exercise book. By two o'clock he was left with only one page. On nine lines of the page he had written a name. A black felt-tipped marker scored out six. This left only three names and in his mind Malone had gone over as much of the personal details of each as he could remember. Finally, just before three o'clock he slowly stood up, stretched and gazed at the drizzle misting the view outside. He felt in exceptionally good form and a little hum hovered on his lips as he pulled on his raincoat. Checking that he had enough small change, he set off for the public telephone box beside the Esso garage. Malone never trusted private telephone lines, very much aware of their potential for bugging by the police. There's no doubt about it, thought Malone as he buttoned his raincoat tightly against the rain, there's nothing like planning a really big job to lift your spirits on a wet winter's day.

After a few false starts when the telephone numbers had been engaged or suspicious voices at the other end of the lines denied the existence of anyone by that name, Tommy Malone finally managed to contact all the members of his 'A-team'. It wasn't the 'A-team' he would have liked but the ravages of drugs, gaol, and a crack down by Gardai on organised crime had taken its toll on the Dublin underworld.

The only people he knew would work with him had listened and finally agreed to meet the following afternoon. Each had been sworn to absolute secrecy and he knew they could be relied on to keep their mouths shut. That's why he'd selected them. They were tough and hungry. More importantly, he knew they were clean from drugs, vital in what he was planning. Experience had taught him one lesson in crime, never work with anyone on drugs. He knew full well all they thought of was the next hit. This job would require clear and experienced heads. After he ticked them off one by one he made one last call.

'Betty?'

'Is that ye, Tommy?'

'Aye. Listen, I won' be around for the next week or so.'

'Where are ye goin'?'

'I was thinkin' of goin' on a business trip.'

At the other end of the line he heard Betty snigger. 'Business me arse. I don' wanna know anyway, Tommy. Gimme a shout when ye're back.'

'Nah, Betty, I was wonderin' if ye'd come with me.'

'Where to?'

'I can't tell ye now. Could ye meet me in Mooney's pub in an hour?'

'What are ye plannin', Tommy?'

'Can't tell ye, Betty. See ye in Mooney's, righ'?'

'Righ'.'

Betty Nolan was Tommy's current girlfriend and one of the few women he'd ever allowed himself to get close to apart from his late long-suffering mother. She and Malone shared beds at weekends when he wasn't plotting or involved in some crime.

Betty was the widow of one of Dublin's petty criminals, dead many years previously, but not by natural causes. Her marriage was doomed from the start as her husband-to-be had to pull an off-licence robbery on the morning of the wedding to pay for the reception. They'd had one child, a girl called Sharon, before Betty became a widow at the age of twenty-three. A robbery planned to pay for a holiday in

Spain went horribly wrong and her husband was shot dead trying to escape. Betty Nolan went back to scrimping and saving to make ends meet.

Tommy Malone muttered to himself as he walked towards the buses on D'Olier Street in the misty rain. This job's just gotta work out. This is the last chance for a really big wan. If I pull this off I'll clear off outa the country somewhere with Betty. It's just gotta work out.

Coat collar pulled up, drizzle misting his face, Tommy Malone waited for a bus to take him to Mooney's pub in the south Dublin suburb of Blackrock.

Tommy Malone had almost gone for the 'big wan' two years earlier. There had been a lot of hype in the papers about a famous painting being discovered in a Jesuit house in Dublin's Leeson Street. Tommy Malone had taken a keen interest immediately, relating the newspaper reports to a fellow hood one morning.

'It's real big stuff. There's some undiscovered treasure that's bin hangin' on the Jesuits' wall for years, and them not knowin' a thing about it all that time. Stupid bastards. Anyway, didn't they go and give it to the National Gallery in Dublin for the people of Ireland to enjoy.' This made them even stupider bastards in Tommy Malone's eyes. 'I mean, it's worth a fuckin' fortune. They're talkin' millions, fuckin' millions. Some eejit on the telly said it was invaluable. Shows ye how much he fuckin' knows.' Tommy Malone didn't know much about painting, neither painting as in painting and decorating, nor painting as in art. But he knew when something was that valuable it would be worth a look at.

Which was how Tommy Malone came to be staring at 'The Taking of Christ' by Michelangelo Merisi, better known as Caravaggio, in Room Nine of the National Art Gallery one Wednesday morning in November 1994. He had come to plot a robbery, *its* robbery.

But he couldn't take his eyes off it, it disturbed him so much. There was Christ, all meek and humble like, about to be dragged away. And there was Judas planting a kiss on his cheek while two heavily armoured soldiers clutched Him, one with dirty hands and nails. The whole painting was dark, gloomy and foreboding. Malone had walked away twice, the second time right down to the front entrance, but each time he had come back to look and wonder. The second time he'd sat down on the bench directly opposite and examined every figure, every facial expression, every detail of clothing. The face of Judas looked repellent, his brow furrowed, eyes open, lips pressed against Christ's cheek. The fucker, Tommy Malone had thought, that Judas was a righ' fucker, righ' enough. Then he noticed another soldier in the background. Three of them! It took fuckin' three of them! And would ye look at yer man! He's not even puttin' up a fight! Malone couldn't take his eyes off the figure of Christ. He kept staring at it, looking at the face, a mixture of betrayal, resignation and sadness. He'd stood up and read the details of the painting: 'The Taking of Christ'. Caravaggio 1573–1610.

So they were takin' him off to be fuckin' crucified and he didn't even put up a fight? He had looked at the hands, clasped together, subdued. Then he'd stared at the eyes. They were closed, not scrunched up or wincing against pain or terror. Just closed. Accepting. Knowing what was coming and accepting it. No resistance.

Is it any wonder I don't believe in God? He had turned for the third time to leave when it suddenly hit him, like a thunderbolt. He suddenly knew why he knew he would never make a move on the painting, why it unsettled him so much.

The scene came back. He was aged about nine years and the family was living in one of the slum flats on the second floor of the Steevens Street complex. He heard again the hammering on the door, watched as his father tried desperately to hide. He remembered so vividly his mother weeping, wiping her eyes repeatedly with a filthy apron tied around her waist. The hammering grew louder and the other children started to cry and scream with fear, with terror.

That was what he remembered most, the sheer sense of terror. Finally the door was broken down and in charged six Gardai, batons drawn. There was a fight in the small kitchen, his father cursing and screaming, the Gardai trying to pin him down, raining blows to his head and arms and shoulders. His father broke free, rushed to the door and out onto the landing, still shouting and screaming. 'Ye won't take me, ye shower of bastards.' He jumped over the small landing wall down the twenty feet to the courtyard below. And to his death. He died from massive brain damage when his skull opened like a coconut as it hit the concrete. And all the time, as the children screamed and roared and the neighbours fought with the Gardai, his mother just sat and wept, wiping her eyes with that filthy apron. Her manner was resigned, as if she had known some day it would all come to this.

Just like Christ.

Tommy Malone had stared at the painting intently. His gaze kept returning to the face of the betrayed Christ, the eyes closed, the brow furrowed, lips slightly open.

'Why didn't ye run?' he'd muttered. 'Just open yer eyes and run. Like me Da.'

He'd looked up at the face of Judas and then at the face of Christ and then at the face of the soldiers.

'We'll I'm fuckin' tellin' ye this,' the words had been whispered. 'They won't crucify me. I'm tellin' ye that. They won't crucify me. There's no way I'm gonna let the rozzers get hold of me again. They won't crucify me.'

He'd suddenly noticed someone standing close to him and looked up. A nice American tourist was admiring the painting as well, an elderly, blue-rinse set woman.

'Isn't it just a magnificent painting?' she'd drawled.

'Would ye ever fuck off?' replied the art critic.

Betty Nolan bustled in, shaking the drips from her umbrella. She was slightly taller than Malone with bleached blonde hair sitting on her head like a beehive. A good looking woman in her day she was slowly going to seed and the dress she was wearing under her heavy overcoat bulged at the front and sides. She sat down and took a quick sip of Malone's whiskey. 'Jaysus it would freeze ye out there.'

Malone smiled and ordered a whiskey and soda from the young bar hand who had followed her into the snug. As soon as he was satisfied they couldn't be overheard Malone turned to Betty, motioning that the conversation was to be kept low.

'D'ye still do the odd bit of cleanin' down at Harry O'Brien's headquarters?'

Betty's eyes narrowed, full of suspicion. 'Why d'ye wanna know?'

Malone avoided the question. 'Are ye fed up cleanin' and scrapin'?'

The bar hand interrupted with the drink and Malone dropped five pound coins in his outstretched hand, waving away the few pence change offered. As soon as they were alone again, Malone continued.

'How'd ye like to make a million, and I'm not talkin' about winnin' the lotto?'

Betty took a sip of her whiskey and then added a little soda. 'What are ye plannin', Tommy?'

'I'll tell ye in a minute. D'ye still do the odd bit of cleanin' down at Harry O'Brien's place. Would ye answer me?'

'I do. Twice a week, Thursdays and Fridays, before the offices open. Why? Waddye wanna know abou' Harry O'Brien?' She sipped at her drink, never once taking her eyes from Malone.

'Would ye like to make a million and fuck off outa the country to somewhere nice and sunny and live it up for a change?' Malone drained the last of his Guinness, wiping the froth from his moustache. 'No more cleanin' and scrapin'.'

Betty said nothing, her eyes still fixed on Malone. She knocked the whiskey and soda back in one gulp, shuddering slightly as she felt it hit her stomach. 'Waddye plannin', Tommy?'

Malone stood up and opened the snug door to make sure no one was listening outside. He waved away the young bar hand moving towards him. 'In a minute, I'll call ye in a minute.' Satisfied, he closed the snug door and sat down, reached across and took one of Betty's hands in his own. She looked down and then back at him. 'Waddye plannin', Tommy,' she whispered uncertainly.

11

Dean Lynch drove from his Ballsbridge flat and parked in
the multistorey car park at the Ilac centre, only a five minute
walk from the hospital. It was a bitterly cold night with
few people on the streets. Those who were out huddled in
doorways sheltering against the wind as they waited for
buses or taxis to take them home. Dublin's Central
Maternity Hospital was located in Whitfield Square, a once
grand square situated only five hundred yards from O'Connell Street, the city's main thoroughfare. The square had
fallen into disrepair over the years and new office blocks
now replaced the old, mainly Georgian buildings. In the
centre was a small overgrown garden, railed off from
the roads and poorly maintained by Dublin Corporation.

The front of the hospital was an impressive grey stone
structure covering three levels. The massive wooden front
door was flanked on both sides by granite columns and the
upper floors had six large windows on each level. The hospital complex was divided into four wings: North, South,
East and West. This had little to do with geography and
everything to do with convenience, the wings added over
the years and pointing in every direction but that which
their names suggested.

The hospital was protected by high walls and there were
usually only two entrances open at any one time, the main
front door and a small service door at the back. Dean Lynch
avoided the main entrance and slipped into the car park

through a side gate, moving quietly along the edge of the building until he found the door that was used by cleaners to dump rubbish. It was open, as usual, and within minutes he was inside the basement. He listened carefully before going any further, but confident of every move. He had been this way many times before. He knew how to slip in and out of the hospital unnoticed and often used this route when he wanted to raid the supply stores for fresh needles and syringes.

Checking carefully, he edged past the pipes and humming turbines of the hospital generator to the stairwell leading to the upper floors. Within minutes he was on the outpatients' level of East Wing and into the corridor alongside his consulting room.

The reception area was in total darkness, the patient chairs scattered aimlessly in every direction. One or two well-worn glossy magazines lay on the floor. Lynch slipped off his shoes and left them inside his room, closing the door quietly. Stealthily he padded along towards the laboratory. There were no lights in any of the examination rooms, the library empty with only a corner light giving a faint glow onto the darkness outside the door. He turned it off, closed the door and moved towards the laboratory. In the gloom the only noise was the soft padding of his feet.

Inside lab assistant Mary Dwyer was finishing off the last blood reports from one of the gynaecology wards. She glanced at her watch for the third time in as many minutes and mentally calculated how long it would take her to get home at this hour. Her parents were very unhappy about the extra duty she had to put in at the hospital. She considered briefly ringing them but dismissed the thought just as quickly. They would have to learn she was a big girl now and able to handle herself. Being an only child sure has its drawbacks she thought as she set up a full blood count screen for Ward Four.

Through the half open door Dean Lynch quickly assessed

the situation. As expected at this time of night there was only one assistant staying late to deal with emergencies. From where he stood he could make out a white coat and a head of reddish-brown hair bent over the desk in front. Lynch squinted closer, double checking no one else was in the lab.

Mary Dwyer stood up briefly to reach for paperwork and Lynch made a note of her frame, slim but not skinny. He checked his watch. It was 9.16 pm. Still in stockinged feet he made his way back to the consulting room, picked up the internal phone and dialled.

'Damn,' fumed Mary Dwyer when she put down the phone. 'Damn, damn. A bloody AIDS test at this hour of the night. It'll take an hour to get a result on that.'

She was still obviously angry when Dean Lynch entered the lab and put the small blood filled bottle down on the counter in front of her.

'Dr Lynch, is this test really necessary tonight? I mean it'll take an hour to get a result. Could it not wait until tomorrow?'

Dean Lynch controlled the urge to smack her across the face.

The bitch.

'I need that result tonight, thank you very much, and no, it will not wait until tomorrow. I need to decide on this woman's management immediately.'

Lynch had taken the sample of blood from himself earlier and labelled it Joan O'Sullivan. He'd completed a standard hospital request form for a HIV test on a Joan O'Sullivan with an address in Crumlin, careful to print the request and not sign the form. He fixed his eyes on the young lab assistant and she averted his gaze.

'Ring me in an hour,' she muttered as she set about processing the test.

'I'll call back.' Lynch closed the lab door behind him.

Mary Dwyer scowled as she heard it shut.

Back in his consulting room, Dean Lynch sat down on the chair in front of his desk and began the long wait. All day long he had gone over in his mind how he could have contracted the AIDS virus. It couldn't have been from injecting himself for he always used fresh needles and syringes for each hit and never shared. It could only have come from one of the many prostitutes he'd hired out over the years.

While he had been overly cautious about safe sex he knew when his mind had been fogged from heroin he wouldn't have known what he was doing. So fogged on occasions he knew he might well have shared a fix with one of the many call girls he had visited in Amsterdam, London and Bangkok.

Half in dread, half in exultant expectancy he stood up, checked his watch and set about preparing.

He had decided already what he would do if the test was positive.

No one must learn he had AIDS.

No matter what had to be done.

The last examination room along the darkened corridor was reserved for minor surgical procedures. It was about six yards from the laboratory. Inside Dean Lynch slipped on a pair of surgical gloves and pulled them tightly across his hands and extended fingers. He clasped both hands together, interlocking the fingers until he felt he had as firm a fit as possible. Then, opening a stainless steel instrument tray, he selected a sterile scalpel handle from inside. On a shelf behind lay boxes of various sized scalpel blades. Lynch peered along each, finally selecting a size twenty-three, the widest blade available.

Opening the foil he snapped the blade onto the scalpel handle and slipped it inside his white coat pocket. The foil was screwed tightly into a ball and pushed inside a trouser pocket. For a moment he leaned against the wall, summoning up all his mental and physical reserves. Sweat formed on his brow and he wiped it away with a sleeve.

Mary Dwyer had her back to the lab door, engrossed in paperwork. With a quick glance along the darkened corridor, Lynch gently opened and closed the door, turning the lock. The click as the bolt engaged alerted Dwyer and she turned sharply.

'Is that test ready yet?' His voice was slightly shaky, his mouth dry. The pounding inside his chest almost rocked his bulky frame.

Mary Dwyer turned back to her paperwork, ignoring the question.

'There's no Joan O'Sullivan at the address you put on this form, Dr Lynch. At least there's no Joan O'Sullivan of that address in the hospital computer records. We have no record of that patient ever having attended here either as an in-patient or outpatient.'

She swivelled her chair round to Lynch.

'I've checked through the past five year records and there's no Joan O'Sullivan of 249 Crumlin Crescent in our system. Do you think she's given you a false name and address?'

Dean Lynch controlled his rage.

The little bitch had actually checked his request form.

She's on to me already.

'It's . . . it's possible, I suppose . . . I mean . . . how can you tell . . . sometimes it's hard to know if some patients are giving you their right name or not.'

He was stammering, fluffing his lines and he knew it. What's more he knew that she knew it. Mary Dwyer stared straight at him, a half smile on her lips.

'Probably some prostitute or bloody drug addict I'll bet,' she snapped as she flicked a switch on the computer terminal beside her. The machine whirred slightly and half stopped, then the printer beside started to click into action. Dean Lynch watched as the test result was printed.

First came the false name and address: JOAN O'SULLIVAN, 249 CRUMLIN CRESCENT, CRUMLIN, DUBLIN.

Then the date of birth: 27/2/76.

Next the test requested under a box labelled: 'Syphilis and HIV1\HIV2 Serology'.

HIV SCREEN.

DOUBLE CHECKED BY SERODIA – HIV.

The printer paused and then started up again.

The words FINAL RESULT appeared.

Then the result.

POSITIVE.

With one hand Mary Dwyer tore the sheet from the printer. 'Well she's going to hell, whoever she is.'

The phone behind her rang, the sudden noise jolting and for a moment they both stared at it, mesmerised. Just as Dwyer reached for the receiver, a surgical gloved hand slammed down over her.

At the other end Nurse Sarah Higgins waited for someone to answer down at the laboratory. Finally the phone was picked up.

'He ... hello ... hello ... is anyone there?'

There was a pause.

The noise that followed she later described as from a wild beast. The animal like snarl of hatred and anger made her blood run cold and she instinctively reached for her throat. The receiver was thrown down and Nurse Higgins could hear the sound of glass breaking, something being knocked over, crashing, more crashing, and finally a door slamming.

She placed the receiver back down slowly and then quickly dialled switch.

'Hi, it's Ward Four, North Wing, Staff Nurse Sarah Higgins here. Look I'm just after hearing something very strange over the phone coming from the lab. Would you ask security to check it out?'

Less than twenty minutes later Dean Lynch started up his car. As he did two security men were breaking open the door into the laboratory. And as Lynch eased his BMW out along the ramps and down to the exit, Mary Dwyer's lifeless eyes stared back at Pat O'Hara, night security officer. 'Jesus

Christ,' he muttered as he staggered backwards. 'Jesus Christ. Jim, call the cops! Quickly! Call the cops!'

For Dublin's Central Maternity Hospital the nightmare had begun.

The cages were starting to rattle.

Day 3

Detective Inspector Jack McGrath hated hospitals.

Maybe it was the smells, or maybe it was the instruments, or maybe it was just the doctors. Whatever it was he hated hospitals. Which was why he was feeling distinctly uneasy sitting in the hospital library watching as Staff Nurse Sarah Higgins was comforted by the night matron. To his right, Detective Sergeant Tony Dowling, his sidekick in the detective division of Store Street Garda station, was conferring with Detective Sergeant Kate Hamilton, one of the new breed of women detectives in the Garda Siochana being trained in serious crime investigations. Dowling finished writing in a notepad, looked up and nodded.

'Okay, Sarah,' began McGrath, 'I'm going to go over this for the last time and you tell me if everything's exactly as you remember. Okay? If there's anything you think you've left out, anything at all, no matter what, stop and tell me.'

Sarah Higgins sniffed and nodded. Her eyes were brimming with tears and she rolled and unrolled a handkerchief from one hand to the other, still shocked with what had been discovered. She dabbed at her eyes, hands shaking.

'At approximately 10.55 pm yesterday you rang Mary Dwyer in the lab looking for the result of a full blood count.' McGrath paused to check his terminology with Dowling. 'When the phone was finally picked up no one spoke for about twenty seconds, and then someone roared at you

71

across the line. You immediately hung up and called security.'

McGrath stopped. Staff Nurse Higgins was sobbing again, her head slumped on Matron's ample bosom. Tony Dowling and Kate Hamilton exchanged weary glances.

A knock on the door mercifully interrupted. McGrath stood up and opened it. Dr Noel Dunne, the state forensic pathologist, stood outside.

'Detective Inspector McGrath, I've finished in there and I'd like to get the body down to the morgue. Is there anything else you want to see before the room's sealed?'

McGrath thought for a moment, stroking his moustache. 'One moment.' He slipped back into the library and whispered something to Dowling, then waved a beckoning finger at Kate Hamilton. McGrath was back beside Dunne.

'Any thoughts?'

Noel Dunne was forty-eight going on a hundred. He had the worn face of someone who spent each day cutting up corpses, trying to determine exact cause of death. Tall but paunchy with steel grey hair, he had a reputation for gallows humour.

That morning there was no attempt at humour. That morning no one was in the mood for jokes. His usual ebullient manner was subdued. From behind Dunne's equally steel grey beard and moustache, McGrath could sense disquiet.

'Nasty one, Detective Inspector, this is a nasty bit of work altogether.'

McGrath stroked his moustache thoughtfully. His moustache matched his hair, grey and bushy. 'Any sign of sexual attack?'

'Nothing immediately obvious. Torn clothes, legs splayed a bit but nothing else. I'll swab her mouth, vagina and rectum.' He paused slightly, and threw a quizzical glance in Kate Hamilton's direction.

'Sorry,' said McGrath, 'I should have introduced you. This is Detective Sergeant Kate Hamilton.'

Dunne took a quick glance at the tall, slim, dark young

woman, snorted then raised his eyes quickly to heaven, not so that Hamilton could see but enough that she could sense his displeasure. Dunne was a man of the old tradition, used to male companions all the time during his work, uneasy at any female presence. He'd been brought up to treat women as ladies, always to stand up when they entered a room, always to offer a seat when none other was available, always to protect their sensitivities from the unpleasantries of life. To have a young lady watching in on a murder investigation was unsettling him, especially at that hour of the morning. He decided to ignore her completely. He slipped a dictaphone inside a jacket pocket. 'Did anyone see anything?'

'Nothing,' said McGrath, his mind revving away in top gear. 'Nobody saw this guy come and nobody saw him go.'

Dunne frowned. 'Can we move the body?'

McGrath nodded. 'I'll have one last look in there before forensics wreck the joint.'

Dunne smirked. Jack McGrath was a good cop, a sharp and experienced detective but one hell of an irritable bugger at times. He always double checked the forensic team, looking out for any sign of slipshod work. He wasn't exactly their favourite detective but he had a reputation within the force, a good reputation. He was considered to be tough but with a liberal sprinkling of common sense: he acted on intelligent hunches and had a mental database on the Dublin underworld that was unrivalled in the Gardai. If anyone needed a quick profile on the most likely mover behind a big robbery or gangland killing, it was Jack McGrath they turned to first. His insider information rarely let him down, his hunches had caused more than a few Dublin criminals to rue their fate. McGrath worked out at a local gym near where he lived and kept his six foot frame in top condition. He carried neither mental nor physical flab.

The laboratory door was slightly ajar and guarded by a lone, uniformed Garda. A yellow incident tape was stretched across it. Ignoring the Garda completely, Dunne pushed the door open with the bottom of a pencil to avoid leaving his own fingerprints and ushered McGrath inside. He was trying to close it again when Kate Hamilton firmly pushed it back and squeezed past, glaring at him. Dunne grinned. Inside the lab fluorescents burned intensely.

Dunne started to sit down on a stool, then paused and offered it to Hamilton without a word. She ignored the gesture and leaned against a bench to watch McGrath's next moves. Dunne shrugged and sat down.

Three of the forensic team were still there, one squatting as he angled a camera for a better position.

He focused.

FLASH!

Mary Dwyer captured, but not one for the family album.

McGrath moved slowly round the scene, eyes darting as he took it in. He deliberately avoided the lifeless body, still lying where it had been discovered. A rack of glass test tubes lay smashed on the floor and the blood each tube had contained was spilled, lying in a thick, congealed, splinterly ooze. The smell of blood and laboratory chemicals irritated McGrath and he popped a peppermint into his mouth and inhaled the vapours. A small PC and its printer lay end up in another corner, bits of their grey plastic casing scattered around. The paper from the printer was pulled out. Two other machines lay where they had fallen. On the benches stood the usual equipment to be found in any hospital laboratory: burners, cooling machines, racks of test tubes, microscopes, Petri dishes and the rest. There was no sign of any surgical equipment.

Dunne glanced at his watch, trying to decide how much longer McGrath would take. Noel Dunne and Jack McGrath had worked together on so many murder investigations they knew each other's routines like the back of their hands. By Dunne's reckoning McGrath might spend another hour in the laboratory trying to get a feel for the actual incident. He knew McGrath often came back to murder scenes on his own, after the forensics had left and there were no distractions, just to try and relive the last pained moments of a victim's life.

'I don't see any blades here,' McGrath said. 'Waddit you

call that thing sticking out of her neck?' He was now standing over the body, crunching and inhaling furiously.

'Scalpel.'

'Yeah, scalpel. I don't see any sign of any others around the place. Do you?'

'No, and I looked.'

The detective went down on his hunkers to inspect more closely. Only his laboured breathing was louder than the background hum of the laboratory machines. The scalpel was deeply embedded in Mary Dwyer's neck with only about an inch of blade handle sticking out. Her face was purple and still slightly swollen. Tiny blood haemorrhages, petechiae, had burst on the skin surface. Her eyes were glazed and lifeless, conjunctival haemorrhaging had caused white to be replaced by red. A pool of blood lay on the floor from a wound to her head. Her neck showed significant bruising and scratch-like marks. Her left leg lay awkwardly, knee upright and splayed to the side, skirt riding up. She was wearing pantyhose, a tear extending from knee to groin. One of her nails was broken and bent.

Standing up McGrath noticed a yellow chalk mark on the edge of the desk. One of the forensics had spotted something and marked the spot. A trace of blood and a small clump of hair clung to the wood.

'Take her away. I'll call down to the morgue later.' He looked at the clock on the wall. 'What time should I call in?'

'About ten, ten thirty. Give me till then. I'll try and start early.'

'See you then.'

Dunne yawned and nodded at the same time.

'Kate,' McGrath turned towards Hamilton who was scribbling notes in a small black pocket book. 'I'd like you to go over the scene on your own now. Forensics will tell you where to look and what not to touch and things like that. We'll go over your impressions later. When you've finished come back to the library, I'll be there with Tony.'

Kate Hamilton didn't move from her position against the

bench for almost ten minutes after Dunne and McGrath had left. Her eyes were fixed firmly on the body of Mary Dwyer. The laboratory had gone strangely quiet with even the forensic team saying little as they squatted and peered and photographed. Finally Hamilton began her own search of the area.

Kate Hamilton was one of only three female detectives being instructed in serious crime investigation within the Garda Siochana. She had been under Jack McGrath's wing for almost six months and he had grudgingly come to accept, then admire her, recognising a natural talent for criminal investigation.

'She's sharp, sharp as a tack,' he'd told Tony Dowling one morning. 'And fierce ambitious. Jesus, it wouldn't surprise me if she wasn't running the force soon.'

Dowling had laughed slightly, then looked McGrath straight in the eyes. 'Tell me, Jack, has yer missus seen her yet?'

McGrath grinned. He had a wife and two teenage boys. 'No, and she's not bloody well going to. One look at her and she'd have me transferred to traffic duty.'

Kate Hamilton had beauty to go with the brains. She was a confident young woman, three inches in height below most of her six foot Garda colleagues, with short dark hair usually pulled back and held in place with two combs at the side. She had deep blue eyes under dark eyebrows and a very pretty face. A very pretty face. So pretty that she was the pin-up girl for many in Store Street Garda station where she was based. While she may have been their pin-up most knew she was unobtainable, still grieving. For Detective Sergeant Kate Hamilton was a single mother with a four-year-old son called Rory whom she adored. The father of Rory she had adored once too, but he was now dead.

Just before she was assigned to Jack McGrath, he'd discussed her background with Chief Superintendent Mike Loughry, his immediate superior in the same division of the force. Loughry was attached to the Serious Crime Squad and McGrath reported to him on all the investigations he was handling.

'She's thirty-two,' Loughry informed him, reading from a file. 'Joined as a cadet aged twenty-four after completing a degree in History and Politics in UCD. She was one of the top students in her final university exams and went through the Garda training college in Templemore winning high praise from all quarters. Showed particular interest in forensics and drug offence detection.'

McGrath listened with a keen interest. He didn't want to have to take on some wally who would follow his every step like a brainless lapdog.

'She was one of five chosen for extra training in the US and spent a year with the Boston drug enforcement squad.' Loughry paused and leaned closer to McGrath as if they were fellow conspirators. 'Unfortunately she became involved with one of the detectives there.'

'Involved? What do you mean involved?'

'Romantically. They were going to get married.'

'What happened? He ditch her?'

'No, he got killed.'

'Christ.'

'Exactly.'

'What happened to him?'

'Drugs bust that went wrong. The heads weren't supposed to be armed.'

'But they were.' McGrath sighed wearily.

'They had a small arsenal. He never stood a chance.'

'So she had to come home and find a nice Irish boy?' McGrath was even surprised himself at his cynicism.

'Except she was pregnant.'

'Christ.'

'Exactly. Apparently there was a lot of pressure to have an abortion. She refused and had the baby back here in Dublin.'

McGrath rested his chin on both hands, flicking at his moustache with the little fingers of both hands. 'A woman with a mind of her own.'

'Very much so. She comes from a long line of Gardai. Her father and grandfather were both in the force. However she's your new generation woman, an independent spirit with her own opinions and certainly not intimidated at being one of the few women detectives in the force.'

So Kate Hamilton had joined the serious crime investigation unit based in Dublin's Store Street Garda station, a woman with a past already marked out as a woman with a future. After some sniffing and circling of one another she and McGrath did hit it off and within six weeks he had come to regard her as part of the team. Even Tony Dowling overcame his misgivings at having women involved in serious crime investigations and went out of his way to make her feel comfortable when confronted by some of the older, hardened officers.

As Hamilton finished her inspection of the crime scene, she knelt down to examine the body of Mary Dwyer, steeling herself against the lifeless eyes, the sight of the scalpel still protruding. She shuddered involuntarily. Jesus, don't let me end up like that, she thought. Not for a long time, anyway. I still have a child to rear.

Dean Lynch had finished the clean up operation by one thirty that morning. Every stitch of clothing, right down to underpants and socks, was sealed in small supermarket plastic bags. There were eight of them laid out on the kitchen table. He had taken off his shoes before getting into the car and they were already in separate plastic bags. He felt strangely calm, relieved almost. Tired but not exhausted. Sleepy. He lay on his bed, flicked off the bedside light and stared at the ceiling. As so often happened, his thoughts returned to her, Mrs Duggan, his personal tormentress.

Elizabeth Anne Duggan was a psychological misfit who should never have been let near children, let alone put in charge of them. She was a tall woman, always dressed in black with jet-black hair pulled back severely, revealing a pinched face and unhealthily pale complexion. The whiteness of her skin against the black uniform coupled with her long, white bony fingers, made her an intimidating figure for many of the children, intimidating and frightening. She was a religious zealot who felt it her personal mission in life to win back to the Lord children born to single mothers.

Elizabeth Anne Duggan was convinced these children were born with sin scorched on their souls. She forced them into acts of worship and penance at all hours of the day and night and made them perform more menial tasks than any of the others. 'This is the Lord's work,' she would often screech when she sensed any slacking. 'Jesus washed the feet of the sinner woman and you shall work as He has done. Let the Lord Our Saviour be your inspiration. Let His light be your beacon in life.'

Duggan had taken an instant dislike to Dean Lynch from the moment she came across him hiding in the kitchens, his pockets stuffed with stale, mouldy bread. That was the first time he'd experienced her favourite punishment, the under-stairs dark room, a four foot square, lightless corner where brushes and pans were kept. The seven-year-old Lynch was dragged, screaming and bucking, to the little room, thrown inside and left in total darkness for hours on end.

From that day on Elizabeth Anne Duggan hounded and haunted Dean Lynch's life. She would set little traps for him like pulling him out in front of the rest of the children at breakfast and accusing him of trying to run away. When the startled and terrified boy didn't deny the charges quickly enough she would order him back to the 'black room', as she called it. Two of the other staff would come forward, and it always took at least two, and drag him off to be squeezed again through the narrow door opening. With his hands and arms and the strength of his legs and the weight of his body he would push against that door as they strained outside to force it closed. 'Don't!' he always pleaded, first in a frightened whimper. But as he felt his legs give way from under him and the door close the light from his life yet again, panic would set in and the pleading would become roars of torment. 'Don't, please don't lock me in here!' And

always, always, he would hear that woman's voice as the
door shut tight, plunging him into total darkness.

'You can sleep in hell now, Dean Lynch, you can sleep in
hell.'

Elizabeth Anne Duggan knew how to turn the screws of
fear.

Kate Hamilton had to plead with her father to take Rory to school and then collect him afterwards. 'Look, dad, I've been up almost all night. You know I need the experience. If I ring in now and say I can't take an active part in the hospital investigation because I can't find someone to look after my son, what do you think'll happen? Huh? I'll be dropped like a hot potato, that's what'll happen and you know it.'

Her father had started to protest but gave up half way. He knew how ambitious she was, how she would move mountains to keep her independence and her child and her career.

'What'll I make for his tea?' he'd sighed.

Kate Hamilton bear-hugged him before rushing out the door. 'There's waffles in the freezer. Throw a poached egg over one, he loves that.' Then she was gone.

Rory had looked up at his grandfather and pulled a face. 'I hate poached eggs.'

Grandad smiled and led the boy back to his bedroom to get him dressed for school. Rory was already up to Grandad's waist, with sallow skin, brown eyes and black hair, courtesy of the Italian blood on his late father's side. He was a slight child with spindly legs and arms that seemed always to be on the go, leaving Grandad exhausted by the end of a day's baby-sitting.

Kate and Rory lived in a red-bricked artisan cottage

situated in a quiet cul-de-sac in the south Dublin suburb of Ranelagh. Keeping up with the mortgage payments swallowed most of her monthly salary and she relied heavily on her father to help out with looking after Rory. Not that he minded. Grandad, as Rory called him, was as much devoted to the boy as his mother and had moved to Dublin to be closer when she arrived back from Boston six months pregnant. She was his only child and indeed his only family, his wife dead almost five years previously. He'd bought a two-bedroomed flat fewer than five minutes' walk away and based his life around the child.

Most mornings Kate would get Rory ready for playschool and drive him the short distance to Grandad's flat. There he would play for about half an hour while Grandad finished off his breakfast and then the two, hand in hand, would walk the short journey to the school gates. Grandad usually picked him up again in the afternoon and took him home. There, while Rory told him all the latest classroom gossip, Grandad would cook his tea and prepare a hot dinner for his mother. He always waited until Kate arrived home and had a chance to eat the meal in peace before leaving.

Often as Grandad walked back to his empty flat from the toy strewn house his heart would be heavy with worry. What's going to become of the two of them? They're just so wrapped up in each other, what's going to become of them? She needs a man to help her out. She should be looking for a husband. That boy needs a father.

But looking for a partner was the last thing on Kate Hamilton's mind as she drove to Store Street Garda station. The murder investigation was the first she'd been allowed to become actively involved in. Despite her revulsion at the murder scene and shock at the viciousness of the attack, she still couldn't suppress the excitement she felt at being so closely involved. She was even more elated when Tony Dowling briefed her on the questioning of the lab staff and suggested she conduct it herself, while he and McGrath listened on.

'Where were you between ten and midnight last night?'

'Can you provide names of people who can confirm where you were?'

'What do you know about Mary Dwyer?'

'Can you think of any reason anyone would want to harm her?'

'Did she have any boyfriends, any male friend that you know about?'

'What sort of work did she do?'

'What kind of tests was she doing last night?'

'Could her murder be in any way related to her work?'

Hamilton fired the questions thick and fast but the answers didn't come as quickly as she or the team had anticipated. The shock on the faces of Mary Dwyer's colleagues was genuine. Reactions ranged between tears and an ashen-faced, stunned, numbed silence. Female staff wept openly, while male staff were subdued, some almost catatonic. Heads were repeatedly shaken, fists clenched, words of disbelief muttered. Hamilton looked towards Dowling, then McGrath. He shook his head slightly. We're getting nowhere fast.

Dean Lynch watched the bin lorry trundle over the bridge down to the shops along Lower Baggot Street. The bin men were running along beside, lifting black plastic bags, bins and boxes full of rubbish, tipping them into the back of the lorry. He calculated that at three-minute intervals the driver tripped a lever setting in motion the giant claws that compressed and then dragged the rubbish inwards.

Easing his BMW slowly forward Lynch glided to a spot ahead of the moving lorry, stopped and suddenly jumped out with the ten plastic bags. Walking quickly along the kerb he watched the claws creak into action and began to count. At two and a half minutes by his own calculations he stepped forward, dropped the bags and stood back. Right on time they were caught and dragged.

He allowed himself a slight smile.

Right again, Dean boyo.

Keep your cool.

You're doing just fine.

Despite the bitterly cold weather he was dressed lightly. He didn't feel the chill.

Dean Lynch was on a rollercoaster of revenge. He knew he was HIV positive, knew he had an advanced stage of AIDS and that the virus was destroying his body. And while the disease might progress only slowly, in his mind Lynch was preparing for the worst.

He believed he was dying.

He decided he wasn't going alone.

There were a few more scores to settle.

But first he had to cover his tracks.

14

'There are almost five hundred people employed here at any one time.'

Luke Conway was trying to explain the logistics of conducting a murder investigation in the Central Maternity Hospital. 'There are forty-two doctors, thirty male and twelve female. We have two hundred and seven nurses, all female. There are no male nurses. The rest of the staff is made up of physiotherapists, laboratory workers, pharmacists, social workers, administrative back-up and various support systems such as security and maintenance etcetera.'

Conway looked pale and drawn and was in a state of shock. At the beginning he could barely believe what was happening. But as dawn broke and the police remained and the lab door stayed sealed off, the awful significance of the yellow incident tape began to sink in.

'I need a list of all male staff members. I also need a list of any males who call on the hospital regularly, especially to the lab. I'm thinking here of couriers, flower deliverers, taxi men, whatever. I want you to sit down now, while your mind is fresh, and make a list. I need that list by lunch time.' Jack McGrath was at his efficient best. 'Also I may need to interview every member of staff individually and privately if we don't get an early break.'

'That's a lot of people, a lot of very busy people.'

'I know,' McGrath's muttered reply was weary. He hadn't slept much. The image of the scalpel sticking out of Mary

85

Dwyer's neck haunted him. 'A cast of thousands. That's what it looks like. A cast of bloody thousands.'

Neither spoke for a while.

'When can the lab staff get back to work?' Conway was determined to keep an air of normality in the hospital but was acutely aware the news had already spread like wildfire. 'There are lab results from yesterday that the staff need for today and tomorrow. I need to know now, otherwise I'll have to farm out all today's tests to a private lab.'

McGrath looked at his watch and slowly stood up. 'Forget the lab for the rest of today. There's a lot of work for my men to do in there. I'll let you know when it's clear to go back into action.' He was about to leave when a thought entered his mind. 'Could we use the medical library for our conferences. It's big enough and it'll save us trudging back and forward to Store Street station. Is that okay?'

Conway hesitated then nodded reluctantly.

Walking along the corridor towards the library, McGrath passed Dean Lynch. Neither man seemed to pay the slightest attention to the other. Lynch pulled the door into his consulting room closed.

Maybe they're going to make their base in the library?

That's right up your street, Dean boyo.

They're looking for you, but all the time you're looking at them.

Keep your cool.

You're doing well.

Plan ahead.

He always planned carefully. That was the secret of his successes. That was how he had first tasted sweet revenge.

Elizabeth Anne Duggan had asthma, everyone in the orphanage knew that. They could hear her coming long before they saw her, wheezing and coughing and panting. She was often seen leaning and grunting against a wall, waiting for her breath to return, fumbling among the layers of her black dress for the tablets that gave her relief. And when any of the children saw her take one, they ran to warn the others, for whatever was in those tablets sent her wild. With a seemingly renewed strength she would scour the corridors and dormitories looking for the slightest scuff mark on a wall or a bed not properly made, a locker not closed or tidy. And with shaking and trembling hands she would find someone, anyone to vent her rage upon. More often than not it was Dean Lynch, more often than not it was he who was made to suffer for her drug-induced rage, for it was the stimulant in the tablets that drove her to such extremes as well as relieving her asthma.

But he finally sorted her out.

He decided he'd had enough, he felt he could take no more. More importantly, he'd discovered by accident how to end his misery, how to end the tormenting, the taunting, the false accusations and beatings. And it was so simple. When he discovered how to do it he was astounded at its simplicity.

He stole six small pink tablets that the gardener used for his high blood pressure. He stole them after he'd read the label on the bottle in which they were kept. *One to be taken twice daily. Never to be taken by asthma sufferers.*

He'd brooded over that warning for weeks before he made his move. And when he'd thought his plan through he felt a quiver of excitement for the first time in his life, an electric tingling of delight as his mind registered the audacity, the sheer danger, of what was to happen. And happen it did, after he switched the tablets.

The shouts along the corridors alerted him to his success. As he followed the older children and staff running towards the noise, the sight of the collapsed and sweating and black-faced Elizabeth Anne Duggan struggling to stand up, struggling to breathe, greeted him. Through the milling crowd that had gathered around wondering how to help, Dean Lynch watched. And smiled. Just before Elizabeth Anne Duggan gave up her last tortured attempt at breathing she looked up to see the twelve-year-old Dean Lynch smiling down at her.

It was a smug, satisfied smile.

It was a job well done.

15 9.55 am
City Morgue, Store Street

Dublin's city morgue was situated on the corner of Store Street and Amiens Street in the north inner city. The building itself was old, part of a complex housing the Garda station in Store Street, the Coroner's office and the morgue itself. The city planners could never have foreseen the dramatic increase in crime that would completely swamp these facilities in later years. The Garda station in Store Street was the busiest in the city, dealing with up to ten thousand arrests each year. The morgue, too, was busier than the planners had originally anticipated.

Much busier.

Jack McGrath hated the morgue even more than he hated hospitals. Whatever it was about hospital smells, the morgue had its own particular odour that clung to clothes and hair. He paced up and down the courtyard separating the Coroner's office from the entrance to the morgue, puffing furiously on the fifth cigarette of the morning. Outside the gates he could hear the morning rush hour traffic as it blared and honked its way across the quays. McGrath ground his butt under a heel and made his way inside.

The main autopsy room was sixty feet long, thirty-five feet wide and as white as could be kept. There were white tiles from floor to roof, white paint on all woodwork and three white marble autopsy tables, each about ten feet from the other, centred and anchored to the middle of the tiled floor. At the head of each table there was a water tap with short hose attachment, while at the bottom a swivel tap, about nine inches tall, was fixed onto a deep sink unit. The room was well lit with natural light from a wire-strengthened opaque glass roof, heightening the overwhelming sense of white.

On the centre autopsy table lay the naked and dissected body of Mary Dwyer, now covered in a green surgical drape. Two white boiler suited forensics stood at an X-ray viewing box, inspecting a group of films. Noel Dunne was standing near the third autopsy table with Dan Harrison, the forensic photographer. Harrison had his Nikon in hand, at the ready. He squatted slightly, focused and suddenly a flash lit up the corner.

'Ah, Detective Inspector McGrath,' greeted Dunne, noticing McGrath out of the corner of his eye. 'You're just in time.' His booming voice echoed off the walls and the small group turned. McGrath nodded to each in turn and they nodded back.

'We've been working very hard here,' continued Dunne as he walked over to the viewing box, 'and we've more or less finished. Haven't we, gentlemen?'

A few grins were exchanged. Dunne was at his expansive best. Give him an audience and he'd perform. He stroked at his beard and moustache as he watched McGrath come closer. He was dressed in surgical greens, green protective gown that buttoned to neck and ankles and over this a long green, thick protective apron. He stood inside green, mid-calf heavy duty rubber boots.

Dunne picked up a wooden-backed clipboard on which lay an A4-sized piece of paper with a drawn outline of the human body. His scribbled handwriting and a number of pencilled arrows noted the observations he'd made as he conducted the postmortem. He slipped off the surgical gloves he was wearing and sat down on a stool beside the X-ray box, motioning McGrath to join him. The two made quite a contrast, McGrath lean and fit, Dunne slightly paunchy and stooped, his beard and moustache masking his facial features, making him look older than he really was.

The white boiler suited forensics shuffled to one side as McGrath moved in.

'Let's start from the top,' began Dunne, pushing a pair of half-moon glasses onto his nose. He frowned slightly and squinted at the clipboard. 'Can't even read my own hand-writing this morning.' A few grins were exchanged again. 'Ah, here we are. Right, let's begin.'

Out of the corner of his eye, McGrath could see one of the X-rays. It showed clearly the scalpel handle and blade embedded in the greyish white outline of Mary Dwyer's neck, the tip of the blade almost coming out the far side of her neck tissue.

'Case number 1473, postmortem of Mary Dwyer.' Dunne flicked on his cassette recorder, speaking as much to it as to the audience.

'She is a young, well nourished female,' he continued, 'aged early twenties approximately. She has short reddish brown hair, blue eyes and weighs eight stones seven pounds. She is five feet nine inches tall.'

Dunne paused briefly to check on a squiggled entry, then continued. The audience listened attentively. Jack McGrath fiddled in his pocket for a peppermint.

'She has a four inch jagged laceration to the left temporal scalp with blood matting of the hair in that area. There was a pool of blood beside her at the incident scene consistent with bleeding from that scalp wound.' Dunne placed the clipboard down and looked up at one of the X-rays lit up by the glow of the viewing box lights. It showed front to back and side to side views of Mary Dwyer's head and upper neck. He stretched a finger out and pointed to a faint silver grey line on one side. 'There's a hairline fracture of the skull underneath that scalp wound. You can just about see it on the X-ray but I found it when I inspected the open skull. She must have been bounced off that bench with some force.'

For the briefest of seconds Dunne's eyes locked on McGrath's. 'I don't always X-ray my patients, Detective Inspector,' explained Dunne. 'Usually only when I'm looking for bullets or shrapnel or such like. I thought this one would make good teaching material though.' He turned back to his notes and continued.

'There are conjunctival haemorrhages in both eyes with multiple petechiae on the face. Three amalgam fillings in the teeth, otherwise the mouth was normal. I've swabbed it as usual,' he added this for McGrath's benefit. 'There is bruising to the left and right of the neck midline with linear scratch markings along the same area. The bruising has two patterns: some are disc shaped, one quarter of an inch wide, the rest are larger and irregular, suggesting movement of the fingers. There are petechiae on the epiglottis and visceral pleura; haemorrhages under the skin of the neck and into the strap muscles.'

Dunne paused, pressed the OFF button on his cassette and shouted, 'Dan, would you get me a shot of this, please? Take one of that X-ray, would you?' He pointed to the X-ray with the scalpel *in situ*. 'Then try and get me a close up of the neck. This *is* very good teaching material,' he added to no one in particular. McGrath took the opportunity to pop another peppermint.

Dunne looked back at his notes. 'There is a half-inch clean stab wound to the right mid-neck area. No bleeding from this wound was found at the crime scene. There is a surgical scalpel embedded in the neck through this stab wound.' All eyes followed Dunne's as he looked up again at the X-ray with the scalpel. He stroked his beard. 'The scalpel handle has Swann hyphen Norton, capital BS 2982 engraved on its side. There are circular, concentric etchings on the lower third of the handle. The scalpel handle shows heavy brown staining.'

Dunne flicked the OFF button again. 'I'll come back to that in a minute. That staining could be significant though.' McGrath looked over sharply but Dunne was off again.

The ON button was flicked. 'There is bruising to the left outer shoulder and mid chest. The right index finger nail is broken and bent back. The rest of the body is unremarkable apart from a few bruises on the back of the upper left shoulder and an old appendectomy scar. There is no sign of sexual interference whatsoever. The girl is virgo intacta.' He stopped recording, still looking at the viewing boxes.

'What does all this add up to?' asked McGrath finally. He noticed that a small group had gathered around behind and to the side of Dunne. They included two uniformed Gardai, and Pat Relihan, the tall, dark, fingerprint expert from Kerry. They were waiting for the final verdict.

Dunne sighed deeply, as if he was taking everything personally. McGrath hadn't seen him so involved in a long time. Dunne had a very simple philosophy. He was a doctor first and foremost who just happened to be a forensic pathologist. Even though his patients were always dead his duty was to protect them and discover their cause of death. He rarely speculated on motive or intent. He left that to the likes of Jack McGrath.

'What it all adds up to is this: the first injury she sustained I believe was the head injury. Her head was cracked off the side of that bench with enough force to fracture the skull and probably dull her reactions. Apart from the broken nail and a few scratch marks on her neck there isn't much sign of a struggle. Next she was strangled. There are deep bruises to the neck and fractures to the superior horns of the thyroid cartilage on both sides. This all fits in with strangulation.' He paused. The audience shuffled slightly. 'Now we come to the gory bit.' All eyes fixed on Dunne. 'The scalpel was stuck into her neck after she was dead.'

'After?' McGrath couldn't hold back.

'Yes, Detective Inspector, after.' Dunne turned to his notes again. 'The blade severed her common carotid artery, among other things,' he added laconically and then explained. 'The common carotid is a major artery carrying blood to the brain. If the blade had severed it while she was alive, in other words while her heart was still technically beating, there would have been a lot of blood in the neck space. Apart from a small amount of seepage there was no blood in the neck space.'

The bastard, thought McGrath.

'Now, the scalpel handle is heavily stained.' Dunne reached into a side pocket and produced a short thin foil which he peeled open. 'This is a standard issue scalpel handle. You can see it's a sort of silver-grey colour. The one we removed from this girl's neck was almost totally brown, a sort of streaked dark brown. I have seen this before – that scalpel handle came out of an old sterilising unit. Most modern sterilising units leave no staining on instruments. But that handle looks like it's been in and out of the same, possibly old, steriliser for some time. Find that steriliser and you'll possibly find where the scalpel handle came from.'

McGrath took out a pocket notebook and scribbled something down.

'Now, Detective Inspector,' continued Dunne. He had a smug grin on his face. 'I've been doing a little detective work myself here this morning. Ably assisted by Garda Phelan here.' He reached round and placed a hand on the dark blue uniformed arm of a young Garda standing behind. McGrath noticed he was almost blushing. 'Garda Phelan did a bit of ringing around earlier. Tell Detective Inspector McGrath what you learned.'

Garda Phelan cleared his throat nervously. 'Well Dr Dunne wanted to find out where the scalpel handle might have come from. So I rang the Central Maternity Hospital surgical stores' department and they told me all their small equipment comes from an agent in Kells. So I rang them and they told me they have the agency for all the main Dublin hospitals and general outlets in the city. Swann-Norton scalpel handles and scalpel blades are fairly easily come by.'

'So what you're telling me,' interrupted McGrath, 'is that scalpels are as common as muck in Dublin.'

Dunne cut across. 'As common as muck, Detective Inspector, if you're a doctor. Make a note of that. As common as muck if you're a doctor. I wouldn't have thought the scalpel was much help apart from the staining. I still believe that narrows down its point of origin, for want of a better phrase.'

'There's no prints on the blade or handle either,' a soft Kerry accent interrupted. Pat Relihan was putting in his tuppenceworth.

'And forensics discovered something interesting at the crime scene.' Dunne turned to one of the white boiler suits and then looked back at McGrath. 'Forensics do a marvellous job, Detective Inspector, they really do.' He was enjoying himself no end.

McGrath grinned ruefully.

'There was a small piece of latex,' said the white boiler suited forensic, 'no more than a quarter of an inch wide and long, lying on the ground just to the side of her right hand. The hand with the broken nail.'

'And?' asked McGrath.

'Dr Dunne thinks it's from a surgical glove.'

The room went suddenly quiet, the only noise coming from one of the water taps as it sluiced along Mary Dwyer's body.

'Yes, it looks very like a piece of latex from a surgical glove. It all adds up. No nail indents on the neck, no fingerprints on the handle. Whoever murdered this girl may well have been wearing surgical gloves. I had a close look at her neck and noticed traces of some fine powder. Most surgical gloves are powdered inside. We've sent that off for forensic examination to see if I'm right but I can tell you, this all fits in.'

For the first time Noel Dunne locked onto and held McGrath's piercing gaze.

'What are you suggesting?'

'I'm not suggesting anything, Detective Inspector, not a thing. That's not my job, that's your job. But I'm going to run a few ideas by you.' Dunne rested his hands on his lap, fingers interlocked. He stared at them for a moment, then began. 'Let's look at what we've got so far: Mary Dwyer was strangled to death. Within minutes the scalpel was stuck into her neck. Now I can't help feeling that action was some sort of statement, a personal mark.' He paused for a moment. 'The scalpel handle and blade are standard hospital and general practice issue. My feeling is that they are not going to be that helpful. Apart from the staining.'

McGrath's eyebrows arched.

'Look at it: a man turns up in the laboratory with a fresh blade attached to an old scalpel handle. From the position on that workbench where her head was bounced I'd say she saw and heard him before he came close enough to grab her. The fact that he attacked her *at* her bench, not at the door, suggests she may have known her attacker and let him into the lab not realising he had her in his sights. I believe that this man actually knew Mary Dwyer and she knew him and was not surprised to find him in the lab so late at night.' Dunne looked up at McGrath to see how he was taking all this in.

'I'm with you all the way.'

'Right. So who's going to turn up in the Central Maternity Hospital laboratory at near eleven at night that she doesn't feel threatened by?' Dunne looked McGrath straight in the eyes again.

McGrath returned the gaze. 'You tell me.'

'I'm not telling you anything, Detective Inspector. But my gut instinct tells me that you shouldn't spend too much time looking for our murderer outside the hospital.'

'You think he actually works in the place?'

'Yes.'

Silence.

'Anything else you feel I should know about or look for? You're the doctor. You know how these places work.'

'Look for the foil that held that blade. Take this one and look out for one similar.'

Dunne reached into his pocket again, producing a small foil. He handed it to McGrath who turned it over two or three times, noting packet size and lettering. *Paragon Sterile Stainless Steel Blade: Sterilised by Gamma Radiation: Sterility Guaranteed if Package is Unbroken: Blade No. 23: Made in Sheffield England.*

'The blade came from a foil like this. It may still be in the lab or even one of the examination rooms along the corridor leading up to the lab. Look for any room on that level or any other level that has an old sterilising unit. Check also for any surgical glove wrappers. Check wastepaper baskets, sink units, anywhere our man might have got careless and dropped the blade foil or glove wrapper.'

McGrath looked at Dunne with obvious dismay. 'I hate hospitals. I was hoping this was going to be a simple case, like some guy looking for drugs or something. The more you tell me the more I don't like what I hear.'

Dunne grinned. He hadn't seen McGrath so uneasy before, and he knew the forensics were loving every minute of his discomfort.

'Did you find anything more about how our man got in and out of the hospital?' Dunne asked.

'Security says he could only have got in and out through the basement or the wards, certainly not the main entrance or he would've had to go past them. He could've sneaked down through the wards and back out that way again. But so far nobody's seen anything.'

Dunne thought this over for a minute. 'I'd say he used the basement. I can't see anyone doing what he did and then ambling back through the wards as if nothing had happened. I'd bet on the basement.'

McGrath stroked his moustache. 'Then he must know that hospital fairly well. He must know how to get in and out without being seen. That's worrying.'

Dunne nodded slowly. 'Now, Detective Inspector, you know I'm not the sort of man to get overly dramatic about murder cases.' McGrath looked at him sharply. 'And I have no great desire to sound overly dramatic this morning – '

'But . . .' interrupted McGrath.

'Indeed. But I have a feeling this isn't one of your ordinary run-of-the-mill murders. This man is too well organised for my liking. He's covered his tracks carefully. He could easily strike again.'

The room went deathly quiet. Outside a car horn blared, nearly lifting Garda Phelan out of his skin.

McGrath slipped the scalpel blade foil into his pocket and

stretched his cramping legs. He looked around at the green cloth covered body on the central autopsy table. 'I hope you're wrong, Dr Dunne. I hope you're wrong. I hate bloody hospitals. I'd like to sort this one out quickly.'

'You'll have my full report this afternoon,' said Dunne standing up. He began to put away instruments.

McGrath walked slowly past the body on the table. A lifeless hand, wax-like, showed from beneath the drapes. I hope there's gonna be no more like you, he thought as he left.

16

Tommy Malone sat in one of the front rooms of Hal's
Snooker Emporium waiting for his A-team to arrive. As he
waited he puffed smoke rings into the air.

Hal's Snooker Emporium was a favourite meeting place
for a number of small time Dublin criminals and was situated
above a group of three shops along a side street in the
south Dublin suburb of Monkstown. One of the shops was
a hairdressing salon run by a girl called Eileen ('Late of
New York'), the second a dry cleaners, while the third was
occupied by a solicitor who specialised in personal injury
litigation. His business was booming.

The entrance to the emporium itself was a reinforced steel
door at the top of a concrete staircase to the side of the
building. Just inside the front door Hal had positioned a
chipped formica-topped desk and stacking chair where one
of his henchmen sat, ostensibly checking membership status,
but in reality keeping an eye out for police raids. The
emporium was divided into a main hall which held eight
full-size snooker tables, and three small rooms to the front
of the building which overlooked the road outside. The hall
was in almost constant use, mainly by the unemployed and
hopeless youths of the surrounding areas. The air was usually
heavy with the smell of cigarette smoke and stale beer,
peaking on dole day, and occasionally was laced with the
sweet aroma of hashish.

The middle of the three front rooms had a specially

strengthened door with strong bolts inside. A fire burned most days, even at the height of summer, in a small cast-iron fireplace and in the middle of the floor stood a half-size snooker table. The fire was kept well stoked by Hal himself, a small weed of a man with a row of nicotine-stained teeth and greasy hair. Hal rented the middle room out on an hourly basis and charged top rates. The strengthened door and strong bolts prevented quick entry to the room in the event of a raid, while the burning fire allowed incriminating evidence to be destroyed. Tommy Malone had used Hal's Emporium on a number of occasions in the past. He had a feel for the place, believing it was lucky for him. No job planned there had gone wrong.

He warmed his bottom in front of the fire, still blowing smoke rings into the air.

'Moonface' Martin Mulligan was the first to arrive. Six feet tall and fifteen stone. Although only in his early thirties, Moonface was almost bald and had the unfortunate habit of dragging his remaining Weetabix-like hair across his pate. His round face added to a final unattractive result. Moonface was a strongman with a vicious temper. No one had ever been known to call him Moonface to his moonface. He was dressed in a Manchester United tracksuit with a red and black scarf around his neck. Moonface was a big soccer fan. While Manchester United was his favourite English premier league team, he reserved all his passion for the Ireland soccer team. He followed Ireland wherever they played and tried to arrange his 'work' around their fixtures. When Ireland played in the 1994 World Cup in the USA, Moonface had robbed three bookies inside two weeks to get the money for the trip. When they had progressed further than even Moonface predicted, he robbed an all-night pharmacy in Orlando, Florida, where the team were playing, to keep his cash flow going. Moonface would die for Ireland if he had to. So far that hadn't proved necessary. Despite his hard-man reputation and activities, Moonface still lived at home with his mother in a corporation housing scheme in the Dublin suburb of Rathmines. To Ma Mulligan, Martin was still her baby – she continued to do all his washing and ironing and fretted when he wasn't home at a sensible hour.

'Howya Tommy? Fuckin' freezin' outside,' said baby Mulligan.

'Howya Martin? Hit a few balls around till the others arrive.'

Next to arrive was Sam Collins, dressed as usual in black. Black trousers, shoes and socks, black turtleneck sweater under a black corduroy jacket. His jet black hair was pulled into a short pigtail at the back. The only break with the colour scheme was a silver ring in the top of his left ear which Collins had the habit of fingering at when he was nervous or excited.

'How's about ye Tommy?' Sam Collins came originally from Newry in Northern Ireland and even though he had been living in Dublin for eight years had never lost his strong Northern twang.

Collins spotted Mulligan and tipped his rolled-up copy of the *Daily Star* at him.

'How's about ye Martin?'

'Notta bother.'

Sam Collins was an edgy, shifty character. He slipped over to the window and squinted out as if he expected the place to be surrounded by police. This wouldn't have been surprising for Collins was an ex-IRA explosives expert who had seen his fair share of house-to-house searches by the RUC. He knew what it was like to be on the run. In fact he was so used to it, it had become second nature. When the IRA declared a ceasefire on midnight 31st August 1994, Sam Collins quickly realised he would have to do a bit of free-lance work to make ends meet. Since he didn't know anything other than guns and explosives, he quickly drifted into the Dublin underworld as a hired hand. When the IRA resumed hostilities with a massive bomb in London's docklands on 8th February 1995 Collins eased himself away from their activities and paid only a token lip service to 'the cause'. He held on to his small cache of weapons and explosives and rented them, or himself and them, to the highest bidder. When the IRA command learned of this the word was put out that Sam Collins was a traitor to the cause and would be eliminated if he continued with his anti-social activities. Collins went into hiding, not keen to present himself for a trial and almost certain execution. Like Tommy Malone, Sam Collins was looking for a 'big job' with a big reward and the chance to get out of the country.

'Have a seat, Sam,' suggested Malone. 'There's wan more to come.'

Collins sat down on a long wooden bench that ran along one wall and flicked open the paper, pretending to read. His eyes took in the scene behind the pages.

Only the crack of billiard ball against billiard ball broke the silence.

After about fifteen minutes a faint tap set Malone to his feet. The door opened slightly and a small, dumpy woman dressed in a cheap fake leopard coat peered inside. 'Is that ye Tommy?'

Malone opened the door further. 'Come on in Peggy.' He closed the door and slid the bolts across, then pulled a chair against the handle, jamming it tight. Mulligan and Collins looked at each other, puzzled. Collins shrugged his shoulders and turned back to the paper.

'How's Monty?' asked Malone.

'Not grea', Tommy. He's not doin' at all well this time.'

'Peggy, this is Martin Mulligan and Sam Collins. Ye remember Sam, he was on that job we pulled with Monty down in Cork a while ago.'

'Howya Sam? Freezin' out.'

Collins nodded. If he was aware of the weather he gave no sign. The woman's presence unsettled him.

'Sit down Peggy. Martin, would ye sit down now? I told Hal we'd be outa here by four.'

Mulligan joined Collins on the bench, sitting about five feet away. Peggy Ryan sat on a chair Malone had pulled up for her.

'This is Peggy Ryan. She's Monty Ryan's wife. Monty's in Mountjoy doing a twelve-year stretch for armed robbery.'

Malone was setting out Peggy Ryan's background. He could sense the two younger men were unhappy at her being there.

She looked at them and said, 'He's not copin' with this stretch at all. He's not copin' at all.'

Neither Collins or Mulligan spoke.

Malone sat up on the billiard table. 'Peggy's an important part of this job. In fact if she doesn' like what I'm gonna say the whole thing's off.'

Collins slowly lowered the paper. He looked again at the woman, this time with more interest. Collins was a bit of a loner and didn't socialise well with women. He sensed he had better take an interest in this one, though.

'I'm gonna set out the background first,' began Malone. 'If anywan doesn' like what he hears then stop me. I don't want anywan pullin' out at the very end. This is the last big job I'm gonna do for a long time and I don't want it fucked up from the beginnin' by somewan backin' out and then shootin' his mouth off.'

Nobody spoke. Peggy Ryan looked at Malone with almost hero worship.

'There's six hundred grand for each of youse within five days of the start.' He paused to let this sink in. 'Anywan want out now?'

Nobody spoke. Moonface picked at his nose and inspected the result.

'It's a kidnappin'.' Pause, long pause. 'Anywan want out now?'

Nobody spoke. Sam Collins rolled up the *Daily Star* and stuck it behind his back. This was sounding interesting.

'It's gonna be a big job and I'm askin' three million. That's six hundred thousand big wans for each of youse and twelve hundred grand for me. That's 'cos I've got all the know how and the perfect hideaway.' Malone shifted slightly on the billiard table. 'Anywan want out now?'

'No, Tommy,' whispered Peggy Ryan. Six hundred thousand big 'wans' was hard to walk away from. She was scrimping and saving desperately now that Monty was back inside.

Still neither Collins nor Mulligan spoke, each trying to take in what Malone was unfolding.

'We're gonna kidnap a baby.' He let this one sink in for much longer. 'Anywan want out now?'

Nobody spoke.

'I need to know now if youse is in from here. Nothin' else comes outa my mouth from here on unless youse is all in. Are ye in Martin?'

'Fuckin' sure. It beats robbin' bookies any day of the week.' Moonface laughed at his own little joke. No one else did.

'What about ye Sam?'

'I'm in, Tommy. It sounds okay to me.' Sam Collins' brain was ticking away in overdrive. This sounded just the sort of job he had been looking out for for a long time, this sounded ideal. What he didn't like about it was Tommy Malone. Even though he had been on two small robberies with Malone that had gone all right, he knew of Malone's reputation as a loser. He decided to hold tight and listen to what else might pan out. But he wasn't sure Malone was the right one for a big job.

'What about ye, Peggy? Now ye know why ye're here.'

Peggy Ryan had eleven of her own children and four grandchildren. Monty Ryan might have spent most of his life behind bars but he'd had an active sex life when outside.

'Sure, Tommy. Whatever ye say, whatever ye say. I could sure do with the money.'

Malone looked at them each again, and then continued.

'Harry O'Brien is a multi-millionaire Christ knows how many times over.' Malone began unveiling his plan. 'He's president of the O'Brien Corporation and it's worth a fuckin' fortune. He married a young wan a while ago and she's just popped a baby. The papers say he's promised to put up two million for the Central Hospital to mark the occasion. If he can put up two million just to mark the occasion he can fuckin' well fork out three to get him back. We're gonna kidnap Harry O'Brien's young fella.'

His co-conspirators listened impassively. Tommy Malone

might have been relating a plan to put Shamrock Rovers back in Milltown for all the expression they showed.

'Look at it,' continued Malone enthusiastically, 'we won't have to go round wearin' masks to stop the young fella from seein' our faces. We don't have to worry about him tryin' to escape. We don't have to worry about movin' him around. We don't have to worry about him pickin' us out in an ID parade. We don't have to worry about leavin' him back when Big Harry's paid over the ransom. He can be dumped outside any hospital. All we have to do is feed the little bollox and change his nappy.'

Both Collins and Mulligan started to protest. They could handle a kidnap, even a bit of heavy muscle if it came to that. But changing nappies was way out of bounds.

'That's where Peggy comes in,' Malone interrupted. 'Peggy knows all about babies, don't ye, Peg?'

'I do Tommy, I do.' Peggy Ryan was delighted. 'Jaysus, all those years of rearin' children might actually come in useful, after all.'

They all managed a grin at that.

'Peggy's in charge of lookin' after the baby,' continued Malone. 'She feeds him, changes him and generally makes sure he's well looked after. The rest of us just have to get him and take him to the cottage.'

'What cottage?' asked Collins. His initial misgivings were fading and he was beginning to look at Malone in a new light. This might be worth a go at after all.

'I've a small cottage outside Newbridge. It used to be me uncle's. He lived in it when he worked in the Polaroid factory in Newbridge. He's dead this years and his children are all in England. I'm the only wan that knows about it or ever uses it. It's tucked well away and surrounded by fields on all sides. There's a narrow lane about three hundred yards long that leads up to it. Nobody can get up that lane without bein' seen. The nearest house is about half a mile away. I've used it a lot when lyin' low. It's only about an hour's drive from Harry O'Brien's mansion in Wicklow but far enough away that the rozzers wouldn't think of lookin' there.'

Malone paused for a moment and looked at the others before continuing. 'I have a...' he paused slightly again, then continued, 'I have a close friend who works in the O'Brien headquarters in Dawson Street.' The way Malone disclosed this made the close friend sound like a member of the board of the O'Brien Corporation. Collins looked impressed and even Moonface stopped picking at his nose.

'Who?' asked Collins.

'I can't tell ye that, Sam. I really can't tell ye that yet. When this is all over the rozzers'll turn that place upside down and I don't want anywan to know me source apart from me. Now I knew youse wouldn't like that but youse is just gonna havta trust me on that.'

Collins looked at Moonface who shrugged his shoulders. 'Doesn't bother me,' he said moving towards the billiard table to take a shot.

Collins wasn't so sure. 'Tommy, if we're gonna land this one we all need to know what we're dealing with from the beginning.' His strong Northern accent had a sharp edge to it. 'How are we to know what you're up to behind our backs if we don't know who you're working with?' Collins liked the sound of the job and the small numbers involved but he wasn't going to take chances.

'Sam, I can't tell ye, that's all. We're all in this together. Nobody's gonna double cross anywan 'cos nobody's gonna get hold of the money unless we're all together. I just can't.'

'When are we gonna move on the house?' Moonface butted in.

'As soon as the child's brought home,' said Malone. He sounded relieved at the distraction. 'The papers say he should be brought home within days. I wanna hit the joint the first night, before they can get inta any routine. Their security would be upset by the change. I think we should go in after midnight.'

A short discussion developed about the best way to get in and out of the house, how to get around the alarm and how to get away. Sam Collins had decided to lay off Malone for the time being. He'd find out later who was in on the inside of the O'Brien Corporation.

'I want youse to steal two good cars,' said Malone. 'A fast, strong wan and a small, family sedan. Mebbe a Range Rover or wan of them patrol jobs. And a Volvo 460. Ye can get those, Sam. Put new plates on each. Put Kildare registration plates on the Volvo.'

Collins nodded.

'Martin,' continued Malone, 'get a fast motorbike. Not too flashy or too big. Check what the couriers use and go for wan of them. Get yerself a courier outfit as well. When we have the baby I want ye to drop Polaroid photos of him all over the place so that the rozzers know he's alive and well.'

'Do I need to do anythin', Tommy?' asked Peggy Ryan.

Malone smiled for the first time. 'Yes, Peg.' He reached into a pocket and pulled out a wad of notes, peeling off ten. 'Go out and buy baby clothes, nappies, bottles, teats ... whatever ye think yer gonna need for the five days. Don't buy it all in one store and don't let any of the family know what yer buyin'. Store it in the garage and keep it well out of sight. When ye've got it ready I'll call and collect.'

She nodded, fingering a strand of her coarse brown hair.

'Ye'd better tell yer family ye're goin' away for a while.'

Peggy thought about this. 'I'll say I'm goin' to me sister in Liverpool.'

'Is she on the phone? If wan of the kids rings lookin' for ye she could give the game away.'

'Not much chance of that at the moment, Tommy. She's in the slammer for passin' dud cheques.'

They all had a good laugh at that.

'But don't the rest of yer family know she's in the slammer?'

'Nah, I've kept it a secret from the rest of them. She's their favourite aunty. I wouldn't want to ruin her reputation.'

They had an even better laugh at that.

Malone was winding up the meeting. Each knew exactly

what to do and what was expected. The ice had broken and they were chatting.

'There's wan final thing,' he announced, 'and this is vital.' They stopped and listened attentively. Even Moonface stopped picking at his nose.

'From the moment we grab that child I don't want anybody drinkin' so much as a can of beer. Youse have gotta keep yer wits about youse and keep yer heads down. The child mustn't come to any harm. No booze, okay?'

They nodded.

'Where's the ransom gonna be dropped?' Sam Collins was checking all angles.

'Tha's the fuckin' best bit, Sam,' smiled Malone. 'I was leavin' that till the end to tell youse. I was up all night workin' it out. Wait'll youse hear.' He couldn't stop smiling. 'First,' he explained, 'we're gonna nick another three cars. Then we're gonna rent six mobile phones from six different companies. Wan of the phones goes inta each of the three cars.'

Moonface's brow furrowed as he tried to keep up with the plan and Peggy looked lost already. She continued to look at Malone with hero worship. Collins never took his eyes from Malone, analysing and processing his every word.

'The cars'll be parked outside three of them multistorey car parks ye see around the city. When the money's gonna be delivered we'll tell the fella to drive to the first car and switch to it. Wan of us'll watch what's goin' on from up in the carpark.' Malone paused for a moment to see how this was going. 'Are youse with me?' Three heads nodded, though two hadn't a clue what Malone was talking about.

'Now if there's any rozzers followin', or there's a heli-copter watchin' from the sky, or if the first car is wired so it can be followed, then we can start to lose them immediately. From the minute the fella has switched to wan of our cars we can direct him where to go over the mobile phone.'

As Malone slowly set out his master plan, Sam Collins was won over. This was sounding very interesting. This was not the plan of a loser. This *could* work.

'Using our mobile phones the fella's directed to the second multistorey car park where the next car's waitin'. He's told to switch inta it and to drive away. Then he's moved on again to the next car. Each time he changes car wan of us can move on to the next car park and watch from up inside to see if he's bein' followed. And while he's drivin' from wan spot to the other Martin'll be followin' him on a bike to make sure there's no funny business along the way like the rozzers stoppin' him and gettin' in or anythin' like that.' Malone flicked his eyes quizzically at Moonface.

'I'm with ye, Tommy, I'm with ye.' He wasn't really but Sam Collins was and he was feeling a quiver of excitement as he realised the plan's potential for success.

'What happens after the switch to the last car?' Collins asked, fingering at the ring in his ear. 'We can't have the bollox driving around Dublin for a week.'

Malone smiled at Collins' interruption. 'Tha's what I was comin' to. That's the good bit.' He looked at each of the three in turn. 'Do youse know Hillcourt Mansions along the quays?'

Three heads nodded in unison. The whole of Dublin knew Hillcourt Mansions, a corporation flat development with a reputation for drug dealing, robbery and violence. The Gardai had more or less declared it a no-go area and rarely ventured inside the quadrangular complex unless in significant numbers. In Dublin criminal circles Hillcourt Mansions was like a cathedral where refuge could be sought. Many a mugger or handbag snatcher had been chased there and managed to avoid the clutches of the Gardai by escaping along one of four narrow lanes that lead out the back and onto busy roads. There was only one main route into the complex wide enough to take a car or delivery van.

'He's told to drive into Hillcourt Mansions where two of us is waitin' and ready. As soon as the car hits the flats out he comes and the money is put inta four big hold-alls. Then we get outa the fuckin' place along the wee lanes on two motorbikes. Wadda youse think?'

Moonface's mouth dropped open with surprise. 'Fuckin'

brilliant,' he offered. 'Fair play to ye Tommy, but that sounds fuckin' brilliant.'

'That's good, Tommy,' agreed Sam Collins. 'That's a good plan, right enough.' He decided there and then to drop his concerns about Malone's contact inside the O'Brien Corporation. He'd work on that later if needed.

Peggy said nothing, she just beamed at Malone as she listened.

'Now get goin',' said Malone confidently.

As Malone paid off Hal and edged his way gingerly down the concrete steps, he was humming to himself again. He was delighted with the way the meeting had gone and was especially pleased that he had won Sam Collins over. He needed Collins badly, for Collins had guns and explosives.

Walking to the public phone box at the corner of Monkstown Hill, Malone slipped a twenty-pence coin into the slot and began dialling.

'Betty?'

'Is that ye, Tommy?'

'Aye.'

'How'd it go?'

'Brillian', brillian'.'

'So it's on then?'

'Fuckin' sure.'

'So I'll see ye in the mornin'?'

'Aye, ye will. Five o'clock, isn' that righ'?'

'Aye, five o'clock. Roun' the back. The black door, like I told ye.'

'Righ'.'

'See ye.'

'Yeah,' said Malone. 'See ye at five.' He lit another cigarette to keep warm.

We're in business.

As Tommy Malone placed the receiver back in its cradle, his intended target was being changed and winded after a feed. Sandra O'Brien held the tiny baby in her arms, crooning gently into his ear. In another corner of the room

June Morrison was testing the water inside a baby bath for the child's first wash. She smiled as she watched Sandra, noting how nervously the young woman was handling the baby.

'Cradle his head in your left hand when you set him down,' she advised and gently took him up to demonstrate.

Gordon O'Brien threw both arms out suddenly as his tiny body felt the change of hands, and his legs kicked inside the oversized blue babygrow. Sandra and Morrison exchanged smiles. Despite the early exchanges between herself and Harry O'Brien, June Morrison had taken a real shine to Sandra and now fussed over her like a brooding chicken. The drama of the emergency birth had abated and the joy she saw every time Big Harry poked his nose inside the room won her over to him as well.

June Morrison decided to put the past unpleasantries aside and concentrate now on helping Sandra become confident in handling her newborn baby and getting used to his touches and cries and understanding his needs.

Jack McGrath was worried.

There was no sign of the blade foil or surgical gloves wrapper anywhere in the hospital. Wastepaper bins, sinks, sluices, backs of radiators, all had been carefully checked. Next, security informed him they were now certain the only way the murderer could have got in and out of the hospital unnoticed at that hour of the night was through the basement. All wards had been checked and double checked. No one had left and reappeared around the time of the murder. Noel Dunne's theory was sounding more and more plausible.

Then the outpatients sister showed McGrath the old fashioned sterilising unit used for all instruments in East Wing. She agreed it caused staining on scalpel handles. 'And a helluva lot of other instruments too,' she added, sounding annoyed. 'I've been asking for months to have a new unit installed here but we're always the last department to be upgraded.'

McGrath asked why.

'Because we're the public wing. Everything new goes into the private wings first.'

'Missing any scalpel handles?'

'I'm sorry, I can't really tell. We never keep a record of the small surgical instruments here. They walk so often it would be impossible to keep up with them all.'

112

'Walk?'

'Yeah, walk. As in nicked.'

The room was sealed off for forensics.

Half an hour later he had a blazing row with Luke Conway who was pressing to have the laboratory back in action.

'I haven't finished checking it yet,' snapped McGrath.

'I need the lab, Inspector. I need that lab. I have a hospital to run.'

'And I've got a murder to investigate.'

The two middle-aged men eyeballed each other, both enraged.

Conway was under a lot of pressure. The hospital's reputation must be preserved at all costs, even if that might mean frustrating the investigating detectives. An attempt to convene the hospital board in an emergency policy meeting had to be scrapped due to non-availability at such short notice of many members. The ball was firmly in Luke Conway's court, it was up to him to minimise any damage to the hospital's reputation.

To make matters worse for McGrath, Tony Dowling reported that Mary Dwyer's background was squeaky clean.

'Nobody can come up with any reason why she might be attacked.' Dowling inspected his notes again. 'We know everything except the name of the bollox who did this and why he did it,' he added unhelpfully.

Tony Dowling was nearing his fifty-seventh birthday when he was due to retire. There were only six weeks to go. He was of medium height, medium build and still had a medium amount of hair. He had a thick Cavan accent that rolled easily off his tongue and wore clothes that were fashionable in the late seventies and threatening to come back into fashion again. Dowling had spent all his life in the Gardai Siochana, first in uniform and later in the detective ranks. He was looking forward to going back home to Cootehill, where he could fish the lakes and walk the back roads, stopping and talking to anyone who'd answer – anything but forcing young thugs up against the wall and frisking them for guns and knives. Dowling was longing for the quiet life of his retirement.

McGrath grinned despite his sombre mood. 'Jesus Tony, there's no doubt about it. You're a bloody genius.'

Dowling grinned back. They had been together in the Serious Crime Squad for almost seven years and worked well as a team. They knew each other's working patterns, eating habits and families.

'What worries me,' said McGrath, 'is that Dunne's probably right. Everything points to this guy knowing that hospital like the back of his hand. He's covered his tracks well. We're gonna have to look carefully at what's under our very noses. We'll have to interview a lot of people.'

'Some of them aren't gonna take too kindly to that,' commented Dowling.

'No,' agreed McGrath thoughtfully, stroking his moustache. 'No. We could have some problems. And I hate bloody hospitals.'

'Ah, would ye ever give over.'

Dean Lynch was not feeling good. The anti-thrush Mycostatin pastilles he had started were working very slowly and his mouth and throat still felt raw.

He stood naked in front of the wall-to-wall mirror in his exercise room, inspecting his body. He had tried to do his usual quota of push-ups but found he became exhausted quickly, much more so than he could remember in the past. He sweated easily. On the floor lay unopened bottles of vitamins and different packets of capsules containing trace mineral preparations. He flexed his muscles, then turned sideways for a better view of his stomach.

You're losing weight, Dean boyo, you're losing weight.

You're fading away.

Don't fade too fast, Dean, don't fade too fast. There's more work to do.

Lynch had had a chance to rest and regain his strength. His operating list had been cancelled because the lab was closed. His outpatients' clinic had been cancelled because of the police investigation there. Patients turning up on a bitterly cold day and told to go home, were incensed. Lynch told his registrar to deal with all his in-patients while he went home early.

You're fading away, Dean, you're fading away.

But you're well ahead of the pack, Dean. Just keep your head down. You're doing well.

He began to do push-ups again, only this time much more slowly.

Don't waste your strength, there's more work to do.

Day 4

18

9.15 am, Thursday, 13th February 1997
South Wing, Central Maternity Hospital

Professor Patrick Armstrong was born middle-aged.

Now aged sixty-six and the only non-gynaecologist on the staff, he had the bearing of a man holding firm to tradition in Irish medicine. Solemn and aloof, arrogant and detached, cold and overbearing, his tall asthenic build was usually dressed in dark sombre suits, starched white shirts and dull muted club ties. He had a hawk-like face with small, dark eyes squinting from under dark, bushy eyebrows as if searching for prey. The only son of a famous father and grandfather in Irish medicine, he had a childhood of stuffy formality and extraordinary boredom, barely knowing what a smile was, a laugh beyond comprehension. What in the world was there to laugh about? Life was too serious.

On the morning of Thursday, 13th February 1997, Armstrong was livid. He held the business card in his left hand, peering at it over half-moon glasses. There was no disguising his disgust.

'He wants to what?' he snapped at his secretary, a boring and aloof middle-aged woman with a face like a hatchet.

'He wants to interview you about that incident yesterday in the laboratory.' Mary Dwyer's death would never be described as murder by the older medical staff. Unwittingly they had begun to talk about 'the incident'. It made them feel better. It was a form of denial.

'He wants to interview *me*?' Incredulous.

'Yes sir.' She always called him 'sir', she knew he liked that.

'Well, Mary, you can tell Detective Inspector Jack McGrath of the Serious Crime Squad based in Store Street Garda station,' Armstrong read from the card, 'that I am a very busy man. He'll have to make an appointment to see me like the rest. When is my next free appointment, Mary?'

Mary scanned the diary she was holding. 'There's nothing free for about a month.' She smirked.

'Tell him that, Mary. Tell him that.'

'Yes sir.'

Professor Armstrong picked up the phone, flipped open a card index, and began dialling.

'Dean, it's Paddy Armstrong here. I'm sorry to trouble you so early this morning but I won't keep you a moment. It's about that incident in the laboratory.'

Lynch stiffened.

'I've just had a request from a Detective Inspector McGrath to interview me,' continued Armstrong, 'and I really find the whole thing quite distasteful. I'm sure you do too, Dean.'

Lynch mumbled.

'Well I think we senior consultant staff should close ranks a little here, Dean, don't you? It's quite appalling that the police should be in this building in the first place. It's doing no good to our public image. What's the place coming to when senior staff have to be interviewed by the police? It really is quite preposterous. Don't you agree?'

'Absolutely.'

In the five years since he had joined the medical staff at the Central Maternity Hospital, Professor Armstrong had never as much as bid Lynch the time of day. He'd ignored him in the corridors, in the wards, in the canteen, everywhere. Suddenly he was all over him like a rash. Dean loved it.

'Well Dean, I think we should put these policemen in their proper places. I mean they are just wasting their time and ours. Why aren't they out looking for the real thug among the drug takers and criminals that have made this country the way it is?'

'I couldn't agree more.'

'Excellent Dean. I hoped you would agree. I'm going to ring a few more colleagues and have this scotched before it gets out of hand. If you see anyone down in East Wing do please tell them of our policy.'

'Of course.'

'Good morning, Dean. Again, sorry to have disturbed you. Like myself, I'm sure you've got a busy day ahead and little time to waste.'

'Indeed.'

Lynch replaced the receiver slowly, a smile creasing his lips.

This is becoming quite extraordinary. I'm causing all sorts of ripples.

Such a *simple* act.

Mary Dwyer shouldn't have smiled. She *just* shouldn't have smiled. If she had done her job, and not interfered, I wouldn't have had to kill her.

But she interfered.

She knew too much.

And she *smiled*.

And now look at all the fuss.

It's really quite extraordinary.

Quite *exciting*.

It'll soon be time to do it again.

Now, what other bitch is going to cross me?

McGrath soon found himself stonewalled at every turn. Too many egos were being challenged, reputations risked.

How to handle an investigation for murder, committed right on your doorstep, was not taught at medical school. Having to produce an alibi, *preposterous*.

The phones in various family solicitors' offices began ringing. The advice was the same from each: say nothing unless your personal legal adviser is present. Be polite but firm in your request for legal advice before answering any questions. The solicitors were emphatic. They could see a decent fee in this.

'Okay. I want you to give me a tour of this place and tell me what happens here.'

McGrath and Dowling were back in the laboratory accompanied by Luke Conway. Kate Hamilton had been assigned to second interviews with hospital security.

'This is haematology and biochemistry.'

'You can stop right there. All this may mean something to you but it's Chinese to me.'

'Bloods. This is where we do all the hospital blood tests. Check blood levels, body chemistry, blood groupings and things like that.' Conway was trying to be polite and patient. He was equally determined to get the laboratory back into action as soon as possible. 'We also do immunology, AIDS testing and such like.'

McGrath said, 'What sort of test was Mary Dwyer working on?'

'We finally tracked down the last test she did that night. It was a full blood count for Ward Four in North Wing.'

'Anything unusual in that?'

'Absolutely nothing. The patient was an elderly lady about to undergo major surgery. Her case and the test were completely routine and uncomplicated.'

'Nothing to kill for?'

Conway shrugged. 'I'm no help here, Inspector. I can't think of anything Mary Dwyer knew or was doing here that would make her a murder victim. I'm as disturbed and

121

puzzled as the rest of my staff. I mean, this sort of thing just doesn't happen in hospitals.'

McGrath and Dowling exchanged looks.

'Could she have been doin' any tests on the quiet. Like could she have been doin' anythin' for a friend that might have been out of the ordinary?' Dowling asked.

Conway pursed his lips, thinking this one over. 'It's possible. It's strictly against hospital policy to perform any unauthorised tests but I know it goes on all the time. It's very hard to police.'

'So she could have been workin' on somethin' that nobody knew anythin' about?'

'It's possible,' agreed Conway, 'but I can't think what she would have been working on that was so important someone would want to kill for.'

McGrath was standing over the rack of broken test tubes still lying undisturbed on the floor.

'Why would he have smashed these?'

Conway shrugged again, trying to hide his annoyance at the repetitive nature of the questions. 'I'm a gynaecologist, Inspector. I don't want to appear unhelpful but I really haven't a clue.'

'Can ye find out what sort of tests were bein' run on those samples?' asked Dowling.

'Sure. The individual bottles are labelled with the patient's name. We keep triplicate copies of all request forms.'

'Where?'

'In a back office.' Conway indicated the general direction with a nod of his head.

'Okay,' interrupted McGrath suddenly. 'Put all the requests against the sample bottles and get me a list of the patients and the tests. Could that be ready within an hour?'

Conway nodded.

'I've had the PC and printer checked,' added McGrath. 'It's bolloxed and we're not gonna get anything useful out of them. Would you check around these offices and see if you can find paper torn out of the printer. There's so much paper in here nobody knows what might be genuine rubbish and what this gook might have been trying to hide or destroy.'

'I'll have to get the chief technician to do that, he'd know that better than me. Is that okay?'

McGrath mulled this over briefly, then nodded. The chief technician had been cleared as a possible suspect. 'The other machines he smashed, any ideas on that?' he asked.

Conway shrugged no.

McGrath peered through a door connecting the first laboratory room to other rooms inside.

'What's down there?'

'Cytology and histopathology. Lots of microscopes for checking glass slides. Containers with pathology specimens.'

McGrath's eyebrows raised quizzically.

'Samples of uterus, samples of breast tissue, samples of ovary, samples of . . .'

'Okay, okay, I get the message.' McGrath was feeling squeamish again. He popped a peppermint. Dowling grinned.

'Any other rooms?' McGrath was beginning to sound tetchy.

'Three,' said Conway. 'There's an office at the very end. Beside that there's a small room where all paperwork from the lab is processed. That's where all hospital requests are stored.' He paused as he watched Dowling scribble something in his notebook. 'Then there's the autopsy room.'

'Autopsy room?' McGrath's peppermint almost dropped out of his mouth. 'This is a maternity hospital. What the hell do you need with an autopsy room?'

Conway cleared his throat. 'People die here too, Detective. Sometimes babies don't make it into the world alive. Sometimes their mothers don't survive labour. We deal with a lot of women who have cancer, cancer of the womb, cancer of the ovaries. Sometimes we don't get them better. Sometimes they die and postmortems are necessary. We need to know why some babies die when we reckon they should have lived. We need to know how diseases progress.'

The room was silent apart from Conway's quietly spoken words. McGrath and Dowling were visibly shaken. Maternity hospitals had always seemed places of joy and life. Babies being born, fathers going in and out clutching flowers and expensive cigars.

Life and living.

Futures.

Not death.

'You have to cut up dead babies?' McGrath mouthed, his words barely audible.

'Indeed that happens on occasions, though I don't do it personally. It's the one thing the staff here find really difficult. Dealing with a baby that never got a chance at life.'

Conway sensed he had touched a raw nerve in both detectives. Now's the time to put a bit of pressure on, he quickly decided.

'You see this hospital has to deal with life and death all the time. Everybody thinks we only deal with delivering babies. But there's a lot more. We have a fifty-bed gynaecology unit, an eight-cot neo-natal intensive care ward and an eight-cot special care unit. That's where we look after the very small, premature babies. We take a lot of pride in that unit. Our success rate in stabilising and nursing those babies to a decent size so that they can go home is among the best in the world. We do a lot of good work here.' He paused. There was no mistaking the expressions on McGrath and Dowling's faces.

They were impressed. Impressed and humbled. This was indeed hallowed ground.

Conway decided to milk the moment.

'That's why this murder is so obscene. We can handle death here, we're used to it. But only when it's from natural causes. To come into a hospital, any hospital, this is traditionally inviolable territory, and then kill someone as innocent and beautiful as Mary Dwyer is diabolical, an obscenity.' His voice sounded strained. 'We all want you to find out who did this and bring him to justice. But we've got to think of the rest of the patients up in the wards. The mothers and their babies. The women waiting for surgery. All of them. We've got to get the hospital back to some sort of normality. We need to get this lab back into action.'

Outside McGrath turned to Dowling. 'For a moment I almost believed every word.'

'Jaysus, Jack but ye're an awful cynic.'

'You need to be cynical in this game, Tony. He was doing well up until he started to cry about his missing lab. That guy should be in equity.'

Detective Inspector Jack McGrath by now had decided he hated doctors as well as hospitals. They were as bad as the common criminals he dealt with all his working life, shifty, evasive and self-protective.

He could sense he was on a collision course.

He was right.

Head high, mind racing, Conway didn't notice Kate Hamilton staring at him as he came towards her. She stopped and did a double take as he came level, then sat down suddenly on a nearby bench, her hands shaking. She grasped at the lapels on her jacket for control and took deep breaths in and out to try to regain her composure. She looked again at the retreating figure who had now stopped to talk briefly with a white-coated doctor. Conway half-turned in mid-conversation and looked back along the corridor to where Hamilton sat. She could see his face clearly, there was no mistaking the features, the tall bearing, the tight red hair, the darting eyes. She remembered him vividly. It all came flooding back and she had to suppress the urge to run up and punch him straight in the nose.

'Don't you think you should put your baby up for adoption?'

She was lying sobbing on the delivery bed only thirty minutes after giving birth. From inside her body she had pushed the most perfectly formed baby boy into the outside world.

It hadn't been an easy birth, physically easy, maybe, but emotionally a nightmare. She could still see the tall man,

125

dressed in green protective gown, masked and with what looked like a J-cloth covering his hair. He had gently eased and controlled the final, bursting stage, coaxing and cajoling.

'Push . . . don't push . . . deep breaths . . . relax . . . push . . . don't push . . . deep breaths . . . you're doing fine . . . one more push . . . that's it. I can see the head coming. No, don't push until I tell you, that's it . . . good girl . . . that's great. Head coming now. One more big breath and then a big, long push . . . excellent. That's it. Scissors please nurse. Lignocaine . . . breathe deeply on the mask now. You're going to feel a sharp sting near your bottom . . . perfect . . . baby's head born. Your baby's head's born. Try and relax. Feel another one coming? Okay, deep breath and push.'

Suddenly it was all over. The relief. Then the joy as the tiny, blood-smeared baby was handed to her, wrapped in hospital greens, his eyes rolling in his head as if stunned by the journey into life.

Squashed and bruised as he was, there was no mistaking. He was his daddy's boy.

Except his daddy would never see him, never see anybody, ever again. There was only his tiny baby to mark his existence in this world.

As Rory was taken away to be weighed, Kate began to sob uncontrollably. There was no one to share this special moment, no family to rush home to and show off her newborn baby. Her own mother was dead and she had strictly forbidden her father to come near the hospital. But the greatest torment was knowing there would be no father coming in later clutching flowers and handing out cigars and wanting to dance with the nurses.

She was one more single mother.

She gradually became aware of the figure leaning over the bed, face mask down, cloth cap removed. Dr Luke Conway had read the signs all wrong, totally and humiliatingly wrong.

'Don't you think you should put your baby up for adoption?'

She started screaming, struggling to climb off the bed. 'Where's my baby? Where's my baby?'

He'd ordered her held down and forcefully sedated.

She'd never seen him since. Until now.

Kate Hamilton slowly stood up, straightened her uniform and dabbed at her eyes with a tissue. With as much control as she could summon she walked towards the library where the rest of the investigation team waited. Relax, relax, she warned, don't let the others see you're upset. Don't let anyone know you now have a personal agenda here.

20

Just after one o'clock that afternoon an RTE NEWS TV crew was wrapping up a 'piece-to-camera' item in front of the Central Maternity Hospital, the reporter outlining the dramatic events overtaking the hospital, starting with the emergency delivery of Gordon O'Brien and ending with the discovery of Mary Dwyer's body fewer than thirty-six hours later. It would be the first of many 'piece-to-camera' items involving the Central Maternity Hospital.

Inside the hospital Luke Conway and Professor Patrick Armstrong were deep in conversation. While Conway was the Master of the hospital and in charge of day-to-day management he quite often conferred with Armstrong. The older man had been attached to the hospital for almost twenty-three years and was on the board of governors. He knew the pulse of the hospital and was a clever manipulator of its staff.

'Let me have a word with the Minister for Health,' suggested Armstrong. 'I'm on quite good terms with him. We'll put a bit of heat on Detective Inspector McGrath.' He almost spat the words out. 'We should have the lab back in action by tomorrow.'

Luke Conway nodded, relieved. Maybe there might be light at the end of this very long tunnel after all. He watched as Armstrong placed the call.

Tommy Malone drove a stolen Volvo 460 along the New-bridge bypass for about two miles before taking the turn off to Kilcullen. Sitting in the back seat, staring out at the passing traffic, was Peggy Ryan. Sam Collins had taken the car from outside a pub in Donnybrook earlier and fitted it with a set of Kildare number plates which Moonface had lifted off a Toyota Corolla parked in the long-term car park at Dublin airport. Moonface had also taken a set of '95 registration Dublin plates from a BMW. He'd been sorely tempted to take the car as well but was under strict instructions to steal only what was ordered and nothing else. 'And that means don't lift a fuckin' thing outa the back seat or nuthin',' Malone had warned.

As Malone and Ryan drove through the village he pointed out the nearest grocery shop, telephone kiosk and public house. Slightly less than a mile past the last bungalow marking the edge of the village, Malone turned off the main road onto a smaller B-road, then turned sharp left again onto a track that led them past fields. Peggy squinted into the enveloping darkness, barely able to make out the top of the hedgerows. Malone slowed to a crawl easing the Volvo up a dirt path. Finally the headlights picked out the front of a small whitewashed cottage with two front windows and a black front door.

'We're here,' grunted Malone as he killed the engine. He climbed out of the car first, advising Peggy not to budge until he had the front door open. 'Ye'll freeze out here. Wait'll I have the door open and a ligh' on.'

Peggy pulled the collar of her coat up around her neck and waited. The blackness of the night was relieved by a weak moon struggling to make itself seen from behind dark clouds. Malone struggled to find the right key and then struggled further to find the lock and turn the bolt. With a kick and a curse the door was slowly pushed in, creaking and groaning. In the gloom Peggy watched Malone grope

129

his way along a wall and suddenly the weak glow of a single lightbulb lit up the inside porch.

Once inside the two looked over the cottage carefully. It was basic, three bedrooms, a kitchen-cum-sitting room and an inside toilet with an old grime-stained bath in the same small room. There was a fireplace in the kitchen. The other rooms were heated by three-bar electric fires. The cottage was freezing and frost hung off their breath as they spoke.

'Ye'll have to get this place heated, Tommy. Ye can' bring a newborn baby into this vault. Jaysus, it wouldn' last an hour.'

Malone nodded, deep in thought.

'We'll light the fire in the kitchen now,' he said, 'and turn on the electric fires in the bedrooms. Better get electric blankets as well.'

Peggy didn't much like what she saw. The cottage was a dump, obviously unlived in for months. A musty smell hung everywhere and the sofa in the kitchen felt damp to the touch.

'Jaysus Tommy, I hope we don' havta stay here long,' she complained. 'We'll all get our deaths a cold here.'

Malone ignored her and continued carrying in boxes of groceries, tins of baby food, firelighters, peat briquettes, bundles of sticks and, finally, a large box of Mini Pampers for boys.

Within half an hour the first smoke from the burning paper and sticks trickled into the frosty air outside. It hadn't snowed yet but there was talk of it. There was little wind even though dark clouds moved slowly across the sky. The fields surrounding the cottage had pockets of frost but, apart from a few sheep and cattle nuzzling the hard earth, there was hardly any movement.

Half a mile away, Brian O'Callaghan was worrying over a sheep he was sure was going to lamb. Wrapped in four sweaters and a long grey oil skin, he could still feel the bitter cold penetrate. The ewe seemed unperturbed, scraping at the frost for any tuft of grass that hadn't been grazed.

Now well into his seventieth year and a farmer all his life, O'Callaghan reckoned any lamb born now, and in the open, stood little chance of surviving. He wasn't at all happy as he watched the sheep, swollen bellied, move off to a more promising looking tuft.

As he turned around towards home he noticed the smoke. That's strange, he thought, I've never seen anyone use that cottage this time of year.

The mood was heavy with anger and frustration.

'Wait'll you hear this one.' One of the detectives assigned to the case was recounting his experience trying to interview a consultant. 'I do the polite thing and ring up his secretary, tell her who I am and why I need to see the great man. Do you know what she says?'

McGrath's team listened, some smirking but others with similar experiences were grim faced.

' "Well," she says, "I'll check and see if there's a window in his diary for next week." A window in his diary,' he mimicked, 'and for next week. I'm trying to investigate a murder and all I get is this crap. A window in his diary for next bloody week!'

A buzz of conversation filled the room as others related similar experiences.

'Okay, okay,' interrupted McGrath as a last straggler entered, sat down and pulled a chair nearer to the large reading table in the middle of the room. McGrath and Dowling sat at the table, tall shelves of medical textbooks on either side. Kate Hamilton glanced at her watch as she shuffled her chair along the reading table to make room. She'd promised Grandad she'd be home by seven. The way things were going she doubted she'd make it.

'It looks as if we're all getting the run around.' McGrath flicked open a notebook and squinted at it briefly. 'However before we go into that I want to run over what we now know about this case.'

The group shifted to more comfortable positions, each consulting individual notepads.

'We know Mary Dwyer was murdered between 10.45 and 10.55 last Tuesday night. Almost certainly the killer knows this hospital like the back of his hand. He got in and out without anyone noticing. There have been no sightings in the hospital, the grounds, the car park or the exits leading into Whitfield Square. Either he went back to doing whatever he usually does in the hospital and continued as though nothing had happened, or ...' A murmur of dissent interrupted McGrath's flow. 'Or ... or,' his voice grew louder, 'more likely, he slipped out the same way he came in, through the basement and out one of the side gates.' He paused as one or two scribbled in their notebooks.

'We also know that the scalpel used, almost certainly, but not definitely, came from the room outside that the docs use for what they call minor surgery.'

Someone sniggered at a comment about Mary Dwyer's minor surgery getting a bit out of hand and Kate Hamilton had to cover her face to hide a smirk.

'There are no prints on the scalpel,' continued McGrath, ignoring the diversion, 'and forensics say the markings and powder on her throat suggest he was wearing gloves. Surgical gloves.'

He paused to let this sink in.

'The guy also smashed a row of blood samples, a small PC and printer and a couple of other machines. The lab staff have double checked the samples with the requests and say there's nothing they can find that would link the murder with the tests. The paper from the printer is individually numbered and there are eight sheets missing, can't be found anywhere. They can't have got out of the hospital by any normal route as we've had all wastepaper bins, sluices and the like checked. The skip outside the basement has been turned over and nothing found.'

He stopped again and looked at the gathering. All eyes were on him.

'Every rubbish bin and skip in a mile radius has been turned over. Every taxi company and bus driver interviewed. Zilch. Nothing.'

He paused and looked at Dowling who nodded back.

'Mary Dwyer is as clean as the driven snow. We've nothing on her. She lives with her parents and she's not into drugs. There's no funny bank accounts, no kinky sex. Nothing.'

McGrath stood up slowly, resting both hands on the desk in front of him, staring at his notebook.

'Nothing that's immediately obvious anyway. But I just can't help feeling she knew something. She might have had some information, something. Something so important she had to be killed for it. She may not even have known how important it was but this guy just couldn't take any chances. She had to go.'

The room was silent.

McGrath looked up from the desk. 'Now,' he continued, his voice raised again, 'we seem to be getting the run around from some of the medical staff here. Some of these guys seem to think it's beneath their dignity to be interviewed by the police.'

'Bloody right they do,' shouted a voice and Kate Hamilton turned to see who had spoken. She was secretly delighted the investigating team were incensed at the doctors' attitudes. Now you know, boys, what we girls go through all the time.

McGrath held up a hand. 'Well let me tell you, and I don't mind you letting this slip out to anyone you feel might like to hear it, but we have the trump card in this game. From what I've heard operations are being cancelled, patients are having to be sent home and some women are being directed to the Rotunda Hospital to have their babies. All because we've closed the lab.'

Something close to a cheer filled the room, followed by 'shooshes' and muted laughs.

'Until we get cooperation that lab stays closed.'

The cheer could be heard down the corridor.

As the detectives filed out of the library, Dean Lynch watched from his consulting room just down the same corridor, the door open only a fraction. He had counted twelve going in and checked that the same number left. There were eleven men and one young woman. Eleven men and one very interesting looking young woman. He had watched her very closely, noting her body language and hand movements.

I'd like to meet you, sometime.

Alone.

When the last murmur of conversation drifted away from the empty and darkened waiting area, he slipped out and entered the library.

He assessed the scene quickly. All the chairs were pulled around the central reading desk. There were only two at the desk, one facing the other. He scanned the book shelves which stood immediately to each side and, using a cloth tape, measured the width of a number of titles before choosing four. They left the hospital with him.

Commissioner Thomas Quinlan, responsible for overall control and management of the Garda Siochana, was sitting in his living room watching TV when the telephone rang. Spread on the carpet at his feet lay the two Dublin evening papers, each carrying banner headlines about the murder investigation.

'Commissioner, this is Alice Martin.'

Quinlan sat bolt upright and flicked the TV off with the remote control.

'Minister, what can I do for you?'

'My sources tell me that a Detective Inspector Jack McGrath is wreaking havoc down at that hospital and the doctors are raising hell.'

Quinlan said nothing. Experience suggested the Minister of Justice was less worried about the murder and its investigation and Jack McGrath than she was about bad publicity.

The government was a shaky coalition, lurching from one badly handled crisis to another. Law and order, or the lack of law and order, was the current hot political potato.

'Did you hear me, Commissioner?' Martin's voice felt like a lash.

'Most certainly, Minister. But I get the impression you want me to do more than tell you what you already seem to know.' Bite on that one, you smart assed bitch.

Martin paused, taken back.

'I think Detective Inspector McGrath should be removed from the investigation.'

Quinlan had sensed this coming.

'That might be a mistake, Minister, if I may say so. It might seem like a panic reaction to the bad publicity.'

'I want him off that case.' It was an icy voiced command, not a suggestion.

'Minister, let me make a few calls tonight and I'll get back to you first thing tomorrow morning. There may be ways around this.'

'Commissioner Quinlan, may I remind you I am the Minister for Justice. You are directly responsible to me.'

'With respect, Minister, you have not ceased to remind me of that since the day you took office.'

'I want Detective Inspector McGrath removed from that investigation.' The phone was slammed down.

Quinlan stared at the earpiece for a moment.

'Hoor,' he muttered and started dialling.

Dean Lynch carefully cut out the insides of the four textbooks to the depth and shape he required. He closed each book in turn and inspected the result. The books looked no different. When opened a neatly carved space was exposed with a thin, narrow space running to the spine. Into the spaces he fitted a Panasonic Voice Activated System dictaphone. Attached by a lead to the top of the dictaphones was a Vivanco EM 116 clip-on microphone. When closed, the books showed no sign of the dictaphone. The tiny clip-on microphone lead was easily threaded through the

136

specially cut tunnel, barely protruding above the book spines.

Lynch admired his handiwork for some time before putting it to the test. He placed the four books upright at various levels inside his kitchen cupboards and then sat down at the kitchen table. He began reading out loud from an instruction book on cooking a casserole in under eight minutes using a microwave oven. After five minutes, as timed on the kitchen clock, he stopped. The books were taken down and the tapes inside the dictaphones checked. They all had responded to his voice as picked up by the microphones. He rewound and played. His voice had been recorded clearly. He rewound the tapes once more and replaced the books in the same positions. The instruction manual was read aloud again, but this time he stopped for a minute every three minutes. Down came the books and the tapes were replayed.

Perfect.

The Voice Activated System had worked perfectly, recording only when he spoke, stopping when there was no noise picked up.

Perfect.

It's looking good, Dean, boyo, it's looking good. Put them in four different sites so you miss nothing. Then you'll be able to keep tabs on whatever's going on in the library.

There's no doubt about it, you're a little genius.

He treated himself to a fix to celebrate.

Day 5

The jeep's headlights pierced the early morning darkness.

Tommy Malone and Sam Collins were delivering heavy artillery. Malone was concerned about developments at the Central Maternity Hospital and rumours that Harry O'Brien might move his wife and newborn son home. He wanted to strike as soon as possible.

Malone had turned up at five o'clock the previous day to the back door of the O'Brien Corporation headquarters in Dawson Street as arranged. Three gentle knocks, repeated at thirty-second intervals, alerted the waiting Betty and within minutes he was inside the building.

Betty had guided him well away from the night security guard and down to Big Harry's personal office. There, at the back of a large swivel chair behind a leather-topped desk, hung an aerial photograph of Beechill, the O'Brien family residence in Wicklow.

Tommy Malone had stared at it for over an hour, noting the front gates, the road leading to the front gates, and in particular the dirt track that ran along one side of the estate. He'd squinted at the gardens close to the house itself and the clumps of bushes nearby. Ideal cover, he decided. Then he'd noted the large trees, singly and in groups, scattered around the twelve-acre site. Fuckin' brilliant, even better. Betty had checked in twice to let him know he was okay and wouldn't be disturbed. When he'd left, just after six

139

thirty, Tommy Malone knew Beechill like the back of his hand. He also knew Big Harry and Theo Dempsey's private home telephone numbers, read off a pad inside a drawer in the desk. In his mind he'd already chosen Dempsey as the go-between and courier for the ransom. All dealings with Big Harry would be through Dempsey, the only telephone calls would be made to Dempsey's number. The rozzers, he reckoned, would bug Beechill first and only get round to Dempsey when they realised the ransom pick-up wasn't being dictated to Big Harry through his telephone.

Malone also learned something very interesting from Betty. 'He's letting all the staff off for a few days to celebrate the baby's birth.'

Malone couldn't believe his luck. 'When?'

'Tomorra. I heard wan of the security men talkin' abou' it and givin' ou' shite tha' he wasn' bein' givin' a few days off as well.'

Tommy Malone hugged her for that little gem of information.

Later that afternoon Sam Collins had driven past Beechill in a newly stolen Cherokee jeep with front ram bars and another set of newly stolen Kildare number plates. Collins had noted the large wrought iron gates attached to an entrance space in a fifteen foot high granite wall. The wall ran for two hundred yards along a small back road that connected in a semi-circle with the main Roundwood to Killiskey road. Checking no one was watching, he'd quickly jumped out and tested the strength of the gates, deciding there and then just how much Semtex he'd need to blow them off their hinges and out of the way.

Then he'd driven the jeep down the dirt track Malone had told him about. The dirt track ran from one end of the front wall down past an older perimeter wall built sixty years previously, finally ending at the water's edge of Vartry Reservoir. Collins discovered the track continued for another fifty yards past the turn off to the reservoir. As he slowly walked he'd noted the estate walls to his left, old and crumbling in places but still essentially sound. Then he came across a wooden gate. The gate had been used for years by previous owners of Beechill as their own path to the fishing in the reservoir. In the dark Collins tested the hinges, first with the tips of his fingers feeling for rust, then with the strength of his left shoulder. He'd smiled as he felt it give slightly. As he drove back to Dublin he made a mental note to collect a sledge hammer.

The sledge hammer was the first item to be unloaded from the back of the jeep at the cottage. Next came a sawn-off double-barrelled twelve-bore shotgun, two .38 Smith & Wesson handguns and a Libyan made AK47 sub-machine-gun. Collins had dipped into his IRA cache. A Smirnoff vodka box containing balaclavas, four pairs of tight-fitting leather gloves and enough ammunition to conduct a small war lay on the front passenger seat. Malone was leaning across the driver's seat to ease this closer to the other door when he accidentally pressed the steering column horn. The sudden blare nearly lifted him out of his skin and woke Peggy Ryan, now staying at the cottage full time, wrapped up in a sleeping bag.

It also woke Brian O'Callaghan.

He slipped out of bed and peered through the early morning gloom just in time to see car headlights being switched off.

O'Callaghan scratched his head and then his arse and went back to bed.

What the hell's goin' on up there? he wondered sleepily as he snuggled down, trying to find his warm spot in the bed.

'We're going in tonigh', righ',' said Tommy Malone over a mug of strong tea. 'We'll take the little bollox tonigh'. Me source tells me Big Harry's bringing him home today and has let the staff off for two days to celebrate the baby. He couldna planned it better for us if he'd tried. Righ'?'

Malone looked at Peggy Ryan and she nodded she was ready.

'That's okay by me,' said Collins. He pressed the trigger on an empty chamber of his Smith & Wesson, aiming the barrel into the distance. 'That's okay by me. The sooner the better. I'm ready.'

In Room Three, North Wing, in Dublin's Central Maternity Hospital, Sandra O'Brien had just fed her baby and was changing his nappy. She continued to croon and smile as she watched his face crease, his nose twitch and his spindly arms flail in protest at the intrusion. He cried for a few seconds and Sandra lifted him and kissed his forehead. The crying stopped and tiny eyes squinted at the blurred face above. Sandra kissed him again, then slipped him back inside his babygrow and laid him on his side in the Moses basket.

She watched his eyes flicker and stare before sleep took over and they closed again. What a beautiful, beautiful baby boy you are. Please God let you grow up to be big and strong like your father.

Outside in the corridor Sandra heard the cries of yet another newborn baby being wheeled to one of the other rooms further along. As she listened she settled back in the bed, massaging Vitamin E oil onto her operation scar for quicker healing. She had never felt more content or fulfilled in her life before.

Dean Lynch was also in the hospital at that time, earlier than usual. Not that there was much work for consultants, with the lab still out of action operations and outpatient clinics were being cancelled. Women in established labour which seemed remotely complicated were directed to other maternity hospitals, some even taken by ambulance from the Central Maternity wards.

Lynch carried with him a briefcase he made look lighter than it felt. Ignoring everyone he made his way to his consulting room.

The corridors, examination rooms and the waiting room were deserted. The library was empty.

He had decided already where the four books with their

concealed listening devices would be placed and lost no time in positioning them. Standing back from the shelves he checked they did not look out of place, that the microphones could not be seen. He grunted with satisfaction.

Back in his room he clicked the combination lock on his briefcase and laid the contents out on an examination couch. There were eight two-hour microcassettes and sixteen Panasonic LR6 replacement batteries. He was taking no chances.

The four Voice Activating System recorders and their clip-on microphones had been bought in different stores, as had the microcassettes and batteries. All had been wiped clean of fingerprints. As he checked the replacement batteries and microcassettes he wore surgical gloves.

No point taking any chances, Dean, boyo.

From his careful observation of the detectives' routine over the previous two days he had noted that they usually gathered in the library for an early morning briefing at about 8.45 am. Lunch was also held there, and he was sure they discussed progress and strategy over junk ordered from the staff canteen. There was usually a summing up at six in the evening. In between, any interviews were also held in the library.

Now he would hear every word spoken. He could watch the comings and goings through the gap in his partly closed consulting room door and replace cassettes and batteries when an opportunity arose. And a lot of opportunities would arise. Due to the lab closure the usually busy waiting room, examination rooms and corridors leading to the laboratory were almost deserted.

You can watch and listen in on your *own* little murder enquiry, Dean boyo.

What fun.

Just after eight thirty Harry O'Brien snapped off the radio he was listening to and stared at it for a moment, deep in thought. Spread out on the desk in front of him was the tabloid *Daily Post*, its lead story an 'EXCLUSIVE' and accompanied by a photograph of the Gardai yellow incident tape across the Central Maternity Hospital laboratory door. The photo was in full colour.

'HOSPITAL IN CRISIS!' ran the banner headline.

The RTE radio early morning news programme, *Morning Ireland*, ran the hospital story as its first news item, later including a six-minute extended report.

Harry O'Brien had had enough.

A few minutes after nine Garda Commissioner Thomas Quinlan met with Chief Superintendent Michael Loughry at Garda headquarters in the Phoenix Park. A heated discussion ensued, lasting slightly over one hour and ending with the politically motivated decision to move Jack McGrath from the murder investigation of Mary Dwyer.

It was Loughry who suggested introducing a woman to take over the enquiry.

Jack McGrath decided to use his trump card.

He was fed up playing games with the doctors.

He was worried about the lack of any half decent break in the case. The more he thought about it the more convinced he was the murderer was one of the hospital staff. The more he thought about that the more he worried.

'The bastard could strike again,' he said to Dowling. 'He could be walking the wards, laughing at our frustrated attempts to catch him. Well it's time to take the gloves off. It's time to put these bastards in their places. This may be their hospital but this is *my* murder enquiry. It's time to kick ass.'

The doctors filed in in groups. There was subdued small talk and nervous glances at the very-out-of-place-looking detectives scanning every face. McGrath had positioned his team at strategic points so that each had a good view of the tiered rows stretching back from the central dais at the front. Kate Hamilton stood halfway down the hall, leaning against the wall, trying hard to look intimidating.

Luke Conway joined McGrath at the lectern without a word and they watched as the last one or two pushed others along in the very back row. Dean Lynch sat three rows from the back, watching every move, waiting for any snippet of conversation. He suddenly spotted Hamilton and a slight

145

smile flickered, then died. He turned so that he had her in view all the time.

Conway spoke first.

'This is Detective Inspector Jack McGrath of the Serious Crime Squad. He is based in Store Street Garda station. Inspector McGrath and his team are investigating the incident that occurred in the laboratory Tuesday night.'

Incident! thought McGrath. *Incident! The girl was murdered!* He could feel his temper rise.

'As you know,' continued Conway, 'we seem to be at loggerheads as to how this investigation should proceed in the hospital. The Inspector, understandably,' Conway paused and looked condescendingly at McGrath, 'wants to find the perpetrator of this crime as soon as possible. We, on the other hand, have to keep the hospital running. As you all know there are twenty-four-hour-a-day activities going on here. Sickness doesn't strike just during office hours, and if my own experience is anything to go by, babies do seem to have that peculiar knack of being born at the most inconsiderate hours of the night.'

A polite ripple of laughter filled the auditorium and heads nodded in agreement. Conway permitted himself a half smile.

'However,' he continued, 'we really cannot carry on our activities without a fully functioning laboratory. Inspector McGrath has seen fit to continue to keep the lab closed, for whatever reasons. But he has informed me that after our little talk here this morning, there's a good chance that yellow incident tape will come down and we can all get back to work.'

There was a small ripple of applause.

'Certainly we need to get this hospital back into action as soon as possible,' Conway added quickly. 'The adverse publicity is having a dreadful effect on patient confidence and staff morale.' He paused significantly and half turned towards McGrath. 'Only this morning I had a telephone call from the Minister for Health wanting to know what was going on and why we weren't working as normal. I had to tell the Minister that the police investigation was stalling our best efforts to restore normality.'

He rounded on McGrath.

'I'll hand you over to the Detective Inspector who wants to say a few words.'

Conway sat down in the front row and waited.

The interruption was carefully stage managed. A side door into the lecture theatre was noisily opened and all heads turned to see Professor Patrick Armstrong stride in followed by a smaller, paunchy man in an expensively tailored pinstripe suit. In his right hand he held a rather battered brown briefcase. The two men walked deliberately in front of the dais and pushed into the far side of the second row. Others squeezed to make room.

Armstrong stood up. 'I'm terribly sorry we're late. The traffic outside is dreadful. My name is Professor Patrick Armstrong and this,' he rested a hand on the smaller man's shoulder, 'is Peter Harrington of Harrington and Partners, the legal representatives for the hospital.'

Armstrong sat down. Harrington snapped the locks on his briefcase noisily and rummaged inside. Heads strained to watch. He produced a dictaphone, making a great show of connecting a microphone and directing it towards the front. He reached inside his jacket pocket for the briefest of seconds but this was merely to start a time recorder. Harrington and Partners billed by the hour. He needed to know how much he would charge at the end of this little diversion. Money for jam, he thought to himself as he settled back to listen.

McGrath began.

'Thank you, Dr Conway. I'm not going to go into the details of this investigation, you all must know them by now. What I will say is that for the first time in the many years I have been working with the Serious Crime Squad I have come up against an extraordinary wall of silence. Requests by my men to interview many of you have been stonewalled. Calls have not been returned. Questions refused. Any information has had to be dragged out. I've learned more from the newspapers.'

A rumble of protest was building up among the tiered rows. Before anyone could interrupt, McGrath played his ace card.

'I can spend the rest of the year scouring every inch of the laboratory for clues. And it will stay closed until I say otherwise.'

The rows erupted in protest. Sitting quietly near the back, Dean Lynch smiled. He glanced towards Kate Hamilton but quickly averted his eyes as he noticed her look in his general direction.

McGrath held up a hand for silence but it came slowly, the deep mutterings continuing for minutes.

The next move McGrath had thought over for hours. It was a gamble, but it was time to gamble. He reached into a side pocket and produced a long brown envelope from which he theatrically drew a folded piece of paper. All eyes followed. McGrath opened the paper, laid it on the lectern and smoothed it out.

'Late last night we received certain information.' He paused. He would never have a more captive audience. 'As we speak that information is being checked. If it proves accurate we may be in a position to make an arrest soon.'

Gasps reverberated round the theatre.

Dean Lynch still smiled. Inside he was laughing. He had already retrieved the first set of tapes and listened to the early morning briefing: he knew they had nothing.

'However,' continued McGrath quickly, desperate to seize the opportunity, 'we cannot proceed on that information until we have screened every male staff member of the hospital. You cooperate with my men and I'll allow your lab to reopen.'

He slipped the paper inside the brown envelope and placed both inside his jacket pocket.

Dowling pulled him to one side as the theatre emptied. 'What information did ye receive last night?'

'Bugger all. The only thing on that paper was yesterday's lunch order.'

Dowling groaned.

The laboratory was cleared for re-opening at three o'clock that afternoon.

A hastily arranged photo call was held in the impressive front lobby of the hospital at five thirty that same afternoon. There was a TV crew from RTE, journalists and photographers from radio, newspapers and a number of glossy magazines. Even *Hello!* magazine had a photographer present.

Luke Conway entered the lobby first and read from a prepared script.

'Thank you ladies and gentlemen for coming along today at such short notice despite the bitterly cold weather. However we did promise you an opportunity to see the happy couple, sorry, happy *family* before they left the hospital.'

Cameras whirred, bulbs flashed.

Into view came a beaming Harry O'Brien, pushing his young wife in a wheelchair. Sandra's personal hairdresser and beautician had worked on her for most of the morning and she looked beautiful, if a little drawn. Her long blonde hair was pulled back revealing high cheek bones, full lips and a dazzling smile. Here was Ireland's most famous model, her beauty untouched by the recent pregnancy and dramatic birth.

Behind followed June Morrison carrying Gordon O'Brien wrapped in a lace shawl, his tiny face and shock of wispy blond hair just barely visible above the bundle of clothes. Morrison carefully handed the baby to his mother and she turned to the cameras.

Bulbs flashed, shutters whirred again.

Harry O'Brien then stood behind the wheel chair for the family photograph. The photographer from *Hello!* magazine switched cameras and fired off another roll.

Then the barrage of questions began.

Harry O'Brien answered as many as he could with good humour, smiling throughout. He was an imposing figure in a charcoal grey pinstripe suit, crisp white shirt and navy and white spotted polka dot tie. His curly hair was almost combed to order and in his breast pocket a dark pink kerchief hung out. Big Harry looked like a man in control and he kept both hands firmly on the back of the wheelchair as he spoke.

No, Sandra and Gordon were not leaving the hospital early because of the police investigation. The weather forecast was not good and he wanted his wife and son home in case it snowed.

No, he had not decided to move them earlier than expected because he feared for their safety.

Yes, he had full confidence in the staff of the Central Maternity Hospital. Wasn't he taking one of them down to Wicklow to help with Sandra and the baby? He pulled June Morrison over and a fresh burst of flash bulbs lit up the lobby. Morrison smiled for the cameras.

Yes, he was delighted to be a father again. He was absolutely and totally delighted to have a *family* again. He threw a big beaming smile towards Sandra who flashed one of her heart stoppers back. The photographers nearly killed one another trying to catch that moment.

Yes, he was deeply appreciative of the care and attention he and Sandra, and now little Gordon as well, had received at the Central Maternity Hospital. He was particularly pleased with the quick response of the staff when Gordon got into difficulties. He wanted to thank Dr Tom Morgan for looking after Sandra throughout the pregnancy. Morgan appeared from behind a small group of onlookers and shook O'Brien's big hand. Bulbs flashed again. Tom Morgan looked so handsome he almost stole Sandra O'Brien's thunder.

There was no mention of Dr Dean Lynch.

And he also wanted to thank the paediatric team who had played such an important role in his son's birth. The tall figure of Paddy Holland briefly joined the group for the camera call. He ran his fingers through his short dark hair and adjusted his glasses, trying to look a little more respectable. He seemed embarrassed at all the attention and shuffled into the background again as soon as he could.

With a final thank you and wave and a few more poses for the photographers, Harry O'Brien wheeled his wife and four-day-old child back along the corridors and out to the waiting Mercedes. June Morrison would follow in the Range Rover driven by Theo Dempsey.

Dempsey felt an overwhelming sense of relief as he drove behind his boss on the hour's journey from central Dublin to the family home in Wicklow. He'd been unhappy about Sandra's safety in the hospital after he'd learned about the murder. Wicklow would be much safer.

It was the final conference for the day.

Every male staff member by now had been accounted for. Eight had no alibis for their whereabouts on the evening of Tuesday, 11th February 1997. This included five doctors and three non-medical staff. Of the five doctors two were Dr Dean Lynch and Dr Tom Morgan.

One of the detectives who checked Morgan's story was unhappy. 'He's a shifty bastard. Very evasive. Hummed and hawed a lot. Said he was at the cinema. "On your own?" I asked. He looked very embarrassed and mumbled that he often went to the movies on his own.'

'Did ye ask him what he went to see?' Dowling asked.

'Yeah. He got that right. But I'm still not happy about him. He deserves closer inspection.'

McGrath noted this. 'What about the others?'

'I checked out a Dr Dean Lynch and a Dr Paddy Holland,' said Kate Hamilton.

'And?'

'Both seemed very straightforward and reasonable to me. Lynch is one of the gynaecologists and lives alone in Ballsbridge.' She consulted her notebook. 'Flat twenty-three, the Elms. That's an apartment block just off Baggot Street.

Says he spent the whole night there, on his own, watching TV.'

'Did ye ask him what he watched?' Dowling interrupted.

'Sure did. Had to think about it but came back with a few programmes. I'll check with the TV guides later.'

'Good.'

The TV guides would confirm Lynch's story. He had set his video to record four different programmes on Tuesday 11th February. He had even looked at them since. Always the careful planner Lynch had decided long before he left the flat that if the worst came to the worst he would have his alibi set up.

'Dr Paddy Holland is a paediatrician who looks after the newborn babies,' continued Hamilton. 'He seemed a helluva nice guy.'

'So did Crippen,' somebody muttered. There were a few laughs, then it was back to business.

'Well, anyway he was on his own in his house in Donny-brook, number four Angelsea Terrace. Lives there with his two small children.'

'No wife?' asked McGrath.

'Died three years ago from cancer.'

'Shit,' somebody groaned, and heads shook in sympathy.

'So what about the kids. Were they with him?'

'No. They were at a slumber party with friends in Black-rock,' replied Hamilton flicking at the pages of her notebook. 'He had the night to himself.'

'Check him again,' ordered McGrath.

One by one the remainder of the non-alibi males were discussed. One of the kitchen chefs seemed a bit flaky to the questioning detective and was marked for further attention. Half of the detectives were assigned to ringing around to confirm alibis, the other half divided up the non-alibis for further checking. They were breaking up when McGrath's mobile phone rang.

'Jack, it's Mike Loughry here. How's that investigation going?'

McGrath's defences went up immediately. Chief Superintendent Loughry rarely called in unless there was trouble.

'Very good. We've finally had some cooperation here.'

'Good. Jack I'd like to talk with you about the case.'

'Okay.' McGrath's defences were up. What's he really want? 'When?'

'How about tomorrow. I know it's Saturday, but there's one or two things I want to run over with you. How about ten o'clock at my office?'

'Fine.'

'Good. See you then.'

The mobile went dead at the other end. McGrath stroked his moustache. Something's up, he thought. Something's up.

Lynch waited for an hour before slipping into the library and recovering the tapes. Fresh batteries and microcassettes were inserted, the books replaced and checked again.

24

10.07 pm
Beechill, the O'Brien residence, nr
Roundwood, Co. Wicklow

Beechill, a Victorian mansion, had been owned for generations by an Anglo-Irish family, the Burges. Some of the most extravagant and lavish social parties ever seen in County Wicklow had been thrown there over the years. Apart from the imposing house itself, there were twelve acres of land, some near the house laid out in formal gardens, the rest natural woodland. For years the St Steven's Day hunt had begun at the front door and ended with the annual hunt ball when socialites from all over Ireland (and some from abroad) converged on the tiny picturesque Wicklow village for an evening of drinking in the local pubs before dancing the night away in a large room at the back of the house. The tradition of the St Steven's Day hunt and ball ended in 1991, the year of the crash, the year Harry O'Brien lost his entire family.

Now, sitting in his study, watching flurries of snow threaten the ground outside, Harry O'Brien decided he would reinstigate the tradition of the hunt ball. It was time for a new beginning.

Never a man to dwell on the past, Harry O'Brien was content again, at peace with the world at last. The dark days of heavy drinking and self-pity were over, the blackness and despair had lifted. Life must go on.

His son had just been fed and was sleeping peacefully in the nursery, images of Winnie the Pooh and Eeyore and

Piglet peering down at him from the wallpaper. His beautiful young wife was asleep in the adjoining room, the painkillers to ease the long scar of the emergency Caesarean section also making her overly drowsy. She had never looked more radiant and Harry had never felt more love for her as when he had peeked in earlier and found her sleeping peacefully, her long blonde hair loose on the pillows.

Then he had gone into the nursery and stood over the cot admiring his son, wondering at the mystery of life. He couldn't remember being so interested, so involved, so intensely caring even with his first family. He was too busy building up the O'Brien Corporation then. Well not this time, he promised the tiny bundle, not this time. This time we'll get to know each other real early. We'll have so much fun together.

He reached down and pulled back a corner of the blanket covering part of the baby's face. For a moment he feared he'd actually woken the baby up and pulled his hand back quickly. Then, as he grew more confident, he reached down and kissed his son's forehead. He recognised immediately the unmistakable smell of babyhood and had to withdraw, a lump forming in his throat as he remembered the last time he had smelt that peculiar smell.

This time, Gordon, we'll go fishing and horse riding and cycling. Hell, we'll have so much fun together. Just you wait and see. So you better eat up all your veggies and grow up big and strong. He brushed a finger along a wisp of hair sticking up. God'll protect you, Gordon. God'll protect you. There'll be no more car accidents, I'll see to that. God and your daddy will protect you.

Harry O'Brien had turned to religion only recently, shortly after the pregnancy had been confirmed and he realised he was going to have a family again. He felt God had given him a second chance, that God would not allow him to be tortured again. No one had suffered the way he had in the past, he had been to Hell and back. It was time to start again, time to live again for he again had a child to live for. God would protect him and his family.

He was wrong.

Tommy Malone didn't believe in God.

The A-team decided to strike well before midnight.

The weather forecast threatened snow over high grounds which meant the Wicklow hills would almost certainly be covered. It also meant their narrow country road escape route might be dangerous. Malone brought the whole operation forward.

Moonface drove the Volvo to the car park of the Stand Hotel at the Curragh, just outside Newbridge in County Kildare. He fastened two large heavy chains to the steering wheel, connecting them to a bar under the driver's seat. He also took the spark plugs from the engine and slipped them into his pocket. Too many car thieves in Kildare.

Finished, he climbed inside the Cherokee jeep, heater full on against the bitter cold outside. Sam Collins drove with Malone in the passenger seat and Peggy Ryan in the back with Moonface. Peggy's heart was racing with a mixture of excitement and fear. Behind them in the spacious luggage area lay a sledge hammer, guns, ammunition, various electronic equipment for by-passing burglar alarms, leather gloves, balaclavas and a baby's travelling cot. Inside the cot rested one pound of Semtex explosive.

'Just as well we went for a four-wheel drive,' muttered Collins as he watched the windscreen wipers flick snow away. The roads looked black but the edges were starting to turn white, as were hedges and fields.

'Aye,' agreed Malone. 'We'll be there soon enough, though.'

Tommy Malone was worried. Not about the weather, but about the job itself. For a man who had involved himself in every criminal activity over years, including murder, extortion and kidnapping, this particular job was beginning to trouble him. It would be easy to carry out, he had no fear of that. But what really concerned Malone most was the target. A newborn baby.

He repeated to himself all the good reasons why a baby was an ideal kidnap target.

We'll get the baby, no sweat, he reasoned. We'll get the money too, I'm sure of that. Big Harry'll cough up. But what'll the reaction be? That's what was worrying him.

No one had ever kidnapped a baby before. Businessmen, bankers, industrialists, wives of wealthy bankers, even a dentist, they'd all been targets before. But never a baby.

He steeled himself as the jeep finally entered Roundwood at 11.05 pm.

There's a first time for everything and this'll be no exception. When the money's paid over and the child returned the fuss'll die down.

The A-team drove to Beechill from Newbridge along back roads over the Wicklow gap. Nobody spoke, each to their own thoughts.

The plan had been rehearsed many times in the cottage, maps of Wicklow and an outline of the house drawn up by Malone pored over for hours. Timing and staging had been discussed and finally agreed – who would do what and when and why, worked out to the last detail. They were ready to strike.

As they drove into Roundwood from Annamoe a four-wheel drive Mitsubishi slowed to let the Cherokee past. It was the only other vehicle they saw all night. The Cherokee was the only other vehicle the driver of the Mitsubishi saw either.

Sam Collins stopped the jeep briefly again at the wrought iron gates and checked the locking mechanism. He squinted through the bars at the driveway then slowly withdrew.

'Any problems?' asked Malone anxiously.

'Nah. Piece of cake. Just don't want the gates blowing onto the driveway and blocking it. No sweat, Tommy. No sweat.'

In the back seat Moonface was picking at his nose and wondering if he'd get a chance to use the handgun Collins had given him. He was itching to shoot somebody, anybody. Just for the experience.

Beside him Peggy Ryan shivered inside a heavy overcoat from cold and anticipation. Even though her husband had been involved in crime from the first day she'd ever met him, this was her first 'job'. As the jeep turned down the dirt track at the end of the front granite wall, Ryan could feel her knees shake.

'Okay, Martin, ye stay here with Peggy till we give ye the word.' Malone and Collins were out of the jeep, hauling equipment from the boot. Moonface nodded and Peggy Ryan snuggled deeper inside her overcoat. 'When youse come make sure youse have gloves and the balas on, righ'?'

'Righ',' agreed Moonface, watching as the two shadowy figures disappeared along the track and out of sight. 'Are ye all righ'?' he turned to Peggy. She just nodded her head in the dark.

The rusting hinges on the wooden gate came away easily with three thumps from Sam Collins' sledge hammer at 11.17 pm on Friday, 14th February 1997. A minute later Tommy Malone was standing inside the perimeter wall of Beechill. He was wearing black leather gloves and a bala-clava and carried a fully loaded .38 Smith & Wesson handgun. Behind him, also gloved and masked, came Sam Collins armed with an AK47 sub-machine-gun and carrying a bag. Inside was his selection of electronics and burgling equipment.

11.21 pm

Harry O'Brien turned the lights off in his study, stretched and yawned and looked out of the window at the whitening lawns. He did not see the shadowy figures moving between the trees towards the conservatory.

Sam Collins first put two sealing cups on one of the large conservatory windows. Looking like door handles they stuck firmly to the glass. Using a small, portable oxy-acetylene welder, he melted the PVC surround until the whole window first loosened, then came away. It did not disturb the burglar alarm. There were no sensors on that window. The security company had sensors only on moveable windows and they hadn't reckoned on that particular window moving.

They hadn't reckoned on Tommy Malone.

11.32 pm

Malone and Collins were ready to move in. Using a two-way radio Malone informed Moonface and he acknowledged.

11.43 pm

Despite the bitter cold Moonface was sweating inside his balaclava by the time he reached the conservatory. He had stuck his handgun firmly inside the belt of his trousers and was carrying a sawn-off shotgun which he passed to Malone. Nodding to each other the three entered the house. Collins had by now by-passed the alarm system. The phone line was cut. As Collins snipped the wires Harry O'Brien heard a short jingling noise on the phone in the study. He was so tired he ignored it.

They moved as planned, Collins and Malone together on the lower levels where they had seen lights, Moonface upstairs where only one light glowed.

'Make wan fuckin' sound and yer brains are over the wall.'

Harry O'Brien's heavy footsteps along the corridor as he made his way to bed had alerted Malone and Collins. He walked round a corner into both barrels of a sawn-off twelve-bore shotgun and Malone forced him back into his study where he was first gagged and then strapped to the legs and arms of a chair.

Tommy Malone always used this trick next, he felt it stamped his authority from the beginning and cowed the victim into submission.

Standing in front of O'Brien, both feet splayed for effect,

arms outstretched and holding the gun very steadily, he deliberately cocked his .38 Smith & Wesson, pressed the front of the barrel against O'Brien's mid-forehead and slowly squeezed the trigger. The wild eyes watching squinted closed.

Click. The hammer hit against an empty chamber.

'The next wan's for real, Harry,' menaced Malone as O'Brien's eyes slowly opened. 'And so are the rest. No heroics or ye'll find out.' Harry O'Brien could barely see the eyes that flitted behind the balaclava.

Theo Dempsey was woken by the cold steel and pressure of another Smith & Wesson as it pushed against the side of his head. Collins quickly moved him downstairs where he joined his boss. They were strapped back to back in separate chairs.

June Morrison was in a half-sleep when Moonface and Collins burst into her bedroom. She started a scream but found it stifled by hands clamped across her face. Other hands lifted her out of bed, pulling her to a chair. Within one minute both feet and both hands were strapped together, a separate strapping covering her mouth. They left her struggling, trying desperately to get enough air through her nose.

It was Malone's decision not to force Sandra O'Brien. The three stood over her and started their routine but found her unresponsive. She swatted at the gun barrel pressing against her ear as if it were an irritating fly. Malone shook her, gently at first and then aggressively. She pushed him back, turned over and started snoring.

'Leave her,' he ordered.

Gordon O'Brien was still asleep when Moonface's rough hands lifted him from the cot. He stirred slightly, both arms flying out and he whimpered. But he didn't wake up.

Harry O'Brien heard the short 'whoomph' as Sam Collins triggered the Semtex attached to the gates. The windows rattled and shook. Moonface darted from room to room, checking. As soon as he heard the Semtex go off he sprinted back to where Sandra O'Brien lay. She hadn't moved.

From where he was positioned Theo Dempsey could see

the Cherokee race up the driveway to the house and screech to a halt. He heard the front door open, its heavy bolts and chains drawn back from inside.

Then the four balaclava'd conspirators were inside the room.

Dempsey felt his boss stiffen in the chair behind him. He strained his head around in time to see the baby being passed from Moonface to Peggy Ryan.

They stood in front of Harry O'Brien and paused to let him take in the full effect. He looked desperately from one to the other finally stopping at his newborn son. His eyes said it all.

Despair.

Despair.

My child!

It was Tommy Malone's policy to keep all exchanges to a minimum, nods rather than words. The four stood silently but menacingly, masked, their guns pointing directly at O'Brien as Malone reached inside his black windcheater and pulled out an A4-size brown envelope.

'It's all in there Harry. Ye won't hear from us again till the money's paid over.' He waved the .38 at the sleeping baby. 'It's all very simple too, Harry. The sooner we get the money the sooner ye get the baby back.'

O'Brien's eyes pleaded, he shook his head violently from side to side.

Malone nodded and Moonface discharged both barrels of the shotgun into the ceiling, showering Dempsey and O'Brien with plaster. Gordon O'Brien awoke and started screeching with fright. His tiny arms threshed.

'No money, no baby,' were Tommy Malone's parting words.

Peggy Ryan stuffed a soother into the baby's mouth but it didn't stop his frightened screeches. Harry O'Brien heard those screeches right up until the child was carried into the back of the Cherokee and driven away.

They drove back towards Kilcullen by the Sally Gap in the higher Wicklow hills, passing through Cloghleagh Bridge and Manor Kilbride. Forty-eight minutes past midnight they arrived in Newbridge, after winding their way along back roads which were now covered by the still falling snow. The transfer in the car park of a nearby hotel to the Volvo was delayed only by Peggy Ryan's increasingly desperate attempts to stop Gordon O'Brien's screeches.

Sam Collins primed the can of petrol with a charge for fifteen minutes after they abandoned the Cherokee. The Volvo was inching up the narrow lane to the cottage when the charge detonated, turning the jeep into a blazing inferno and waking up most of the hotel residents.

Just after one o'clock on the morning of Saturday, 15th February 1997, Tommy Malone's A-team sat in the kitchen of the cottage drinking tea, their faces reflecting the elation each felt. Gordon O'Brien was sucking contentedly on a bottle of formula milk Peggy Ryan had heated, his screeching over for the moment at least.

Tommy Malone held up a mug of tea in a toast.

'Well done team. Well done.'

They smiled at one another.

Back in Wicklow Sandra O'Brien's demented screams echoed throughout the mansion.

Day 6

25

6.45 am
Saturday, 15th February 1997

Kate Hamilton was already half awake when the phone rang.

In the bed beside her lay Rory, who had crawled in at 4.17 am exactly as she noted on the digital clock. She had spent the rest of the night trying to find a spot in the bed that his kicking legs wouldn't reach. She snatched at the receiver before a second ring woke the sleeping child.

'Hello.'

'Is that Kate Hamilton, Detective Sergeant Kate Hamilton?'

'Yes. Who's that?'

'Detective Hamilton, it's Mike Loughry.'

She sat upright in the bed, hand cupped over the mouthpiece.

'Who?' Her voice reflected her incredulity. *Mike Loughry ringing me?*

'Mike Loughry. Chief Superintendent Mike Loughry.'

For a split second she thought it was someone playing a joke, then quickly decided to run with the caller just in case.

'Yes ... what can I do for you?' It was as much as she could think of saying, and even then it was whispered.

'Kate,' Loughry decided to drop the formalities, 'I'm sorry but you'll have to come in today. Something big blew up last night and we have to call everyone in. Also the Commissioner wants to have a word with you.'

'The Commissioner? You mean Commissioner Quinlan?' Hamilton was astonished, then worried. *What the hell have I done? This had better not be a prank. I'll kill if someone's setting me up.*

'Yeah. It's something about that case down at the maternity hospital. You might be asked to take it over.'

'Take it over?' The words were almost shouted.

'Look Kate, I can't go into this over the phone. I'm sorry. It's just that the Commissioner has to make some very big and sudden changes and you're part of those changes. I can't tell you any more at this stage and I've gotta go. I've half the force to ring up.'

'What happened last night?'

'Listen to the news at seven.'

Click. The phone went dead. She barely had a chance to let this sink in when it rang again and Loughry's voice barked: 'Room Twenty-Four, Garda HQ in the Phoenix Park at ten o'clock exactly. Don't be late for Christ's sake.'

She was still staring at the receiver when Rory woke up.

Kate Hamilton didn't get a chance to listen to the seven o'clock news. Rory threw a tantrum when she tried to explain she had to go to work. Again. Today of all days, the first free day she was supposed to have off after ten in a row on duty and a Saturday at that. Saturday and Sundays were precious to Rory, the days when his mother allowed him to lie on beside her until breakfast. Then she would bring up a tray with two bowls of cornflakes and toast and tea to the bed. The two would cuddle up while Rory watched cartoons on the portable TV that balanced precariously on the tiny dressing table. And as he lay beside her with his thumb in his mouth Kate Hamilton would gaze at him, wondering at the mystery of life, admiring his petite features.

That morning Rory's petite features were marred by tears and tantrums. He was howling. He howled while she showered, while she rushed to get the breakfast, while she rang her father to come over and mind him. He even howled through all of Sesame Street.

'Damn!' cursed Hamilton as she tried to blow dry her

hair, Rory clinging to her dressing gown. 'The joys of being a single mother.'

He only stopped howling when she bribed him with a trip to the zoo with Grandad. She just had to figure out now how to persuade Grandad to take him to the zoo.

'I hate the zoo. And it's trying to snow out there, did you know that?' Grandad was none too impressed. 'It would cut you in two out there,' he grumbled as an afterthought.

'Look Dad, he nearly had a fit when I told him I had to go in today. I'd have offered him a trip to the moon to shut him up.'

'Might have been warmer than the bloody zoo.'

She stood in front of the only long mirror in the house, trying to decide what best to wear, and finally chose a navy skirt, sky-blue blouse and navy linen jacket. Look like a policewoman, she told herself, let them know you know where you're coming from. She checked herself one more time in the mirror, tucking her blouse in under her skirt band at the same time. She bared her teeth to make sure there was no lipstick staining, then pouted.

You haven't lost it, she said to the mirror. There was no one else to admire the view.

She kissed Rory and her Dad and flew out the door, aware of the disapproving frowns that followed. She was back again within seconds.

'Keep an eye on him, for God's sake, if you do go to the zoo. Don't let him out of your sight. Make sure he's got Ted with him and don't lose it.' Ted had once been a cloth teddy bear and was now Rory's comfort rag. Four years of washing it and clutching at it and rubbing it along the ground had reduced Ted to no more than a greyish square. Still there was no going anywhere without Ted and no consoling the boy when it went missing. During any tantrum or crisis Hamilton had only to show the rag and Rory's right thumb would disappear into his mouth and he would settle. For Rory there was no life without Ted.

Grandad and Rory watched open mouthed as she disappeared again.

'Right, Rory, let's get the house tidied up and we'll have some breakfast.' Grandad looked around at the mess and sighed. Rory's train set was laid out in the small living room, the tracks stretching back into the kitchen and under the breakfast table. There were stations with tiny men holding up flags, other stations where make-believe coal was being dropped and two sheds where engines were in for repair. 'Are you going to help me tidy up?'

Rory was down on his knees shunting an engine into a siding. 'In a minute, Grandad, in a minute. You go and have your breakfast first.'

Grandad smiled and knelt down beside the boy, sensing his unhappiness. 'Don't worry, Rory, we'll have a great time at the zoo.'

Rory said nothing and continued pushing engines and carriages along the tracks. He didn't look up until Grandad started climbing to his feet.

'Grandad, why does mummy have to go to work?'

Grandad started to answer then decided better of it. 'I'll get the breakfast.'

'Grandad, where's my daddy?' Rory had stopped shunting engines and was looking straight into his grandfather's eyes. There was no mistaking this was a *big* question for the boy, one he probably had been brooding on for some time.

Grandad sighed deeply. He wanted to answer honestly, just as Kate had asked him to if the subject ever cropped up. She was emphatic the boy should know everything about life, told honestly and openly. Grandad just wasn't up to it.

'I'll tell you after breakfast,' he lied.

Rory went back to shunting.

Alice Martin, Minister for Justice, was a small, tidy-looking woman who kept her years at bay with weekly root treatments, allowing just enough grey to creep into her hair to make her look slightly younger than her fifty-two summers. For twelve years she had sat on the opposition benches complaining about no fewer than three governments and their inadequacies. When her coalition staggered into power on the strength of a three deputy majority in the Dáil she soon discovered it was much easier to criticise from the opposite side of the house than to enact changes in government. Her portfolio brought her to the cutting edge of society. It also brought her into regular contact with Commissioner Quinlan and the two made little attempt to hide their intense personal dislike for each other. Quinlan was tall and statesman-like in his manner, always looking good in his Commissioner's uniform. She, by contrast, appeared frequently to be a woman out of her depth wearing clothes that were out of fashion. To compensate for the profound physical difference in stature she wielded her icy wit and barbed tongue like a blunt instrument during their frequent exchanges.

At nine fifteen that morning Martin was being briefed on overnight developments. She quickly decided this was not a day for scoring points.

The news on Gordon O'Brien's kidnap had begun filtering through to Garda HQ just after three o'clock that morning. At each level a decision was made to inform the next immediate superior. Commissioner Quinlan was finally telephoned at four o'clock. He listened, a sinking feeling filling his stomach, as the details were related. Then he acted.

A meeting of all senior ranking officers and the special Jaguar Unit was arranged for ten o'clock that morning in the Phoenix Park. The Jaguar Rapid Reaction Unit was the force's response to the increasing crime wave that had swept the country in 1996. With the breakdown in the IRA ceasefire in February 1995 and threats of Loyalist bombs in Dublin, the Gardai were stretched to their limits policing paramilitarists as well as common criminals. Throughout 1996 a series of brutal murders rocked the country provoking calls for the government to act to stem the rising tide of lawlessness. But worse was to come that same year, two more dreadful events would shock everyone.

Before the summer had even begun, on 7th June, a serving member of the Garda Siochana, Jerry McCabe, was gunned down by an IRA unit involved in the robbery of a post office van. Weeks later Veronica Guerin, an investigative journalist with *Independent* newspapers, was shot dead by a contract killer as she sat in her car at a set of traffic lights. The revulsion at her murder swamped the government and a set of emergency proposals was announced in parliament. As emergency legislation to seize the assets of known criminals was being enacted another crisis erupted in October. On the day one of Dublin's gang lords was being brought to trial, the star prosecution witness was almost abducted. There was a lot of criticism of the way the Gardai handled the event by the then opposition, now government. Alice Martin had been the most outspoken.

Twenty senior detectives with experience in subversive activity and major crime were identified. They spent ten weeks' extra training in rapid reaction manoeuvres and heavy firearms experience, and each was assigned specialist areas of activities. Eight of the unit then spent two months attached to an Israeli elite anti-terrorist squad. The other twelve spent Christmas at an FBI training camp in Virginia, USA, being trained in the latest anti-personnel armaments. On their return the full Jaguar Unit held a series of strategy meetings at the Garda training college in Templemore in County Tipperary before returning to normal duties. They blended back quickly and few in the force ever knew the reason behind their sudden absence. The unit was kept on a constant state of alert to move in if something big erupted.

The formation of the Jaguar Unit had been a political rather than operational decision, the incoming government promising such a unit in its election manifesto. It was very much Alice Martin's baby.

It's time for you to meet your baby, thought Quinlan as he telephoned Martin just before six o'clock that morning.

The details of the kidnapping were more or less complete. Quinlan related the sequence of events and as much extra information as was available. He was dressed in full formal uniform with braided hat on the desk in front as he spoke. Martin listened impassively, noting how tired and drawn

Quinlan looked. He was in no mood for a fight either. Martin's fingers gripped and ungripped a ballpoint pen which never wrote a word on the blank paper laid out in front of her.

'What happens now?' she asked finally.

'There's an incident room already set up in Wicklow town Garda station under the command of Superintendent Peter Andrews. He's a good man, very experienced. The O'Brien mansion's sealed off and a forensic team are already working on gathering evidence. There were only four people in the place when this gang struck, five if you count the baby. Apparently there's usually a staff of ten.'

'Where were the rest last night?'

'From what I gather Harry O'Brien let them all go for a short break to celebrate the baby's birth. They're due back tomorrow morning.'

Martin massaged her temples. 'Sounds suspicious to me. An inside job?'

'Everything's possible. Anything's possible.'

'Go on.'

'I've ordered the kidnapping group from Jaguar Unit to meet us here at ten o'clock. We'll go over operational details first and then they move down to Wicklow immediately to support and advise the local command.'

Martin looked at her watch. It was now ten minutes to ten.

'Jesus what's the country coming to?' She sighed, almost as if in pain.

Quinlan shook his head in agreement as he leaned back in his chair. He stretched forward again.

'You'll have a chance now to meet Jack McGrath himself. The detective you insisted we transfer off that hospital investigation. He's our kidnap expert on the Jaguar Unit. He can be moved now without anyone knowing any different.'

'And who's going to take over?'

'Right up your street, Minister.' There was a barely subdued glee despite the circumstances. 'We're going to promote one of our finest young women detectives and let her deal with the hospital enquiry.'

'Who?'

'Detective Kate Hamilton.' Quinlan opened a file and went over Hamilton's details. Martin listened closely, never interrupting once. She liked what she was hearing, though.

'Sounds very impressive,' she said finally. 'Very impressive indeed. A single-minded young woman.'

'She's that, I can tell you,' agreed Quinlan. 'She doesn't think twice about questioning orders or decisions she doesn't agree with.'

'You mean she doesn't take any crap from a male-dominated force that has a senior command structure without a woman in it.'

Quinlan smiled. He'd heard all this before. First in the election speeches, then in their many acrimonious exchanges since Martin became Minister for Justice.

'Apart from your good self, Minister.'

Martin scowled, then looked again at her watch. 'It's almost ten. Where's this meeting being held?'

Quinlan stood up smartly and opened the door. With a grand flourish he pointed along the outside corridor. 'After you, Minister. Room Twenty-Four, on your right. After you.'

As Martin strode out she growled out the corner of her mouth. 'Don't try taking the piss, Quinlan. It doesn't suit you.'

Just after ten o'clock Jack McGrath began outlining the history of kidnappings in the state.

He was first in and had watched the others arrive and take their seats at the large circular oak table in the centre of the room. Around the table sat Garda Commissioner Quinlan and his Deputy Commissioner with Chief Superintendent Mike Loughry in a chair opposite. The Minister for Justice sat to the right of the Commissioner. Then Tony Dowling and himself. And Kate Hamilton.

McGrath looked quizzically towards Dowling who shrugged back. Then he looked at Hamilton but she had her eyes fixed firmly on the table in front of her. What the hell's she doing here? he thought.

'The last attempted kidnap or abduction happened last October,' began McGrath. He had a confidential file open in front of him on the desk. 'Halfway through the trial of Paddy O'Hara, our main prosecution witness was grabbed. You know the rest yourselves. There was a shoot out in Malahide and the whole gang was taken. Our witness caught one and nearly died. He spent months in hospital and delayed the trial just as long.'

Everybody in the room knew the details and a few shifted uncomfortably in their chairs. Alice Martin had a 'don't remind me' look on her face.

'Before that,' continued McGrath, 'banker Jim Lacey and his family were kidnapped in November 1993 and only released after a ransom of three hundred and forty thousand pounds was handed over the same day. That was one of Dublin gangster Martin Cahill's efforts. Not that it did him any good.'

He flicked through a bunch of papers he was holding and continued.

'October '87, dentist John O'Grady taken and held by "Border Fox" Dessie O'Hare. O'Grady was recovered safely apart from the tip of one of his fingers. O'Hare is still in Portlaoise gaol. April '86 Jennifer Guinness was taken from her home in Howth. She was recovered safely and the gang were all caught. In December '83 supermarket executive Don Tidey was recovered after being taken by an IRA gang. We lost a young recruit, Peter Sheehan, and the army lost Private Peter Kelly in a shoot out. In '81 supermarket tycoon Ben Dunne was kidnapped and taken across the border. There was a substantial ransom paid over before he was released, reckoned to be about seven hundred and fifty thousand pounds in '81 money. Then we're going back into the mid-70s, Tiede Herrema the Dutch industrialist and earlier Lord and Lady Donoughmore.'

McGrath paused and looked at Quinlan. 'Do you want any further details on these?'

'No. What's the analysis on all this though?'

That was the bad news, thought McGrath. Here's a bit of good news.

'Kidnapping generally ends in disaster for criminals. We have a very good record in this area. We've caught most involved, recovered most of the money. We've also headed a few operations off at the pass before the target even knew there was a problem. We caught a whole IRA unit in 1983 who were planning to kidnap Galen Weston, the supermarket magnate. There was a helluva shoot out. Even so, apart from some of Martin Cahill's wilder schemes, kidnapping has more or less ceased as a method for raising money.'

Alice Martin interrupted. 'Inspector, what sort of wild schemes was Cahill planning?'

A few knowing smiles were exchanged across the table.

McGrath placed his papers down. 'Well, believe it or not, he planned to steal one of our national treasures, The Book of Kells.'

Martin's eyes widened. There was no disguising the look of astonishment on her face. 'Jesus Christ.'

Quinlan blew his nose to mask the smirk.

Martin threw him a withering look and turned back to McGrath. 'Go on.'

'My reading of the information so far is that this could be the work of one of the big players or just a bunch of hoods trying to break into the big time. The target is so high profile they might as well have taken the Man in the Moon. By picking on a baby they have, knowingly or unknowingly, risked bringing the whole of the underworld out against them. There's going to be a big shake up. There are check points all over the place already. There'll be raids on known criminal gangs and their haunts. There won't be a crook, from mobster to pickpocket, who won't curse this kidnapping. Mouths will open, hopefully. Kidnapping is bad for business. Kidnapping a newborn baby will put crook against crook.'

'Any ideas who might have done this?'

'Not yet. There were four involved and they were heavily armed. The place must have been staked out for some time for they knew where and when to strike. Either that or somebody on the inside has been feeding them all the information they need. Harry O'Brien hasn't been off the front of the newspapers this past few days so it wouldn't have been hard for them to know when to make their move.'

Somebody along the table muttered agreement.

'We have a report of a four-wheel drive in Roundwood not long before the raid and we know a four-wheel drive was used to take the gang and the baby away. They used some type of plastic explosive to break open the entrance gates. That suggests an ex-IRA involvement, somebody used to explosives.'

Quinlan whispered something to the Assistant Commissioner on his left who nodded.

McGrath continued. 'There's a report of a burned-out jeep in the car park of the Stand Hotel at the Curragh. Local Gardai say there are tracks and footprints suggesting a second car was parked there with movement between the two. That's a good place for a changeover. They could be on the motorway to Dublin within minutes or turn south towards Portlaoise. They could have gone along the motorway for part of the way and then turned off. They could be anywhere.'

There was a sombre silence around the table. Alice Martin listened intently, eyes fixed on McGrath. 'Have you any thoughts on where they might be?' she asked quietly.

McGrath sat back in his chair, his eyes lowered while he thought about this. 'If I had to take a guess I'd say this is a Dublin gang. They used guns and explosives. These sort never feel happy out of Dublin, they hate the countryside. I'd say they're back in Dublin somewhere.'

A ripple of muted conversation broke out.

'There's one final thing.'

The room quietened again and all heads turned towards McGrath.

'How this goes depends a lot on whether Harry O'Brien has kidnap insurance. Many top businessmen have "risk management" policies which include kidnap insurance. If O'Brien has kidnap insurance we could find ourselves trying to keep one step ahead of him and his advisers. Past experience suggests deals may be done behind our backs.'

There were groans all round.

'Anything else?'

'Not at this point.'

Quinlan interrupted. 'Jack we want you down in Wicklow immediately. Superintendent Peter Andrews is in charge of overall operations but has requested the assistance of the Jaguar Unit.' He hadn't. It was never going to be a case of waiting for a request. Alice Martin's baby had to go to work.

McGrath nodded and then started to speak when Quinlan cut across. 'Detective Sergeant Dowling will remain on the hospital murder inquiry.' He stood up and walked down the table to where Kate Hamilton was sitting and stopped behind her. 'I would like you all to meet Detective Sergeant Kate Hamilton. Many of you know her already.' He rested a hand lightly on her right shoulder. 'Detective Sergeant Hamilton will join Dowling. However, she is now in overall control of the investigation. Let me repeat that, she is now in overall control of the hospital investigation. She will report to Mike Loughry as usual. Detective Sergeant Dowling will remain on the case to maintain continuity and provide the necessary experience.'

Kate Hamilton could hardly believe her ears. She swallowed deeply. Keep your cool, keep your head up. She fixed her eyes firmly somewhere in the distance, apparently unruffled. This sort of thing happens all the time, guys, don't expect me to look surprised.

Alice Martin just couldn't resist the temptation. 'If I may say so, Commissioner, it's not before time a woman was given the opportunity to show her paces in the force.'

Watch it, thought Hamilton. You're on trial.

Quinlan couldn't resist the temptation either. 'I'm sure

the minister will take particular interest in how the hospital investigation develops from here on.'

Oh God, thought Hamilton. I'm piggy in the middle here. This is some sort of power play.

Martin felt she just must have the last word on the subject. 'I won't have to, Commissioner. I have full confidence in Detective Sergeant Hamilton. She'll bring a woman's touch to what has been a very heavy handed investigation up to this point.' She looked directly at McGrath and the whole table followed the deliberate confrontation. McGrath started to reply, then noticed the warning sign from Mike Loughry. He decided to hold his peace. Another day perhaps.

Martin, unfortunately, took this as a sign of weakness. She reached into a bag at her feet and pulled out the *Daily Post*. 'I read in this morning's paper, Inspector McGrath, that you announced a breakthrough in the case yesterday.' She laid the paper on the table, face down. The kidnap story broke too late for the morning papers, their headlines still dwelt on the hospital investigation. 'Can you share this information? Are we to expect an early arrest?'

McGrath arched his hands and spread his fingers open, resting the tips on the table. He stared at them for a moment as if he was about to perform some trick. He chose his next words carefully, very much aware all eyes were on him.

'Minister, with the greatest respect, there are operational ploys every detective uses from time to time to shake up a stalled investigation. I can't remember a murder investigation as bizarre as this. We have a young woman brutally murdered in a hospital and the whole medical staff treat it like it's some sort of inconvenience. I can't remember a case where I've had less cooperation. I've got more information out of crooks than the doctors down there.'

He paused to let this sink in. There was total silence around the table. Kate Hamilton watched every move, beginning to understand why she had been called in on the investigation.

McGrath looked up to find Alice Martin's eyes boring

down on him. 'I read that newspaper too, Minister. My words are reported verbatim. None of my men leaked those details to the press. But somebody did. There's more to that hospital than meets the eye. There are a lot of personal agendas there. Detective Sergeant Hamilton will have her work cut out unravelling them all.'

Afterwards she wondered how the words left her mouth. But Kate Hamilton was never a woman to be patronised or advised when she never asked for it. She always spoke her mind, often impulsively.

'I'm quite sure I'll be able to maintain the high standards Detective Inspector McGrath has set. However the case has stalled, we all know that. But sometimes it's useful to have a fresh head look over the evidence and maybe come up with a different approach.'

She looked directly at McGrath, defiance sparkling in her eyes. McGrath grinned back. Touché. For a brief moment they both smiled at one another.

Alice Martin could have swept her up and kissed her. She just smiled, triumphantly. Even Commissioner Quinlan was impressed.

Mike Loughry interrupted. 'I'm afraid, Kate, you'll be working with a smaller team. We've pulled almost everyone onto this kidnapping. There'll be a lot of door-to-door enquiries, surveillance of known criminals, road checks, the lot. We need every spare man. I've had to reduce your operating team to six for the immediate future. I'll review that this day week if there are no fresh developments.'

Hamilton nodded. Dowling shrugged and exchanged knowing looks with McGrath as the meeting broke up.

Luke Conway heard directly from the Minister for Health that Jack McGrath had been taken off the case. It was the only good news that morning.

The hospital was thunderstruck by Gordon O'Brien's kidnapping. Staff listened anxiously to every news bulletin and became even more incensed when they learned that June Morrison, one of their own, had been taken to hospital unconscious. The admitting doctor suggested the gag pulled over her mouth had blocked her ability to breathe adequately and she had collapsed from lack of oxygen.

Sky television carried the first pictures from Wicklow on their noon news. Helicopter shots picked up Gardai moving throughout the estate, some with tracker dogs, their dark uniforms standing out in perfect contrast with the snow-covered ground. Squad cars were parked at all angles in front of the house. Telephoto lenses picked out forensics, in their white boiler suits, moving past windows. Two uniformed Gardai were standing beside a squad car which blocked the entrance, only moving when authorised personnel called. The Sky news bulletin mentioned the ongoing murder investigation at the Central Maternity Hospital and wondered about any link. Luke Conway groaned as he listened to that. Kidnap experts, paediatricians, ex-policemen, anything and anybody who might be an expert or hold an opinion were dragged into the studio and interviewed. The shots of Harry O'Brien wheeling his wife into the lobby of the Central Maternity Hospital were beamed across the world to other news bureaus.

'I think you'll find this young woman a refreshing change from Detective Inspector McGrath, Dr Conway. She should bring a woman's touch to this investigation. After all, it is a women's hospital.'

Luke Conway had thanked the minister.

But he was still a worried man. The hospital was in the eye of the storm again. The sort of publicity he was hoping desperately would die down had returned with a vengeance. And his favourite midwife, June Morrison, was in intensive care and still unconscious according to the latest bulletins.

Maybe Detective Kate Hamilton will be easier to deal with, he thought. I've spent all my working life dealing with women. I know how they think, how they behave. I'll soon have her under control.

Just before one o'clock Kate Hamilton waited outside the Master's Office with Tony Dowling. The two had already gone over the details of the case, forensic findings and progress. McGrath had given her connected paperwork and later she'd listened closely as Tony Dowling explained the confrontational difficulties experienced, giving her inside information on some details previously only he and McGrath had known about.

She'd frowned when he related McGrath's ploy to open up the wall of silence and play the dummy card of a breakthrough and possible early arrest. That was the first she'd known the ace card was nothing more than a blank. The more she thought about the way the case was being investigated, the more concerned she became. It *was* time for a fresh approach.

'Dr Conway, my name is Detective Sergeant Kate Hamilton. I'm usually attached to Store Street Garda station. You already know Detective Sergeant Dowling.'

Conway stood up, reached across and shook her hand. He nodded to Dowling. There was absolutely no flicker of recognition as he inspected the young detective sitting opposite.

'Dr Conway, I have been asked to take over the investigation of Mary Dwyer's murder.' Conway flinched at the word murder. 'Detective Sergeant Dowling has briefed me on progress so far . . .'

Conway interrupted. 'Is there any progress, Detective? Are we any closer to that early arrest Detective Inspector McGrath promised?'

'For operational reasons I can't divulge any details, Dr Conway. Let me just say immediately we are as anxious as you and the rest of the staff here to bring this case to an early conclusion. With that dreadful kidnapping last night, the force is stretched to breaking. I've had my investigating team reduced to six.'

'I'm sorry to hear that,' lied Conway.

'All the more reason, with respect Dr Conway, for us to get total cooperation. I have less men to work the case. We're all going to have to work much harder. I'd like your personal assurance that you will persuade your staff to cooperate with us as much as possible. That way you'll get to keep your hospital moving and we'll get to find the killer.'

Conway spread his long fingers out and rested them on the desk. Hamilton stared at them briefly, fascinated. The long fingers that lifted my baby from inside my body.

'Let me assure you, Detective Sergeant, I and all of my staff will move mountains to help end this investigation.' He smiled. It was a sweet smile, but too sweet, sickly sweet.

'Would you mind if I asked you a few questions now?'

There was a smug look on his face. 'Not at all.'

Hamilton lifted a briefcase onto the table, reached inside and produced a small black notebook which she flicked open. Beside it on the table she settled the paperwork and clippings McGrath had produced on the case.

Dowling sat beside her, mute.

'I've been looking through the list of medical staff.' She paused and looked up.

Conway nodded, chin resting on those long fingers, now curled. 'Yes.' It was a slow, wary yes.

'There are no women consultants.'

Conway looked puzzled. 'I'm sorry. I didn't quite get that.'

'There are no women consultants on the staff here.'

'So?'

'No woman has ever applied for a job as a consultant here?'

Tony Dowling suddenly sat forward, a bemused look on his face.

'No, that's not true. We have had a number of applications from women when any consultancy position has arisen.'

'Why are there no women consultants on your staff then?'

Conway was beginning to get ruffled. 'Because the applicants weren't up to the high standard we require of a consultant at this hospital.' The reply was sharp, razor sharp.

'But the male applicants always were?'

Conway fiddled with his bow tie, trying to control his anger.

'Detective Sergeant Hamilton, would you like to tell me what on earth the hospital policy on consultancy application has to do with your murder investigation?'

Dowling turned around in his seat to take a closer look at the young woman, his face clearly showing puzzlement and concern.

'It may have nothing to do with it all, Dr Conway. Then again it might. I was just wondering if there is a deliberate policy to prevent female applicants achieving consultancy posts in this hospital?'

I'm lying. I just want to see you squirm, you bastard. I didn't put my baby up for adoption, did you ever find that out?

'That's an outrageous suggestion, Detective. What the hell do you think you're getting at?' Conway was obviously livid.

'I'm just wondering why a hospital that is almost two hundred years old and deals exclusively with women and babies has never, even once, appointed a woman as a consultant. Doesn't seem that strange a question to me. Does it seem so strange to you, Tony?'

Dowling lifted his eyes to heaven.

Conway started to reply when she cut across.

'You see, from the moment we've been called in on this case there has been a wall of silence. Detective Inspector McGrath told me he'd never experienced anything like it in all his career. And he's had a long and distinguished career.'

Conway seethed as he listened.

'But as I said at the beginning I'm having to work this case with a lot less manpower. Only six detectives to do the work of the twelve-man team originally assigned. So let's get the ground rules established immediately. We expect full and total cooperation from now and until this case is closed. Anything less than that and I'll make sure the newspapers know just what we're up against. I don't really think you could take much more bad publicity.'

Tony Dowling could hardly believe his ears. He sat with the face of a Buddha and the insides of the QE2 on full throttle.

Conway jumped to his feet and leaned across the table menacingly, his face purple with rage. 'I have never heard anything so outrageous in all my life. I'll ring the Minister for Justice immediately. I'll have you taken off this case so quickly you won't have time to powder your nose on the way out.'

Hamilton slowly began packing her notebook and paperwork away. She didn't as much as look up to acknowledge Conway's outburst. Her movements were slow and deliberate, so slow that the shouted words had dissipated by the time she replied. When she did speak her voice was calm and controlled. But ice cold.

'Well, Dr Conway, I don't think that would be so wise really. You see I've been particularly chosen to take over. I've just come from a meeting with the Minister for Justice. She's delighted to have a woman working a major case. Somehow I don't think she'd be too pleased to remove me as quickly as she's seen me appointed. She's very much a feminist is our Minister for Justice and likes to see women seek high office. I don't think she'd be much pleased to hear we got off to a bad start just because I asked you why there are no women consultants in this hospital. She might start to wonder the same thing herself and start to ask questions in the Dáil. More bad publicity.'

Conway sat back slowly in his chair, fuming.

'Actually there is one very big reason I asked why there are no women consultants in this hospital.'

Conway's eyes narrowed suspiciously. Dowling almost fell out of his seat to hear.

'If there is a policy, deliberate or not, in this hospital to keep women in their place then it will cause major problems for me. I do not take to condescending or patronising gestures. When I ask questions I want answers. I do not want anyone to think that because I'm a woman they're going to get an easier time than if Detective Inspector McGrath was still in charge. I would like you to put the word out, Dr Conway. I'm here to stay until this case is closed. And I'd like it closed quickly.'

Conway stared at her in amazement.

'A lot of work has gone into this case already, Dr Conway,' continued Hamilton, waving a hand across the reams of paper she had stuffed into her briefcase. 'Don't let's ruin it all by getting upset with the new ground rules. I'm here and I'm here to stay. Let's get on with it, shall we?' She smiled at him, delighting in his obvious discomfort. Then she gathered up her briefcase and reached across with outstretched hand. Conway instinctively took it, surprised at the firmness of the grip.

Dowling struggled to his feet awkwardly.

'Myself and Detective Sergeant Dowling are going down to the laboratory to question the staff again. I'd like it if you would accompany us and I'd prefer if you didn't let them know in advance.'

She walked out the door followed by Dowling, like a lapdog.

'Jaysus, Kate . . .' started Dowling outside, but she grabbed his arm and shushed him. She held on to it. He stared at the gripping fingers.

She counted to twenty, then opened the door again.

'I'd really much prefer if you didn't let them know, Dr Conway. As I asked. And when you're ready we'll see you outside the lab.'

Conway's mouth dropped, the receiver already in his hand.

As Kate Hamilton and Tony Dowling were making their way along the hospital corridors towards the lab just after one o'clock, back in County Wicklow Jack McGrath was pacing the corridors of Beechill trying to piece together the exact details of the kidnap. He'd arrived at mid-day and went into immediate conference with the officers in charge from the local Garda station. What time were you called? What was the place like when you arrived? Were there any sightings of the getaway? Did anyone nearby hear the explosion? Have there been any suspicious sightings near the house recently? How did they get in? Where and when did the first road blocks go up? The ground work had been good, those first on the scene doing everything right. An ambulance had transferred June Morrison to the nearest hospital within half an hour of the Gardai entering the house. McGrath complimented them on their speed and thoroughness. But he was now encountering the first major obstacle in the investigation – Harry O'Brien. Big Harry had lost his mind.

When Sandra O'Brien had finally climbed out of bed to feed her child it was the pressure and discomfort of the surging milk in her breasts that woke her. Not the cries of a hungry baby. That worried her immediately. She had gone first to the nursery and discovered the empty cot, then rushed to where June Morrison was supposed to be sleeping and found her lying on the ground and unconscious. Quickly releasing the gag and barely daring to believe what was happening she'd rushed downstairs to find Big Harry and Theo Dempsey tied back to back in the study, struggling against the gags, their hair and clothes showered in ceiling plaster. By the time she'd cut them free and discovered what had happened she was so distraught she ran from room to room, bursting open doors, screaming for her baby. Big Harry was little better. He had charged out of the house in a frenzy and was discovered half an hour later by the first squad car on the scene, rambling and barely coherent, frozen and shivering.

Only Theo Dempsey had kept his head. The ex-army sergeant who'd seen two tours of duty with the Irish peace-keeping force in Lebanon had been down many dark alleys before and was trained to handle emergencies. It was Dempsey who made the first call to the Roundwood Garda station on his mobile phone and who also had the wit to immediately contact Garda headquarters and arrange for an all out alert for the kidnappers. And it was Dempsey who'd placed June Morrison in the recovery position, just as he'd been shown during army first aid lectures, who'd finally restrained Sandra from also chasing off into the night and who'd telephoned the local doctor to come and help out with the immediate chaos.

When the rambling and demented looking Harry O'Brien was finally brought back to Beechill it was Theo Dempsey who'd dealt with him and was eventually able to settle him and persuade him to put on warm clothes. He had never seen his boss as agitated, as distraught, as disturbed as he was when he was brought back inside the house. Even in the darkest of the dark drinking days, Big Harry had kept some semblance of sanity. But not now. The local doctor had become so concerned that he injected a strong, long-acting sedative and ordered him to bed. Sandra O'Brien was finally persuaded to go back to bed an hour later after the Gardai had gleaned as much useful information as they felt they would get.

Jack McGrath paced the floor of the study as he listened to Theo Dempsey recount the night's events yet again. Dempsey had lost count of how many times he'd told the story.

'There were four. Two tall, one medium and one small. You're sure the small one was a woman?' asked McGrath.

'I could see her stockings, pudgy ankles and flat shoes. The feet were too small to be a man's. I know it's not much but it's as much as I can tell you.'

'The smaller man seemed to be the one in charge.' McGrath was going over Dempsey's first statement.

'Yeah, but they hardly spoke. Most of the communication was done by nods when they were in the room with us but the small man was the one who did all the talking at the end.'

'Dublin accent?'

'Definitely. Strong Dublin accent.'

'But you did hear one of the others and he spoke with a Northern accent. You're certain about that?'

'Yeah. I've been up North a lot with Mr O'Brien on business and I know a Northern accent when I hear one. He definitely had a Northern accent, a distinct Northern accent.'

McGrath wasn't surprised at this, he'd suspected as much when he had inspected the gates. Semtex had been used, strongly suggesting ex-IRA involvement. Fits in with the Northern accent, he thought. Do a little homework on that. Not too many of that crowd we don't know about.

'Anything else?'

'Not a lot. It was all over so quickly.'

Dempsey looked haggard. His crew cut hair glistened with sweat and his usual upright army stance had deserted him. He hadn't slept, hadn't washed, hadn't shaved and hadn't eaten. He had never seen big Harry so bad. He was very worried about him.

McGrath sat down heavily on the chair behind Harry O'Brien's desk. Resting on the top was a clean A4 sheet of paper. Pasted across the sheet were various letters and clippings from a newspaper. HARRY'S BOY ... £3M ... OR DEAD HARRY'S BOY. MOVE SOON ... OR DEAD BABY.

'Are you sure this is all that they left? No mention of a contact, no mention of when they'd get back?'

Dempsey shook his head. 'No, nothing.'

'Did they say anything about a deadline?'

'Not a thing. Whatever was in that envelope was all they left. They certainly didn't say anything else to Mr O'Brien or I would have heard it. I was strapped to the chair with him.'

The door to the study slowly opened. A haggard and distraught Sandra O'Brien, one hand resting against the frame for support, swayed and almost collapsed. Theo Dempsey rushed to grab her before her knees buckled.

'Get me my baby,' she mumbled. 'Get me my baby back.'

Two Ban Gardai took her from Dempsey's grasp and led her gently back to her bedroom.

McGrath and Dempsey exchanged glances as they watched her disappear up the stairs.

'Stay here,' ordered McGrath. 'I'll be back in an hour. Hang on here in case these bastards make contact. You're the only one on your feet that knows anything about this place at the moment.'

Dempsey slumped into a chair and rested his head in his hands. What a night. What a fucking awful night.

Dempsey could still hear the screeches of Gordon O'Brien as he was carried out into the freezing night and of Sandra O'Brien as she rushed from room to room, crashing doors open. 'Where's my baby? Where's my baby?'

He felt drained, totally exhausted, totally defeated. Where *was* her baby?

The hospital staff had agreed to work over the weekend to clear the backlog. Theatres were returning to normal, wards were buzzing again with activity. Babies were being born in a more settled hospital atmosphere.

The laboratory was fully stretched. Bloods, swabs, urines, cervical smears, tissue samples for histology: all had to be collected, analysed and reported on. The staff were back in action and chasing their tails to make up for lost time. They needed Kate Hamilton like a hole in the head.

But that's what they got at two thirty, accompanied by a grim-looking Luke Conway, still smarting from their first encounter.

'I'd like to speak with all the staff for a moment,' she told him in the outside corridor. 'Then I'd like it if we could speak with them individually.'

Conway sighed deeply, an air of resigned compliance. 'Do you have to do this now? They're only just getting back to some sort of normality. There's an enormous backlog of work here, you know.'

Hamilton rounded on him angrily. 'Now, this minute. Not tomorrow or next week. This minute.'

Conway wasn't that surprised at her outburst, he knew he was up against a formidable young woman and one who was in the driving seat.

The staff turned when the three entered the lab. Nervous glances were exchanged. Hamilton and Dowling walked over to the spot where Mary Dwyer's body had been found. Inspecting it closely, Hamilton took out her black notebook to compare what she had written on the first night. She frowned. Dowling watched and a faint flicker of an amused smile crossed his face.

As the lab became quieter, Conway cleared his throat. 'Okay, everybody. We'll have to break for a moment. You can stop everything and put it on hold for a few minutes.'

More faces turned, roughly fifty-fifty male to female. Hamilton looked at each, her mind buzzing. She counted eight in white coats around the benches.

'Eh, I'd like to introduce you to Detective Sergeant Kate Hamilton.' Conway began. 'She's now in charge of the incident, eh, the murder investigation.' He almost choked on the words and paused as if he was trying to think of a better way to continue. Then he suddenly realised he was now standing on the exact spot where Mary Dwyer had been found and couldn't stop himself looking at it. Eight sets of eyes followed his to the floor and there were involuntary shudders all round, two of the girls clutching at their throats, as if ghostly hands were slipping around them.

'Detective Hamilton wants to say a few words.' Conway finally ended.

Hamilton waited until she was certain of full attention.

'Hi. I'm sorry to interrupt you all and I know you're all trying to get the hospital back into some sort of routine and working all day Saturday and Sunday isn't exactly fun.' She paused, noticing a few nervous smiles. 'However, the more I've looked at the information we've got so far the more convinced I am there's something missing that's staring us in the face. And I think it's something to do with this lab.'

Worried glances were exchanged all round.

'So what I'd like you all to do is go over the ground you've already gone over when Detective Inspector McGrath was here. Is there anything, anything at all, no matter how remote or irrelevant you may think, that you maybe didn't mention?'

She stopped to let that sink in.

'In particular can you think of any way of finding out what test Mary Dwyer was working on that night that maybe we don't know about? Could she have been doing one for a friend as a favour? Why was the PC she was working on smashed? There were several sheets of paper torn away from the printer. Any ideas why? Why was the printer smashed as well? Why did the murderer deliberately drop all the blood samples onto the floor? Were the other machines smashed randomly or was one chosen in particular, maybe to destroy the information it contained?'

She stopped to look again at the faces. This time she looked very closely, as did Dowling. They both agreed later if it was one of them he sure kept it back. A more numbed and anxious group of faces would be hard to find anywhere.

Hamilton continued. 'Are your PCs networked? If they are do you have back-up facilities at the central server?'

A voice cut through. 'We do.'

All eyes turned to a young, desperately young face, pock marked with acne. He had long dark hair tied in a ponytail. Both his hands were folded across his chest and he was wearing a white coat that had seen better days.

He continued. 'I tried to explain that to the other detective.' Hamilton looked towards Dowling. 'No, not him. The other one. With the moustache.'

'Detective Inspector McGrath?'

'Whatever his name was. I started to explain that to him but he got into an argument over the phone with somebody and next thing we knew the lab was closed and nobody could get in or out. I mean what's the point in asking for our cooperation if you're not going to listen to what we have to say?'

Luke Conway smirked.

Hamilton didn't want to alienate this group any further. Go carefully, she thought.

'I'm sorry about that, er . . . sorry what's your name?'

'Hogan, Ben Hogan. All our tests are computerised. We get the request form with the sample and enter all details into PCs at the benches. All this is carried back to a central server. There's an automatic back-up in case of power failure and the like. So even though the bench PC was broken the information is still recorded and kept. Same with all the other machines.'

'So anything Mary Dwyer was working on last Tuesday is stored and can be retrieved?'

'Absolutely.'

Hamilton turned to Conway and smiled sweetly. 'Dr Conway I know you're already overstretched but do you think I could get Ben to do a little computer work for me. Like now?'

'All this could have been sorted out much earlier, you know,' complained Conway, jumping on the aggrieved bandwagon, 'if Detective Inspector McGrath had done his job properly.'

'Let's forget about all that for the moment.' She motioned to Hogan. 'Okay, Ben, let's go to work.'

Dowling listened closely to all this and concluded two very important things. One, he was delighted to be retiring soon. All this talk of networking and back-ups was way out of his depth. He still used an old battered portable typewriter for reports. And two, Kate Hamilton was one helluva smart cookie. A third thing then crossed his mind. Jack McGrath could well end up as the scapegoat if this investigation screws up.

5.07 pm
The Cottage, nr Kilcullen, Co. Kildare

Gordon O'Brien, five days and five hours old, was a very unhappy baby.

A newborn baby is the most delicate and vulnerable animal on earth. For the previous ten months Gordon O'Brien had grown and slowly developed into a fully formed baby. He had bounced gently in the protective waters surrounding him in his mother's womb. He had heard her heart beat, felt her movements, even heard her voice. He had been in a warm, loving environment. He was content. Unborn, but happy, growing and developing normally. He was never hungry and never frightened.

All that changed on Monday, 10th February 1997, the day he was born. He had struggled for life then and almost lost. He had been lifted roughly into the outside world and felt pain for the first time as needles entered his skin. He'd heard loud, anxious voices and then slowly realised he could not hear the comforting noise of his mother's heartbeat, the sound of her voice.

He had screamed in his own little way, struggled to scream, fought desperately for the breath to scream. But finally screamed.

Then she was back again. He was feeding from her breast and heard again her heart, her voice. He felt for the first time her touch as she caressed his face and body and stroked his hair.

He was content once more. Happy. He had his mother.

Now she was gone. Again. He screamed in his own little way.

'Can you not shut that bloody child up?' Sam Collins was near the end of his tether.

None of them had slept much the night before. The elation of the successful kidnap had kept them awake, the adrenalin still flowing from the noise of the explosives, the excitement as they drove back to Newbridge.

But the baby wouldn't stop crying, screeching in fact. And Sam Collins had had enough. He didn't like babies at the best of times and this one was really getting on his nerves.

'Peggy? For fuck's sake would you shut the little bollox up.'

They were all edgy. Tommy Malone had tuned in to all the news bulletins throughout the day, wanting to hear everything about the night's work. Like all criminals, he loved reading in the papers or watching on TV or listening on the radio to reports of his latest job. He wouldn't be disappointed on all three.

The news was broadcast in sombre tones and given extra time. Appeals were made to the kidnappers for the safe return of the baby and separate appeals were made to the general public for help. The Minister for Justice would make a nationwide appeal on the 6.01 News tonight. Sandra O'Brien and her husband were under police guard and medical attention, both heavily sedated, unable to make any personal TV appeals at this stage.

'Fuck,' muttered Tommy Malone. He hadn't reckoned Big Harry would go off the deep end. 'Maybe he'll come round tomarra? Well he'd better fuckin' hurry, I can't stand that screechin' child meself. Hope Peggy's up to this.'

Peggy Ryan was up to it. About fifteen years ago, but not any longer. Even she was getting agitated with the baby's incessant crying. She stuck soothers in his mouth but that didn't work. She tried winding him, but that didn't work either. She tried feeding him. No good. She was tempted to smack him one. But not while Tommy Malone was around.

Gordon O'Brien was very frightened. His mother's soft caresses were replaced by rough hands, the comfort and warmth of his mother's breast replaced with cold rubber teats. Her voice was gone. All he could hear were loud shouts, abusive shouts. Angry voices.

His nose and chest were becoming irritated already and he began to snuffle and cough, the result of inhaling smoke from Tommy Malone's cigarettes.

Malone flicked the radio off. The baby was asleep. A bit of fuckin' peace for a change. He threw Peggy Ryan a threatening look. Shut him up or else, his eyes said.

'Okay. As far as I can see Big Harry won't be in any fit state to get the money organised until Monday by the earliest. That's two days from now. Youse may as well ignore all that crap on the wireless. It's the usual crap after any big job. By tomorra they'll be singin' a different tune. Big Harry'll want his baby back.'

'He's fuckin' welcome to him. Noisy little bollox.' Moonface was getting fed up too. He picked at his nose and wiped the result on the back of his trousers.

Malone ignored him. 'We're stuck here until the money's paid over so youse may as well make the best of it. I'm gonna go out and get more groceries in. Write down anything youse want. Remember, no booze. Peggy stays with the baby all the time.'

Fuck, thought Peggy.

'I don't want anywan leavin' the cottage. Or only go as far as halfway down the lane. I don't want anywan seein' who's here or nebbin' at what we're doin'. Okay?'

Heads nodded. The same heads cursed their luck. Fuckin' screamin' child and not as much as a can of beer to calm the nerves.

'Can I come with yah?' asked Moonface. 'I need to get a bit of air. Those fuckin' cigarettes of yours is deadly.'

Collins wasn't sure about letting the two of them out of his sight but decided to let it go. They wouldn't disappear without the baby. Pity, almost, he thought.

Moonface was packing the boot of the Volvo with groceries and baby food and nappies.

'Ah Christ, Tommy. Why do I have to ge' them?'

'Because I'd look fuckin' suspicious buyin' baby things at my age. Didn't ye hear the news? Everybody's lookin' crossways at anywan buyin' baby stuff. Ye look the age. I don't.'

So Moonface paraded up and down the aisles in the big Quinnsworth in Newbridge, looking for tins of Cow & Gate and packets of Pampers for boys. He had a terrible time working out the right size.

Inside the Volvo, Tommy Malone scanned both evening papers. He'd hit the headlines in a big way. SNATCHED! KIDNAPPED!

The *Evening Herald* and *Evening Post* had the family photo, taken in the lobby of the Central Maternity Hospital, splashed across their front pages. Inside each continued the story with more photos and big close-ups of Gordon O'Brien, his tiny head and small crop of hair sticking up, wrapped in his shawl and sleeping contentedly in his mother's arms. There was a map of North Wicklow with Roundwood arrowed, aerial shots of Beechill and more on the Garda presence. The articles contained 'on-the-spot' reports with photos of the on-the-spot reporters, photos of the TV crews, even a close-up of a CNN crew filming. Reports on the kidnap story were being beamed live across all CNN networks with a history of Harry O'Brien and each bulletin was accompanied with a potted history of previous kidnappings in the state.

Malone didn't read that in case it would annoy or worry him. He didn't like the way this was all blowing up. He watched as Moonface pushed an empty trolley back to the shop, then slipped out of the car and stuffed the papers in a rubbish bin.

'Did ye bring the papers with ye?'

'Ah bugger it, I musta left them on the boot of the car when we were drivin' off. Musta got blown away.'

'Righ',' said Moonface. I didn't see them on the boot though, he thought suspiciously.

Brian O'Callaghan came round the corner just too late to see more than the tail of the Volvo as it turned into the lane.

They're still here, he thought. I wonder who they are?

Ben Hogan looked at the monitor screen, puzzled.

He'd done a print-out of all tests carried out in the lab on Tuesday 11th February 1997, then checked them against the official hospital request forms. All matched up, except one. There was no request form corresponding to one of the tests.

He then scanned the records, which was even funnier. Funny unusual, not funny ha ha. There was no patient registered by that name, the name on the screen he was now staring at. Joan O'Sullivan, 249 Crumlin Crescent, Crumlin. Date of Birth: 27/2/76.

He did a search by name, then by initials, then by date of birth. Nothing. There was no Joan O'Sullivan, at that address, with that date of birth, in the hospital records.

But what was funnier, funny peculiar and definitely not funny ha ha, was the fact that there was no name of technician entered. Or of doctor ordering the test. Which was unusual, most unusual. But there was litle doubt who had carried out the test. It had to be Mary Dwyer. Because it was set up, as recorded on the screen, at 21.23, 11/2/97, when Mary Dwyer had been on duty. The only one on duty.

Ben could feel his heart race as he walked to the back office. He pulled open a filing cabinet and rustled through until he found what he was looking for, the list of names and test requests for the broken rack of test tubes. Then he sat down and began checking names against tests ordered. At the end of the first check one didn't match up. He checked again. It still didn't match up. He rang Luke Conway and asked him to come back down to the lab. Immediately.

Conway was back in the lab within minutes.

'Remember we had to collect all the names on those test tubes? You know, the ones broken on the floor last Tuesday night.'

Conway studied Hogan closely, wondering what exactly he had discovered. 'Yes.'

'And we had to check the names against the test ordered?'

'Yes.' Clipped, precise.

'Well, there's something funny here I can't make out. One of them doesn't match up.'

'Explain it to me slowly. Very, very slowly.' Kate Hamilton had called all the team together in the library to listen in on the development.

Ben Hogan and Conway outlined the problem. Conway was markedly subdued, very aware of the significance of what was about to be revealed.

'Mary Dwyer set up an AIDS test at exactly twenty-three minutes past nine last Tuesday night,' began Hogan.

'Exactly?'

'Yeah. It's recorded on the computer. Exact minute the test kicks in.'

'Right.'

'Now when we routinely type in requests we put the requesting doctor's name and ward. Or if it's outpatients, we type in OPD. We also type in the technician's initials. That's whoever's setting up the test in the first place. Are you with me?'

Hamilton nodded.

'Now when we set up a test we need to know whether it's for a patient already on the hospital records or for a new patient. If she's already on record there's less typing to do. You just add the request to her file.' He paused to look at Hamilton and she motioned him to go on.

'Now when Mary Dwyer set up that test,' continued

Hogan, 'she would have routinely scanned the records to see whether the patient was already in the system. But she wasn't.' He stopped and took in a deep breath, sensing everyone was hanging off his every word.

'So, she was a new patient,' interrupted Dowling.

'Not at half nine at night. She'd have been in the wards if she was a new patient, and even if she had just been admitted, she would still be in the system. All her details would have been entered at reception. More importantly, I can't see anyone ordering an AIDS test at that hour of the night. After hours requests are for emergencies only.'

'And an AIDS test isn't an emergency?' one of the team interrupted, real surprised like.

'No. I know that sounds strange to you but really AIDS tests are expensive and time consuming. We try and do them during normal hours. I've just never heard of anyone requesting an out-of-hours AIDS test.'

'Maybe she was a new outpatient?' offered Hamilton.

'Still not at half nine at night.' Hogan had thought this all through. He knew what he was talking about. 'Outpatient clinics are well over by six, six thirty at the latest.'

'Okay,' interrupted Hamilton. She knew by now there was something important in all this. Very important. 'She sets up an AIDS test at nine thirty or thereabouts, which is way out of line, but what's the big deal? I mean from what I hear some of you do little tests on the quiet for family and friends. You know yourself, it goes on all the time, you know that.'

Luke Conway came in on that one. 'It does, but not out of hours. It's too easily spotted then. We check on this fairly regularly. It's part of hospital procedures, trying to keep our budget in line. Most are done when the lab is busy. That way the test's buried in among all the other stuff.'

Hamilton turned this over. 'Okay, anything else?' She couldn't help but notice Conway's change in attitude.

'Yes. There's no request form. Ben couldn't find a request for that test. We don't know which doctor ordered the test. And if she was doing that test for a friend, or even herself, she would have gone ahead and carried out the test but not entered a false name and address into the hospital system. She wouldn't have entered anything, she'd just've gone ahead and done the test. But she set up the test in a patient's name.'

'Why didn't she enter the doctor's name and her own initials? You said that was routine.'

Ben Hogan answered. 'I know.' All eyes switched to him. 'That's something we do all the time when the request doesn't tally. It saves on unnecessary typing and correcting. If the request form isn't properly written or the requesting doctor's name can't be made out, and that happens a lot believe me, we hold back on the paperwork until everything's correct.'

Dowling looked confused. He was confused. 'All ye're tellin' us is that she may not have carried out the paperwork because she couldn't find the patient in the hospital records. I still don't get it. What's the big deal?'

'The big deal, as far as I can see, is this,' Conway interrupted and began to explain. 'One, Dwyer set up an AIDS test out of hours, which is most unusual. Two, the test was set up on a patient who wasn't already registered in the hospital. Three, the test request form is missing. And four, and this is the bit I was really coming to, the blood sample is missing also.'

'Missing?' Hamilton's voice lifted an octave.

'Yes, missing. All samples are kept and stored. Ben and I thought the sample would have been in among the ones smashed on the ground. But we've checked and double checked on them. All are accounted for.'

Hamilton and Dowling exchanged glances, as did the rest of the team. 'So where's it gone?'

'I don't know. It was definitely not in the lab. Everything was searched that night and the next day. Every bin, every disposal unit, behind every radiator. Everywhere. I know that for certain for your Inspector McGrath made a point of closing off almost half the hospital to look. It was definitely not in the lab.'

'So he took it with him?'

'That's what I think.'

'What was the address for the patient?' John Doyle, one of the detectives, asked. He was leaning against the bookshelves.

Ben Hogan read from the computer print-out. '249 Crumlin Crescent, Crumlin.'

'Say that again,' asked Doyle, straining forward to be sure he heard correctly.

'249 Crumlin Crescent, Crumlin.'

'Is that Dublin? Is that supposed to be in Dublin? Dublin 12?'

Hogan looked down. 'I think so. Mind you it's got Dublin 16 on the print-out.'

Doyle straightened sharply. 'That's wrong, that's totally wrong, Kate. I used to work the Crumlin area. I know Crumlin Crescent. It's only about twenty houses facing one another down a wee cul-de-sac. There couldn't be a 249 in Crumlin Crescent. Not in a million years. Couldn't be any more than a number twenty or a . . . a number nineteen.'

Silence.

Luke Conway was distinctly uneasy and shifted uncomfortably in his chair. Ben Hogan's discovery could mean one thing and one thing only and he could hardly bring himself to say it. But Kate Hamilton left him no room for evasion.

'What's your assessment of this Dr Conway? What do you make of all this?'

Conway moistened his lips and curled his long fingers in an arc in front of him. He deliberately avoided looking up as he spoke.

'The only way I can fit all this together is for someone inside the hospital to have killed Mary Dwyer.'

The room fell silent again, a long, dead silence.

'Why?' It was a very slow why from Detective Sergeant Kate Hamilton.

Conway paused to get his wits about him.

'Mary Dwyer was a great kid, a good worker. She was sensible, down to earth. She would only have started up an AIDS test at that hour if specifically requested. It could have been one of the doctors, even one of the porters, anyone. But it had to be someone from inside the hospital. Anyone could have forged a hospital request form, brought their own blood sample in and said Dr so-and-so's just sent me down with this and wants that test done immediately. She was a very obliging girl. I can just see her going ahead and doing it, setting it up along with the other tests she was doing and only getting around to the paperwork at the end.'

Nobody spoke for a moment.

'So you're telling us that anybody from the hospital could have come down to the lab last Tuesday night and could have duped Mary Dwyer into setting up an AIDS test. Only she twigged something was wrong when she tried to check the patient through the hospital computer?'

'That's what I think.'

'But why was she killed?' Dowling asked the obvious. They were all thinking the same thing, but they wanted Conway to spell it out for them. Why was she killed?

'I think it's because she discovered something he didn't want to get out.'

'Like what?' Kate Hamilton's face was grim.

'That he's got AIDS.'

Crunch.

'The test was positive.'

Each word was recorded by the microcassettes. They clicked on to any noise. They clicked off to each silence.

Dean Lynch knew how to listen in. And listen in he would.

'This is one dangerous bastard.' Kate Hamilton was angry. Her voice sounded very, very angry, as recorded on the microcassettes.

'This is one dangerous bastard. I hope he rots in hell.' When Dean Lynch listened later, those words tormented him. 'I hope he rots in hell.'

He played it back, again and again.

'I hope he rots in hell.'

Like a wounded animal, Dean Lynch began to howl.

*

'There are eight members of staff who don't have alibis for last Tuesday night.' Kate Hamilton was reading from notes. 'I know it's Saturday and we'd all like to get home but let's pull in three and take them down to the station for questioning.'

There were a lot of silent curses.

'There's the kitchen chef who was very flaky about his whereabouts according to the interview report. Get him. Will you take him, John?'

Doyle nodded and collected the original interview statement.

'Paddy Holland has no alibi. He's one of the doctors.' She paused slightly, feeling inexplicably flustered. 'I'll take him with Tony. Is that okay by you?'

'Okay.'

'There's a Dr Tom Morgan who's story sounds way off according to the interview report. Let's call on him first though.'

Tony Dowling looked at her aghast. 'Are ye and I goin' to deal with both of them tonight?'

Hamilton frowned. She no more wanted to be running into overtime at the weekend than the rest but felt they had to press ahead while the momentum was building.

She collected her bag. 'The rest of you can go home. I'd like us all back here tomorrow at one o'clock.' Groans filled the air. 'Yeah, I know it's the weekend but we've got to move on this while it's hot.'

She paused.

Unbeknown to her the microcassettes clicked off.

She spoke.

The microcassettes clicked on.

'Also I think we should interview that nurse again, the one who heard this guy's voice. Get her to listen in on any questioning. We could put up a screen in an interview room down at the station. Fire the questions and have her listen. Maybe if she hears the voice again it'll jog her memory. Also I want to get legal advice on doing an AIDS test on male staff members. We could wrap this up very soon if we screened them all.'

Later, when he listened to this, for the first time Dean Lynch began to worry.

Before she left Kate Hamilton joined Luke Conway where he sat in the outside corridor. There was no mistaking the worry on the man's face. This nightmare was deepening, not easing.

'I'd like to arrange an AIDS test on all male staff members. We could get to the bottom of this case very quickly with that information.'

Conway shook his head slowly. 'I've been thinking that myself, that thought's been going through my head from the moment Ben Hogan told me about this.' He looked at her and she sensed deep, deep concern and worry. 'There are two problems though,' he continued. Hamilton listened intently. 'One, if word gets out that someone in this hospital is HIV positive and possibly working here, all hell will break loose. The wards will empty in minutes.' He paused as the significance of his words shook him yet again. 'Secondly, anyone having an AIDS test would have to give permission first and you might find legal problems there. I'm going to have to get advice on this from our solicitors.' He stood up to go. 'I suggest you do too. You might find the law slowing you down. I just know some of the doctors will want to take legal advice before agreeing to this. This isn't going to happen overnight.'

29 *6.01 pm*
Studio 4, RTE television centre,
Donnybrook, Dublin 4

'Roll with intro jingle.'

The 6.01 News jingle began, the 6.01 News logo appeared.

'Cut to intro clip.'

The clip of Harry O'Brien wheeling his wife into the lobby of the Central Maternity Hospital was shown in slow motion. The intro jingle continued. Across the nation's screens the clip ran with sound but no voice-over.

On screen, Harry O'Brien stopped and posed behind the wheelchair. Flashes, like bursts of lightning, silver-greyed the faces. There was still no voice-over. June Morrison came into view carrying Gordon O'Brien, wrapped in shawl. More flashes. Then came the hand over in slow, slow motion. Sandra O'Brien gently took the little bundle, resting him in her arms. Her face looked down lovingly at the tiny head, barely visible. Harry O'Brien looked over her shoulder and poked a finger down to gently lift the shawl back for a better view.

FLASH! FLASH! FLASH! FLASH! FLASH!

The viewers could see the silver-grey lightning but could not hear the thunder yet to come. There was still no voice-over, just a flickering TV screen, intro jingle running without a commentary.

Harry O'Brien stood up and rested both hands on the back of the wheelchair. The camera zoomed in as the beautiful face of Sandra O'Brien slowly lifted. Then came that smile, that million dollar smile. FLASH! FLASH!

The camera pulled back to take in the family unit. Big Harry, his beautiful wife and their newborn baby. There was lots of lightning as the flashing cameras lit up the scene.

'Hold that frame. Voice-over.'

'The infant son of Harry and Sandra O'Brien was kidnapped from their family home in County Wicklow in the early hours of this morning.' The news was read in a voice that would do justice to a preacher at a funeral. Hardly a television set in the country wasn't tuned to the bulletin. In pubs and game halls, clubs and sports centres, people gathered around, shushing and pushing for a better view.

'Three masked and armed men entered the house just before midnight, tied up the occupants and lifted the sleeping baby from his cot. The front gate of the O'Brien mansion was blown open, probably by some form of plastic explosive. The raiders made their getaway in a four-wheel drive, later found abandoned and burned out in the car park of the Stand Hotel at the Curragh in County Kildare. A midwife from the Central Maternity Hospital staying at the house was found unconscious and is in intensive care in Wicklow General Hospital. Gardai are appealing to the public for any information to help track down these men, believed to be members of a Dublin criminal gang. A fourth member, thought to be a woman, was also involved. As yet, Gardai have released no details of any ransom demand.'

Women held their children tightly, men cursed and swore. This was the worst crime in the nation's history, worse even than the Monaghan and Dublin bombings in the mid-70s, worse than all the shootings and knivings and bludgeoning. He's only a baby, for Christ's sake. He's only a few days old, the poor little bollox. There was open talk supporting hanging, even a firing squad, if the kidnap gang was caught.

There was no mistaking the public anger. We're disgraced again as a nation. All this is being beamed across the world, just when we thought the country was getting back to some sort of normality. They've disgraced us in the eyes of the world. The bastards!

The newscaster went on to relate the sequence of events. There were clips of Gardai on the estate with helicopter views coming in over the Wicklow hills, still covered in a light layer of snow. It could almost have been a travel documentary, it looked so beautiful.

The reports were accompanied by a number of 'piece-to-camera' on-the-spot reports at Beechill while others were relayed from the incident centre in Wicklow town and included a shot of Jack McGrath climbing into a squad car, ignoring the microphones thrust at his face.

'Is the Jaguar Unit involved? Have the Gardai any leads? How is Harry O'Brien? Is his wife safe? Was anyone hurt? Has any ransom been demanded?'

'No comment.'

The on-the-spot reporter returned the viewer to the studio where interviews with members of the opposition, baying for the blood of the Minister for Justice, followed. Arguments soon broke out on the panel with political experts disagreeing on the way the government was handling the affair. Lots of hot air and strong opinions but not an ounce of common sense, the panellists so caught up in political point scoring they couldn't have given a damn if Gordon O'Brien was found face down in the Liffey. It might have helped, in fact. That would have given them more ammunition to get back into government and then hold a public inquiry.

Alice Martin, grim faced and wearing a very sombre suit, appealed to the nation from the Dáil TV studio. Her speech was beautiful, almost poetic, the content full of passion. As she neared the end, her face contorted, as if suppressing tears. She looked beyond the camera, reached into a pocket and pulled out a white handkerchief. She dabbed at her eyes and let her shoulders shake a little. She continued with more appeals, finally ending with a prayer, a good, well-recognised Catholic only prayer.

'Thank you. And may God protect you Gordon O'Brien

wherever you are.' It was a magnificent performance, Oscar potential.

'Jesus, will somebody get me a drink,' said Alice Martin, Minister for Justice, at the end. I wonder how that went down? Hope I didn't ruin my make-up.

Dean Lynch watched the news.

Somebody's stealing my thunder.

'Is your daddy in?'

Hamilton and Dowling stood at the door of the magnificent redbrick house in Sandymount where Dr Tom Morgan lived, or was supposed to live. Certainly that was the address he gave. As they waited both stomped their feet to keep away the numbing cold.

'Who's that at the door?' a slurred female voice called out.

The little boy looked over his shoulder anxiously. 'I don't know.'

The sound of footsteps was heard, tripping footsteps.

'Get inside.' A hand grabbed the child's shoulder roughly and he was pulled back from the door as it swung slightly open, revealing a woman who was long past her 'best before' date. A cigarette dangled from her lower lip and she was clutching a bottle of vodka with her right hand. She looked them up and down.

'Who're you?' Before Hamilton could answer the woman began a fit of coughing, resting her right hand on her right knee as she bent down for support, careful not to spill the vodka. 'What do you want?'

'I'm sorry to disturb you. I'm Detective Sergeant Kate Hamilton from Store Street Garda station. This here's Detective Sergeant Tony Dowling. We were wondering if your husband was in? We'd like to have a few words with him, if that's at all possible?'

The drunken laughter rang in their ears all night. When the woman finished enjoying that little bit she went into another fit of coughing, letting go the door which slowly opened fully, revealing the frightened faces of three children.

Two boys, aged about seven and five, and the most beautiful looking little girl, no more than three years old, if even that. They were all crying, obviously frightened.

'Why don't you look down in the animal shelter? He's probably screwing every alley cat they've got.' There was no mistaking the bitterness and anger in her voice.

The door slammed in their faces. Dr Tom Morgan was obviously not at home.

Hamilton knocked again and waited. Dowling stomped his feet rapidly and blew into his hands to stave off the biting cold. The door opened again and the woman leaned against the frame.

'How long are you going to keep annoying me? He's not here, I told you that.'

Hamilton stepped forward and pressed against the door slightly. She felt the woman push it back against her.

'Look I'm real sorry to be bothering you, but it'll only take a minute. We just want to ask a few questions. Can we come in?'

'No.' Even though the voice was slurred the tone was emphatic. 'If you have anything to ask about, ask it here.'

'Jaysus Kate, get on with it,' grumbled Dowling. 'I'm freezin' here.'

'Eh, Mrs Morgan . . . am I right, are you Mrs Morgan?'

'You are right. I am Mrs Morgan. For all the bloody good it does me.'

'Well, Mrs Morgan,' continued Hamilton quickly, grasping at the morsel of cooperation, 'we're trying to tidy up a few loose ends. It's about the young girl who was murdered at the Central Maternity Hospital. I'm sure you've read all about it?'

If Mrs Morgan had read about it she was not letting on. She swayed slightly and Hamilton watched as she gripped tightly onto the frame for support. 'Go on,' she slurred.

'Well we just wanted to check out something your husband told us.'

'What exactly did he tell you?'

Hamilton flicked open a notebook and squinted at it in

the gloom. Suddenly the porch light was flicked on and Hamilton could see Tom Morgan's wife clearly for the first time. She was around the same height as Hamilton but with a careworn and wrinkled face. Her streaked blonde hair lay in a mess around her shoulders and the tracksuit she was wearing reeked of cigarettes and spilt vodka. She noticed Hamilton sizing her up and stepped back further so that she was halfway in and halfway out the door. Hamilton glanced up at the light and smiled. 'Thanks.'

'Forget it. Now get on with whatever you want to know, I'm getting cold standing here.'

From inside the screams and roars of children bickering could be heard and the woman turned and shouted a mouthful of abuse at them. The screams died instantly. She turned back. 'Get on with it for Christ's sake.'

'Your husband said he was at the movies on the night Mary Dwyer was murdered. Can you remember that night? Maybe you were with him or you remember him going out?'

The drunken laughter started again. 'At the movies. Jesus I don't believe it, at the movies. That bastard wouldn't sit through a movie if you were to pay him. I dunno where he was that night but I can bloody well tell you he wasn't here and he certainly wasn't at the movies.'

The door was slammed back in their faces again.

Tony Dowling rubbed his frozen hands against one another. 'Charmin' lady, isn't she?'

Kate Hamilton frowned. Dr Tom Morgan would certainly need to be questioned again.

9.47 pm

Inside a public phone booth in Sandymount Green the surgically gloved finger of Dean Lynch dialled a number.

'Hullo?'

'I want to speak to John.'

Pause. Breathing clearly heard at the other end.

'This is John speaking.' Cautious, wary.

'Hello John. This is Bobby.'

Little laugh.

'I thought it was you, Bobby boy. Thought I recognised the accent. You're early. I wasn't expecting to hear from you so soon.'

'I have a problem.'

'Haven't we all, Bobby boy, haven't we all. These are difficult times we live in.' Short pause, too short for Lynch to come back. 'What's up?'

'I need a gun.'

Long pause.

Finally. 'No problem, Bobby boy. If the price is right you can get whatever you want. I'll get you a Sherman tank if you know how to drive it.' Lynch heard a grunt that might have been a laugh.

'I need a small gun.'

'Like a handgun?'

'Yeah.'

'Is this defensive or offensive? Are you thinking of starting your own little war, Bobby boy?'

'I may need to be positive.'

Slight chuckle. 'Need to be positive. I like that, Bobby boy, I like that. Need to be positive.' The Cockney twang sounded lighter than usual.

'Can you get me one?'

'No sweat, Bobby boy. No sweat. I know just the one for you. Will you be taking it home with you?'

'Yeah.'

'Then you'll need something to carry it in that won't look suspicious.'

'Yeah.'

'Leave it with me, Bobby boy. Leave it with me.' Short pause. 'When do you need it for?'

'Can I get it tomorrow?'

'This is very sudden for you, Bobby boy. You usually give me lots of notice. Something big happening?'

'Kind of.'

'Very good, Bobby boy. Ring me as soon as you get to the airport. What time do you think you'll be arriving?'

'Late in the morning.'

'See you then, Bobby boy. See you then. Bring a grand in cash for the gun. And another grand for ammunition and secure travel bag.'

'See you tomorrow.'

'Need anything else?'

'No.'

Both phones clicked.

Dean Lynch made his way back to his flat, deep in thought. They were deep, deep thoughts, black, black thoughts.

He had been feeling unwell all day, sweating even in the cold. His mouth was sore again, his appetite non-existent. He felt dreadful.

I'm dying.

He wasn't planning on going alone.

The door bell at Dr Paddy Holland's two storey redbricked terraced house rang at ten thirty exactly. The house was set back from the pavement by a small garden in which a few withered rose bushes struggled to survive. There were black railings and a small half-open gate leading to the front door. Kate Hamilton and Tony Dowling had driven there immediately after questioning Tom Morgan's wife. They'd agreed they would only call on Holland if they saw lights on inside the house. Dowling groaned as the car pulled up. Not only was the light on in the front room but the curtains were only half pulled and the tall frame of Paddy Holland could be clearly seen sitting at a table.

He ushered them in, apologising for the state of the house in one breath and then warning them not to talk too loudly in the next. 'You'll wake the children,' he hissed.

Kate Hamilton warmed to him again, just as she had when first she'd interviewed him. She warmed to the house as well, recognising the disorganised chaos of children. Two bicycles rested awkwardly in the hall and cycle helmets lay halfway up a staircase. A door led into a kitchen and even in the poor light Hamilton could make out a table with dishes not cleared away. A kindred soul, she thought. Here's someone like myself, struggling to make a home for the children and hold down a job at the same time.

'How old are the kids?' she asked, trying to break the ice. She'd sensed immediately his concern at being called on so late at night.

'Anna's seven and Laura's nine. They're good kids really, but they know how to run rings around me.' Holland smiled ruefully. 'It takes me ages to get them down at night and then I only have these few hours before I go to bed to catch up on my hospital work.' He took off his glasses, breathed on the lenses quickly then cleaned them with the end of his tie.

'Sorry,' offered Hamilton. 'We'll get this over quickly.'

Tea was offered and refused as Dowling began going over Holland's story in detail, checking it against the original statement. It matched. Any worries about Holland's whereabouts on the night Mary Dwyer was murdered were quickly dispelled. Holland mentioned he had made a number of telephone calls that night, two of them around the time of the actual event. When Dowling asked if he could check the telephone company records on this Holland had no objections and sounded relieved there was a way to confirm his story.

'I suppose this murder has caused all sorts of problems at the hospital,' Dowling suggested finally, fishing for gossip.

'Dreadful,' agreed Holland. He was sitting on a sofa, one leg draped across the other.

He looked and sounded tired. Paddy Holland was taller than Kate Hamilton and quite young-looking for his forty-two years. He was in denims and checked shirt with a rather worn looking cardigan thrown over for warmth. A gas fire burned in a fireplace beside where he sat and Dowling pulled his chair closer for heat.

Holland kicked off a suede boot and wrinkled his toes for comfort before slipping the boot back on again. 'The nurses are very worried. We've had two girls refuse to do night duty already, they're too frightened to come in on their own in the dark.' He looked towards Hamilton and noticed her suddenly avert her eyes from him. He glanced quickly at her ringless hands as they fiddled awkwardly with a pen and notebook.

'And,' he continued, 'I've had to sit down with Anna and Laura to try and explain everything to them. Somebody at school got to them and the next thing I find is them waiting up for me to come home and crying because they were told I was going to be killed next.' He shook his head sadly. 'Kids and their exaggerated scare stories.'

Hamilton made a few sympathetic murmurings.

'It's having a dreadful effect on some of the staff and their families,' he added finally, looking back again at Kate Hamilton who was watching him closely. This time she didn't look away. 'You don't have any kids so I suppose this doesn't mean a great deal to you,' he said.

Tony Dowling tried to defuse the gaffe with a sudden burst of coughing.

'Wrong, very wrong,' said Hamilton. She stood up to go. 'I have a four-year-old boy.'

Holland looked flustered and embarrassed and started to mouth apologies.

'Don't worry, you weren't to know. His father and I were planning to get married but he died.'

The room fell silent, Dowling studied his hands for a moment. There was a short but very pained silence.

'Can I ask how?' Holland asked.

Hamilton began packing her notebook, unclipped the biro, slipping it inside her jacket, anything to distract. She finally looked up and straight at Holland, her emotions running riot but her features controlled. Tired and worn out as he was she could see care and sympathy in his eyes.

'He was gunned down in a drugs bust in Boston. I worked there for a short while. It was supposed to be a simple drugs bust, but they got it wrong. He died instantly.'

'I'm sorry.'

212

'No need to be. I know you've lost your wife. I've seen your interview file. You know what it's like trying to hold down a job, rear your children, be there for them and at the same time keep your independence.'

Holland looked surprised at the insights to his life Hamilton knew.

'Is it worth it, Detective Sergeant?' he said. 'Sometimes I ask myself that. Do you? Is it worth it?'

'Is it worth it for you?' Hamilton felt unsure of herself and embarrassed she was discussing her private life so openly in front of Tony Dowling.

'Yes. The hospital and my children are my life, they're all I've got. And the hospital is bigger than all of us. Bigger than every member of staff, bigger even than the egos of some of the doctors who walk its corridors. It's been serving the people of Dublin for centuries. Not for ten years, or fifty years, or even a hundred years. For two centuries. Rich and poor alike. It's more than a maternity hospital, it's a national institution. And now some bastard's brought it to its knees.' His voice was now full of anger.

Tony Dowling watched and listened in silence. He could sense the raw emotions in both and could almost feel the shared grief.

'Nice fella,' said Dowling when he and Hamilton were back in the car. Kate Hamilton was glad the darkness hid her blushes. As Dowling waited for a break in traffic to get out onto Donnybrook Road, he was grinning. 'And he's unattached.'

Hamilton waited until the car was safely onto the main road. 'Tony, you're way outa line on this.'

The two briefly smiled to one another.

Tommy Malone made contact for the first time just before midnight. He drove into Kilcullen and parked on the main road close to the public phone box with the car lights off. He waited for twenty minutes and during that time no one appeared on the road. Only two cars passed by.

The telephone rang out once and Malone redialled. Finally it was answered by a sleepy voice at the other end.

'Is Theo Dempsey in?' Malone had the mouthpiece covered with a cloth to disguise his voice.

There was a pause. 'No, he's not. Who's speaking?'

'Can you take a message for him?'

'Yes. Who's speaking please?' The sleepiness had gone out of the voice.

'Listen and listen very carefully to what I have to say. I won't say it twice. Are ye with me?'

There was silence at the other end for almost a minute.

'Are ye still there?' Malone didn't conceal his annoyance. 'Yes.'

'Tell Theo to take this message to his boss. If he wants his baby back he'll have to come up with three million in cash. Three million. Cash. Tell Theo I'll ring him tomorra at this number. Tell him to get Big Harry movin' for we want the money by Tuesday at the latest. When I call tomorra I'll tell Theo how we're gonna collect it.'

He hung up.

At the other end Theo Dempsey's wife, Marie, scribbled furiously, trying to remember every word. Then she rang Beechill.

Day 7

A little hand brushed against Kate Hamilton's face. 'Mummy, I'm frightened.'

Half asleep she reached out and tugged Rory in beside her and he nestled down, put his thumb in his mouth and fell asleep again. Hamilton edged away slightly to give herself more space and turned to lie on her back and stare at the ceiling. Outside she heard a rumble of thunder and minutes later the steady streaming of rain against a skylight. It was at moments like this that she felt the loneliness so much, so strongly.

She reached across and shifted the sleeping child's body slightly for more room and held her breath as she watched him stir in the darkness. Then his breathing settled again. You're all I've got, Rory. You're all I've got. You and Grandad. Tears pricked behind her eyes and for a fleeting moment the face of Paddy Holland flashed through her mind. She turned to one side and closed her eyes and tried to drift back to sleep.

A little hand pulled her face back to the other side. Rory was awake again. 'Close your eyes, now. It's very early. Mummy wants to sleep.' Rory began brushing Ted across his mother's face. 'Rory, go to sleep. Stop that. Mummy's very tired.' She cocked an eye at the digital clock and groaned. 'Go to sleep Rory.'

Rory rested one arm on her shoulder and closed his eyes

again. He was content. He was with his mother. He could feel her warmth, hear her breathing.

Gordon O'Brien could not. He was awake too, crying. He was hungry and frightened and in his own little way he knew there was something wrong. There was no warmth, no tenderness, no caresses. There was no mother's milk, no comfort of the breast nor sound of his mother's heartbeat as he fed, nor warmth of her breath against his cheek. He cried loudly. Too loudly.

'Take tha' ye little bollox.' Peggy Ryan was beginning to regret the whole episode. Jesus, I'm well past gettin' up at nigh', feedin' babies, changin' nappies, walkin' the floors. She stuck a half-warmed bottle of milk in the child's mouth and pulled the sleeping bag tightly around her shoulders. Jesus, it's freezin'. We'd better get outa this kip soon before we all get our deaths. The smell of damp and must was beginning to get to her. The smell of Tommy Malone's cigarettes hung everywhere. What a kip.

At around the same time Dean Lynch was staring at his naked body in the long mirror in his exercise room. The rash was spreading. He had noticed it two days previously for the first time, but knew it may well have been there longer. It was red and scaly in both large and small patches, mainly on his chest where it almost covered the tattoo there, and whatever part of his back he could see. He noticed some on his forehead and eyebrows.

Disease progression. It's catching up on you, Dean boyo. You'll have to move a little faster. You've some unfinished business to do. Like that little nurse. And that new detective.

Yes, her in particular.

Rot in hell, will I?

I'll see you on the way down the elevator.

The phone rang and he jumped. Heart pounding, he snatched at the receiver.

'Dr Lynch?'

'Yes. Speaking.'

'Doctor I'm very sorry to wake you so early but we've got a deep transverse arrest in Labour Ward Three in East Wing. Dr Sharif's doing an emergency Caesarean section in theatre at the moment. There's nobody else in the house to do this.'

'I'll be in within ten minutes.'

It worked to his advantage.

Oh lucky man!

5.32 am

It was a difficult delivery, but skilfully and successfully completed. The mother, a thirty-three-year-old in her second pregnancy, was trying to push out a nine-pound baby and had become exhausted. The baby's head arrested at mid-pelvis, occipito-posterior presentation. Her baby's head was arriving into the world the wrong way round and was stuck. Only a skilled and expert obstetrician could turn the head around and ensure a normal delivery. Fortunately she had an epidural in place and could not feel the manipulations going on inside her body.

Lynch slipped the Kielland's forceps inside, up to and around the sides of the baby's head. After locking the blades, he pulled gently to ensure a proper fit. Then, in tandem with the contractions, the baby's head was gently turned and then eased lower into his mother's pelvis, right way round. Eventually, and safely, the child was born. But Lynch became aware halfway through how draining the effort was. He didn't usually feel so fatigued, the delivery wasn't that difficult. He noticed also he was perspiring heavily. Very heavily.

Before he left the labour ward he took three scalpel handles and three size twenty-three scalpel blades from the stores.

6.12 am

He slipped into the library and retrieved one of the medical textbooks containing his microcassettes. He had plans for it.

6.27 am

He gently and slowly opened the door into Matron's office which was deserted and unlit. He'd carefully checked there was no one along the corridor likely to disturb or see him before closing the door quietly. With a pen torch he scanned the walls until he found what he was looking for. The nurses' duty roster. He flicked off the torch for a minute and listened. The only sounds were from his own breathing and the pounding of his heart. The noises reassured him and he flicked the pen torch on again and read, finally coming to the name he was looking for. Staff Nurse Sarah Higgins. Apartment 7, the Hawthorns, Rock Road, Blackrock. He scribbled the address and telephone number onto the back of his hand. Then he scanned further. Sunday 16/2/97: 2–11 pm shift.

In the dark, he smiled slightly.

7.49 am

He was back in his flat staring at the reflection in the mirror. It was perfect. His usual disguise, jet black, well-fitting wig with the hair swept back severely. The wig was long, over collar at the back, covering his own, slightly lighter and totally grey. There was no sign of Dean Lynch's hair anywhere. He fixed a short but thick black moustache onto his upper lip with mastic spirit gum, pressing firmly along its length until he was sure it held well. Then he placed a pair of thick horn-rimmed glasses on his nose, pushing them into position. There were no actual lenses in the frames, just clear glass. He was dressed in a neat, casual jacket and trousers with roll neck sweater, all black. A dark grey scarf would be pulled up over his lower face later to protect against the cold and to complete the disguise. He pulled on black leather gloves and a heavy overcoat.

I'm dressed to kill. The Dean Lynch thin smile flickered.

It was his usual routine when he visited London John. He was always careful, always on guard, the art of disguise mastered to the last detail. He had taken trips to London twice on the same day in different outfits and no one at the airports or on the flights would have recognised him. It was London John who'd suggested this once, a long time ago. It was London John who had actually arranged for the wig fitting, the glasses, the moustache.

'Never let anyone know your business, Bobby boy. Keep yourself to yourself. Never let the girls see your face.'

They never did. All they ever saw was the black wig, the black moustache, and the horn-rimmed glasses. And the eyes. It was the eyes that frightened them most.

He left a message on his answering machine, to be on the safe side. But he had already cleared with Dr Sharif to cover any emergencies, which was usual in gynaecological practice. He'd told everyone he was going to take the day off and relax, maybe take in a movie later tonight. The film started at quarter past ten and went on until after midnight, suiting his plans nicely. He'd mentioned some of this, casual like, to Dr Sharif and a few nurses as they sipped tea in the rest room of East Wing after the forceps delivery. He was setting up his alibi.

He checked the flat door peephole. There was nobody in the corridor outside. He turned on the burglar alarm, then the back-up burglar alarm, before slipping outside and gently closing the door behind him. Then down the stairs to the ground floor, stopping and checking again before leaving through the fire escape. He inserted a small metal bar, no longer than six inches, no thicker than a quarter of an inch, into the inner frame of the fire escape door. The door closed against it but didn't lock. He had done this before, many times. He knew how to get in and out of the flats without using the front door. It was a useful trick.

He walked briskly along Baggot Street and hailed a taxi.

'Airport, please.'

Those were the only words the taxi man got out of him throughout the thirty-minute journey, despite his usual attempts at conversation. He was paid, in cash, without a word. Miserable little bollox, thought the taxi man as he drove off without a tip.

Lynch bought a ticket on the next flight out, an Aer Lingus to Heathrow, using the name Julian Nutley.

He sat in a window seat, staring out at the clouds, throughout the flight, looking neither left nor right and ignoring the hostess.

'Coffee, sir?'

'No.'

'Paper, sir?'

'No.'

Odd bollox, thought the air hostess.

11.24 am

'Hullo?'

'I want to speak to John.'

Pause. Breathing clearly heard over the line.

'This is John speaking.'

'Hello John. This is Bobby. I've arrived.'

1.17 pm

London John sat in the foyer of the Hilton Hotel, Park Lane, reading the *Sunday Times*. It was full of details of Gordon O'Brien's kidnap with banner headlines and half of the front page devoted to the story. London John read with interest. He couldn't give a toss, really, but always found it fascinating what others would do to get money.

London John was a tall good-looking Cockney in his late fifties. His grey hair was fashionably short at the front and fashionably just that little bit long and thick at the back, covering the collar of his crisp white shirt. He was wearing a navy-blue suit, cashmere and wool navy overcoat with a red Liberty cashmere scarf. A club tie set off the image perfectly, giving him a slightly raffish look, like someone about to climb into an open-hooded Mercedes and zoom up to his weekend retreat in East Anglia. Except London John wouldn't know where East Anglia was if you asked him to point it out on the map.

A Londoner all his life he rarely left home territory except on short business trips to Amsterdam or Turkey. London John was a big business man who controlled most of the pornography and hard drugs in South London. Starting as a small crook in his late teens London John had become involved first in London vice dens, then pornography, then procurement. He'd befriended girls and boys hanging around the bright lights of Soho, offering them somewhere to stay, then offering them money and gradually buying their confidence. It wasn't long before he owned them. Within ten years he had established a formidable reputation in the sex trade. He then moved into drugs. With the profits from drugs he acquired the heavy back-up necessary to keep pretenders to his developing empire at bay. He also needed the heavies to collect debts.

By 1996 London John had the reputation of a man who could get anything you wanted, at a price. He was a businessman of sorts. He could provide boys and girls of any age and drugs of every kind. He could also provide the hardware, and the heavies to go with the hardware if necessary, at a price. He was not cheap.

Dean Lynch had first met up with London John in a Soho sex shop. He was putting out feelers for a good dealer, one who wouldn't rip him off. London John heard through the grapevine and had him checked out. When his spies declared Lynch clean a meeting was arranged and from then on a very sensible business arrangement was agreed. No names were exchanged, just code tags. London John. Bobby. Nice and simple.

In exchange for cash London John would provide all the heroin Dean Lynch required and all the girls he felt he could handle. Dean Lynch was a good customer, never failing to come up with the money. His income from the Central Maternity Hospital was good and he had few or no outgoings. He could easily afford his little treats. He usually rang two weeks in advance of any purchase to the memorised number London John had provided. His requests were clear and unambiguous, heroin at first, the exact quantity and at the going rate. Then, as he came to trust his dealer, he began pushing for something extra. Girls. Always slightly older girls, always dark and taller than Lynch himself.

To London John such requests sounded normal. In fact he dealt with so many weirdos, Lynch sounded refreshingly normal. 'I'd like a dark-haired girl, mid-thirties or older. No older than forty. Get her to put on lots of deep red lipstick.' 'Whatever you say, Bobby boy, you're paying. You'll always get what you order from me.' The requests never varied and while some of the girls asked not to go with him again, many felt they made their money real easy. 'He just sat and stared at me for two bloody hours,' one reported back to London John. She would be one of the lucky few. All the girls' reports had one thing in common. Lynch frightened the life out of them. The bastard was dangerous. Those eyes were full of hate.

Then Lynch became violent. Not too rough at first, but progressively more so with each visit. It got so that London John would only put junkies down for Lynch; desperate for money they usually put up with anything. But the last girl had been badly beaten. Battered in fact. It had cost London John over three hundred pounds to have her sorted out in the private clinic he used for all his girls and boys. The surgeon there was a customer of London John's. 'Whoever did this really got stuck in,' he related to London John over a fix afterwards. 'He broke her nose and nearly ripped the scalp right off her head. It took me hours to get her sorted out.'

Which was why London John had decided to have a little word with Bobby. He'd been keeping tags on him and a pattern was emerging. He was using more heroin, the calls were more frequent and the times in between had lessened. From one score every two months, Bob had progressed in four years to one score every two weeks. But even that didn't worry London John. It's usual really, he considered after the previous evening's telephone call. The little scumbag's hooked. That's usual and that's his funeral. He knows the rules, he knows the game. The girls mean nothing, they're just dirt anyway. But I don't like to see them get roughed up. It costs me money and they're out of action for a long time. It costs me money. Bobby boy is beginning to cost *me* money, and that's just ridiculous. It's not on and I'll have to tell him. Nothing too heavy today, it's Sunday and I'm in a good mood and he's been a good client for a long time. He's stayed with me longer than most and always comes up with the money without the slightest quibble. But the little scumbag needs putting in his place. He needs to know what he's doing to my profit margins.

London John continued to read. He noticed a connecting report to the Gordon O'Brien kidnap story. It was all about a murder inquiry at the hospital where Gordon O'Brien had been born. There were accompanying photographs. One of the photographs showed two people coming down the front steps of the hospital. London John squinted at it closely.

He stared at one of the two people with particular interest, even taking the paper over to a large plate-glass window in the hotel lobby for a better look. He squinted at the photograph from about five different angles, before dropping the paper into a wastepaper bin. Do you know, thought London John to himself, if I was a betting man I'd put a grand on that being Bobby boy.

Lynch sat down beside John on the deep, expensive sofa parked in the middle of the hotel lobby. London John pretended to examine his hands, splaying his fingers out for effect.

'Nice to see you again, Bobby boy. Shall we go for lunch?'

'I'm not hungry.'

London John turned round and inspected the much smaller man sitting so quietly and still on the sofa beside him.

'You should eat, Bobby boy. You've lost weight since I saw you last. On a diet?'

'I'm just not hungry.'

London John hailed a taxi and they sat in the back, not a word exchanged. The cabbie left them at the back of Harrods and London John walked, Lynch beside, along Basil Street to Walton Street and into Lennox Gardens to his parked Saab. They drove back to Kensington Road then along Kensington High Street to Hammersmith where London John owned a two-storey over-basement redbricked terrace house. This was where he held his business meetings, stored his business goods and kept his hardware. Like many big-time criminals, London John lived well away from his office. He had an expensive luxury flat in Holland Park where he spent all his free time with whatever woman was in favour and wasn't using his main source of income, heroin and cocaine.

The Hammersmith office basement had double brick walling on each side, the bricks of a special sound-proof material where the house abutted its neighbour. These little extras had all been added after purchase and included one room with a twelve-foot long, six-foot wide and ten-foot deep sandpit, the heavy artillery room where London John tested his hardware.

And murdered his enemies.

'I've got you a Walther PPK handgun.' London John was explaining the hardware. Lynch looked on intently as London John held the weapon in the palm of his left hand.

'It's a .38 double-action automatic pistol, weighs just under two pounds, so it's reasonably light. As you can see it's quite small, about seven inches long, ideal for carrying around. It's an old style gun, but still very reliable. It was popular among the police in the seventies but they've moved up a few gears since. I still like this type though. Small, not too heavy, easily concealed and carried about. Reliable.' His Cockney tones rolled off the gun's merits as if he was a salesman extolling the virtues of a high-tech microwave oven.

'There's one problem with it though.'

Lynch looked up sharply, eyes narrowed.

London John looked into his eyes, briefly. Headcase, he thought.

'It can jam. The bullets can stick in the magazine clip and either not get into the firing chamber or just stick there too and not discharge properly.'

He ran metal against metal, as if feeding a round into the firing chamber, then slowly squeezed the trigger. The hammer hit against an empty chamber.

'The gun has to be kept clean, so do the bullets. Any small traces of dirt can interfere with the magazine spring and the bullets won't move into the chamber. Are you with me?'

Lynch nodded.

'Also you've gotta look after the bullets. Don't let them get overheated or too cold. Keep them clean and never put a dropped bullet into the magazine without first cleaning it properly. Are you still with me?'

Lynch nodded again. All the time his eyes were fixed on the gun in London John's hand.

London John handed him a spare magazine and showed him how to load the bullets. They slipped in easily.

'Only ever put seven bullets in the magazine, never try and squeeze another one in, you'll overload the spring mechanism. If you want an extra round put it up the breech first.'

Lynch looked up at London John, his eyes reflecting his query.

'Okay, what that means is you load the magazine like I showed you. Then clip it into place and feed a round into the firing chamber.' The sound of metal against metal followed the action. 'This puts one round into the breech, ready for firing, gottit? Then unclip the magazine, you've only six rounds inside it now so you can slip another one in.' His long, delicate fingers handled the gun and bullets with the ease of experience. 'Now you've got the firing power of eight rounds in quick succession instead of seven.' He smiled. 'Neat, isn't it?'

Lynch looked impressed.

'When you're using it don't try firing off rounds in quick succession like you see in some Wild West movie. Take it slowly and deliberately. Squeeze the trigger gently and give yourself at least two seconds before you shoot again. Don't try one of your cowboy shoot outs. Keep it controlled.'

Lynch scratched at his nose, his eyes flicking up to acknowledge all he had heard.

The gun was passed over and Lynch weighed it carefully first in one hand then the other, then back again, getting used to the feel and the weight. He inspected it carefully, noting the firing chamber, the cocking mechanism and the magazine-clip insert.

'Now, Bobby boy, if you're gonna use it you better try it out a few times. There's no point in you deciding to get positive and not knowing the first thing about shooting, is there?'

Lynch looked up, still passing the gun from one hand to the other.

London John went over to a cupboard and took out two sets of ear protectors, slipping one on himself, handing the other to Lynch. In his right hand he carried a small box of live ammunition. He slowly went through the motions again of slipping the bullets into the magazine and then clipping it onto the gun. Lynch watched on with an intensity that was almost palpable.

'Now, Bobby boy. If you're gonna be positive, do it properly. When you're gonna shoot stand like you see them do in the movies. Both feet splayed apart, two hands on the gun. One hand for the trigger, the other to steady.'

London John adopted the correct pose. 'This is what is known as the "cup-and-saucer" hand position. The cup hand holds the gun handle with the index finger on the trigger. The saucer hand sits underneath the magazine feed, holding and steadying. Gottit?' The gun seemed smothered inside London John's larger, more delicate hands. 'Aim at the chest. Don't try going for head shots. Heads can duck quickly. It's harder to get your body out of the way.'

Dean Lynch was the model of attention.

London John adopted the shooter's pose again, talking to his student out of the corner of his mouth. They had both shed overcoats and jackets, now dressed for business.

The business of killing.

'If your target has his back to you, hit him there and then. If he's facing you keep the gun down by your side up to the last minute. Always shout, real loud, to distract him. He's wondering so much what's going on he won't have time to duck when he sees Bobby boy taking positive action.'

Lynch didn't move, his eyes never left the gun.

'Squeeze the trigger, don't snatch at it. Squeeze it slowly and firmly. That might sound daft to you, Bobby boy, but you'll be surprised how quickly these things go off. Don't try rushing it. It'll do the business. But don't rush at it. You'll only lose your aim. If you have time to get your target in the sights, then use them. They're at the front and back of the barrel. Don't anticipate the noise, that'll only put you off and make you fire down and sideways.'

For the first time Lynch looked up. He'd put away his see-through lenses and London John could see his eyes clearly, even in the gloom of the basement. For the first time he began to feel uneasy.

'Put your ear muffs on.'

London John aimed the gun at the sandpit and gently squeezed the trigger. The basement echoed to the deafening sound and he looked to see Lynch's reaction. There wasn't any. He just stared at the gun and then at the dimple in the sandpit.

'Watch again,' London John mouthed at Lynch.

London John adopted the shooter's pose again and fired off three more rounds in quick succession. The padded walls couldn't dull the noise and Lynch felt his ears ring.

'Try it yourself.'

Lynch loaded, showing London John each move. He adopted the shooter's stance, one hand holding the gun with the other supporting. His index finger was poised over the trigger.

'Okay,' London John mouthed.

Lynch squeezed and the gun jumped in his hands.

London John smiled and placed both his hands over Lynch's to show him how to steady.

'Go.'

Lynch squeezed and both their hands felt the power but this time the gun didn't jump as much.

'On your own.'

Lynch slowly fired off another four rounds, balancing the recoil and adjusting for the pull after each discharge.

London John slipped the muffs off his ears and Lynch followed suit.

'Okay. Load it up again. No ear muffs for you this time.' London John slipped his muffs on, noticing how easily Lynch loaded the magazine and fed a round into the firing chamber. He was a fast learner.

Lynch turned to the sandpit again, took aim and squeezed. He fired off two more without the muffs and then stopped, mouthing he wanted the protectors again. The muffs went back on and four more dimples formed, the sand dancing with each round.

'You look good, Bobby boy. Look real good indeed. You look the part.' London John was real pleased with his student.

'I got you a special case to take it back with you, Bobby boy.' London John went to the back of the room and opened a press, returning with a brown leather Samsonite briefcase.

He clicked the lock and opened the top. Inside, the case was filled with standard businessman type material, a business card in the name Andrew Kelly at an address in

Hammersmith and an accompanying false telephone and fax number. The card declared Andrew Kelly to be a computer software salesman for a non-existent company based in Southampton. There was a false fax and telephone number for Southampton as well. There were some glossy brochures on computer software with lots of Microsoft Windows '95 material. An A4 notebook, ballpoint pens, three thick red, green and black magic markers filled more space. Paperwork had been stuck in the filing space of the upper lid, with pen scribblings clearly seen. The bottom of the case looked straightforward, a cloth cover firmly stuck down.

'The lower space comes away in one piece. You see the little tabs on each corner?'

Lynch inspected and nodded, watching intently again.

'These peel off.' London John peeled. Underneath the tabs were four small screws. 'The screws hold the unit in place.' He handed Lynch a small screwdriver.

The screws came away easily and Lynch lifted the unit. It stuck slightly and he had to rock the case. Suddenly the bottom came away in one piece revealing a recessed space with moulding in the shape of the Walther. There was more moulding to take a box of ammunition. The design was perfect, ensuring that no amount of heavy handling would discharge one.

'What do you think, Bobby boy? Neat, isn't it?'

Lynch nodded his agreement. Without speaking he placed the gun into the mould, then gently slipped the box of ammunition into its moulding. It stayed firm. A velcro strap could be pulled across to ensure a steady fit.

London John watched. 'Whatever you do don't take that on board as hand luggage. The scanners'll pick it up. Let them put it in the hold and only pick it up from baggage collection. There's a combination lock. The combination's written on the corner of that brochure.' He pointed and Lynch squinted closely, noting the number.

He closed the case and flipped the combination numbers randomly, then tried to open but the lock held. He clicked the exact combination sequence and the lock snapped open.

London John watched every move, trying to decide when to get down to the real business of the day.

'When are you thinking of going positive, Bobby boy?'

Lynch said nothing, easing a fresh, unopened box of nine millimetre Browning FN Court bullets into the moulding. He tied the velcro across.

'I was reading the paper this morning, Bobby boy. That country of yours is going to the dogs. Kidnapping little babies now, they are.'

Lynch said nothing. He placed the gun in its mould again and admired the neat fit. He removed it and checked the chamber. There was one round still inside. Unused. Live.

'And there was something about a murder in one of the hospitals.'

Lynch stiffened.

'And there was a photo of the hospital, Bobby boy. Two guys coming down the front steps. One of them looked a lot like you.'

Lynch turned and looked up at London John, a thin smile on his face for the first time. 'Really? Did it?'

'Yeah. It was the image of you, Bobby boy. The spitting image. You wouldn't be thinking of getting positive in that hospital? Again?'

Maybe if he hadn't said 'again' Lynch wouldn't have cared so much. But he said 'again' and Lynch decided London John knew already.

'Look out!'

The howling roar took London John by surprise and he turned slightly as if someone was behind. He had only half-turned when he realised he had read Bobby boy all wrong. Completely wrong.

The walls echoed again but this time it wasn't the sand that jumped. This time it was London John's brain as the bullet entered just beneath his left eye and exited through the right of the back of his skull.

'Never tell anyone your business!' Lynch screamed at the convulsing body lying sprawled against the bottom of the sandpit, blood pouring from entrance and exit wounds. 'Keep yourself to yourself!'

He fitted the Walther and the box of ammunition into the mould and gently placed the inside casing back, ignoring totally the gurgling and grunting of London John's last efforts at life. He screwed the case down carefully, replacing the concealing tabs. Then a quick check of the combination lock, before closing the case and flicking the numbers. He looked around, found the car keys and said his goodbyes to London John before going out into the bitterly cold Hammersmith air, scarf wrapped up against his nose. He drove London John's Saab to Heathrow and booked a last minute flight to Dublin in the name Andrew Kelly. The briefcase was checked in as baggage and went into the aircraft hold.

He patted the bulge in his jacket pocket where he had the two thousand pounds cash which London John would not now be using. Some of it went in the airport shops.

'Coffee?'
'No.'
'Paper?'
'No.'
Odd bollox, thought a different air hostess.

On the afternoon of Sunday, 16th February 1997, in the interview room of Store Street Garda station, Kate Hamilton and the investigating team thought they were on to something.

The call was registered at nine thirty that morning and the details noted by the duty Garda. A woman was ringing on the confidential telephone line. She was distressed and pleaded with the Garda not to reveal her name. He promised as much as he could.

'What information do you have? Don't forget, everything's confidential at this point. All you have to do is hang up and nobody'll be any the wiser, but please tell me whatever it is that's caused you to ring in.'

'It's about that girl who was murdered at the hospital.'

'Yes.'

'I saw her removal to the church on the TV last night. God love her parents. They were devastated.'

'Yes they were. It's a terrible tragedy.'

There was a lot of crying on the other end of the phone. The Garda said nothing, but everything was being recorded.

Finally he asked, 'Do you know anything about that girl or anything that might help us with the investigation?'

More sobbing. 'Are you sure this is confidential?' Sniff, sniff.

'Absolutely. This is a totally confidential line. Whatever you tell me is between ourselves.'

'I think my husband killed that girl. Oh Jesus!' She burst into tears again.

'Can you tell me who you are?'

The answer couldn't be made out over the convulsive sobbing. The tape was still rolling.

'Please, can you tell me your name?'

Gasping sobs then came from the other end.

'Why do you think your husband killed the girl?'

Then it all poured out.

'He's violent, very violent. He drinks heavily and beats me up a lot. He stays out regularly and some nights never comes home. He taunts me about all the nurses he's screwing down at the hospital, where he works. He's a chef there. Sometimes he comes home, ties me up and describes in detail what he's been up to. Or says he's been up to. He didn't come home at all the night that girl was murdered. He came home the next night, though, drunk out of his mind and knocked me around a bit. Warned me I'd get the same treatment as that girl. "Watch your step," he shouted at me. "You'll end up with a scalpel stuck in your neck too. Just like I did to that other bitch." '

The duty Garda noted all this and the tape recorded.

'He'll kill me if he finds out I told you this. Don't let anyone know I told you this. He'll kill me.'

Which was why Anthony Francis O'Loughlin, the flaky chef who couldn't account for his movements on the night Mary Dwyer was killed, was sitting in the interview room being grilled.

Dowling spent the first hour with him, going over the alibi which didn't make sense and which was significantly different from what he'd told the first time round. Then he started to get stubborn and refused to say anything. So Dowling told him he'd been heard boasting he killed the girl.

Anthony Francis O'Loughlin's jaw dropped in total surprise. Dowling sensed he'd been hit between the eyes with that one.

'What eejit told you that shite?' O'Loughlin was a thin

weed of a man who smelt of cooking fat. He was still dressed in his working clothes, checked trousers, white tee shirt covered by a stained and greasy denim jacket.

Dowling tapped his nose. 'Sources, Tony. Me sources tell me ye know all about how Mary Dwyer was murdered. Ye know more than we do. Ye've been shoutin' yer mouth off about how she was killed. And, do ye know what, Tony? Nobody knows as much detail as ye seem to. So tell me now, Tony, why did ye do it?'

'Fuck off!' screamed Anthony Francis O'Loughlin, the hard man at home.

Dowling sat down opposite him, across the interview table. Kate Hamilton stood well behind O'Loughlin's back, leaning against the wall. John Doyle smoked and watched from the other corner. He could see O'Loughlin and made sure O'Loughlin could see him. Doyle and Dowling took it in turns. O'Loughlin began to wear down. He was getting tired, exhausted in fact. He'd been on a binge the night before and felt dreadful. Now he was sitting in a police station being grilled about a murder he hadn't committed. As far as he could remember.

'Why did ye do it, Tony? What did she do to deserve it? Turn ye down? Say ye weren't up to it?'

But as the interview progressed they all began to realise that it couldn't have been Anthony Francis O'Loughlin who killed Mary Dwyer. He was all mouth and no brain. He'd have left a trail of broken bottles all the way from the lab to his front door.

What a wasted day. It was indeed.

But not for Dean Lynch.

While Kate Hamilton and her team were barking up the wrong tree, the real McCoy was back in his flat and planning his next move.

And they wouldn't hear him boasting about it in the pubs.

Tommy Malone's telephone call to Theo Dempsey's house the previous night sparked the kidnap investigation alight.

Jack McGrath and his men now knew they were dealing with a determined gang.

'Hardly anyone has my telephone number,' Dempsey told them. 'I'm ex-directory and have been for years. Anyone who wants to contact me does so through headquarters in Dawson Street. There's very few outside the family who know that number.'

Dempsey's wife and three teenage boys were then subjected to a gruelling interrogation by one of the Jaguar Unit. Who knows your telephone number? Can you remember anyone ringing you recently that you didn't know? Anyone ring recently and say they had dialled a wrong number? Did you give your number out to any girlfriends, lads on the soccer team or even the team coach? Their answers were checked and then double checked and the names mentioned fielded out for further evaluation and back up from central computer records in Garda HQ.

Then all the staff in Beechill and at the O'Brien Corporation headquarters were grilled for signs of involvement or carelessness with privileged information. Twenty extra detectives were pulled in and worked throughout the day dealing with their statements. Betty Nolan and the rest of the part-time cleaning staff were given only a fleeting evaluation.

An angle being explored seriously was that the kidnap was merely a ploy by a business rival to unhinge and destabilise Harry O'Brien. The financial pages in the *Evening Post* carried a story about a takeover bid by the O'Brien Corporation for one of the UK pharmaceutical middle-weights and the resistance to the effort. Could the kidnapping have been planned and financed from somewhere inside the City of London? The *Evening Post* advised caution before jumping to such conclusions but made a good story out of the speculation anyway.

Then one of Harry O'Brien's ex-managers, sacked by the big man months previously, shot his mouth off in a pub suggesting to anyone who'd listen that he himself was in on the kidnap and knew exactly where the gang were holed up.

Someone *was* listening and before he had a chance to sober up the ex-manager found himself sitting across the table from one of the Jaguar Unit in Waterford Garda station. He wasn't released for six hours.

All leads had to be followed up, all angles explored. Jack McGrath and his men wore the leather off their shoes chasing such diversions. The houses around Roundwood were visited and the householders questioned about suspicious sightings or unusual queries by strangers about directions around the area. Outhouses and cottages within a five mile radius of Beechill were searched. The caravan park in Roundwood was searched and the owner quizzed about recent lettings. Bed and breakfast houses had their books scanned for names. Then they had their other books scanned as well, the books they kept hidden from the tax man. A number of known criminals in the immediate vicinity were rounded up, questioned and released under surveillance. Their phones were tapped.

In Beechill and at Theo Dempsey's house the phones were wired to record all incoming calls and the telephone company primed to track them.

Jack McGrath wanted Dempsey to return to his house and wait for the kidnappers' next call. 'They're going to use you as the go-between, I'm sure of that. There's no other reason they would have rung your house. You'll have to sit by the phone and try to keep them talking when they ring again.'

Dempsey wasn't at all happy with this suggestion. 'I can't, I just can't. You've seen the state of my boss. He's on the edge of a complete breakdown. I caught him at the drinks cabinet and he hasn't taken a drop for the past three years. Sandra's had all the booze taken out of the house just in case.'

Sandra was holding up despite all her body signals. Her breasts ached from engorgement of milk that had no mouth to feed. The pain of her operation scar still ached. More importantly, her heart ached for the child she had given

236

birth to and lost so quickly. She wanted him back, no matter what it cost.

'Harry, we've got to pay that ransom.' She sat with Harry on the edge of the bed in the master bedroom as she tried to talk some sense into him. 'He's too young, Harry. He's only a newborn baby. If they don't look after him properly he could die before the police ever find him. Harry, we've got to pay whatever they want.' She was down on her knees in front of her husband, grasping his hands, imploring. The first time she'd ever begged him for anything. His eyes were dull and lifeless like his heart and he said nothing, just staring into space. 'Come on Harry, come on,' Sandra shook him by the shoulders. 'We've got to move on this fast. We've got to get our baby back.'

She felt an overwhelming despair.

'Get Theo.'

Those were the first sensible words Harry O'Brien had spoken for days. 'Get Theo to come up. He'll know what to do.'

Jack McGrath watched as Theo Dempsey followed Sandra upstairs. Then he watched as a renewed Theo Dempsey suddenly appeared at the bottom of the staircase fifteen minutes later, a sense of urgency about him. Dempsey disappeared into Big Harry's study. Within minutes a fax was on its way to London.

Jack McGrath sensed deals were going to be done behind his back.

The first spasm had gripped Gordon O'Brien after his third feed before noon. It was mild compared to what would follow. Anxious and fretful as he was, he still needed regular feeds and his cries of hunger were coming every four hours. But at the noon feed when Peggy Ryan put the teat in his mouth he had seemed distressed. His head rocked to and fro as if trying to dislodge the bottle. After two or three sucks his arms started threshing about, his face contorted in pain. Tiny legs kicked furiously inside the babygrow. Knees were drawn up. He screeched.

The screeching pierced the small cottage and Peggy Ryan had to walk the floor for an hour before he finally slumped into an exhausted sleep. She changed his nappy, muttering and cursing to herself, quietly at first and then more audibly.

Moonface watched.

So did Sam Collins.

Both of them were fed up with Peggy. Had she got the bottle? Could she stick the pace? Could she not shut the fuck up and stop talking to herself? They were also fed up with the cottage. Even with the fire in the kitchen burning all day and the electric fires on in the bedrooms, the place still reeked of damp and mould and must. A broken pane of glass in one of the bedrooms allowed freezing air inside and they all had to wear their outdoor clothes to keep warm. The front and back doors let in draughts adding to the discomfort. Then Moonface had spotted a mouse in the toilet and began kicking at the walls. 'Come ou', ye little bastard,' he had shouted, waving a gun at the hole in the skirting board he'd discovered. Only the smell of bacon and eggs, cooked by Peggy Ryan for tea, lifted the mood of unpleasantness in the cottage.

Tommy Malone had been out earlier, returning with arms full of the Sunday papers.

He knew there was little point trying to hide the huge public outcry from the rest of the A-team. They'd get to know sooner or later and it was better he controlled how the news broke and his interpretation.

'Jaysus, we've hit the jackpot all righ'.'

He dropped the *Sunday Independent* into Moonface's hands, the *Sunday Post* to Collins while he devoured the *Sunday Tribune*. Peggy Ryan was left staring at the football results on the back pages. She began talking to herself again.

Excitedly the others exchanged papers, engrossing themselves in anything to do with the kidnap, laughing at their descriptions as reported differently. In one Sam Collins was the mastermind, described as an ex-IRA explosives expert from Derry. Moonface was described as the 'animal' who had knocked June Morrison about, leaving her in a coma. There were lots of laughs at that and Collins started barking at Moonface to send him up.

Peggy Ryan gave him a lash of her tongue. 'If ye waken tha' baby I'll bloody well swing for ye.'

Collins glowered at her and she glowered back. Tommy Malone noticed and intervened to keep the peace. Secretly they were all very worried about the June Morrison development. That wasn't supposed to happen. But the three men had all checked her before they left and each knew they were as much to blame as the other.

If Peggy Ryan wasn't allowed to share the newspapers it wasn't because she had been ignored by the reporters. GARDAI SEEK MYSTERY WOMAN IN KIDNAP. WHAT WOMAN WOULD DO THIS? KIDNAP BITCH! One of the English tabloids featured a photo of Gordon

O'Brien wrapped in the now famous shawl. Superimposed were a pair of hands in a snatch pose.

IRISH POLICE SEEK KIDNAP BITCH!

They didn't pull any punches. This was right up their street, a big story on their doorsteps with lots of glamour and drama.

The cottage was quiet for a spell, the A-team huddled in front of the coal and briquette fire in the kitchen, absorbed in the papers. Moonface switched to the sports pages and was reading all about the Ireland vs England soccer international on the coming Wednesday night. Moonface had tickets for the match. He was hoping the job would be finished by then.

Peggy Ryan made a pot of tea and they sat, each to their own thoughts, staring at the flames. Tommy Malone read something he didn't like about Big Harry which could slow everything down. This is not what I wanna hear, he thought. Tommy Malone was very much aware of the tension that had crept in among his A-team. The cottage was too small, everyone was bumping into one another, hanging out of one another. And they couldn't stand the screeches of the baby. It seemed to ring in their ears for hours. He hadn't thought about that, hadn't thought about that at all. He sneaked a look at each.

Moonface was holding up. Collins was getting edgy but still holding in there. Peggy looked awful. That screamin' child's gettin' to her. Jaysus, we've only got the little bollox two days and already they wanna get rid of him.

He read the bit about Big Harry again. It worried him even more the second time.

Tommy Malone had to make some decisions. It was time to speed things up before Big Harry finally did crack. We gotta shake him up, get him to start movin' money. We can't stay in this shaggin' cottage for ever. Time to move to the next phase.

He looked at Collins and decided to take him, instead of Moonface, who he'd planned on doing most of the drops.

He decided Collins needed to get out of the cottage for a break, especially if the child started screeching again.

'Okay.' Malone broke the silence. 'Time we put a bit of pressure on.'

They all looked up.

'Photo call. Martin, put your balaclava on. We're gonna drop a few Polaroids.'

Peggy Ryan didn't want the sleeping child disturbed, but Malone wanted to get the pictures while the baby was asleep. He especially didn't want Polaroids of the child screaming. It's bad enough as it is. Jaysus, if the papers get hold of wan of him screamin' we'll be lynched.

So Moonface put on his balaclava, Peggy Ryan lifted Gordon O'Brien from the travel cot as if he were Waterford crystal, and placed the sleeping bundle in Moonface's arms. The baby didn't wake up, just threw his arms out at the disturbance, scrunched up his face and sneezed.

Tommy Malone set up position and flashed a shot. They all waited as it slowly unwound from the camera. It was a good one of Moonface holding the baby with the *Sunday Post* held beside him by Collins, out of picture. The banner headlines confirmed the day the Polaroid was taken.

'He should be in the shawl, Tommy,' said Peggy Ryan. 'He could be any baby. Put the shawl aroun' him and they'll know it's the real thing.'

Malone, Collins and Moonface were taken aback, impressed.

'Good thinkin', Peggy,' said Malone, 'ye're on the ball, Peggy. Good thinkin'.'

Malone shot three more, this time with the famous lace shawl wrapped firmly around the sleeping baby. Moonface looked the part of a kidnapper. Big thick arms and big thick head inside black, intimidating balaclava. Big thick brain wondering would it all be over in time for the football match?

Malone told Collins to come with him.

'Jaysus, Tommy, ye said I'd do the drops,' Moonface protested.

'From tomorra on. From tomorra we'll be droppin' Polaroids all over Dublin. We'll need the bike then. Ye'll be out most of the day. Sam needs a break.'

'You're dead right,' agreed Collins, his Northern accent now grating on Moonface's ears.

'You're dead right I do.'

They wrapped up against the cold and climbed into the Volvo, inching it slowly down the lane, careful of black ice. Collins drove, allowing Malone time to think.

Brian O'Callaghan spotted the headlights from his own cottage. *They're still here. I wonder who they are?* He picked up the Sunday paper again and continued reading. There was little in it apart from the kidnap story and the hospital murder investigation. He sucked at his spit through false teeth and began a silent prayer for the safe return of Gordon O'Brien.

Malone decided on four drops, all in Dublin and well away from Kilcullen to confuse the Gardai. One was slipped into a letter box in Gardiner Street where collection wasn't until the next day. Another fell in through the letter box of the *Sunday Post* along Burgh Quay, while a third dropped into the letter box of Dillon's pub in Clonskeagh. The final one he delivered himself to the letter box of the O'Brien Corporation headquarters in Dawson Street.

Then, in a public phone booth in Tallaght town centre, Tommy Malone rang the Garda confidential phone line. Satisfied the big thick culchie at the other end of the line got the details right, he then dialled Theo Dempsey's number.

'Ye've got 'till tomorra to get the money. If ye want that child back ye better get ready to part with the money. I'll ring tomorra afternoon and tell ye how to move it.' He heard the sharp intake of breath at the other end of the line as he hung up.

As the Volvo began the journey back to Kilcullen, squad cars were screeching to all four drop-off points and Jack

McGrath was listening to a play back of Tommy Malone's disguised voice.

And Gordon O'Brien was screaming with colic in the cottage.

Peggy Ryan was walking the floors again, rightly fed up and talking to herself like she was in a speaking competition. Moonface had plugged in a walkman and was listening to an old U2 tape. He picked at his nose with a vengeance, rightly fed up. He even drew blood.

In Beechill, Harry O'Brien sat mute and motionless near the front door. He had positioned himself there after he learned of the second telephone call from the kidnappers.

'I'm waiting for my baby to come home,' he told a uniformed Garda who went to enquire if he was all right. So the young Garda sat opposite and watched with him, like a faithful labrador.

And while the big man sat downstairs, upstairs Sandra O'Brien was being watched over and comforted by a young uniformed Ban Garda who had a baby of her own at home and who just couldn't stop ringing to check she was okay. Almost every hour.

And this was happening all over the country. Every news bulletin was listened in on, a nation's desperate hopes of a breakthrough hanging on every word. Some couldn't bring themselves to watch the TV pictures any longer, they were so distressing and disturbing. Many still couldn't believe what was actually happening. It was like a bad dream, a nightmare.

Top industrialists started contacting their parent companies, putting in formal requests for transfers from Ireland, their wives refusing point blank to stay. Bodyguards were doubled, new bodyguards hired and old bodyguards double checked to make sure they weren't planning any copycat kidnappings.

'Mummy, will you read me a story?' Rory was clutching a new Thomas the Tank Engine story, her guilt present for being out all day. Grandad glared at the clock when she arrived back, exhausted. The house was in a mess. Toys were scattered in every room, with pages of Rory's childish scrawls lying on the couch. Grandad had obviously been busy trying to keep Rory amused.

'Now don't start. I've just had a dreadful day. I'm tired, I'm hungry and I'm fed up.'

Kate Hamilton had good reason to be especially fed up. Gardai legal advisers had informed her any AIDS test would have to be done voluntarily. If she wanted to check on anyone in particular she would have to allow them to seek legal advice first. Everything suggested seemed guaranteed to frustrate and delay.

She slumped down in an armchair, fit to cry, and Rory climbed up onto her knee. She stroked his cheek, stroked his hair, kissed his forehead. Then she kicked off her soaking wet shoes and pulled down her soaking wet tights, dropping them onto the already crowded floor.

'Hi,' she said.

Rory sensed something was wrong. He put his thumb in mouth, took Ted out from inside his pyjamas and ran it along his mother's face. She kissed him again, trying to freeze out the image of his dead father, which she saw so often now that he was growing and filling out.

'Has Rory had his tea?'

Grandad was fixing up bacon and eggs in the kitchen and shouted a 'yes'. The smell of the cooking rumbled her stomach and Rory giggled. They both had a good giggle. They cuddled up and she held him tightly.

'Don't, Mummy, you're hurting me.'

She spotted the Sunday paper with its headlines about the kidnapping and couldn't stop herself clutching him closer. They snuggled down in each other's arms, content and happy.

Grandad brought the bacon and eggs out to find Kate and Rory fast asleep, curled in each other's arms. He looked at them and decided not to disturb them, sitting down to eat the tea himself. Waste not, want not. He looked at them again from the table.

Jesus, what a life for her, he thought. How long can she keep this up before something gives?

Standing in front of his exercise mirror in number twenty-three, the Elms, Dean Lynch was planning to help Kate Hamilton ease her workload. He held the Walther PPK in a positive-action pose and clicked the hammer against an empty chamber. He'd been doing this for the past hour, getting the feel of the steel, the weight of the metal, learning the firing mechanism. He was getting ready for phase two of being positively active. And he was looking forward to it.

He slowly lowered the gun and inspected his body. I am losing weight. London John is right.

London John *was* right.

Dean Lynch stood in the queue, lit up like a lighthouse in a lurid green tracksuit top and bottom, yellow roll neck sweater poking above the tracksuit top and red baseball hat with the Chicago Bears written in black across it. He was wearing white runners and yellow mittens, all bought at Heathrow airport shops with the money meant for London John. He had also bought a cheap sports bag there, completely black, which lay at his feet as he shuffled along with the queue. Inside was his black wig, clear-lens glasses, false black moustache, black roll neck sweater, black tracksuit top and bottoms, black socks, black trainers. There were also two pairs of surgical gloves, one Walther PPK double-action automatic pistol and twenty rounds of ammunition carefully packed so as not to be suddenly discharged. Wrapped carefully inside a towel was an eight pound hammer bought earlier in Woodies hardware store along with four feet of strong blue binding twine. It was primed for action. One end had a firm knot into and through which he had already threaded the other end so that it looked like a mini lassoo, easily slipped over a head and around a neck.

He also had something else, his *pièce de résistance*, his trademark.

The Savoy was running a season of late night tributes to Francis Ford Coppola. This week it was the Godfather movies, *The Godfather*, *The Godfather Part II* and *The Godfather Part III*. There were big crowds with last minute rushes from buses discharging their loads onto O'Connell Street. Lynch beamed at them, like some half-wit. They just couldn't have failed to notice him.

'I'm awfully sorry, I've nothing smaller than this.' He offered the cashier a fifty-pound note for a four-pound-fifty ticket. She glared at him and he smiled sweetly back, removing his baseball hat to give her a good look at his face. Remember me, won't you? When they ask, won't you?

'Would you even have a fifty-pence piece?' she snapped.

'Sorry. Nothing other than that. I came away without any small change.'

The queue behind was getting restless and he turned to 'sorry' them all and let them get a good look at his face. A lot of dirty looks were thrown in his direction, and the ticket collector stared at him with an undisguised contempt.

Lynch finally collected his ticket and change and shuffled the bag at his feet away from the ticket booth. He waited until a few more bought tickets and the crowd had started building up. Then the beaming smile disappeared as, head down, he lifted the bag and made his way to the toilets. There was nobody inside. He was in luck.

Oh, lucky man!

Again.

By the time the foyer was full with crowds thronging up the two opposite sets of stairs to the cinemas above, Dean Lynch was ready. The lighthouse effects were in the black sports bag and a small man in black emerged from one of the cubicles. He checked himself in the mirror and quietly left the toilet, quick, furtive glances ensuring no one had noticed him. Within minutes he was out on O'Connell Street again, nudging his way past the crowds, head well down. Nobody so much as glanced at him. Nobody paid the slightest attention to the small man in black clothes, black shoes, with his black soul and black intentions.

He walked briskly around the corner to Eccles Street where his BMW was parked and checked the double alarms were set correctly. Then he flagged a taxi.

In subdued tones he asked to be driven to the Blackrock

Clinic, saying he was visiting a friend in hospital there. 'She's had her appendix out,' he added quickly before the taxi man started looking for the life story and operating details in all their gory splendour. Throughout the journey all he could think was that he was going to miss the scene in *The Godfather* where Luco Brazzi was strangled from behind. He relived the scene in his mind as the taxi passed the RDS.

I wonder will it be like that?

He glanced at his watch.

At about 11.30 pm.

I wonder will it be like that?

Will her eyes bulge?

On the way out they were stopped briefly in a queue of traffic, a Garda checkpoint looking for Gordon O'Brien. The Garda waved them through without looking and Lynch sighed inwardly with relief. The taxi man started giving out about the kidnapping and the state of the country generally and the bloody government who couldn't organise a piss up in a brewery. All comments were ignored, his anger wasted on the passenger whose mind was elsewhere. Lynch was completely oblivious to the fact that the nation and world's attention was focused on the baby he had delivered himself. It had completely gone out of his head. He was preoccupied with other events. He had his own fish to fry.

He was dropped off outside the Blackrock Clinic hospital and made a show of going towards the door until the taxi man drove away. Then he made his slow but steady way down Rock Road towards the Hawthorns, where Staff Nurse Sarah Higgins lived. It was frosty and as he walked his breath misted. He could smell turf burning and flared his nostrils as it irritated.

He had checked the Hawthorns out earlier. It was an old imposing family home converted into flats, set back slightly from the busy Rock Road, with car parking spaces at the back, each space numbered for the flat occupant. There were eight flats. The car spaces for flats seven and eight were separated by a large chestnut tree trunk, its branches overhanging the tarmacked park. There were no leaves on the tree, just frost on its bare branches.

He had rung the telephone number on five separate occasions throughout the day, after two o'clock, by which time Staff Nurse Higgins should have left for work. There was no reply on each occasion. He gave a final ring now, from the telephone booth in Mooney's pub, only two hundred yards from the flat. There was no reply.

He checked his watch. It was now 11.05 pm.

'Time, gentlemen, please. Have yiz no homes to go to?' The barman in Mooney's was trying to clear the pub and go home for a good night's rest. A peaceful sleep. Which was what Lynch was planning for Staff Nurse Higgins.

More or less.

He had decided earlier not to use the Walther PPK. He would have loved to have used it and was very, very disappointed at not being able to. Bitterly disappointed, annoyingly disappointed. Angrily disappointed. But he decided it would be too noisy and there was no point drawing attention, possibly even putting himself unnecessarily at risk of being caught.

There's more work to be done after tonight, he told himself. Much more.

He stood behind the massive trunk of the chestnut tree, black bag at his feet, Walther PPK loaded and resting on top of the bag in case of an emergency. A pair of surgical gloves covered both hands, one of which grasped the Woodies hammer tightly. The blue lassoo lay innocently on the ground, collecting frost.

A set of headlights suddenly pierced the blackness of the car park and he quickly glanced at his watch. It was 11.17 pm. Christ, she's early. His heart raced in anticipation. Christ, she's gone to the wrong space. A Toyota Corolla swung into parking space three and two people climbed out, a young man and younger woman. The doors closed shut and Lynch heard the locking mechanisms engage. The man skipped around the front of the car, grabbed his now giggling passenger and the next minute they were indulging in some heavy petting, tongues down one another's throat. Moans of pleasure floated across the night air.

Fuck off! Lynch almost screamed. Fuck off!

By now the young woman was leaning up against the side of the car, her driver all over her, hands pushed inside her coat.

Lynch reached down and picked up the Walther PPK, preparing for positive action.

Suddenly she broke free, and with a sexy, inviting laugh made a half-hearted attempt to run away. He ran after and the two staggered, groping and tonguing, around to the front of the building.

Lynch relaxed. When he heard the front door opening and slamming shut he gently placed the gun back on the sports bag, checking no one else had entered the car park.

The wait was beginning to annoy him. It was freezing and the cold seemed to penetrate his bones. He peered at his watch, catching the hands in the street lights. It was 11.37 pm. Come on Staff Nurse Higgins, where are you? A light suddenly came on in one of the flats at the back and he looked up in time to see the young lust birds before the curtains were drawn.

Just as the light from the window was shut out, the car park was flooded with the headlights of a Mazda 626, driven by Staff Nurse Higgins.

The car eased slowly to space seven beside the chestnut trunk and the lights were turned off. An inside light flicked on and Lynch could see the young nurse fiddling with keys and handbag. The inside light flicked off and the driver's door opened. A white nurse's shoe stepped out, followed by a white stockinged leg, a long white stockinged leg. Then came a white uniform partly covered by a three-quarter-length thick padded dark anorak. Staff Nurse Sarah Higgins turned to lock the driver's side door and flicked the car alarm. The warning lights flicked on and off twice. She coughed slightly as the cold night air caught her throat and she pulled the anorak tighter around her chest.

She turned towards the flats and half-stopped. A twig snapped behind her, then came a faint rustling.

Fifteen minutes later Dean Lynch sat in the back of a taxi on its way into Dublin city centre. He'd flagged it down on the Rock Road and grunted his instructions before settling his black bag in the back seat and climbing in himself. The taxi man couldn't give a stuff that his passenger said nothing more. It was his last run and he was glad to be going home, anyway he'd spent all day mouthing to half-wits.

Lynch arrived outside the Savoy in time to mingle with the crowds coming out after the movie had finished. Head down he pushed his way against the flow and back to the first floor toilets. In an empty cubicle he changed gear again, reappearing in the lurid green tracksuit, complete with Chicago Bears baseball cap. The black sports bag was held well out of sight. He made a special point of saying goodnight to the same ticket collector who watched him come in.

'Brilliant movie,' he enthused.

'Piss off,' suggested the ticket collector under his breath. 'Little moron.'

Lynch drove his BMW slowly back to Ballsbridge, stopping only to drop some of the incriminating evidence in various litter bins along the way.

It was another day's work well done for Dean Lynch.

Day 8

You're late, thought Kate Hamilton as Rory drifted into her consciousness. She could feel him cuddle up beside her, check for her face and turn it round so he could see her clearly. Contented, he settled, thumb in mouth, Ted in hand. Then she was dragged back from the enveloping sleep again.

'Mummy, can we get a puppy?'

She groaned and turned onto her other side. 'Go to sleep, Rory. Go to sleep. It's too early. Go to sleep.'

It was too early in Kilcullen also but the A-team was wide awake, cursing and fuming.

Gordon O'Brien hadn't slept well. He fed just after midnight without any problems, then awoke at 4.47 am, hungry and whimpering to be fed again. Peggy Ryan had the bottle heated and ready within minutes, but with almost the first suck the spasms returned and he drew away. Then the colic hit him like a lightning bolt and he screeched. Tiny legs threshed, knees were drawn up, his little fists shook with pain.

'Oh sweet Jaysus,' muttered Peggy Ryan out loud. 'Oh sweet Jaysus, not again.' She began walking the floors, cursing and muttering to herself. She jiggled the baby up and down, stopping to massage his board-like tummy, laying him over her shoulder and patting his back. But nothing worked. Gordon O'Brien screeched. His screeches echoed

253

and re-echoed around the cottage walls, penetrating the pillows that Moonface and Tommy Malone and Sam Collins had pulled over their heads in a desperate attempt to drown out the noise. But a colicky baby's cries have great powers of penetration, especially when Peggy walked into their rooms with the child over her shoulder. 'Will somebody take him from me before I kill him,' she screamed. There were no takers.

Before long the A-team was up, bumping and snarling, cursing and swearing. Moonface took himself to the toilet to escape the noise and began poking at the mouse hole with the tip of his boot. 'Come ou', ye little bollox, come ou'.' Sam Collins sat himself down at the kitchen table nervously fingering his earring, wondering how it was all going to end. Peggy Ryan carried the child to the back door to escape the glares and black looks thrown at her. Only for the bitter cold outside she might have walked across the fields, and never returned.

'Tommy, should we not give the little bollox back and go home?' Moonface had had enough. He'd have preferred half a dozen armed bank robberies to this carry on. At least they'd be over quickly, the money split and eveybody could go out and have a good time. But this carry on, this is just fuckin' ridiculous, he cursed to himself.

Sam Collins turned his earring round and round as he listened to the exchange. He watched to see Tommy Malone's reaction, wondering how he'd handle this.

'Nah, nah. We're in this too deep. The Gards'll come after us wan way or the other. What's the point of startin' somethin' and not gettin' paid for it at the end?'

Moonface shrugged. He was unhappy, as in very unhappy. He could see this dragging on all week, and there was the match on Wednesday. He sat down at the kitchen table, now covered in unwashed dishes with cigarette butts stuck in empty milk bottles and ash scattered everywhere. Moonface sniffed sour milk in one of the bottles and pulled a face.

'We'll have to do something, Tommy.' Sam Collins decided to put his tuppenceworth in. 'That screeching has us all demented. If he was any older I'd bloody well plug him one. That'd shut the little bollox up.' He sounded edgy.

From the back door, the screeches reached a new peak as Peggy Ryan jiggled the baby violently. Her patience was at an end and her soothing sounds were now replaced by curses. This made the baby even more upset. He screeched again and for the first time Peggy Ryan slapped him across the face stunning and momentarily stopping his cries. Then he let out an intense and even more piercing scream.

For help.

Peggy Ryan screwed up her fist for another, stronger blow but slackened as she saw Tommy Malone staring at her from the door.

'Put the baby down in his cot, Peggy. Let him scream it off.' She avoided Malone's questioning eyes.

Not for the first time Tommy Malone was wondering himself how this was all going to end. His A-team was showing signs of cracking. It's time to drop off a few more Polaroids and put the pressure on Big Harry. This job better be over soon.

In Beechill Harry O'Brien was planning to end it. The ransom demand deadline had been relayed to him by Theo Dempsey and the decision to pay agreed between himself and Sandra. Jack McGrath had asked if Sandra would make an emotional TV appeal for the release of the baby but this had been refused. Harry O'Brien decided it was pay-out time and had made contact with Security Risks, the English insurance company with which he had taken out his kidnap policy. The policy at first covered only the big man himself, then Sandra when they were married, and only two months previously, the as yet unborn Gordon O'Brien. They had even joked about adding him to the policy.

'God, he's not even born and you have him down as a risk,' Sandra had said one morning as they lay in bed watching her swollen belly ripple with the unborn baby's movements inside.

'I know, I know. I know I'm being silly. But all the same,

the way this country's going I'd feel safer if he was in from the word go.' Big Harry had held the palms of both hands on her belly, feeling the movements of the baby, wondering at the mystery of life.

So the unborn Gordon O'Brien had been added to the insurance policy. Now it was time to cash it in.

7.27 am

Quality time.

Sometimes when Rory was fast asleep and she had a few precious moments before work, Kate Hamilton would lie beside him, listening to his breathing, stroking his hair, the mystery of life overcoming her. She would think back to the day she gave birth and first saw his scrunched-up face, heard his newborn cries, felt his tiny body. She would lie and wonder at the marvel of it all, how that act of giving birth had changed her for ever. She had a partner in life, and her life now was all consumed with the child. That morning she wondered all those wonders again, as she lifted his sleeping body and tried to stir him awake.

'Mummy, can we get a puppy?'

End of quality time.

The puppy was talked about while she was in the shower, while she was drying her hair, while she was putting on her make-up and all through breakfast.

'No, Rory. For the last time, no. There's no room for a puppy here and I have no time to start training one and running around cleaning up after him.'

'But I'll look after him. I'll clean up if he makes a mess.'

She put her spoon down firmly and loudly on the table and looked directly into the child's eyes. 'No, Rory. That's a definite No, no. Now don't let me hear anything more about it. Eat your breakfast. We'll be late.'

Big tears filled his eyes and he sat sobbing into his cornflakes, his shoulders shaking and shuddering. Then he hit her with the killer punch, the heart piercer.

'I've nobody to play with. You're never at home. I've nobody to play with. At least a puppy would be home with me.'

The two of them cried into one another's arms until it was almost too late. Then came a mad rush to get him dressed, sandwiches made and last minute wees before he was bundled into the car. She strapped him in carefully, handed him Ted and watched as his thumb disappeared into his mouth. She decided to take him to playschool herself and rang Grandad to tell him. Grandad would pick him up later, make his tea, sit down and play with him for a while, then make her tea. God, she thought, I can't keep this up for much longer.

Just after nine in the library of the Central Maternity Hospital, Kate Hamilton sat across the table from Tony Dowling.

'Rory wants a puppy.'

'Now Kate, I don't wannabe the baddie who ruins his day but don't get a puppy if ye've half a brain on ye.' Dowling came from a farming family in Cavan and grew up with dogs, real dogs. 'Ye can't give a dog a decent life in the city. Dogs need to run free and wild, chasin' rabbits and hares and stoats and foxes. Not chasin' the bloody traffic along the Stillorgan dual carriageway.'

Hamilton was only half-listening. Staff Nurse Higgins was supposed to meet them on the dot of nine. She glanced at her watch, then turned back to listen to Dowling.

'City dogs are a constipated lot. They never get a half-decent run at anythin' before they're being called to heel. "Sit, heel, roll over, beg." All that oul shite. Now ye look at a country dog.' He was off again, warming to the topic. 'Country dogs are usually black collies with a patch of white on their snout or heads. Ye'll see them lollin' about on oul farm walls or at the side of the road, one ear cocked up in the air listenin' for anythin' unusual. And at the first rustle they're off like a greyhound. Country dogs have a bit of character, a bit of style about them. City dogs all look as if they should be seein' psychiatrists.' He had a bit of a laugh at that little joke himself.

'You've got egg on your tie,' informed Hamilton as she glanced at her watch for the third time since coming in. 'Where the hell is that nurse?'

Dowling started rubbing at the stain. 'Do ye know what I was thinkin' as I was comin' in this mornin'?'

Hamilton dialled Nurse Higgins' number on her mobile, listening to the ringing tone. 'What?'

'We should get up and about in the wards in here. Get a feel for the place. There's somethin' we still haven't put our fingers on. I can't help feelin' there's more these bloody doctors know than they're lettin' on about.'

The number continued to ring, unanswered.

'Maybe she's on her way in. The traffic was bad comin' in from Blanchardstown. Road blocks everywhere, lookin' for that baby.'

'Yeah. Maybe you're right.' Hamilton studied her notes. 'There's two of the doctors I think we should push for immediate AIDS testing. There's two I'm not happy about.'

Dowling laughed. 'Only two? That's a bit better than Jack McGrath. He couldn' stand any goddamn one of them.'

Hamilton smiled.

'Morgan and Lynch. Morgan's been lying, I'm sure of that. His wife more or less said that when we called. And he's been avoiding us ever since. I've sent John Doyle twice to get him and each time he couldn't be found. The other fella Lynch's story seemed a bit too exact for my liking. I think we should ask both of them to come down to the station today. Get the nurse to listen in on them and at the same time ask them why they're stalling taking the AIDS test.' Hamilton collected her bag. 'I'm going to suss out the place until she comes in. Let's meet back here at ten o'clock.'

'Where are ye gonna be in case I need ye?'

Hamilton was halfway out the door already, checking along the corridor for any sign of Nurse Higgins. 'Dr Tom Morgan. I'm going to have a look at him. I want to see him in action.'

Dowling chuckled. 'From what I've heard ye'll be bloody lucky not to feel him in action.'

Dr Tom Morgan was in his private rooms. Hamilton was directed by an orderly, then re-directed by a nurse. She opened the waiting room door gently, not wanting to make herself too obvious to the waiting patients, very much aware how Jack McGrath's heavy-handed police presence had alienated so many. Christ, she thought to herself, the last time I went to see a gynaecologist I made sure I had my legs waxed first.

The first thing that struck her was she was not in a doctor's waiting room at all, so much so that she opened the door again and checked the name. *Dr Tom Morgan, Private Clinic* was written in navy-blue italics on a canary-yellow backed sign. Very trendy.

But when she went back inside she couldn't help but feel she was in a modelling agency. Sitting on various chairs in the quite small waiting room were five young women with long, long legs that just seemed to go on for ever. It was obvious each had gone to great lengths to make herself look as attractive as possible. One wore a short, clinging leather skirt pulled up as high as could be decently allowed. She draped one leg seductively over the other. Two of the others had long black eyelashes that fluttered across the pages of glossy magazines. They wore tight-fitting denim jeans. Another wore the latest from the Paul Costelloe range of fashions and flicked at her hair repeatedly as if trying to decide which was the best side for the day. All five glanced up as Hamilton walked in, eyeing her carefully from head to toe. The eyes returned to the glossy magazines, apparently. All five were sizing one another up, like tigresses, claws sheathed. Given the right opportunity they'd rake across a face in seconds.

Dr Tom Morgan's secretary appeared at the door leading to his consulting room. She was a stunner with long blonde crimped hair, lying lazily over a low-necked tight-fitting cream coloured cotton body-suit top that pushed her young

259

breasts out for all to see. And her rivals in the room to envy. She wore a mid-calf-length pleated skirt over tan shoes with sexy tights which had little diamonds that caught the eye. And the eye that was most frequently caught was that of Dr Tom Morgan. Every woman who attended Morgan hated his secretary, secretly fantasising about what the two got up to when the rooms were empty. There were rumours of them being seen wrapped around one another at a hospital party, other stories of her being caught rushing out from the inner consulting room looking flushed and embarrassed when an unexpected visitor had called.

'Anne Cantwell? Dr Morgan's ready for you now.' One of the women stood up, smoothed her creased skirt, flicked her hair back and entered the consulting room. She stalked rather than walked inside, like a cat after prey.

Kate Hamilton felt almost drawn into this menagerie, fascinated and yet repelled at the same time.

'Can I help you?'

The eyes swivelled.

'Yes. I'd like a word with Dr Morgan.'

'Do you have an appointment?'

'No.' She slipped her card onto the reception desk and crimped blonde studied it briefly before looking up.

'If you'd like to wait I'll speak to him after he finishes with the patient just gone in.'

The waiting women turned towards Hamilton. Who's she with her pretty face and slim body inside that plain, stuffy navy uniform? A silence fell in the waiting room which was broken only by the strumming fingers of crimped blonde.

Tom Morgan's consulting room reflected the generosity of the pharmaceutical industry in Ireland. A calendar on the wall behind his chair not only gave the date but also the role of hormone replacement therapy in peri-menopausal women. Two mugs stuffed with biros confirmed that Disodene was the contraceptive of choice in today's young woman. A writing pad on his desk was surrounded on its outer margins with the logos and trademarks of a number of companies specialising in gynaecological problems. The pens that he wrote with extolled the virtues of the latest NSAID in dysmenorrhoea and even the soap that washed his hands and the towel that dried them were covered in trade names. Only ethical constraints forbidding the pharmaceutical industry putting their logos on Armani suits, shirts and ties prevented Tom Morgan looking like a Formula One racing driver at a pit stop.

'Good morning, Detective Hamilton, I believe you were looking for me the other night. My secretary tells me one of your officers has also been trying to contact me. Something about a blood test?' Morgan sounded concerned and anxious to cooperate. He looked perplexed by the whole business. His pretty face wrinkled, so concerned and perplexed was he. 'It's just that I've been out of town for the past few days and didn't get a chance to get back to you.'

Kate Hamilton had to admit he was quite gorgeous. He had the body and face of Adonis and probably the other bits to go with it. His every movement exuded sexuality as he rested his chin on long, delicate, intertwined fingers and gazed provocatively into her eyes.

'However, now you've found me,' he continued slowly, tauntingly. 'What can I do for you?'

Hamilton was about to go into her prepared speech when the door was burst open by Tony Dowling. He was ashen faced.

'Kate, I need to talk to ye immediately. Ye better come this minute. Something's happened.'

It was the young lust birds who discovered something amiss in Staff Nurse Higgins' life. The continual ringing of the phone in the flat above finally woke them up after a night of passion. The phone would ring off, then start up again, the noise slowly penetrating their sleep, then their wakefulness. It began to irritate.

'She's usually gone by now,' he muttered as he felt a hand slowly advance up between his thighs. 'Again?'

'Yeah.'

'You're an animal.'

'Yeah.'

But the phone rang again, ruining the moment. He slipped out of bed and padded over to the window to check if her car had gone. It hadn't. He rubbed at the steamed-up glass with a corner of the curtain.

'Nah, she's still here.'

Then he noticed something out of the corner of his eye as he turned to go back to bed. He wiped more of the glass with more of the curtain and squinted, this time seeing clearly the patch of red beside the parked car. It was a large patch of red with something lying slightly to the front of this patch of red. Something that looked very like a hammer. He strained to see the car and noticed the windows totally misted. For a moment his eyes dropped as his brain tried to analyse what he had seen. He was puzzled. Then, slightly alarmed he looked back again and this time became even more alarmed.

'Look, I'm just gonna check that car outside. I'll be back in a minute.'

She was lying with the bedclothes pulled full back revealing the morning's anticipated activity areas. 'Hurry. I'll be waiting.' He pulled on a dressing gown, stepped into his slippers, then dragged a thick sweater over his head.

She went to the window to watch.

He came into her view from around the side of the building, his breath misting in the morning frost, both hands inside the opposite sleeve of the dressing gown. She tapped at the window but he didn't look up. She noticed he was edging slowly towards the car, very slowly, really, considering how cold it looked outside. Then he was down peering at something on the ground and, still on his hunkers, crab-stepped his way to something else.

He stood up slowly, still staring at the ground. She tapped at the window again, this time more forcefully, but he still didn't turn round. She watched as he moved backwards, still looking downwards. Slowly, very slowly, he went round to the passenger side of the car and started squinting inside, rubbing a sleeve against the glass. There was frost on all smooth surfaces and on the grass and branches of trees. Suddenly he darted to the back passenger-side window, his sleeve rubbing agitatedly at the window. His head jerked up, breath steaming in the air in short, quick gasps. He looked back in again.

Then he ran like a man possessed, even dropping one slipper.

What the hell is he doing? What is going on? What has he seen?

Hamilton and Dowling arrived just before eleven. Three squad cars, white with distinctive yellow stripe and blue flashing lights, were pulled up and parked randomly in the flats complex car park. Six uniformed Gardai moved briskly about to keep warm, one of them talking into a two-way radio. The driver's side door of one of the squad cars was open and a crackling voice spilled out confirming details and movements of the investigation team. Spindly shadows of the tree branches suddenly cast themselves across the car park as the sun came out from behind a cloud. The momentary brightness dazzled passing motorists and they had to shield their eyes to see what was going on.

Kate Hamilton knew already it was Staff Nurse Higgins' car. Over her mobile phone she learned there was a body in the boot that could be seen through the back window, as one of the back seats was pulled forward flat with a leg resting awkwardly on it. A very still leg. A deadly still, white stockinged leg with red staining, could be clearly seen. It didn't look very good for whoever was inside that boot. And Hamilton knew in her heart it was Staff Nurse Higgins.

In the distance, but coming closer, a police car siren announced the imminent arrival of the forensic back-up squad.

Dowling had separated and was talking rapidly to one of the uniformed Gardai who motioned towards a window in the flats complex. Up there, and looking out, was a Ban Garda, the curtains pulled back, a window slightly open for ventilation. The young lust birds had had their ardour dampened. His teeth were still chattering, despite three heavy sweaters and the radiators on full blast. She was sitting mute on a chair in the kitchen, chain-smoking.

'Kate? Kate? I'm goin' up to have a word with the young fella who spotted the blood.'

Hamilton nodded and pulled her heavy-duty navy overcoat tighter against the cold. She watched as a Garda mini van screeched to a halt only feet from where she stood, its siren suddenly killed. The back door opened and out came the forensic team, two in white boiler suits over heavy sweaters and leggings, followed by forensic photographer Dan Harrison, Nikon already in hand, fiddling to take the lens shutter off. He was followed slowly by Dr Noel Dunne, forensic pathologist.

Dunne put one foot down gingerly on the tarmac, then the other and turned back to the inside, dragging two black doctor-type bags to the edge. Wearily he pulled one open, fiddling about, cursing and grunting until he finally found what he was looking for. He reached back inside the van again and pulled a heavy-duty oil-skin coat on against the cold. Standing up, he arched his back, then turned to get on with the job. He was holding a dictaphone and an A4-size clipboard.

'Get some screens around the car,' he barked and two uniformed Gardai jumped into the mini van and were back out again with remarkable speed. They started erecting a fold-away yellow plastic screen. One of the forensics was already unrolling a yellow Garda incident tape, attaching it to the chestnut tree trunk and a number of self-supporting poles from the van. Within minutes Nurse Higgins' Mazda 626 was hidden from view.

'Dr Dunne, my name is Detective Sergeant Kate Hamilton. We met briefly the night you were called in to the Central Maternity Hospital.' Dunne looked her up and down with obvious distaste. Hamilton ignored this. 'I've taken over the maternity hospital murder inquiry.' She paused to make sure he had heard this clearly and understood. She made sure she accentuated the words 'taken over'. 'I have reason to believe the body in the back of the car may be related to that inquiry.'

Dunne eyeballed her. His breath frosting in the air making him look like a dragon breathing steam. 'You took over from Detective Inspector McGrath?'

'Yes. He was transferred to the kidnap investigation. He's the kidnap expert in the Jaguar Unit.'

'Is he,' grunted Dunne as he started towards the yellow screen. 'Is he indeed.' He stopped and turned suddenly to Hamilton. 'And what are you the expert in?' There was no disguising the tone of his voice. Intimidating.

Hamilton knew his legendary reputation. He hated newcomers on investigations, hated rookie detectives, feeling they wasted his time asking stupid questions. He particularly didn't like women trying to do a man's job. She sensed he would much prefer to be dealing with someone else.

'Cooking. I do very good scrambled eggs.' Suck on that, you old bollox.

Dunne grinned. 'Okay, Detective Sergeant Hamilton, let's get going.' He pulled aside one of the yellow screens, holding it until she was inside the inner sanctum. Then he dragged it closed.

Already a TV crew had pulled up, fiddling with equipment. One of the uniformed Gardai had his arms outstretched, forbidding them any further, as the reporter tried to negotiate a closer spot.

'The doors are locked.' One of the white-suited forensics, wearing surgical gloves, had checked and printed the door handles. Then he had tried the locks but they were all secure. 'Back in a second.'

He ran over to the mini van, returning with a car robber's delight, the complete set of master keys for the most popular cars driven in Ireland. He inserted one after another until suddenly the door locks clicked. Inside the windows small buttons jumped up.

Dunne started dictating. Walking around he noted type of car, registration, colour, inside misting, even scratches on the bodywork. Then he went down on his hunkers, peering closely at a large blood pool, measuring and describing it. Only two feet away lay a blood-stained hammer. Dunne crouched down and inspected it closely, dictating as he went. Dan Harrison followed close behind, snapping at anything Dunne ordered. Dunne spent some time examining and recording tracks and smears of blood along the back and boot of the car. Palm and finger outlines on the edge of the boot were noted, measured and photographed. The forensics dusted and peered as Kate Hamilton watched.

Dunne finished the external examination of the car and its immediate surrounds. He was ready to record the rest.

'Dan, have you got everything?'

Harrison, ace forensic photographer, nodded. Dan Harrison was not a man of many words. His work was not the sort most people liked to hear about, nor the sort he liked to talk about.

Dunne had his own special 'scene of crime' form on which he started to scribble.

NAME OF DECEASED – he left blank, for the moment.

ADDRESS OF SCENE. 'Where are we anyway?' He looked around and one of the uniformed Gardai shouted out the exact address. Dunne wrote it down.

DATE AND TIME CONTACTED. He glanced at his watch and wrote 17\2\97 at 9.57 am.

DATE AND TIME ARRIVED. 17\2\97 at 10.32 am. He had been in the city morgue looking at a body fished out from the Liffey when re-routed. The journey out to Blackrock hadn't taken long with his motorcycle escort, their sirens full on.

OFFICER IN CHARGE. He looked at Kate Hamilton. 'What's your name again?' As Kate Hamilton called out her name, loudly and clearly for all to hear, Dunne made grumbling noises into his beard, registering again his disapproval. He sighed deeply and everyone turned to look. He seemed unusually tired this morning, not his usual ebullient self.

DECEASED LAST SEEN ALIVE – Dunne left this blank.

RECTAL TEMPERATURE – also blank, for the moment.

ATMOSPHERIC TEMPERATURE. He took out his own 'air thermometer' instrument, placing it on the car roof, first laying a square white linen cloth down. 'Nobody knock that over.' The group shuffled back.

RIGOR MORTIS. Blank.

LIPOSTATIC LIVIDITY. Blank.

SUMMARY OF LESIONS. He paused, put the clipboard under his left arm and sighed deeply again.

'Okay, open it up.'

One of the forensics nodded to the other. He slipped off the surgical gloves he was wearing, stuffed them in his pocket, then tugged out a second pair and pulled them on. The small audience gathered round the back of the Mazda. It seemed they were all reluctant to take the next step. Hey, how about we all go and have a cup of coffee and warm ourselves up, maybe go for a boozy lunch? Anything but the next step.

The forensic looked to Dunne and he nodded, eyes resigned to what he was going to see.

The forensic looked at Hamilton, now joined by Tony Dowling, who had slipped noiselessly through a gap in the yellow screen.

Kate nodded, pulling her heavy coat collar up around her ears, clutching it firmly at the front. She wasn't sure she really wanted to see the next bit, but knew she had to. She couldn't turn away. Typical, they'd say, typical of a bloody woman.

The forensic had already checked the lock mechanism and Dan Harrison also had it in his roll of film.

Delicately, one fingered, the lock was clicked open. In the silence it sounded like a pistol shot. Then, with a two finger-tip pressure at each edge the boot was slowly lifted. At about halfway the spring mechanism took over and it suddenly flew up.

'Oh, shit!'

'Christ!'

'Jesus!'

Noel Dunne said nothing, he just stared. Kate Hamilton said nothing, but couldn't help averting her eyes from the bent head, with its long, blonde, blood-streaked and matted hair. The body of Staff Nurse Sarah Higgins had been forced into an almost foetal position, with one white stockinged leg pulled back at the knee so the limb filled one corner of the boot. The other lay along the back of the pushed forward seat. The face was squashed up against a sports bag, the features mercifully hidden from the staring eyes of the audience.

But what was not hidden was the blue twine wrapped around the neck, pulled so tightly it was embedded in the skin. A small collection of blood lay in the visible right ear space.

And in her once voluptuous neck, a scalpel was deeply embedded.

'Dan, get as many close-ups as possible. Get an overall shot of the boot from a few feet back. Right side angles and left side too. One straight on and one from above.' He turned to one of the uniformed Gardai. 'What's your name?'

'Garda Carter.'

'Well, Garda Carter, go to the back of the van and you'll find a small stepladder. Bring it over here, like a good man. Whatever you do, don't go near that pool of blood or kick any gravel or leaves near that hammer. Go round the other side, in fact.' He turned back to Harrison. 'Dan, get as many as you can from above, before we move the body. And get as many decent close-ups of that scalpel holder as you can. The rest of you, stand well back. Give him all the space he needs.'

He turned to Hamilton. 'Detective Sergeant, I'd like a word with you.'

Hamilton and Dowling joined Dunne in a huddle about twenty feet from the right side of the car. For a moment Dunne said nothing, pausing to watch Harrison's Nikon record the scene. He shouted a few more instructions, ordering one of the uniformed Garda well away. Finally he turned to Hamilton as Dowling watched and listened respectfully.

'Detective Sergeant this is the second body I've had to

deal with in the past week that has had a surgical scalpel stuck in the neck. Both victims young women. Do you know who this girl is?'

'It looks like a nurse from the Central Maternity Hospital called Sarah Higgins.'

'Why? How do you know?'

'She was supposed to meet us at nine o'clock. She was supposed to sit in on alibi interviews today. That's her car and that's her uniform.'

'Is she the one who heard the voice over the phone last week? Jack McGrath mentioned one to me.'

'Yes.'

'Would you recognise her if I turned the face around?'

Hamilton swallowed deeply. 'Yes, I've spoken with her.'

'Okay, let's go look. Two scalpels in the neck inside a week is a bit of a record, even for me.'

Dunne walked slowly towards the open boot. Harrison was standing halfway up the small stepladder, snapping away.

'I'm finished.' Harrison climbed down, pressed a small button on the camera base whirring the film into rewind. He was already fishing inside a pocket for a fresh roll.

Dunne lifted the ladder aside and bent down to peer closely at the body. He started dictating. After about ten minutes he turned to Hamilton, who was standing slightly behind and to his right.

'Ready?'

She nodded. A shiver ran down her spine and she struggled hard not to let the rest see her unease. It wouldn't sound good when retold later, in the pub.

Dunne slipped on a pair of surgical gloves and gently prodded the body, first the exposed neck area, then that part of the right side of the face he could see without disturbing. Next he bent the knees. 'No rigor,' he muttered, then turned to Dowling. 'What's the temperature of that thermometer on the roof?' Dowling inspected.

'Four degrees.'

'Thank God there's no wind or we'd all be frozen,' muttered Dunne.

'Any idea how long she's been dead?' Hamilton asked.

Without looking up, Dunne prodded further. 'Not yet, Detective Sergeant. Not yet. There's no rigor yet. It was near freezing last night and most of this morning. Rigor mortis hasn't set in yet because of the cold. I'll be able to give you a better idea after I've measured rectal temperature. I want you to look at her face and tell me if it's your nurse.'

He gently manipulated the head in both gloved hands until the waxen-like face came into view.

For a moment Kate Hamilton couldn't be sure. The beautiful and lively face that had discussed boyfriends and dances and rock bands while Hamilton had tried to persuade her to cooperate during her interview was now lifeless, the spirit gone. The basic features remained, but the sparkle, the life, had left. For ever.

'That's her,' Tony Dowling spoke. He was peering over Dunne's left shoulder. 'That's her all right, isn't it Kate?'

Hamilton straightened. 'Yes it is, unfortunately. Yes, it's definitely her.'

'Well, Detective Sergeant, I think he's used a clean scalpel this time, but it looks as if it's our friend from the hospital again. You've got one hell of an investigation on your hands.'

'Good morning, Southside Town Houses. Lesley Cairns speaking.'

'Ah, good morning. I was hoping to rent one of your houses for a week.'

'Certainly sir. Have you any area in mind or any particular price range you'd like to stay within?'

'Well, it's for a business client coming to Dublin for a week. He'll be based around the southside for most of the time and he'll be on his own. Maybe you could suggest somewhere?'

'Well, we have a new flats complex in Dun Laoghaire that's very reasonably priced.'

'No, that's too far out.'

'Hmm, let me see.' Buttons clicked on a PC. 'How about Booterstown? We have a mixture of town houses and one or two bedroom flats in Mourne Court just off Booterstown Avenue. That's very central really. Not too expensive either.'

'Yes, that sounds fine. Have you a one-bedroomed flat there?'

Click. Click. Noise of humming.

'Yes. We have a one-bedroomed flat with kitchen-cum-dining area. There's a bathroom and toilet and small sitting room. That one's free until the beginning of March.'

'Sounds fine. How much is that?'

It was all on the screen in front of her.

'That one's three hundred pounds per week. The electricity and gas is metered so you pay for that as you go. There's also a three hundred pounds breakages and damage deposit. That's refunded within one week of departure. You can collect that here at our offices or we can post it to you. We can arrange to have it posted in whatever currency you wish at no extra charge.'

'That sounds perfect. Can I book that and I'll call down within the next hour and pay you?'

'Certainly sir. Will you be paying cash, cheque or credit card? If it's by cheque we'll need a cheque card and details of your bank account.'

'I'll pay the lot in cash, if you don't mind. If you just give me a receipt I'll get a refund from my company.'

'That's fine, sir. What name shall I hold the flat in?'

'Andrew Kelly. You can book it in Andrew's name, Andrew Kelly. He's a computer software sales representative based in Southampton. He's over on a business trip to Microsoft in Sandyford. I'll leave you his business card when I call.'

'I'll have the keys and a map of how to get there when you arrive. Our offices are in Mount Street. You can't miss us, there's a large red sign just above the entrance.'

'Great. See you within an hour.'

Lynch flicked through the Yellow Pages again until he

found second-hand car sales. He looked along the list, finally choosing one he knew and had passed by lots of times. He picked up the phone again and dialled. Within ten minutes he learned there was a 'real wee gem, only fifty-six thousand miles on the clock, in perfect condition, new tyres and battery, only two safe drivers as well' awaiting him at Donnie's Motors in Ringsend. He took a taxi to Donnie, dressed in his false wig and moustache, clear-lens glasses and black tracksuit outfit. Donnie was all over him, lying through his teeth about the car mileage, owners, total lack of accidents and 'just serviced' yesterday.

Lynch knew he was lying. Pathetic, really.

They haggled over the price but eventually Donnie was paid cash for a 1995 Dublin-registered Mitsubishi Colt, in which Lynch drove off after supplying the delighted Donnie with a false name and address for the vehicle change of ownership form. Lynch also bought a thick steel chain and padlock which Donnie, now so concerned for his customer, advised. 'Wrap that around the steering wheel and the bar under the driver's seat. It won't stop them nicking it if they really want it, but it might just make them move on to some other, easier car.'

Donnie was real concerned.

Lynch made a mental note to wrap the same chain around Donnie's neck when next they met.

Tommy Malone and Moonface decided in the end to take the train from Newbridge to Heuston station rather than drive to Dublin direct. They'd listened all morning on the radio to news of the kidnap and the continuing hype was secretly worrying each of them. Their uneasiness grew by the hour. By the time fresh Polaroids of the baby with one of the morning papers had been taken, Malone decided it was too risky for himself and Moonface to travel in the car together. 'Too many road blocks. Some Garda will be sure to recognise us and start askin' awkward questions. Martin and I'll go and I'll check out what's goin' on generally. I'll put the frighteners on Big Harry. We'll go for the pick up tomorra, okay?'

So the plan was changed. Sam Collins stayed behind with Peggy Ryan and the baby, Malone and Moonface drove the Volvo to Newbridge railway station where Moonface again chained the wheel and removed the spark plugs. Standing in the morning cold they said little to each other. Malone carried a large thick brown envelope containing six smaller envelopes each of which contained a Polaroid of the bala-clava'd Moonface holding Gordon O'Brien. Over his shoulder Collins had again held a newspaper, clearly ident-ifying the date and headlines.

The short journey to Heuston station was silent for both. Malone advised against them sharing the same seat, even the same carriage. They sat well apart, staring at the headlines on other people's newspapers, trying to read the smaller print. Malone sat beside a young couple with a baby who struck up a conversation with an elderly man sitting opposite.

Very soon they started discussing the kidnapping. The anger from each side unsettled Malone even more and he moved away.

Moonface couldn't have cared less about the papers or the headlines. He borrowed a copy of the *Star* and spent the last minutes of the journey reading about the big match. The more he read the more excited he became. The managers were trading insults, the players admitting it was a grudge match. 'We're taking no prisoners,' ran one quote from the new Irish midfield star. 'Don't expect us to hold back,' returned the opposition striker.

A separate report related how English police had warned Gardai that a large number of National Front bully boys were expected to arrive in Dublin without tickets, their sole purpose to stir up trouble. This was their planned revenge for the baton charge that had ended the last England vs Ireland soccer match, before full time. There was a half-page photo in the *Star* of one English yobbo wearing a Union Jack tee shirt, Union Jack tattoo on his forehead with a Union Jack flag draped over his shoulders and a two-finger salute for the camera. 'Paddy slime will suffer this time.' Quote, unquote. Moonface's blood began to boil. British bastards. English scum. Just wait'll the big night. We'll see who'll suffer.

Malone sidled up to him in the crowded Heuston station with a few brief final words. Moonface nodded at all Malone's words of wisdom. 'Don' worry, Tommy. It's as good as done. I've the bike and courier outfit in a lock-up garage in Ballyfermot. They'll be dropped off within an hour or so. Wha' time do you wanna go back?'

Moonface was in no rush to head back to the cottage and the screaming child. He hoped Malone would drag the day out in Dublin as long as possible. Malone felt the same but didn't say it. Secretly he was very worried about the potent cocktail of Sam Collins, Peggy Ryan and the screeching Gordon O'Brien. It was an explosive mixture. If the baby started acting up again he could see Collins losing his rag altogether. And Peggy was in no great shape either, she was losing her cool. A-team! he thought, some A-team. They're a bunch of fuckin' losers. Jesus, what would've the B-team been like.

Malone and Moonface took separate taxis, Moonface to Ballyfermot, while Malone headed towards his house along the quays. He had to bail out when he spotted a Garda check point with a long line of traffic banked up. 'I'll get out here and walk, it'll be quicker.' The taxi man nodded. He'd just given Malone an ear bashing on the kidnapping and what he personally would bloody well do if he got his hands on the bastards. Gardai are useless. Spot checks all over the place. As if the kidnappers are gonna drive right up to one and wait in the queue to be searched. Malone had heard enough.

He walked past the check point and hailed another taxi only to get an even more vitriolic ear bashing, this time from a woman cabbie who had three small children herself and what she would do to the bastards who kidnapped that innocent wee baby was not worth repeating. She even apologised to Malone for using such bad language but she was sure he'd understand and she was equally sure he must feel much the same. Didn't he?

'Yeah,' said Malone, 'let me out here.'

He spotted the special branch detectives before they spotted him. He was walking along Anderson's Quay and stopped short. There was no mistaking it, the unmarked car with its telltale short aerial, parked only about fifty yards from his house. There were two in the front, one smoking. Malone ducked into a shop and bought a packet of Sweet Afton, lighting one nervously. He felt his heart pounding, noticed his hands trembling. Either they're onto me already or it's just a routine surveillance. He walked back out onto the road, real casual like, back through some side streets and away from the area. Fuck it, fuck it! I'd better make a few calls. He walked until he came to Connolly station where he took the next Dart train back to Westland Row.

As he sat in the carriage he noticed a familiar face, an old Steevens Street flats pal. But the man's face shocked Malone. It was battered, almost war torn, ravaged by lack of decent food and years of booze. He was rambling to himself, his head nodding as one part of whatever still constituted brain conversed with the other. He was wrapped tightly inside an oversized overcoat that was tattered and torn and stained from too much South African sherry. He stank, the smell pervading the carriage so much that fellow passengers moved away. Shamefacedly, Malone sneaked to a distant window seat where he watched the next station slip by until he reached Westland Row. Outside again he stared as the train pulled away, carrying its one cargo of human misery.

The last time he had seen someone so down and out, so destitute and useless, was when his mother had collected his father from the cells in Blackrock Garda station after he'd been arrested for drunkenness. He'd gone on a futile drunken attempt at breaking and entering during yet another losing streak leaving his wife weeks without enough money to put food on the table or clothes on the backs of her seven children. Jaysus, thought Malone as the Dart disappeared around the corner towards Landsdown Road Station, is it any wonder I'm the way I am today? How else am I supposed to live? I'll be fucked if I'll end up like me Da or that poor, simple bollox on the train. He didn't like to admit it, but recognising the down-and-out had unsettled him. That and spotting the special branch car. There's no way I'm goin' back to the flats. There's no way I'm goin' back to beggin' in the streets. No way.

He left the station and walked along with the usual traffic as far as the Davenport Hotel where he found a secluded phone booth. He wanted to ring Betty Nolan and find out what was going on down at the O'Brien headquarters but the two had already agreed a plan on contact. He couldn't reach her until six when she would sit beside the public phone in Mooney's pub in Blackrock in case he had to make contact.

He decided to ring Richie Murphy, an old hand from Mountjoy and one of the few fellow criminals Malone kept in contact with. The news from Richie Murphy was not good at all. The Gardai had turned the Dublin underworld upside down looking for the baby or any leads on who had taken him.

'Do *you* know, Tommy?' asked Richie.

'Nah, havin' a clue. Sure I'm as bad as yourself. I was only ringin' to see if I was the only wan bein' watched.'

'Ah Christ no, Tommy, everybody's bein' screwed, it's deadly.' Then Richie told Malone about no less than three, 'three for Christ's sake', good bank jobs that had to be called off. 'There's just too many cops about. The fuckers are swarmin' all over the place.'

Malone listened with a sinking heart. Then he finally heard what worried him most. The general opinion among fellow hoods, according to Richie, was that the sooner the baby was handed back the better.

'The Gards are puttin' on so much pressure, some bloody eejits are tellin' anythin' to get them off their backs,' he complained. 'A lot of hot information is leakin' out and a lot of hot heads are gettin' rightly fed up. If anybody hears who's got this baby they're gonna dob them in. Rattin' or no rattin', this kidnappin' is fuckin' bad news for business. Anythin' I can do for you?'

'Nah, I was just checkin' that's all. Just checkin'.'

Just after three o'clock a very worried looking Tommy Malone walked out from the Davenport Hotel towards Merrion Square. He glanced at his watch. There was still a lot of time to kill before he met Moonface again. He looked around and noticed he was standing near the National Art Gallery. He tried to walk past it, but felt himself drawn inside. He looked at his watch. I'll kill a few minutes in here. I'll have a look at that paintin' again by yer man.

Tommy Malone had become an ardent Caravaggio fan. After his first unsettling visit he'd returned to the National Art Gallery on a number of occasions to see if there were any other paintings that might be worth stealing but soon decided the security was too strong and not worth the effort. On one occasion to make his visit look legitimate he'd bought a glossy catalogue detailing Caravaggio's life and works. He'd flicked through it idly as he sized up the security system, but becoming astounded and delighted with what he read. Caravaggio had been a bit of a thug himself, Malone learned, and had been in trouble with the police of the day. Now *that's* my kind of painter.

He read further that Caravaggio was in and out of fights and arguments regularly and knew how to lie to the rozzers. 'Once, when interrogated while bedridden with sword wounds,' the catalogue recalled, 'Caravaggio had replied, "I wounded myself with my sword in falling on the streets. I don't know where it happened, and no one was present." ' Ah fuckin' brilliant, Malone had crowed to himself. A fuckin' brilliant painter is yer man. Then he read that Caravaggio had had to flee Rome after killing an antagonist in a brawl. Tommy Malone didn't know what an antagonist was exactly but felt the bollox had deserved all he got if 'yer man' had done it. 'Yer man' was an okay painter in Tommy Malone's eyes and he went back to his masterpiece and studied it in greater detail.

And as he looked and squinted he came to one earth-shattering conclusion. That Judas shoulda bin fuckin' crucified himself. Years spent in gaol listening to cellmates complain how they'd been let down by some snitch reinforced powerfully the fear of betrayal. He'd even wondered if one day he too would be let down by a Judas.

He sat in the coffee shop smoking Sweet Aftons one after the other, ignoring the disapproving glances from adjoining tables. His mind was in turmoil, wondering how the 'big wan' was all going to end. He stared out the window at the pouring rain. He felt very uneasy. Something inside was sounding alarm bells. The kidnapping had been a mistake. I'll give it wan more day and then we'll bail out he decided as he stood up to leave. Just wan more day.

*

Moonface had completed all the drops by three o'clock despite the rain. He'd watched the dark grey clouds form and swirl in over the city but decided to run with the job anyway. Dripping wet he'd delivered one envelope to the TV studios of RTE in Donnybrook, another to the front desk of the *Daily Post*, the rest to various post boxes, media sources and even Fitzgibbon Street Garda station. He dropped his bike and courier gear back at the lock-up then checked his watch. Fuckin' great, he thought, plenty of time to kill. He decided to nip home and collect his supporters' gear for the big match, in case he had to go direct from Kilcullen. On the way he bumped into one of his buddies, sheltering from another shower in the porch of a pub. 'Howya Martin, havin' seen ye for days, where've ye been? Fancy a pint?' 'Just the wan.' 'How's the crack? Anythin' happenin'?' 'Jaysus, wait'll ye hear.' Moonface broke Tommy Malone's first golden rule and had a pint. In fact he had a lot more than one before he remembered Malone's words. But by then it was too late. By then he couldn't give a stuff.

Sam Collins had had enough. Gordon O'Brien's screeching seemed to penetrate the depths of his brain. Peggy Ryan was desperately trying to quieten him, pacify him, settle him, anything him but what he was doing. Anything but that screeching, that loud piercing screeching of pain. The screeching of colic and hunger and fear and terror and lack of comfort and where's-my-mother screeching. All that was just too much for Sam Collins. And he just couldn't stand coming round the corner into one of Peggy Ryan's personal conversations with herself, it unnerved him no end. Gordon O'Brien was too much for Peggy Ryan as well but he was her baby, so to speak, and it was up to her to shut him up. But those screeches just bounced off the cottage walls and finally Sam Collins angrily ordered her outside.

'Take the little bollox down the lane for a few minutes and see does that shut him.'

'Jaysus, Sam, it's freezin' ou' there.'

'I don't give a stuff. Get him outa here before I lift him one.'

The sudden blast of frosty air took the baby's breath away and he actually stopped screeching. He actually stopped for a moment. Then another spasm gripped and he filled his lungs, letting roar again. His screams carried across the quiet country fields on that freezing February afternoon. The very definite and unmistakable screeches of a baby who shouldn't have been out in that sort of weather at all. In a field nearby Brian O'Callaghan could hardly believe his ears. A baby outside in the bitter cold? He had just finished cleaning a newborn lamb with straw and had wrapped it in rags, planning to take it back to the shed for the next few days. Then he heard the screeches, carried so clearly across the fields. He set the lamb down gently and set off in search. He nestled down at the side of the hedge separating his property from the laneway leading to the stone cottage and watched Peggy Ryan walking the baby up and down, up and down. The baby's cries settled, eventually, as the shivering Peggy grew tired from all the jiggling.

God, she looks awful old for a baby that young, thought O'Callaghan.

He was just about to turn away when he spotted Sam Collins walking down the laneway. He walked to within ten feet of where O'Callaghan lay, close enough for him to see his face clearly. It was not a face he knew and wondered again who they were. The thought crossed his mind they might be connected to the kidnap gang and that he should let the Gardai know. Then he remembered about his uninsured and untaxed car with its bald tyres and decided the risk wasn't worth it. If he was wrong all that'd happen was that the Gardai would start nebbing at him and then he'd be out of pocket and have his name in the local paper. He decided to mind his own business.

'I watched the nine o'clock news, then the weather forecast. As far as I can remember I switched to BBC for a programme on new developments in medical technology going on in the States. I might have watched something else after that. No, I remember watching a few minutes of soccer on Sky Sports. Man United and Sheffield as far as I can recall. Wasn't much of a game so I flicked off and went to bed.'

Dean Lynch was recounting his alibi for Kate Hamilton and the team in interview room two of Store Street Garda station.

As soon as the body of Nurse Higgins had been identified all hell broke loose. First Kate Hamilton rang Chief Superintendent Mike Loughry and informed him of developments. He immediately transferred twenty extra detectives onto the case and the new team descended on the Central Maternity Hospital like a marauding army. Its corridors echoed again to the sound of heavy feet. Doors that had never been opened were burst open and desks rifled. Those whose alibis had been shaky or uneven or in any way suspicious for Mary Dwyer's death were invited to Store Street Garda station to help with the ongoing inquiry. And they were invited in such a fashion that no one was in any doubt that the gloves were off. Kate Hamilton meant business. None of them knew about Nurse Higgins, yet, except Dean Lynch, who acted the picture of aggrieved innocence in the interview room.

'And no one was with you overnight?'

Hamilton sat across the table, watching intently. There was something about him that didn't add up. She couldn't figure out what it was but she just wasn't happy. His shirt collar was a size too big, his face looked as if it had lost flesh recently. He had a slight turkey-like loose fold under the chin and a distinct unhealthy looking pallor. His hair was combed back flatly to the back of his head and above his eyebrows she could see tiny beads of perspiration. He also had a slight cough which kept interrupting his answers and irritating the hell out of her.

'There's no one with me any night. I live alone. I always have done. And do you know it's never been a problem for me or anyone else up until this week. I hope you don't expect me to get married just to have someone provide me with an alibi for every crime committed in Dublin.'

He smiled his thin smile which Hamilton tried to ignore but found she couldn't. She had scanned the notes taken at the first interview and could find no flaw at all. Nothing. And now, being interviewed, he was impressively vague when you would expect vagueness and impressively accurate when you would expect accuracy. He was impressively confident and unruffled, not a bit like a man who had committed two murders, two brutal murders, within a week.

He coughed again, a deep throaty and phlegmy cough.

'Got a cold?'

'No, just some bug I picked up. I'm taking some antibiotics. Should be clear within days.'

He looked at her closely, his eyes never leaving her face. She sensed his gaze and felt distinctly uncomfortable.

'Where were you last night?' She decided on a sudden change in tack, hoping to catch him off guard. He was ready for her.

'Last night?' The voice was full of surprise.

'Yes, last night. From around ten to say one o'clock this morning?'

Lynch looked very puzzled. He sat back in the uncomfortable chair and looked directly at Kate Hamilton again. It's those eyes, she thought as she tried to avoid his gaze, there's something about those eyes I don't like.

'Well, actually, I was out for most of last night.'

The room quietened. Dowling and Doyle were both listening in on this interview.

'Oh, where?'

'I was at the pictures. The Savoy. I went to the late night showing of *The Godfather. Godfather Part I*. You know, the good one.'

'What time did it start?'

'God, I don't exactly know. I think it was about half past ten. I queued early to be sure to get a good seat. They don't take credit card bookings for the late show, so I had to go down earlier.'

'And what time did it finish?'

'I really don't know. I wasn't watching the time. Suppose about one, one thirty. Something like that. I drove straight home.'

The questions went on and on. The answers come back just as assured and innocent. Behind Lynch's back Hamilton could see Dowling shake his head at her. We're gettin' nowhere. Move on.

'Dr Lynch would you be prepared to take an AIDS test? We believe we could eliminate you from our enquiries with the result of a simple AIDS test.'

Lynch leaned forward and rested both hands on the desk in front of him. His movements were slow and deliberate and he paused as if thinking through his response. Hamilton watched closely.

'Detective . . . sorry, I've forgotten your name again.'

'Hamilton, Detective Sergeant Kate Hamilton.' Her reply did not sound friendly.

'Yes, Detective Sergeant Hamilton.' Lynch rolled the words around his mouth as if he were savouring them. He looked straight into Kate Hamilton's eyes and she couldn't help but drop her gaze. 'I have no objection, at all, to taking any sort of test that will help. Especially one that would allow me to be, as you say, eliminated from your enquiry. However Professor Armstrong has directed senior staff not to become any more involved in your investigation unless they have a legal representative present. Indeed Professor Armstrong has actually advised us not to cooperate at all.' Lynch finished with a slight flourish.

Kate Hamilton couldn't contain her fury. 'Armstrong did what?'

Lynch leaned back in his chair, trying hard to suppress a self-satisfied smirk. 'Just as I said, Detective Sergeant. Professor Armstrong has directed all senior staff not to cooperate with the investigation. He's the one who does the hiring and firing at the hospital and all of us are more or less under orders to keep our contact with you to the bare minimum. I'll be happy to have a blood sample taken, but not until I've cleared it with him and had legal advice.'

Lynch's revelation about Professor Patrick Armstrong's interference with the investigation disrupted the interview completely. Kate Hamilton went into an immediate huddle with Tony Dowling and then despatched John Doyle to locate Armstrong immediately. The diversion also let Dean Lynch off the hook as the train of questioning was broken. Just as Hamilton was returning to him a knock sounded at the door and one of the investigating team looked in. He spotted Hamilton and beckoned her into the corridor where there was a hurried conversation. Her eyes lit up as she listened and she walked smartly back into the room and started packing away her interview notes.

Dean Lynch watched and then coughed slightly for attention. 'Is there anything else I can do to help?' He was the model of cooperation.

'No, that seems to be all for the moment, Dr Lynch. Thank you very much for being so helpful. I hope we didn't upset your routine too much?'

Lynch stood up, pushing the chair with the backs of his legs. 'Not at all. No problem. Sorry I can't be of more help. I keep myself to myself. Don't really get to hear hospital gossip so I can't really tell you much more.'

Hamilton forced a smile. 'No, you've been very helpful, really. Thank you. I'll have one of the officers show you out.'

'Don't bother. I'll find the way.'

He had his hand on the door when Dowling tried one last shot in the dark.

'Eh, Dr Lynch, did anyone actually tell ye how Mary Dwyer was murdered? Like did ye hear anyone say *exactly* how she died?'

Lynch paused, his hand almost stuck to the door. 'No. I didn't ask and I prefer not to indulge in idle gossip. The hospital's full of it. I didn't ask and no one asked me.'

Dowling stroked his chin thoughtfully. 'No one?'

'No, no one.' He looked at Dowling, then at Hamilton. 'Is that all?'

Dowling nodded. 'Thank you, Dr Lynch.'

As the door closed behind him Kate Hamilton turned to Dowling. 'He's made contact, Tom Morgan's made contact,' she announced gleefully.

'When?' Dowling almost shouted.

'Just now. His solicitor rang and said he'd like to come in and make a voluntary statement.'

This will be interesting, she thought, this will be very interesting. She smiled slightly as she packed her handbag. She would like to have smiled more but there was something about Dean Lynch that unsettled her. She decided to put him out of her mind for the moment.

Kate Hamilton wasn't out of Dean Lynch's mind as he walked along the pavement outside in Store Street.

What a little genius you are, Dean boyo.

He slipped past a huddle of women gathered round a uniformed Garda, each trying to outdo the other with their complaints about some grievance. The Garda pulled one of the women aside to let Dean Lynch by.

As Lynch made his way back to his car a spluttering and indignant Professor Patrick Armstrong was being led unceremoniously down the front steps of the Central Maternity Hospital to a waiting squad car for the short journey to Store Street Garda station. There he would be detained and questioned remorselessly before finally being released without charge. But not before a photographer and journalist from the *Evening Post* had been tipped off. They were waiting to record the man's humiliation.

Dean Lynch was settling all scores.

Jack McGrath wasn't at all happy.

There was very little information coming out of the wood-work. The underworld was being shaken to the roots but nobody seemed to know who had Gordon O'Brien, nor did anyone seem to have the faintest idea where he was being held.

The Jaguar Unit had swooped on every major and not so major criminal and subversive in the country. Their colleagues in the RUC in Northern Ireland had cooperated fully and a number of possible gangsters and paramilitarists had been rounded up and interrogated. Nothing came out of that particular piece of woodwork either.

Small-time criminals in Dublin and some of the major cities such as Cork and Galway and Limerick were taken into custody and grilled for information. Still nothing concrete or positive turned up. McGrath and his team finally decided the kidnap gang was not one of the big players in the criminal scene. They'd rattled so many of their trees that something would have shaken out by now. No, this had to be an opportunist gang, a bunch who didn't know what they had let themselves in for and were possibly now scared stiff. They would be aware of the national uproar and might well be panicking. They might panic so much they'd abandon the baby and make a run for it. And they might not abandon him somewhere safe. Jack McGrath's nightmare was of Gordon O'Brien being found dead in some ditch or bin and the gang melting back into the underworld whence he was sure they had come.

The Jaguar Unit held conference updates every twelve hours. Nothing. The Minister for Justice was in almost hourly contact with the incident room, her calls becoming more and more frantic.

Jack McGrath felt he just needed something out of Big Harry, a name, a description, an accent, some little clue as to who was behind this. He called over to Beechill again and asked for a meeting.

'Is there anything, anything at all, you can remember about the first two men?'

Harry O'Brien was sitting in his study in the same seat he had been strapped into the night his child was stolen. He looked much better than when McGrath had first seen him. The gibbering and ranting and wild-eyed hysterics had abated. Big Harry was back at the helm. Haggard, drawn and worried as he was, he had dressed smartly in casual slacks and Aran sweater over Viyella shirt. His hair was combed to order and there was life back in his eyes. But it was obvious he was struggling to maintain his composure. He wanted everyone to know he was pulling the strings, calling the shots. Theo Dempsey was at home on a round the clock vigil beside the telephone awaiting instructions from the kidnappers. Sandra sat on a leather sofa to the side watching anxiously, her beautiful features contorted by worry and fear and lack of sleep. As far as she was concerned the die was cast and she didn't want anyone trying to change Harry's mind or stalling the ransom pay off. She wanted her baby back. Before it was too late.

'Mr O'Brien,' McGrath asked again, 'please try and help us. Is there anything, anything at all you can remember about the first two men.'

Harry O'Brien looked up and held McGrath's gaze defiantly. 'No.' His voice was strong and even, his demeanour controlled. But his brain was still in turmoil, a mixture of terror, shame, sleeplessness, and defeat. He was finding it difficult to focus on anything other than getting

Gordon back. He had listened to Sandra crying unconsolably night after night, unable to sleep or eat properly. He had developed severe chest pains, so bad the local Roundwood doctor had to be called out immediately. An ECG confirmed what everyone suspected, Big Harry wasn't having a heart attack, just a stress attack. The big man knew then that he'd had enough. He'd like to help catch the bastards who had brought him and his family to their knees but he'd had enough. He wanted his baby back.

'You said one of them was a slightly smaller man,' McGrath pressed. 'Said he did all the talking?'

Harry nodded yes, then no, then yes again. Then he shrugged his shoulders. 'I can't remember.'

'Did he do anything or say anything? Was he wearing anything you could see that you can remember now? It doesn't matter how simple it might seem to you. His shoes, a glimpse of hair, smell of tobacco? Anything? Mr O'Brien, you've got to think. We won't find this gang if you don't give us any information. You were the one who saw most that night.' McGrath slumped back, exasperated and frustrated. He felt defeated for the first time in his many years in the force. He got up and walked slowly towards the door and was halfway out when Big Harry finally spoke, although everyone later remembered it as more of a whisper.

'He nearly shot me.'

The room went suddenly quiet, nobody daring to move or speak.

'The small one put a gun to my head.' Big Harry pointed an index finger to the exact spot, as if he could still feel the metal. 'He cocked it and pulled the trigger. I thought I was dead. But it mustn't have been loaded. I just heard a noise, like a snap.' He clicked his second finger as if he was pulling a trigger. His pointing index finger was the barrel, the finger still pushed against the middle of his forehead. 'Then he said, "The next one's for real".'

McGrath couldn't believe his luck, he just couldn't believe his luck.

'Tell me that again, Mr O'Brien,' he said gently, desperate

not to confuse the big man, desperate himself not to misinterpret the words. 'What did he do exactly?'

'The small one put a gun to my head.' Big Harry went through the motions again, pointing his index finger to his forehead. The room had gone deathly silent. Sandra O'Brien felt she shouldn't breathe at all lest she disturb Harry. She stared open-mouthed at Jack McGrath, watching the intensity on his face as he listened. 'He cocked it and pulled the trigger. I swear to God I thought I was a goner. But it mustn't have been loaded. It just seemed to ... to sort of make a snap.' He looked up at Jack McGrath as he finished. 'Do you think that's important?'

'What did he say then? You said he said something about the next one being the real thing, or something like that?' McGrath's eyes were half-closed, the lids flickering with the intensity of the moment.

Big Harry thought for about a minute, his brow furrowed, then he nodded his head. 'Yes, I'm sure of that, it's not something you're likely to forget. He said, "The next one's for real".'

Jack McGrath had come up trumps. 'That's Tommy Malone, that's Tommy Malone's trademark. That's who's got him, Tommy fucking Malone. That's how we got him the last time.' McGrath couldn't contain his excitement. 'The little bastard.'

He snatched the phone on the desk and punched ten numbers in quick succession. His excitement was infectious and everyone in the room strained to listen. Sandra rushed to Big Harry, kissed him on the forehead, grasped both his hands in her own and knelt down beside him. Her lips moved as she began to pray. Please God, let me get my baby back. She felt her hands squeezed and looked up to find her husband crying softly. She squeezed him back and continued praying. Please God, please God, give us our baby back.

The phone was answered and Jack McGrath shouted his instructions. 'Search the records immediately, then double check with Jaguar Unit sightings. Search under "seek and locate". Search under Thomas Malone, if nothing shows up under that name search under "Tommy Malone".' He turned his back on the audience and began a silent prayer himself, one hand cupped over the mouthpiece. The wait seemed ages but the voice at the other end came back with the confirmation he expected, the confirmation he was praying for. Thomas Malone had not turned up in the 'search and locate' part of the kidnap investigation. He was one of thirty-two known criminals who had still not been tracked down. He had been seen in Hal's Snooker Emporium recently. Hal himself had been questioned about criminal activities and meetings in his front room but had been his usual uncooperative self.

'Put out an immediate search for Tommy Malone. Contact all members of the Jaguar Unit and have them meet me in an hour in Pearse Street Garda station,' shouted McGrath.

He didn't even stop to explain to the open-mouthed audience what was happening. He was out the door and into his waiting squad car before they could react.

The hunt for Tommy Malone had begun.

At that precise moment Tommy Malone was waiting at Heuston station for Moonface to turn up. He was in exceptionally bad form. He had telephoned Theo Dempsey at three o'clock exactly and started to lay down the rules when Dempsey interrupted.

'We haven't got the money yet.'

'Waddye mean ye haven' got the money?' Malone had screamed into the phone. He couldn't control his agitation. 'If ye want that baby back alive ye better get the fuckin' money soon.'

'We're trying as fast as we can,' Dempsey tried to explain. He sensed the anger at the other end of the line. 'The courts have blocked our bankers from moving anything over fifty thousand out. I'm not making this up, you gotta believe me. Harry O'Brien wants his baby back and he's prepared to pay but the banks can't move the money, it's as simple as that. We're getting money in from an offshore account in

Jersey but it's going to take another day at least. You've got to give us another day.'

Tommy Malone stood in the phone booth, teeth chattering from cold and fear. Outside cars and container lorries moved slowly through the narrow roads along the quays. He wished he was in one going somewhere, anywhere. Anywhere but back to the cottage in Kilcullen armed with the news he was hearing. 'Tell yer boss from me he'll find his baby in the river if he doesn't have the money ready be tomorra, righ'? D'ye hear me?'

'I hear you.'

'I'll ring this time tomorrow. If there's no money I'll put Harry O'Brien's baby in a sack and drop him in the Liffey.' He hung up, cursing. And I fuckin' well will too, he decided.

He was in bad enough form even before he reached Heuston station, but was in worse form when Moonface didn't turn up for the 4.45 train to Newbridge. Nor the 5.20. He finally swaggered into the station just after 5.40, singing 'Olé, Olé, Olé' and wearing an Irish soccer team shirt under an Irish soccer team tracksuit topped off with an Irish colours scarf. He stood out like a beacon. 'Olé, Olé, Olé,' cheered Moonface to passers-by. Malone groaned. Moonface could see immediately that his boss was less than pleased. 'Cheer up Tommy, we're gonna knock the shite outa Englan'. Olé, Olé, Olé.'

It was 'Olé' all the way to Newbridge as people on the train looked and smiled at the simple-looking big oaf. If only they knew, he'd kill for thruppence. He was even warned by a uniformed Gardai on the train to behave himself. Oh, God, groaned Tommy Malone, half the shaggin' rozzers in the country lookin' for him and he's lurchin' about like a drunken sailor.

Whatever about Tommy Malone's reaction, when they got back to the cottage Sam Collins was fit to kill. 'The stupid, stupid bastard.' He turned on Malone. 'How did you let him get in that state?'

'Now don't annoy me, Sam, just don't annoy me.'

'What do you mean "don't annoy me"?' Collins mocked

291

Malone's Dublin accent as he shouted. The mixture of his Northern voice and attempt at Dublinese riled Malone and he took a swipe at Collins who just ducked out of the way in time.

'I'll fuckin' swing for ye,' Malone shouted and lunged at Collins, grabbing him by the shirt, tearing it slightly.

Moonface made a half-hearted drunken attempt to intervene and was pushed back against the sink by Collins who had squared up to Malone.

It was Peggy Ryan who broke them up with a lash of her tongue. 'Ye stupid bastards, I'll knock the shite outa the two of ye if ye don' stop fightin'. That child's not well in there and I think he needs a doctor.' She was screaming at the top of her voice and Malone let go Collins' shirt, scowling at him. Collins scowled back. 'Get yer act together, Tommy,' she shouted angrily, surprising even herself with her outburst. 'There'll be no money to collect if somethin' happens to tha' baby.'

The A-team was splitting at the seams. It hadn't burst, but it was definitely showing signs of severe wear and tear.

The row with Tommy Malone was the final straw for Sam Collins. 'I've had enough,' he snarled through gritted teeth. 'I'm fed up with this freezing cottage and with that squawking baby.'

The beery Moonface threw his hat in the ring. 'Sam's righ', Tommy. I'm fuckin' fed up too with this kip.' Moonface wanted it all to be over so he could go to the match. 'Olé, Olé, Olé. Any sign of the money bein' paid over yet?'

Malone was dreading that question. 'No, nothin'. I rang but Dempsey says it'll be tomorra before they're ready. Can youse not wait until tomorra? We'll be laughin' after tomorra.'

'They're not gonna pay, Tommy,' Collins shouted angrily. 'This was a mistake from the beginning. Let's get the fuck outa here, give them back their baby and let's go home.'

'Yeah,' agreed Moonface. 'Olé, Olé, Olé, I wanna go to the match. Stuff the baby. Come on Irelan'.' He made a scoring shot with his right foot and punched the air as he mentally watched the ball hit the back of the net. 'Olé, Olé, Olé.'

Collins looked at him with contempt. 'Let's call it a day, Tommy.'

By now Tommy Malone saw little point in arguing. The whole country was against them and now *they* were ganging up on him. 'Waddyou think Peggy? Where's Peggy? Peggy, where are ye?' Peggy was in one of the bedrooms staring at the baby. Malone came to the door. 'Ye better come out, Peggy. We've somethin' to discuss.'

Peggy looked up anxiously. 'There's somethin' wrong with the baby, Tommy. He doesn' look a bit well.'

Gordon O'Brien was not well, not well at all. He wasn't hungry, his breathing was rapid and shallow, he was tiring. He had bacteria in the bottom of both lungs and they were multiplying. Gordon O'Brien was developing pneumonia, thanks to the constant inhaling of Tommy Malone's cigarettes and the half-hour walk in the bitterly cold air, courtesy of Sam Collins.

Brian O'Callaghan was quite right. A tiny baby shouldn't have been out in that weather.

And Gordon O'Brien was a tiny baby, who'd had enough. He was tired of this life already. I'm too tired, too sick to carry on much longer, he'd say, if he could.

The *Evening Post* had yet another scoop. NURSE MURDERED. It carried exclusive reports and pictures including a half-page colour of the murder scene complete with yellow tape, yellow screen, white-suited forensics and Dan Harrison snapping away. A leader column made much of the state of the nation with biting comments on kidnappers, murderers, drug barons and the like. There was also a quarter-page photo of the Central Maternity Hospital, with the dramatic headline: IS THE KILLER STILL IN THERE?

This was more or less what many anxious patients in the wards were wondering themselves. They started to look at the doctors and nurses and security men and hospital porters with an intensity that unsettled. Some mothers were putting two and two together and coming up with a hundred. And it would only take one to start the stampede.

At 6.20 the Gardai broke down the door of Tommy Malone's house in Anderson's Quay. Tommy was so used to this in the past that he never left any incriminating information or evidence. While milk cartons were emptied and their insides examined, floorboards lifted, the roof space inspected, the supervising Jack McGrath knew already he wasn't going to find anything. He left five men to continue and drove with a team of six from the Jaguar Unit to Hal's Snooker Emporium, well known as Tommy Malone's favourite haunt.

Hal was leaning against a pool table admiring the bottom of one of the female players when Jack McGrath and five of the Jaguar Unit burst inside, two of them carrying the doorman by the armpits. McGrath made straight for Hal who backed away as he watched McGrath first spot and then run towards him. Hal turned to escape but ran straight into the waiting grasp of two of the unit who bundled him unceremoniously out the door and down the concrete steps. A small crowd of the pool players ran to the windows and watched as the protesting Hal was pushed roughly into the back of a waiting squad car.

'Waddyiz wan' with me?' shouted Hal as he tried to scramble out the other side of the car. A heavy hand grabbed him by the hair and thrust him back inside.

'I'd like you to assist us with our enquiries into the kidnapping of Gordon O'Brien,' Jack McGrath said politely, his voice restrained at first. Then he grabbed Hal by the throat and shouted into his face. 'We know already, Hal, so no fucking bullshit. This is one of Tommy Malone's jobs. We know that Hal, and this is big, Hal. We're not talking here about GBH, or a bank job, or a drug deal, or anything like that. We're talking about the biggest crime ever.' To emphasise the point McGrath stuck a newspaper up against Hal's face. 'You've seen the papers, Hal, and you know every dog on the street is baying for this gang's blood. So let me put it to you this way, you either help us or we'll put the word out that you were in on it from the beginning.' The blood drained from Hal's face. 'Waddyou say, Hal? There's a lot of hoods out there going crazy the way the place is shaking. A lotta hard men are ready to sell their grannies down the river to get us off their backs. If the word gets out that you were in on this, Hal, you'll not be playing snooker, you'll be playing the fucking harp. And it won't be in the National fucking Concert Hall.'

Hal identified Moonface and Sam Collins from a collection of mug shots at the Serious Crime Squad HQ in Harcourt Square. He didn't know who the woman was. 'I don' know. Okay? I just don' fuckin' know.'

McGrath believed him. He had enough anyway. He took the three mug shots to Phoenix Park and an emergency meeting with Commissioner Quinlan, the squad cars screaming through the late evening traffic.

Quinlan didn't hesitate. 'Release them to the press and TV channels. Get them on the nine o'clock news. I'll ring the Director General of RTE immediately and clear it. I'll ring Alice Martin as well so she can confirm this with RTE. Now go, for Christ's sake go.'

37

'My name is John Buckley of Buckley and Partners, Solicitors. Here is my card. I have been asked by Dr Tom Morgan to represent him here this evening. I would like immediately to put on record that Dr Morgan has come to this station on a purely voluntary basis. After discussing the situation very carefully with him I have advised a full and frank disclosure of his activities to clear the air so that you can rule him out of any involvement in the murder of the lab assistant, Mary Dwyer. I believe that is the reason you wish to interview him?' The solicitor smiled, putting a row of uneven teeth on display.

Dr Tom Morgan was dressed in a muted pinstripe suit, unlike one of his usual Armani or Hugo Boss collection. He wore a plain white shirt, navy and white flecked quiet tie, his handsome face was still and strained and he looked as subdued as the clothes he was wearing. John Buckley sat beside him, a small, fat man squeezed into a suit he'd long grown out of.

'My client is aware the investigating team wishes to interview him in particular.' Buckley settled some papers on the formica-topped desk, followed by a thick legal textbook, pages noted by slips of paper sticking out. 'Before you ask my client any questions, I would like to make a short statement on his behalf.'

Kate Hamilton frowned. There was no mention yet of

Nurse Higgins. She decided to let that ride for the moment. Dowling and Doyle sat behind Morgan and his solicitor.

'Dr Morgan gave incorrect information to the investigating detective as to his whereabouts on the night of Tuesday, 11th February 1997.' Buckley read from a prepared text on the paper in front. 'Dr Morgan is a married man with three small children. His marriage is not a happy one and indeed has not been so for many years. Mrs Morgan is an alcoholic who has been in and out of treatment many times. She is currently going through a bad spell.' He coughed slightly. Morgan stared at the table, his face expressionless.

'On the night of Tuesday 11th February, Dr Morgan was in the company of a friend from around nine pm and spent the whole night with that person.'

'Who? Where?' Hamilton butted in.

Morgan looked up suddenly at her but just as quickly turned back to an absolutely fascinating scrape in the corner of the formica-topped table.

'Dr Morgan was in room one hundred and eleven of the Gresham Hotel with a Dutch national all night.'

'What was her name?'

Buckley coughed slightly again. '*His* name is Jan Pietersen. He is an old friend of Dr Morgan and they often meet up when he's in Dublin on business. On the night in question Mr Pietersen and Dr Morgan met in the bar of the Gresham and had drinks. They then had a meal and later went to Mr Pietersen's room for a few more drinks.'

Hamilton tried to keep a straight face, not as much as a flicker of surprise showed. Behind, Dowling and Doyle's mouths dropped open.

Buckley paused, then continued. 'Dr Morgan was too drunk to drive home and decided to stay the night in the room with Mr Pietersen. We have been trying to contact Mr Pietersen all day to confirm these details but his office in Amsterdam informed us that he is out of the country on business again and not expected back for two weeks.' He consulted another page of paper. 'He's apparently in the west coast of America. We have sent faxes to all possible destinations but they have not yet been answered.' Buckley paused again and looked up.

Kate Hamilton maintained her Buddha-like expression.

'My client,' continued Buckley, 'recognises the stupidity of his action in not disclosing exactly his actions and where-abouts but he was trying to protect his wife and children and did not want it known that he might be so inebriated himself that he would be unable to drive.' Buckley looked up and a weak smile flickered. 'I mean it's bad enough having one drunk in the house.'

Buddha Hamilton said nothing.

'Dr Morgan would like to apologise for his behaviour and hopes that, when taken in the context outlined, it may be understood. Not accepted, but at least understood.' He stopped.

'This is off the record, Detective Sergeant, but there is no way, just no way, that Dr Morgan could have been involved in that young girl's death. While we have been unable to contact Mr Pietersen today we will be able to contact him sometime. Maybe not tomorrow or the next day, but some-time. And he'll be able to corroborate Dr Morgan's story. And when he does it will be patently obvious that he couldn't possibly have been in the hospital during the hours that murder took place.'

Buckley sat back on his chair, felt how uncomfortable it was, and leaned forward again. Tom Morgan had found a chip in the formica in which he was now engrossed.

'Are there any questions you would like to ask of my client at this juncture?'

Hamilton reached down and retrieved a thick brown paper bag which was resting at her feet. She placed it on the table. Buckley and Morgan watched closely, as if a rabbit was about to leap out. The bag was turned so that its open end faced towards Morgan. He tried to ignore it.

'Dr Morgan, where were you between the hours of eleven o'clock and one this morning?'

Buckley's face creased in a puzzled frown. 'I'm sorry, but what ha – '

'Forgive me, Mr Buckley, but I would appreciate if you didn't interrupt. You did ask if we wanted to ask Dr Morgan any questions.'

'Only relating to the incident on Tuesday, 11th February.'

'You didn't stipulate that Mr Buckley, and we have a separate inquiry on our hands which I would now like to discuss with Dr Morgan.'

'If you don't mind, I'd like to confer with my client first. I had no idea we were dealing with anything other than the events of last Tuesday. Dr Morgan came here on a purely voluntary basis to clear the air about the incident last Tuesday night.'

'Murder, Mr Buckley. The "incident" as you so delicately describe it was a very brutal murder.' Hamilton looked at her watch. 'Are you aware of any other incident your client may wish to discuss here and now?' She gently pushed at the paper bag, easing out a see-through plastic Evidence Bag containing a thick medical textbook. Buckley looked at it.

'I'd like to confer with my client for a moment if I may?'

Hamilton took off her watch and set it on the table in front of her. 'You have five minutes, not a second longer. Before you go perhaps Dr Morgan would like to have a closer look at this?'

Buckley looked sharply at Morgan but he had the look of a stunned mullet. Hamilton slipped on a pair of surgical gloves she had pulled from the side pocket of her navy jacket. Delicately and dramatically she pulled apart the top of the plastic bag and let the book slip onto the desk. She pulled a pen from her inside breast pocket and flipped open the front cover, revealing a cut out recess in which rested a Panasonic VAS cassette recorder with clip-on microphone extending to the spine. Buckley and Morgan stared. And stared. Their faces were scrutinised closely by Hamilton, Dowling and Doyle. Buckley quickly recovered his composure, cleared his throat and coughed nervously.

'Five minutes. Not a second longer.'

While Buckley and Morgan conferred frantically in the outside corridor, Hamilton conferred with her two colleagues. They agreed it was going well so far, but Dowling voiced a suspicious doubt that was niggling at the back of each of their minds. 'He's either a superb actor or he's clean. When ye opened that book he didn't look to me like a man who knew the game was up.'

'Let's hope he's an actor,' muttered Doyle.

'Yeah,' agreed Hamilton, but not wholeheartedly. There was still something wrong with this.

The door opened and Buckley and Morgan came back to the desk again, this time looking a lot less confident.

'I'd like to remind you, Detective Sergeant, Dr Morgan is here on a voluntary basis. I may advise him to leave at any point to seek further clarification if I'm unhappy with the way this interview is going.' Buckley had on his best stern face.

Hamilton was back to being a Buddha. Still wearing her surgical gloves she pressed the rewind button on the cassette player, watching as Buckley and Morgan followed her every movement. She pressed play and turned up the volume. The voices of the investigating team could be heard, not distinctly, but enough to get the gist of what was going on. What they heard was a discussion about Staff Nurse Sarah Higgins and how she had agreed to turn up at nine o'clock to be taken down to Store Street station to listen in on alibi interview checks.

'Where were you between eleven o'clock last night and one o'clock this morning?'

Morgan looked at Buckley who nodded. Go on, tell them, his eyes said.

'I was in Guys Club in Dodder Street.'

Hamilton's Buddha crumbled. Dowling and Doyle almost fell out of their chairs. Guys was Dublin's most notorious gay club. It was a small basement unit with tiny bar and lounge, steam rooms and saunas at the back. Indeed there were enough steam rooms and saunas for about twenty people. The bar and lounge couldn't hold that many, so the steam rooms and saunas were in fairly constant use. One of the tabloids had done an in depth investigation on Guys and reported it as the only steam/sauna complex that had a condom dispensing unit prominently displayed.

Hamilton regained her composure slightly. Buckley had now taken to inspecting the same fascinating scrape on the formica table.

'Guys? You spent the whole night in Guys?' There was no disguising the disbelief in her voice.

'Yes.'

'On your own?'

'No.'

'Well?'

'Sorry?'

'Well if you weren't on your own, who was with you?'

'I can't remember.'

Buckley couldn't suppress the groan.

'You can't remember?'

'No. I honestly can't remember their names.' Morgan was embarrassed, as embarrassed as hell.

'*Their* names. Was there more than one?'

'Yes.'

'Like how many?'

'Three.'

'Three? Male or female?'

There was a nervous cough and fiddling with tie. Stud Morgan caught out. And how.

'Male. They were all male.'

Hamilton changed tack quickly. 'Do you know a nurse who works at the Central Maternity Hospital called Sarah Higgins?'

Morgan looked real worried now. 'Yes.'

'How well do you know her?' Hamilton was leaning over the desk, towering over the once proud Adonis, now a nervous wreck.

'Well, sort of, eh . . . well I once had a drink with her.'

'Cut the crap. Weren't you at one time sleeping with her?'

All this was gleaned that afternoon from Morgan's wife, slurred and all as she was, and from Higgins' nursing friends at the hospital.

'Yes. But what's that to do with Mary Dwyer?'

'Dr Morgan, are you homosexual? No, let me change that. Are you bisexual? Do you have sexual relationships with men as well as women?'

The interview room went stony silent. Buckley wanted to interrupt but recognised it would be futile.

'Yes. Yes I do.'

'Dr Morgan, do you have AIDS?'

Buckley exploded. 'This is a voluntary interview,' he shouted at Hamilton. He was on his feet, clutching the edge of the desk to restrain his rage. 'If you don't explain why this line of questioning is being pursued I'll have no option but to advise my client not to answer any further.'

Hamilton sat down slowly and gently, motioning to Buckley to sit down as well. His body language showed his disgust with her but he sat down, scowling. Morgan slumped in his chair, hands trembling.

'Let me explain why I am so interested in Dr Morgan's movements last night.' Hamilton stretched her surgically gloved hands out fully on the table. Buckley and Morgan waited expectantly.

'Sometime between eleven and midnight last night, Staff Nurse Sarah Higgins was murdered. Her body was found in the boot of her car. She had been struck from behind with a hammer which fractured her skull. She was then strangled with blue binding twine.' She stopped. Buckley's mouth dropped open and he gulped, like a fish in a water tank. Tom Morgan seemed to crumple further inside his suit, like a slow puncture in a balloon.

'When we opened the boot of the car this morning, stuck into her neck was a scalpel blade. It was buried so deeply that only about an inch of the scalpel holder was visible. And that's what we found in Mary Dwyer's neck too, the night she was murdered. And we've been wondering all day why Nurse Higgins was singled out. And now we know. Someone has been recording every word we spoke down in the library where we held our conferences. We discovered no less than three thick textbooks that had been hollowed out deliberately and inside each was a cassette recorder and microphone. And what did we find in your room today, Dr Morgan, but a hollowed out textbook and cassette with our words clearly recorded? And a scalpel and size twenty-three blade. Who was this one for, Dr Morgan?'

Buckley was on his feet again. There was less heart in his anger, though, it was more resigned. 'Detective Sergeant Hamilton, I am terminating this interview. Dr Morgan came to make a voluntary statement and I am now advising him to leave this station immediately and not answer any more questions. Come on, Tom.' He snapped his fingers and Morgan struggled like a man who'd been hit by a sledge hammer. He turned to go towards the door and then turned back. 'I didn't do . . .'

'Tom, don't say another word. Get out of there this minute.'

But Tom Morgan only got as far as the outside footpath where he suddenly felt the restraining hand of Kate Hamilton on his right shoulder. He turned around, scared and bewildered. Buckley looked on, shaking his head.

'Tom Morgan, I am arresting you on suspicion of the murder of Sarah Higgins on 16th February. I must inform you you are not obliged to say anything unless you wish to do so, but anything you do say will be taken down in writing and may be given in evidence.'

Morgan's mouth opened and closed, but nothing came out. Kate Hamilton was already in deep conversation with the Member in Charge. He listened carefully, noting Morgan and his solicitor. He noted in particular that Doyle was keeping a very close eye on Morgan. Finally he nodded his agreement and turned to Morgan.

'Tom Morgan, I am satisfied there are sufficient grounds to detain you under Section Four of the Criminal Justice

Act 1984 for the proper investigation of the crime for which you have been arrested. You may be held for a period of six hours. You may be held for a further period of six hours with the Superintendent's authorisation. You may also, with his authorisation, be asked to provide a blood or other sample for testing in connection with the offence. If you obstruct the taking of any such sample you may be charged with such obstruction under Section Two of the Criminal Justice Forensic Evidence Act 1990. I should warn you that charge alone carries a twelve-month gaol sentence and or a fine of one thousand pounds.'

Tom Morgan almost collapsed.

Moonface was fast asleep, the beer having dulled his already dull brain to the point of stupor. He lay on his small bed, curled up for heat. Even though the electric fire was on full it had barely taken the chill out of the air.

Peggy Ryan was still worried about the baby. He hadn't cried for a feed for almost eight hours and his breathing seemed very rapid. She put the back of her hand against his tiny forehead, it felt hot. It was very hot. Gordon O'Brien had developed a fever, he was even more unwell than Peggy Ryan thought.

'Tommy, I think we should get outa here tomorrow. Leave the baby outside some hospital and let's go home.' Sam Collins had made his mind up definitely. The squawking baby was one thing, the freezing, damp kip of a cottage was another, but seeing Moonface stagger in shouting 'Olé, Olé, Olé' was more than he could take. Malone's losing it, he'd decided earlier. He was always a loser and he'll always be a loser. It's time to bail out. It won't be the first time one of his jobs has gone wrong and it definitely won't be the last. But gone wrong it certainly has and I'm getting out before that stupid big bollox pulls the rozzers on top of us. Malone's a loser. He's not gonna drag me down with him.

Collins by now couldn't stand the sight of Moonface and he hated the look of Peggy Ryan and her mutterings. He was rationalising his position in his mind, planning his exit.

'Are ye out then?' Malone asked angrily.

'I am, Tommy, I've had enough. I've been listening to the radio all day and we're bad news. Every rozzer in the country is after us. They won't pay that money out Tommy, and you know it. We shouldn't have rushed into this, we should've thought it out better.'

Malone knew there was no point arguing with Collins, he was too headstrong. He decided on one more try, one more attempt to keep his A-team together and salvage his 'big wan' from total disintegration.

'Sam, Dempsey said they'll have the money by tomorra. Jaysus, it's only wan more day. Could ye not give it wan more day?'

'Tommy, I'm not gonna give it one more night. I'm gonna get outa here as soon as we can. I'm telling you, Tommy, we're bad news, the whole country's looking for us. I'm getting outa here in the next few hours, just as soon as I think it's safe to move.'

'Look, Sam,' pleaded Malone, 'lemme give Dempsey wan more call and then we'll decide wan way or the other. I mean he could have the fuckin' money in a bag as we're arguin'. He could be waitin' for us to call. Lemme give him wan more call.'

'Suit yourself, Tommy. But I'm warning you,' Collins wagged a finger, 'if he doesn't have the goods, I'm off. Right?'

Malone was already pulling his coat on, searching among the dirty dishes for the car keys. 'Righ', Sam. Just wait'll I give him wan more call.' He turned towards Peggy. 'Is that all righ' with ye, Peggy?'

'Righ',' said Peggy. She felt she owed Malone the few hours more he was asking. But she was more worried about the baby at that point. She wanted out as well. Out and away from the baby. 'Tommy, I'm worried about tha' baby. He's very pasty lookin'. Hasn' takin' a bottle nearly all day.'

Malone inspected Gordon O'Brien who was asleep, mouth slightly open, and breathing rapidly. His lips were slightly blue, which Malone put down to the poor light.

It wasn't.

'We'll leave him till the mornin'. If he's no better we'll drop him outside Naas hospital and make a run for it.'

Peggy felt a bit better about this, but Sam Collins couldn't have given a toss one way or the other. As far as he was concerned they could dump him on the moon. The little bollox hadn't shut his mouth since the night he was lifted.

'Will ye stay with Peggy and hang on until I'm back?' Malone asked Collins. 'If Moonface wakes up he'll go spare if he's left on his own.'

Collins didn't like this one bit, but listened as Malone explained why two of them couldn't go out together.

'The place is swarmin' with cops. Nah, let me do wha' I have to do and I'll be back within the hour. I'm only goin' as far as Firhouse. It's only twenty minutes down the road. I don't wanna use the phone in the village again in case somewan spots me and wonders why I use it so often. Somebody has to stay and keep an eye out. Ye can't expect Peggy to, not with Moonface in a fuckin' coma.'

Tommy Malone eased the Volvo down the lane, headlights lighting the hedgerows. As he did the Nine O'Clock news on RTE scooped the world with the first pictures of Gordon O'Brien's kidnappers.

'Gardai have released the first pictures of three men they would like to interview in connection with the kidnapping of baby Gordon O'Brien, son of Harry and Sandra O'Brien. They are Thomas, better known as Tommy, Malone originally from Dublin's inner city and now with an address in Anderson's Quay in Dublin; Martin, also known as "Moonface", Mulligan originally from Limerick but now thought to be based in the Rathmines area of Dublin; and Sam Collins, originally from Newry in County Down but last known to be living in Swords, County Dublin. The men are described as . . .'

As the Volvo moved out on to the Kilcullen road, in his cottage across the fields Brian O'Callaghan stared at the photographs intently.

*

'Gardai have warned that these men are heavily armed and very dangerous. If any member of the public sees them, or knows of their whereabouts, they should on no account approach. Instead they should contact their nearest Garda station or telephone the Garda confidential hotline. The number will appear on your screens now and will be repeated throughout this news bulletin. Gardai are also looking for the woman who took part in this kidnapping. It is possible she may be an older woman, possibly with children of her own or well used to children.'

The newsreader sifted through the pages in front of him and turned to autocue again.

'In other developments Gardai in Store Street confirmed they are holding a man for questioning about the recent murders of two female members of staff of the Central Maternity Hospital. It is understood the man in question is one of the doctors attached to the hospital.'

Dean Lynch threw his head back and howled with laughter. He howled like an animal over prey. It's worked! It's fucking well worked! Dean, boyo, you're a little genius. It's worked!

He was sitting in his flat, bags packed and ready around him. He checked again all drawers, clothes and under the floorboards and laughed again, a sort of a howling laugh. He went through the motion of carrying the bags, working out the best combination. Three in his right hand, two in his left hand. He walked around the flat holding them until he reached the point where he felt he had to stop. He practised this for another hour until he had the plan worked out to the last minute. Then he sat down, turned off the TV, turned off all the lights and switched on the burglar alarm. Sitting in the dark, resting, relaxed, for all the world he looked like an animal saving its strength for a long hunt.

Which is more or less what he was planning.

'Now I don't want to be botherin' ye people and God knows ye have enough to be doin' without me takin' yer time up. But . . .'

'Yeah?'

'Well it's about that wee kidnapped baby. Now I don't want to be gettin' people inta trouble and mebbe they're right dacent people really. But . . .' said Brian O'Callaghan again.

That was how the Gardai found out where Gordon O'Brien was being held.

10.05 pm

'Betty? Is that ye?'

There was a sudden intake of breath at the other end of the line. 'What's yer number? Gimme yer number an' I'll ring ye back.'

'Wha's goin' on, wha's – ?'

'Gimme the bloody number,' Betty screamed.

Tommy Malone squinted at the number on the box in front of him and called it back. 'Betty wha' . . .' The line went dead. Malone stood looking at the mouthpiece for almost a minute before he had the wit to hang up and wait for the return call. What the fuck's goin' on?

Less than three minutes later the phone rang and he snatched at the receiver.

'Jaysus, Tommy, ye're all over the news.'

'What?'

'Ye're all over the news. Yer picture was on the nine o'clock news with the other two fellas. The kidnappin'. The police are on to ye for the kidnappin'.'

'Christ!'

'Jaysus, Tommy, ye better come up with somethin' better than tha'. I'm tellin' ye, half the country's lookin' for ye and those other two.'

'Betty, can ye put me up for a coupla days?'

'Jaysus, Tommy, ye better not come next nor near me. I'll pick ye up. Don't ye put a step near me until I've checked. Where are ye ringin' from?'

Tommy Malone looked around desperately. 'I'm in a call box in a pub along the Naas dual carriageway.'

'Stay there, don' move. I'll come and collect ye when I've checked.'

'I'm gonna warn the others. I'll ring ye back. I'll ring ye back in an hour.'

'Tommy, for Christ's sake don' come near me an' don' ring me at the house. Ring me in Mooney's in half an hour.'

'Righ'.'

It was already too late.

As Tommy Malone drove back towards Newbridge and the turn off to Kilcullen he was overtaken by eight different squad cars, their lights flashing but their sirens quiet. He followed at a respectable distance, his heart sinking as he watched them take every turn he was just about to take. Finally he pulled into a lay-by when he spotted them setting up road blocks on the road into Kilcullen.

'Jaysus, I'm sorry, Sam. I'm sorry, Moonface. I'm very, very sorry, Peggy. It just didn't work out. It's goin' wrong for me again. I'm a fuckin' loser, that's all there is to it. I'm a fuckin' loser.' He actually whispered the words in the dark as he watched two plainclothes detectives with their UZI sub-machine-guns join the checkpoint.

Jaysus, I better lie low.

As Tommy Malone planned his next move, six detectives walked down the narrow steps that lead to Guys Club, just off Dodder Street. Never would so many be frightened by so few in such a short space of time. The small bar and lounge was relatively quiet but in the steam rooms it was standing room only, so to speak.

'This is not a raid, so you needn't panic.'

The barman panicked, his eyes flitting all over the place.

One old man holding the hand of one much younger suddenly developed an intense interest in his empty glass of beer, while the rest turned sideways, backways and anyways to shield their faces.

John Doyle dropped a photograph of Tom Morgan onto the counter.

'Have you ever seen this man before?'

The barman put on a real studious look, as if he was actually examining the photograph, then shook his head, stopped as if to rethink, then firmly shook it again. 'No, I can't say I have.'

'That's funny, because he says he was here late last night with three other men.'

'Did he?' The reply sounded so surprised, eyebrows disappearing under fringe for effect. He re-examined the face closely, turning the photograph this way and that in the dim light.

Two of the club members tried to make a hasty exit but were restrained. The barman noticed this and decided to be a bit more forceful. 'No, I've never seen this man here, ever.'

'Are you sure? This is real important for him. And if you're not straight with me I can tell you it might turn out to be very important for you too.'

'I've never seen him in my life before. I was here all last night and I can tell you he was definitely not here.' This time he was most emphatic. And so were the rest of the club members when shown the photo. The detectives just couldn't believe how many were in the back steam rooms as they politely asked them to come out, one by one, and have a look at the photograph of Tom Morgan. John Doyle said later that if he had shown each of them a photograph of themselves they still wouldn't have seen that face before.

The membership book was inspected and all the false names scanned. If Tom Morgan had been there the previous night he either didn't sign in or did so, like the rest, as James Murphy. The team had never seen so many James Murphys under the one roof at the same time.

'Big Murphy fan club, haven't you?'

The barman just smiled and offered a drink on the house. The team decided to take up the offer and discussed, real loudly, about how sad it was no one could remember seeing the man in the photograph. 'Because he's in big trouble now. Now he mustn't have been here, in Guys, as he said, but somewhere else instead.'

They finished their beers and let those words linger in the smoke and steam after them.

Things weren't looking good for Tom Morgan.

But things were looking very good for Dean Lynch.

He had waited until the corridor outside his flat was quiet for almost an hour and all lights quenched. Then he silently opened the door, placed the bags outside and turned on the TV and the double burglar alarm before slipping down the fire escape to the fire door. Here he placed the bags down and eased the door open, courtesy of the small metal bar in place, then placed the bags outside. Gently, but firmly, he closed the door and set off towards his new car, the 'wee beauty' from Dinny. No one noticed the small, bulky frame, dressed in black and wearing clear-lens glasses, as he noiselessly skirted the back of the apartment block. Within minutes he was on the quiet road beside the complex, then into the car, bags thrown along the back seat. Gently and carefully, he lay the briefcase on the passenger's seat. Dinny's 'wee beauty' started after a few chugs and was soon on its way to Booterstown. As Lynch drove he threw a backward glance at his flat window, where one light still glowed and the TV churned out whatever rubbish the all-night cable channel had to offer.

Dean Lynch arrived in Booterstown just before midnight and was soon inside his new rented flat.

It was time for the final stage, the settling of all scores.

It was time to go into positive action.

It was time for revenge, the mother of all revenges. Every hurt, every slight, every unkind comment had been noted. The enemy had been identified.

It was time for the enemy to suffer, to suffer as much as he had done.

And he had suffered a lot.

'Is the baby all righ'?'

Tommy Malone climbed into the Datsun.

'Yeah, yeah. He's fine.'

'Jaysus I hope so, Tommy. The whole country's up in arms abou' this. They're bayin' for yer blood. We'll swing for this wan, we'll swing for it if they don' get tha' baby back.'

'Just drive the fuckin' car, will ye? Get me the fuck outa here. The road's swarmin' with cops.'

Betty gave him a filthy look, switched on the engine and eased the car out and back along the Naas dual carriageway. She noticed she seemed to be driving against the main flow of traffic. Everyone seemed to be heading towards Newbridge, and everyone seemed to be in a squad car.

'Are ye sure that child's all righ'?'

Tommy rounded on her angrily. 'Didn't I tell ye he was fine? He's fine. I'm tellin' ye. Fuckin' sight better than me.'

But Tommy Malone was wrong. Gordon O'Brien was very unwell. The bacteria spreading throughout his lungs were already spilling into his blood stream.

Tommy Malone had misjudged the baby, misread all the signals.

Day 9

The Jaguar Unit was in place.

Jack McGrath had been notified by the local Gardai in Newbridge of a possible sighting of the kidnap gang. He scrambled the full Jaguar Unit and they assembled in Brian O'Callaghan's farm cottage. O'Callaghan was beside himself, dishing out pots of tea and sandwiches, fussing around like an old woman.

It was decided that a reconnaissance group of three would approach the other cottage and place two listening devices near the front and back windows. They slipped out into the moonlit night and across the fields. The ground was hard and frosted, there was hardly a breeze. As they moved sheep bleated in surprise and cantered to the shelter of the surrounding hedges. There they stopped and watched as the three shadowy figures climbed over a bank that separated part of the field from the whitewashed cottage. One of the group made a positive identification of Sam Collins and reported back.

'Collins definitely, a woman carrying a bundle, probably the baby, though there wasn't as much as a whimper out of him. There's no sign of Mulligan and definitely no sign of Tommy Malone.'

A detailed discussion then followed on methods and when and how. Front door or back? Stun grenades or not?

'Better not,' said McGrath. 'We don't know how that might affect the baby.'

The final group of six detectives decided on an armed assault.

'There's no use trying to reason with them, or telling them they're surrounded and to come out unarmed,' McGrath explair.ed. 'There's no knowing how they might react. They're dangerous and probably desperate. The chances are they'll hold the baby as some sort of shield and try and make a break for it. The baby could get hurt.'

What really forced the issue, what really determined an early, rather than prolonged siege, was the woman. She'd been picked up on one of the listening devices. 'Tha' child's lookin' very sick. I'm very worried abou' him.'

Back-up ambulances were ordered, one to be staffed by a nurse trained in paediatrics. A decision was made to transfer Gordon O'Brien as soon as possible to the Central Maternity Hospital paediatric wing, no matter what condition he was in.

The six detectives dressed themselves in black from head to toe. They wore black cloth caps firmly pulled down over their heads, black vests, thin black sweaters, thicker black sweaters over that, and black tracksuit tops. Finally came black flak jackets, a special order from the RUC in Northern Ireland. Their faces were then smeared with black camouflage polish. Each carried a Smith & Wesson .459 automatic pistol. Three had these strapped just above ankle level, freeing their hands for heavier artillery. One chose an UZI sub-machine-gun as his main fire power while the other two decided on Hechler & Koch MP5 machine-guns. The three-man reconnaissance group advised gloves against the bitter cold and all six slipped on tight conforming black leather gloves.

'Right,' said Jack McGrath grimly. 'Let's go.'

Brian O'Callaghan went down on his knees with a pair of rosary beads and prayed like he had never prayed in his life before.

The plan was simple. It had been rehearsed in a mock-up cottage near the Templemore training barracks in Tipperary many times. The Jaguar Unit knew how to storm buildings ranging from cow sheds to five-star hotels.

Two would take the front door with a small explosive charge, while three would go in through the back door. One would go through the only window that looked vulnerable. The baby complicated and compromised the plan a great deal, there could be no smoke bombs, no stun grenades, no wild shooting. In addition to the six-man assault squad there was a back-up of seven other armed detectives, primed to go in at the first sign of difficulty. There were at least twenty unarmed uniformed Gardai deployed around the target. There would be no escape route for the gang.

They went in just before one am.

Moonface had woken from his drunken slumber in a foul mood. 'Where's Malone?' It wasn't *Tommy* any more, it was now *Malone*, as in I'm pissed off and fed up and freezin' and where's Malone to get us outa here? He picked up his handgun and started cleaning it at the kitchen table. There was still heat in the fire and he pulled closer for warmth.

Outside, through the kitchen window, Jack McGrath watched carefully, noting the gun. He motioned his partner to watch out for it and he nodded back. There was no sign of Collins or the woman or the baby, but the outsiders looking in now knew the layout of the house. There were three bedrooms, one with a window that could be entered quickly. The other two rooms had windows that were too high or too small to be of any use.

Inside, Sam Collins had taken himself to bed, wrapped in a sleeping bag and as many blankets as he could find, including those he had pulled off Tommy Malone's bed. He promised to kill him when he came back, he'd been gone well over four hours. For a while Collins wondered whether Malone had actually done a runner, then dismissed it out of hand. Apart from the baby, he wouldn't leave Peggy Ryan, the two were old buddies. Even in Dublin underworld circles where personal feuds erupted regularly, you still looked after your own during a job. What you did with them afterwards was a different matter.

As the explosion blew the front door off its hinges and into the small entrance porch, Jack McGrath hit the back door with a large sledge hammer and it gave way immediately. The sound of breaking glass confirmed one of the unit was on his way into the side bedroom. In his still recovering drunken state, Moonface's reflexes were just that bit slower than usual.

Which was a pity.

For Moonface.

He stood up, big mouth wide open with surprise, desperately fiddling with his handgun to get off a shot. Jack McGrath's reflexes were razor sharp and a short burst from the UZI ended Moonface's chances of going to the big match. For ever.

Sam Collins couldn't get out of the sleeping bag in time to put up a struggle. Within seconds he was pinned to the floor, a heavy boot rammed against his neck and the tip of the barrel of a Smith & Wesson .459 dangerously wedged inside one of his nostrils. 'Move and your head comes off.' Which was an unnecessary warning in the circumstances.

They found Peggy Ryan in tears, beyond being frightened, peering into the travel cot. She knew it was all over and she was glad, she'd had enough. She looked up at the blackened face.

'Ge' a doctor quick. I think he's dyin'.'

1.47 am

'Help, Mummy, help! Stop, stop! Stop him Mummy!' Rory woke up screaming.

Kate Hamilton ran and lifted him with one movement, feeling his tiny body tremble with fear. 'Shush, shush, it's all right, Rory, it's all right. Shush, shush, Mummy's here. It's only a bad dream. You're all right, Mummy's here, shush.' She held him like there was no tomorrow.

'What's the matter? Were you having a bad dream?'

Rory was still sobbing, his fingers gripping her arm so tightly it pained. He could hardly get the words out.

'What's wrong, pet? You're all right, Mummy's here.'

But Rory let out a wild shriek that chilled the marrow. 'He's after you! Look out Mummy! He's after you!'

She clasped him tighter, feeling his heart pound so strongly it almost matched her own. My God what a shriek, what was he dreaming about? What the hell did he see on TV? Thankfully Rory slumped back to sleep, thumb in mouth, Ted in hand. She placed him gently back in his own bed and stroked his head in the dark, kissing his forehead. Even in the gloom as she watched his tiny chest rise and fall she could make out his father's features in him.

'Don't worry, Rory,' she whispered. 'Mummy's going to be all right. I have to look after you. There's no one else to look after you. There's just the two of us. Don't worry, Mummy's going to be all right.'

2.17 am

Dean Lynch woke up soaked in sweat. The nightmare was back and she was after him. Again.

'Come back here, Dean Lynch! Come back here!' She was chasing him along the darkened corridors of the orphanage. He ran and ran but he knew she would catch him, she always did. He looked behind to see her gaining, the black hair shaken free and loose, her long white bony hands stretching out towards him.

'Come back here, Dean Lynch. Come back here.'

'No, no, no! Leave me alone, leave me alone.'

He ran round another corridor, then another, then suddenly realised her footsteps had stopped. He stopped and listened, all he could hear was his laboured breathing and his laboured heartbeat. Where is she? He crept slowly and quietly to the next corner, peering around. No one. He crept to the next, past open doors that led only to blackness. He peered around. No one. Then he started around the final corner. It was always the final corner in his dream as it had been in real life. Slowly, but surely, dragged as if by some powerful force, he came closer to the under-stairs door.

His own Hell. Where the blackness always seemed so black, the darkness so dark. He turned to run away.

Straight into her grasp.

That white, white face with those dark, black, wild strands of hair. Those thin, long, bony hands that held him fast and hard. There would be no escape. He tried to scream, then tried again, but the noise would not come out, as if stuck in his throat. One bony hand restrained his strongest struggles while the other pulled the door open.

'No, no! Please! No, no!' He thought he was shouting, but still the words would not come out. His struggles were no use, she was stronger.

Bucking and threshing he was forced inside the small under-stairs space, his arms and legs pushing against the closing door which squeezed him back.

'No, no!' His screams finally came out, his pain burst. 'Stop, stop!'

But the door always closed, it *always* closed, against his weak and weakened body. He slumped down behind it, sobbing and pleading. And always, always he heard that voice.

'You can sleep in hell now, Dean Lynch. You can sleep in hell.'

But this time the voice was different, this morning the face had changed.

It was Kate Hamilton who was persecuting him.

He walked around the floor, agitated and trembling, his heart racing, his body drenched in sweat. He pulled open the briefcase and unsteadily rocked at the inset until it came free. The gun was sitting snugly, the bullets well secured.

He fixed a syringe of heroin and injected slowly. Very slowly, very, very slowly and as he drifted into oblivion he smiled. He could see the gun, he knew how to use it and he knew who was going to feel its might.

'He's dead. There wasn't much chance of him surviving that, he's dead.'

A white-coated and exhausted-looking doctor was staring at the ambulance trolley in the corridor outside the casualty department of Naas General Hospital. On the trolley lay the body of 'Moonface' Michael Mulligan, late of Limerick, Rathmines and this world. He placed two fingers on Moonface's carotid pulse and shook his head wearily. Then he shone a light into the pupils of Moonface's eyes, noting their lack of response. He looked again under the red blanket draped across the body and saw the green soccer tracksuit top, now heavily blood stained.

'There's not much point bringing him in here,' he said to the two ambulance men.

'We need you to confirm it, Doctor. Once you give us the nod we'll take him over to the hospital morgue.'

He gave the nod.

'You'll have to notify Dr Noel Dunne. He'll need to be informed about this.'

The doctor looked at his watch and yawned. 'I'll ring him later this morning. I can't see him climbing out of bed at this hour. Take him to the morgue and ask one of the Garda to stay with him all night.' He yawned again, it had been a difficult and long night.

'I can't get a vein, I can't get a vein! His veins are totally shut down.' Inside the casualty department of Naas General Hospital five doctors were gathered round the tiny body of Gordon O'Brien. He was lying on an examination couch, wrapped in what looked like tin foil in a desperate attempt to raise his body temperature.

He was a very sick baby. A chest X-ray showed pneumonia with consolidation throughout both lung fields. An oxygen-saturation monitor strapped to his foot showed his blood oxygen level was very poor. His breathing was fast, laboured and shallow, his lips blue, his body cold, his core temperature low. They couldn't get a vein for an IV line, his circulatory system was so severely compromised from septicaemia and shock. The bacteria had spilled into his general blood system and were multiplying fast.

He was in grave danger of dying.

'Get me a sterile instruments tray and cannula and fresh frozen plasma,' barked the senior doctor on duty as he washed his hands under hot running water. He dried them quickly and slipped on a pair of sterile surgical gloves, watching as nurses made their own basic observations on the ominously still baby. One was recording time and temperature while another unpacked green drapes, preparing for surgery. A third nurse had already set up IV fluids on a stand and was waiting for the next order.

One of the other doctors began swabbing Gordon O'Brien's neck area, noting how unresponsive the child was. The green drapes were then drawn around the baby's neck, leaving only a small area exposed. Within three minutes a cannula had been inserted through the neck and into the jugular vein. 'Okay, run in the plasma. Give him fifteen millilitres per kilogram stat over the next ten minutes.' The fluids started dripping in. Blood was taken for culture and sensitivity, other bloods taken for biochemistry and haematology. Volume expanders, antibiotics and dopamine were next in line for intravenous infusion.

When the Naas resuscitation team felt they had done all they possibly could, the still limp body of Gordon O'Brien was laid inside a pre-warmed incubator and transferred to a waiting ambulance. The IV lines were attached to a small infusion pump, then carefully strapped so as not to be disturbed.

'Go, for God's sake. Go like the clappers and don't stop for anything.' A nurse rushed out, clutching the blood samples, and jumped into the back of the already moving ambulance just before the doors shut closed.

The siren started.

The ambulance screamed along the Naas dual carriageway towards Dublin with a four-man motorcycle escort. Ahead at every junction, a uniformed Garda was waiting to stop any traffic, ensuring a safe and steady passage for Gordon O'Brien who was going back to where he had come from on the first day of his life.

A second siren-screaming cavalcade had passed that same way only an hour earlier. In the middle was a reinforced Garda mini van with bars on the windows and special seating which allowed for the occupants to be handcuffed. Inside sat the mute Sam Collins and the sobbing Peggy Ryan accompanied by four of the Jaguar Unit, their guns still cocked and ready for action. Their elation at the successful mission was marred only by the state of the baby. Going through each of their minds was the dreadful thought: we're too late. Some of the unit had small children, others had had small children now grown up. All could remember them as babies and the anger they felt threatened to spill over. Four sets of angry eyes drilled in on Sam Collins. Just one stupid move, just give us one excuse.

4.32 am

Dr Paddy Holland snatched at the telephone through a blur of sleep.

'Yes, yes, who is it?'

'Dr Holland?'

'Yes, speaking.'

'Dr Holland this is Staff Nurse Angela Matthews in ICU. We have an emergency coming in by ambulance and the baby's supposed to be in a very bad way. Dr Conway told me to contact you immediately and ask you to come in.'

Holland sat up slightly in bed, resting on one elbow. 'Dr Conway? Dr Luke Conway?'

'Yes. He rang a moment ago and told me to ring you immediately.'

'But why? What's Dr Conway got to do with this?'

'He just told me to ring you and ask you to come in immediately. Apparently the baby's very sick.'

Holland swung his legs over the side of the bed, yawning and scratching, still holding on to the handpiece. 'Do you know anything more?'

'Can you wait one second, I'm going to close the door?'

The phone was laid down at the other end and Holland could hear voices, then the sound of a door closing. He wondered what was going on. The phone was picked up again.

'I'm terribly sorry, Dr Holland, but I couldn't let anyone else hear. It's baby Gordon O'Brien, he's been found. There's an ambulance bringing him in right this minute. He was found in a cottage in Kilcullen. A doctor from Naas hospital rang and said he looked very sick.' She paused slightly and then whispered, 'He said he didn't think he'd make it.'

Holland was already half way into his trousers. 'I'll be there in five minutes.'

He pressed on the receiver to get back the dialling tone and quickly punched in seven numbers. After ten rings a sleepy and annoyed voice answered. 'Yes, who's that?'

'Conor, it's me, Paddy. Paddy Holland. Look I'm desperately sorry to ring you but could Mary come down immediately and mind the children?'

'What!' Incredulous. 'At this hour of the morning?'

'Yeah. Look I'm real sorry, Conor, but I've just been called in on an emergency. I shouldn't be on duty but this is something very big.'

At the other end of the line a mixture of curses and mumblings could be heard. All the time Holland kept an eye on the digital clock at the side of his bed, watching it tick away the seconds. 'Conor, it's the little kidnap baby. I shouldn't be telling you this. But it's the little O'Brien baby. They've found him and he's on his way to the hospital. He's supposed to be in a bad way.'

There was a stunned silence at the other end.

'She'll be down in about half an hour. Give me enough time to get her up and dressed.'

'Conor, I'm going now. I'll leave the front door key under

the mat. Ask her to ring me when she gets here. And Conor, I'm real sorry about this. Tell her I'll make it up to her somehow.' Mutter, mutter. 'And you too, Conor.'

5.07 am

'Oh my God, he looks dreadful.'

Paddy Holland's first assessment of the limp body of Gordon O'Brien as it was carried into the ICU of the Central Maternity Hospital was not good. Then he swung into action immediately.

'Okay, get core rectal temperature and record it. I want two fully trained ICU nurses with him at all times. I'll need to set up a radial arterial line. Get a full blood count, biochemistry and arterial blood gases on those first samples now. I'm gonna take a fresh set this minute. I want all results phoned through here immediately they become available and let me know straight away, even if I'm not here, even if I'm in the toilet.' As he spoke the nurses were already working from intuition and experience. Blood sample bottles were in place, their request form details filled in. A line to establish the baby's central venous pressure and stabilise it was ready for insertion. There were two technicians waiting down in the laboratory for any fresh specimens; they had already started on the samples taken in Naas. It was an early start that morning.

'Double the drip rate of the antibiotics. Did they weigh him in Naas?'

'Yes.'

'Good, work out the dose of dopamine and check it with me.' He turned to look at the baby, still inside the incubator. He was flat and unresponsive, without even a whimper of protest or hunger. His eyes were sunken, there was only an occasional twitch of an arm or a leg.

I don't think you're gonna make it, thought Holland.

Gordon O'Brien was fighting for his life again.

5.32 am

'They've got him! They've got him! Harry, quickly, get dressed. They've got him. They've just rung from the hospital. He's there! He's there!' Sandra was half-sobbing, half-screaming as she shook her husband.

Big Harry was stumbling round the plush white bedroom trying to get into the clothes Sandra threw at him.

'Is he all right?' he shouted as he struggled to fasten the belt around his waist and at the same time slip his feet into a pair of shoes.

'Yes, yes, he's in an incubator and has some sort of infection but he's alive. Come on Harry, let's go! He's alive! They've got him!'

She was right on both counts.

They had him and he was alive.

But only just.

The bacteria were still multiplying.

6.01 am

'Tom Morgan? You can't be serious? You're joking me?'

Paddy Holland and one of his ICU nurses were sipping tea and munching on toast in the office beside ICU. A window gave them a direct view of all incubators inside and Gordon O'Brien's incubator had been moved so that he could be seen at all times. He was connected to three separate monitors, one for his heart, the blue tracing flickering across the screen constantly while a second recorded the CVP line and the third recorded his respiratory rate. At present all three were stable. There was one other baby in the unit, a little girl under close observation after her difficult birth.

'No, I'm not. One of the girls is married to one of the detectives in Store Street and she told me last night.'

'I just don't believe it.'

'Well I'm telling you, it's true.'

'My God.' Holland chewed on another slice of toast and sipped on his tea. He caught a momentary glimpse of his own reflection in the office window and groaned. Dammit, I look awful. He hadn't had a chance to wash or shave before he rushed in.

The phone beside him rang. It was his niece, Mary, ringing to confirm she had reached the house.

'How are the children?' Holland asked anxiously.

'They're fine, Uncle Paddy. They're fine. They're still fast asleep.'

'Thanks, Mary.'

'Don't worry, Uncle Paddy, I'll mebbe get the day off school. How's the wee baby?'

'Not great, Mary, he's not great.'

'Will I pray for him, Uncle Paddy?'

'That's a good idea, Mary, that's a very good idea. Say a decade of the rosary for him. Bye.'

'Bye, Uncle Paddy.'

The kids hate it, absolutely hate it, when they wake up and find I'm gone, thought Holland as he tried to put some semblance of order back into his bedraggled hair. He sighed deeply, the toast like sawdust in his mouth. What a bloody awful existence for them. No mother and a father who disappears like a thief in the night. What a life for them.

'Apparently they found something in his room when they raided it yesterday.'

'Oh, what?'

'I haven't a clue, he didn't know that bit, but apparently it was all to do with something they found in his rooms.'

Holland looked inside the ICU, catching one of the nurse's eyes and she so-so'd to him and turned back to the baby.

'They nearly pulled the place apart. Dr Conway was furious. I mean the wards are half-empty as it is but when they started walking through the corridors, hauling boxes of stuff out from here and there, it was more than most people could take. I heard another twenty-three discharged themselves against advice last night.'

'Oh no,' groaned Holland. 'I don't believe you.'

'I don't know what the place is coming to. The girls are scared stiff. There's no one wants to do night duty. If something doesn't happen soon I can see the whole hospital closing down. I mean it's hard to believe Dr Morgan would do such things but I hope it is him.'

Holland turned to her, astonished. 'Why?'

'Because it'll mean they've caught him. It means we can all sleep peacefully in our beds, not worrying the next night duty we're on we'll need a Garda escort to take us home.' The young nurse wiped her mouth with a paper towel, the anger in her voice barely suppressed. 'I just hope it is Dr Morgan, that's all. It'll mean they've finally got him.'

Paddy Holland stared through the window into ICU, confused and concerned. 'Well I'm telling you it just doesn't fit in,' he said, his brow deeply furrowed. 'I know Tom Morgan, I went to college with him. Sure he's a bit of a bollox, always thinking through his dick, but a murderer? No. That doesn't make sense, that just doesn't fit in.'

The nurse giggled at his language. She had never seen him like this before, so concerned about something other than his children or his work.

If anyone had asked me I'd have said Dean Lynch, thought Holland. Now he even scares the hell outa me. That's who I would have picked if I was in the detective business.

'It can't be Tom Morgan,' he stated again. 'Tom's too fond of women. He might screw them to death, but kill them, never.'

'Well I'm only telling you what's going on,' the nurse said defiantly. She was no great fan of Tom Morgan. She considered him a randy, irresponsible, reckless, feckless bollox. And anyway he'd stood her up on a date once.

Paddy Holland poured himself another cup of tea, sipped and pulled a face. The tea was cold. While he waited for the blood results and the nurses monitored Gordon O'Brien's battle for life, he had time to think about it a lot. It can't be Tom Morgan, it just can't be. And what could they have found in his room? Slowly but pressingly a vision came into his head. He looked into ICU again, trying to dislodge the image but the vision became stronger and he felt his heart beat slightly faster than usual. Oh my God, maybe that's it! Oh my God! Maybe that's it!

He pulled at the drawers furiously, throwing aside pathology forms and prescription pads until he found what he was looking for, the Dublin telephone directory. He flicked it open and tore at the pages until he reached G. 'Garda, Garda, Garda, where the hell are you? Gottit! Garda stations.' His finger ran down until he came to Store Street and he scribbled the number down on the back of his hand with a biro, then stood up quickly and went into ICU.

'Well?'

'No change.'

'BP okay?'

'So-so.'

'Okay, I have to make a quick telephone call. I'm just going down to my office. You can get me there.'

'Fine.'

In his office he shut the door and dialled.

'I'd like to speak to the duty officer.'

There was a pause, then apologies came back down the line.

'Okay, could I speak to Kate Hamilton, eh ... Detective Sergeant Kate Hamilton. The detective in charge of the Central Maternity Hospital murder investigation.'

The cautious voice at the other end wondered why.

'My name is Dr Paddy Holland. I'm a paediatrician at the hospital. There's something I've just thought of that may be important and if you don't mind I'd prefer not to explain it over the phone. Is there anyone from the case there at the moment I could talk to?'

The cautious voice said no, but offered to get in touch immediately with Detective Sergeant Hamilton.

'Could you? That would be great, thanks very much. I'll be at the hospital all morning. Tell her to tell switch to put her through directly to ICU.'

The phone rang again three minutes later.

*

Kate Hamilton was sitting on the side of her bed, half-awake, half-asleep, half-dead from exhaustion. The Garda from Store Street Garda station with the cautious voice had rung and passed on the message from Holland. He also told her they had finally got a doctor to do the AIDS test on Tom Morgan. They'd tried all the previous evening but somehow each of their usual duty doctors became unavailable, or had the flu, suddenly developing anything and everything as soon as they heard it was a blood test on another doctor. The shutters had slammed down and a different policy of non-cooperation was enacted. This time it was no master plan, just that inbuilt sense of self-preservation inherent in the medical profession when one of their own is having trouble.

The Garda also relayed the news of a fax just in from LA, from a Mr Jan Pietersen, confirming he and Tom Morgan had been together all of the evening and night of Tuesday, 11th February 1997. The fax added that Mr Pietersen could confirm this by affadavit or in person, but that would take about a week. Mr Pietersen had asked for confirmation that his fax had been received.

'Damn and blast it,' ranted Hamilton. 'Ring me as soon as you get that AIDS result, call me on my mobile.'

'Could I speak to Dr Paddy Holland?' She could hear a lot of commotion in the background, a woman crying and what sounded like a man sobbing. God almighty, what's going on there?

'Detective Hamilton? Hi, it's Dr Paddy Holland here. Look something's just after coming into my head about this murder enquiry. It may or may not be important but I think you should know about it.'

'Know about what?' Hamilton was trying to speak gently so as not to waken Rory yet urgently so as not to let Holland feel his information wasn't important.

'I'm sorry, I can't go into it over the phone, it's too delicate and important. And we have an emergency going on here.

We've a very sick baby and the parents have just arrived. Could you come in and meet me?'

Hamilton was already fishing for her clothes. 'I'll be in in an hour, is that okay?'

More crying could be heard down the line and Hamilton sensed a hand going over the mouthpiece of the telephone. Then Holland was back. 'Yeah, that'd be great. I'll be in ICU or the Special Care Unit.'

'What's that?'

'That's where we look after the low birth-weight babies. Second floor, West Wing. Okay?'

'Okay,' said Hamilton as she turned to wake Rory.

'Come on Rory, time to get up. Come on sleepy head, wakey, wakey.' Kate Hamilton lifted the still sleeping child and cuddled him awake. He yawned and clasped her tightly, pushed his thumb into his mouth and snuggled against her chest. She stroked his hair, stroked his head, stroked his face and kissed him. For some strange reason, she held him tighter than usual. For some strange reason she didn't want that moment to end but for some strange reason she felt it would. Kate Hamilton, for some strange reason, had a sense of foreboding, of impending doom. A shudder ran down her back and she found herself shivering, even though the radiators were on full blast and the room was warm. The two staggered over plastic railway tracks and engines into the kitchen where Hamilton rushed to get the breakfast cooked and get herself ready for the day at the same time. She glanced at the mess around her feet, then decided to ignore it.

'Come on Rory, finish off your toast, I have to go to work.'

Rory cocked an eye at her, one hand resting his head, the other inspecting the toast. 'Mummy?'

'Come on, Rory, I'll be late.'

'Mummy?'

'What is it? I hope you're not going to ask about a puppy again. I told you we're not getting a dog.'

Rory's face dropped, the toast dropped, a tear dropped.

'Damn!'

Half an hour later she dropped Rory off at playschool. 'See you later, give me a kiss.'

'Mummy?'

'Yes?'

'When can we get a puppy?'

'I'll talk to you later. I must fly. I'll talk to you later.'

Paddy Holland was talking to Harry and Sandra O'Brien at that very moment, trying desperately to comfort them.

'Your child is seriously ill, dangerously ill. We're doing all we can but he arrived here a very sick baby. The next twenty-four hours will be crucial.' Sandra fell to her knees at the side of the incubator; she was white and silent, but Big Harry couldn't hold back the well of tears he had been suppressing for days. He leaned against one of the walls and wept. Holland motioned to a nurse who came up and put an arm around Sandra, trying to console her as best she could. When Big Harry finally regained some form of composure, Holland sat him down on a chair and looked him straight in the eyes.

'Mr O'Brien, your baby's very ill but he's not, let me repeat that, *not*, dead. We'll do everything we can, we'll move mountains if we have to. But we'll not let him go without a fight. You and Sandra have got to help us, you've got to help *him*, as well.' He paused to let that sink in.

Somewhere in Harry O'Brien's mind a light flickered and then glowed. 'Tell us what to do, Doctor.' He wiped at his eyes with a handkerchief, then blew his nose. He stood up and went over to his wife and gently lifted her to her feet. He gathered her to him and held her tightly. 'What do you want us to do?'

Paddy Holland pulled two chairs over beside the incubator where Gordon O'Brien lay. His tiny chest was rising and falling rapidly, his limbs barely moving. His colour had improved somewhat, though.

'Sit there,' Holland pointed and then physically directed the parents to the chairs. 'Sit there and talk to him, stroke him, kiss him. Let him know he's back with his mother and father again. Let him know he's loved again. Give him something to live for. Make him want to live.' He turned to Sandra. 'Make that little boy want to live for his mother. Let him know you're beside him from now on. Let him feel your touch and hear your voice. Let him know he's home again.'

The change in both Sandra and Harry O'Brien was impressive. They turned back towards the incubator and began to fight for the life of their only child. Paddy Holland ushered the nursing staff outside. 'Keep an eye on his basic observations and let me know if anything changes. We've done all we can. It's up to God whether that child lives or not. But at least they . . .' he nodded inside, ' . . . at least they can feel they're doing something. If that child dies they'll know they were with him right to the end, battling with him.'

8.32 am

Tommy Malone was lying in bed in Betty's Greystones house listening to the news on Morning Ireland. Betty came in, ashen faced. She had listened in on the radio from the kitchen.

'D'ye wanna try some breakfast?'

Malone flicked a cigarette out of a packet and lit up, deep in thought. 'Nah. Thanks Betty all the same. Nah. I've some thinkin' to do.'

Ye sure have, thought Betty.

Some nurses called it the Life Chamber, their distinction
from the Death Chamber in execution-happy states in the
USA. It was a large room of about thirty-by-thirty feet with
eight separate open-topped incubators on which rested those
tiny babies born sooner than expected. Some of the babies
were connected to whooshing ventilators which artificially
breathed the oxygen they needed but did not have the
strength to obtain themselves. Most were under special
heating machines and oxygen-pumping machines. Each baby
had parchment-thin skin stretched over bones and tendons.

Each baby shared one distinct challenge: the fight for life.

The Life Chamber was where Kate Hamilton found
herself waiting for Paddy Holland.

'You can't come in. Would you mind waiting in the office?'
a nurse had asked.

'No, of course.'

The office had large clear glass windows allowing staff to
keep an eye on all activity inside the Special Care Unit.
Kate Hamilton stood and watched. She could remember so
vividly her own confinement and one day wandering lost
along this very corridor, coming to ask for directions and
stumbling across the Special Care Unit. She hadn't been
able to take her eyes away from it then and she still couldn't
that morning, the fight for life she witnessed was so dramatic,
the balance so delicate.

'Will he be long?'

'Hard to say. There's one little baby in there we're not too happy about. She's just had a brain scan. He's waiting on the result.'

'Which one?' Hamilton strained to see in further.

The nurse squinted inside. 'See the incubator he's at now? Well the one to his left, as you're looking. That one, on the left and at the back.'

Hamilton watched as Holland stooped to listen through a stethoscope to a small bundle lying under glaring lights. He stood up and gave a slight smile and she noticed the anxious look on the mother's face. He seemed unaware of the power he commanded. The nurses seemed unaware of the power they commanded. Their knowledge, skills and experience were powerful forces that moved among the cots and incubators. The forces of life.

Holland moved towards the at-risk baby and Hamilton could see him murmuring to the mother. He took off his glasses and massaged the bridge of his nose as he spoke. She noticed the woman's chest heaving, then watched her sobbing, clutching at a rolled up handkerchief. Holland then placed a hand on the shoulder of the father who was staring down at the incubator where his child lay, his face contorted.

'He's had a lousy day already and it's only just gone nine.'

Hamilton turned back to the nurse, now watching the drama as well. 'Why?'

'He's been in since about five, down in ICU with that little kidnap baby most of the time.'

'How's the baby doing?'

'Not great, from what I hear.' Oh God, thought Hamilton. 'Then we had this little girl deteriorating. He's been up and down between here and ICU since I came on duty.'

Hamilton looked back. Holland was now talking with one of the nurses who nodded as she drew something into a syringe, then double checked it with him. He turned around, noticed Kate for the first time and raised a finger, acknowledging he had seen her. Don't go away, the finger suggested.

'Then one of his children rang and gave out to him for

335

not being there when she woke up.' The nurse half-smiled. 'She certainly gave him a rough time.'

Hamilton smiled wryly. Don't I know all about that sort of pressure.

'Hi, thanks for calling in. Look I'm real sorry to keep you hanging around but things have got a little bit out of control here this morning.' He looked haggard and drawn, his face almost grey from tiredness and strain. Hamilton couldn't help but notice he was embarrassed about his appearance as he pulled self-consciously at the white coat he was wearing. His tall frame was slumped with worry and concern. He turned to the nurse.

'Call me when the scan result comes in. I'm going down to my office with Detective Sergeant Hamilton.'

'Kate'll do,' Hamilton interrupted.

Holland smiled and Hamilton found herself smiling back and being embarrassed at doing so, like being caught admiring a man and him suddenly noticing.

'Kate, you and I are basically in the same business,' Holland began, cleaning his glasses with the end of his tie.

Hamilton's eyebrows almost disappeared into her hair.

'We're detectives. You go around all day looking for little bits of information to try and piece together who did this and who did that and why they did it in the first place. You look for clues all the time.'

Hamilton nodded, not sure where this was all leading.

'I'm a detective too. When I'm dealing with some of my patients I look for little clues as to how they're progressing or why they're not progressing. I grasp at little bits of information, tiny scraps can give me an insight as to what disease I'm dealing with. Does this make sense?'

'I'm listening.'

'Okay.' He sat back slightly and then leaned forward suddenly and with an intensity that surprised her. His eyes were half-closed, the eye lashes fluttering as he recounted in the correct order his observations and conclusions. Both his hands were clasped together as if in prayer.

336

'You're looking for a murderer. I know many of the doctors here have been less than helpful and maybe held back from speaking their mind out of fear of leading you up the wrong path or incriminating one of their colleagues incorrectly and finding themselves in the High Court next year.' He stopped and looked directly at her.

Hamilton said nothing.

'So I'm going to come out and tell you, on the record, my thoughts on this whole dreadful mess, right?'

'I'm all ears.' She opened up her notebook and clipped a ballpoint pen into action. 'Fire away.'

'Some time ago one of the consultants who works here accidentally let his car battery go flat. He'd been called for a delivery in the middle of the night and forgot to turn the headlights off. When he finally came back to it, later on, I was pulling into the car park and he asked if he could get a set of jump leads onto his battery from mine. When he got the power back two sets of alarms went off at once in his car. Two *different* sets of alarms. The noise nearly lifted the heart out of me.'

He paused. Hamilton hadn't written a word yet, not sure she wanted a lesson in jump leads.

'Now I was real surprised at this. I don't know anyone who has two sets of alarms on their car, especially as the car itself was worth less than the cost of the alarm systems themselves.'

'How do you know?' Hamilton was taking a sudden interest.

'I checked. I was so surprised I made a note of who fitted the alarms and rang them. I wanted something like that for myself. I've had two cars broken into, one finally stolen. You get to be a bit fed up with that.'

'Don't I know.' Hamilton once had the embarrassment of having her Special Branch car stolen from right outside Store Street Garda station.

'Well the car alarm company remembered it as a special job. They told me they'd never had a request like that before, not even on a new Merc and especially not on an old BMW.

Like eight years old. The fella told me the alarm system almost cost more than the car itself. We had a good laugh at that. And then he said something strange.' He paused briefly, as if trying to collect his thoughts before proceeding.

Hamilton sat rigid in the chair, listening. 'What did he say?'

'He said he had never met anyone as unusual as this man. He said he was secretive and meticulous about tiny details, careful with every word. He said he thought he was a bit of a weirdo, hovering around while the alarms were being installed. He felt threatened by the man, and he was only doing a simple alarm job for him. Why should he feel threatened?'

Hamilton had a feeling of dread in her stomach as she listened. That earlier foreboding returned, the sense of impending doom.

'But he also said that when he was fitting the car alarm he accidentally dislodged a secret compartment in the door panel. He was threading some wires or something and the compartment came loose and fell apart. Now there was nothing inside the compartment when he looked but he couldn't help feel that compartment and the expensive alarms on the not-so-expensive BMW were linked.'

'Did he do anything, tell anyone?'

'No, that's the funny thing. He said that when he thought about it and weighed it all up he reckoned it was none of his business. But when I pressed him on this he finally admitted.' Holland paused slightly again.

'What? Admitted what?'

'That he was scared of this man. He said he was so frightened he preferred to keep what he'd discovered to himself and leave it. Life's too short, he said, to be stirring up trouble.'

Hamilton now knew this was it, *this* was the break they had been looking for.

'Then he asked me did I know who the guy was. And do you know what?'

'What?'

'I suddenly realised I felt the same way as the car alarm fella. I said no. And I said no because I felt threatened by him too. And I work with him, he's supposed to be a colleague. I couldn't for the life of me figure out why I should feel threatened, but I did. And that's why I said no, like the car alarm fella.'

'And who is the man. Who is this consultant?'

Holland didn't hesitate. 'His name is Dr Dean Lynch.'

Hamilton tried not to show any emotion. 'With respect, Dr Holland, it's not a crime to have two alarms on a car, even if it is a banger.'

'No, I accept that. But it's like I said a minute ago, it's a clue. We're grasping at straws, I know that.'

'What do you mean?'

'I know you've got Tom Morgan in gaol at the minute under suspicion of committing those murders.'

Hamilton started to interrupt but Holland continued.

'Don't ask me how I know, just take it I know. And I know something else, I know Tom Morgan from way back. He's a bollox, a womaniser, a horny bastard who'd screw the top on a bottle if he thought it'd give him a thrill. But he's not a killer. I rarely read people wrong. Certainly not that wrong.'

'Dr Holland . . .'

'Call me Paddy, if I'm to call you Kate. We're in this together, we've got to help each other.'

'Paddy, I appreciate your information, I really do. But without giving too much away I've got more hanging over Dr Morgan than a double car alarm.'

'Yes, I know that. You discovered something in his room, I believe.'

Hamilton looked at him sharply.

'Don't ask me how I know that either. I just know. So let me tell you another little scrap of possibly helpful information. It may mean nothing, it may mean something. I'm going to tell it anyway.'

He stopped again, cleared his throat and inspected his hands. 'I was called in yesterday morning early as well. We have a little pre-term baby girl who's not in good shape and I was asked to check on her. I slipped out of the house and was back within an hour, the kids didn't even know I'd been out.'

That wouldn't happen in my house, thought Hamilton. Rory would be clinging to me like a leech.

'I left the unit and went up to my office in the private wing to collect some paperwork. I didn't bother to turn the light on as there was enough from the corridors. I had just gone in when I heard a door close, the door next to mine and on the left as you come in. Now I don't know why I looked out but I guess I was surprised anyone else would be around at that hour of the morning. I just caught sight of enough of him to recognise who he was.'

'Dr Lynch?'

'Exactly.'

'So what's the big deal?'

'Dr Lynch doesn't have a private office. Dr Lynch makes a big deal about that. Dr Lynch makes a big thing about one thing and one thing only in this hospital, and that's that Dr Lynch does not see private patients at all. He's strictly a public patients' consultant only.'

'So he doesn't need an office in the private wing?'

'Exactly. He's just never in the private wing consulting offices. *Never*. He makes no bones about the fact that he loathes the place.'

'So why was he sneaking round them so early in the morning?'

'Well, Kate, that's what I was asking myself all day yesterday. And then it slipped my mind and only came back to me earlier when I heard about Tom Morgan. I do know Lynch was in early for a difficult forceps delivery, but that should have been it. He should have delivered the baby and quit. There was certainly no need for him to go up to the private wing.'

Hamilton frowned. She was getting nervous. This was sounding spooky.

340

'It was when I learned your team discovered something in Tom Morgan's room that it suddenly hit me.'

'What hit you?'

'That's where Lynch was so early in the morning.'

Her heart thumped. 'Are you sure?'

'Certain. You see Morgan's room is the last along that corridor. Lynch had to be coming out of it and nowhere else. There's nothing else along that corridor.'

Hamilton nodded quickly, remembering the geography of the private wing when she'd called on Morgan.

'So you think he planted something in his office?'

'I don't know what he was doing there any more than you do. I'm only telling you what I saw. The rest is up to you, you're the detective.'

'That's not what you said earlier.' She managed a grin.

'That was earlier. I do the observations. You'll have to find out whether they're relevant or not.'

Hamilton scribbled in her notebook and glanced quickly at her watch. 'Aren't the office doors locked in the private wing?'

'No, we were broken into once and three doors were knocked off their hinges. It's a hospital rule now not to lock doors or filing cabinets except in the security zone. That way if anyone breaks in they do less damage.'

'Anything else?'

'Yes. Lynch hates Morgan, hates the sight of him. It's common knowledge they'd be at each other's throats except for some careful rearranging of outpatient clinics and theatre duties so they're never in the same area at the same time.'

'Is this for serious? Doctors behaving like this? I mean it's bad enough having criminals carry on like this but you don't expect this sort of stuff from doctors.'

'It's unusual, I agree. Unusual but not impossible. I'm saying no more.' He allowed himself a grin at that. 'I don't want to end up in the High Court.'

'The High Court seems to have you guys by the balls.'

'I couldn't have put it more eloquently myself.'

For a split second their eyes met.

The phone on his desk suddenly rang and he snatched at it, annoyed at the interruption. 'Yes?'

She recognised the nurse's voice at the other end and watched Holland's face slowly drop. He sighed and massaged his forehead with his free hand.

'Okay. Ask the parents to come into the office and clear it. I just want myself and them. No one else. Anything from ICU?' More mutterings came down the line. 'Okay, I'll be there in about three minutes.' He put the receiver down slowly, his mind obviously elsewhere.

'Bad news?'

Holland looked back. 'Yes, very bad news. Our little pre-term baby girl isn't going to make it. She's had a massive intra-ventricular bleed.'

'Is that real bad?' Massive intra-ventricular bleed didn't sound great but it meant as much to Hamilton as a heavy nose bleed.

'I'm afraid so. It means there's been a large haemorrhage into one area of her brain, so large she won't survive it. She's really only being kept alive by the ventilator. As soon as it's turned off that's it, I'm afraid.'

'Can nothing be done at all?' Hamilton could see the parents' faces again and the way they'd stared at the little bundle in the incubator.

'No, not a thing. She was born at twenty-one weeks. We have a policy here of doing all we possibly can for babies born twenty-five weeks and over. Below that we can keep them alive but the end result isn't always great. You can hand over a severely mentally handicapped baby if you get too caught up trying to resuscitate very young, low birth-weight babies. We have one of the lowest infant mortality rates in the world in this country. We like to keep it that way and maybe even improve on it. But there's no use moving mountains to hand over a badly brain-damaged baby at the end. Parents appreciate your best efforts but they'd still like a normal, healthy baby at the end. We thought we could do more for this little girl.'

'God, isn't life a bitch?'

'That's not very politically correct language, but I'd have to say I agree with you.'

Hamilton was thinking about Rory and that dreadful nightmare. She wished she was home with him that very minute, just the two of them, maybe have a whole day to themselves, rather than the snatches of life they had to grab at.

'I'm gonna tell you something else, Kate. It's nothing to do with Dean Lynch,' he quickly added as he watched her eyes suddenly narrow. 'Whoever's killed those girls had better be caught quick. This hospital's in a mess, there's a total loss of confidence throughout the house. The nurses are now refusing point blank to do night duty.'

'We could arrange a Garda escort.'

'Yeah, I suggested as much. They still weren't happy. But the real crunch came about an hour ago. One of the mothers asked if she could take her baby out of here, out of the pre-term unit. The baby's wired to every monitor we've got, is on continuous ventilation, is doing well but still very much dependent on us. And still she wanted him moved to another unit.' His voice rose slightly. 'That child would die within five minutes if he was disconnected. I told her that. But she kept insisting she felt he was in more danger here than the hazard of a journey across the city to one of the other pre-term units. And all because of the bastard who's done this.' He leaned towards Hamilton. 'Find this man, Kate. Get him. It's not just me, it's every baby who's here, every mother still left in the wards, those fretting at home, feeling labour pains and wondering if she's going to come into a place of refuge or a hell hole.'

The phone rang again. 'Yes, yes, sorry. I'm coming straight away.' He looked back at Hamilton.

'Sorry, I've got to go. Hope what I told you is of some help.' He opened the door to go, then turned back. He looked straight at Hamilton, started to say something, then stopped. He looked embarrassed. 'Maybe . . . maybe when this is all over . . . eh . . . maybe we could go for a drink or something?' he mumbled awkwardly.

Hamilton smiled. 'Yeah, that'd be nice.'

Then he was gone.

'Hello switch? Can you put me through to Dr Dean Lynch? He's not in yet? Should he not be in by now? Anyone know where he is? Would you ask one of the security men to check and see if his car's in the car park? Sorry, my name's Detective Sergeant Kate Hamilton. No, no, don't say who's looking for him. I don't want to upset his hospital routine. This is a simple matter. I just want to ask him something.'

But Dean Lynch was not in the house.

Yes, he should have been as he had an operating list at ten and they were waiting for him up in theatre.

No, he didn't ring in sick or anything.

He was just not there.

He was five miles away, in Djouce woods outside Enniskerry, practising at being positive. Even at about fifteen feet from the target, Lynch had managed six out of thirteen hits so far. Two through the eyes, each eye. Three through the forehead. And one through the mouth. He liked that one particularly. He had red felt-tipped the lips carefully, making them extra thick.

Dean Lynch was being positive, and enjoying every minute of it.

As Kate Hamilton walked back along the corridor she heard the sobbing well before she saw the parents. They passed her in the corridor, comforted by a nurse.

Inside the Life Chamber Paddy Holland walked slowly to the incubator at the left and back of the room. The others, mothers on their own, mothers and fathers together beside their own tiny babies, turned their backs, they couldn't bear to watch. Holland looked down for a minute, maybe longer, before slowly and deliberately turning off the life support machines.

The lights went out.

Tom Morgan was released from custody just before eleven o'clock. He was allowed to slip out through a back door and away from the TV crews, photographers and journalists stalking the station since daybreak when word of an arrest in the hospital murders leaked fully. They were left kicking their heels, walking briskly and stomping at the ground to keep out the cold. The only movement was from one of Massey's funeral cars as it took some poor soul out from the adjacent morgue to his final resting place. A few of the photographers snapped at it anyway. What the hell, they reckoned, it might come in useful later.

It would.

Morgan's release was a blow to the investigating team initially. But with the fax from LA, his negative AIDS test result and the barman from Guys finally coming clean and admitting he had been in the club for most of Monday evening, they decided they were backing the wrong horse.

Hamilton briefed them on her conversation with Holland and a new, urgent, plan was drawn up. The target was Dean Lynch. Find and interview.

Lynch drove back from Enniskerry and parked on a side road well away from the flat in Booterstown. He had coughed a lot out in the cold, damp woods, coughed an awful lot. At one stage he coughed up blood. The cold air didn't bother him, in fact he was sweating. But the persisting cough, the blood and the sweats worried him.

Inside the flat he checked carefully no one else had been in before hiding the gun and the rest of the box of bullets under a floorboard he had prised up earlier and in which lay his syringes, needles and heroin. It was gently tapped back into place and a loose rug thrown over. He counted out two hundred pounds cash, slipped it into his pocket and set off for Dunnes Store in the nearby Stillorgan shopping centre. There he bought a fresh set of warm clothes in dark, muted colours, fresh warm underwear and socks and two pairs of black trainers. He also added a black tracksuit with hood to the shopping basket and a new crisp white shirt and dark tie. The collar size turned out to be one inch less than he usually took.

'I think you'll have to go for a smaller size. That one's hanging off you.'

The shop assistant was trying to be helpful. Lynch glanced briefly in the mirror, noticing for the first time just how much weight he had lost. His face was gaunt.

'Yeah, maybe I'll take a smaller size.' But even the next size down didn't fit.

'Look, I'm real sorry.' The shop assistant was embarrassed. 'You'll have to go into the juvenile section for the size you're looking for.'

Which is where he finally got the size to fit. The shop assistant remembered all this later. His small frame, his unusual, wild looking eyes, his persisting cough. She remembered it exactly.

All paid for, he spent a short while in Bewley's café sipping on a coffee. Then he made his way to the nearby chemist and bought a bottle of black hair dye before slipping round the corner to Arnotts shoe shop where he chose a pair of flatteringly thick-heeled black shoes, just enough to give him an extra two inches height. Careful planning. Dean Lynch was planning and was almost ready for the final stage. He was planning to get positive, real positive.

*

'What're ye gonna do, Tommy?'

Betty had been listening to the news on the hour and had brought in all the morning papers. Tommy Malone's face was splashed across the front of each.

There was plenty of the same with lots of background material and details of past jobs. His criminal history was set out in detail: 'Grew up in Dublin's slums and fought his way out . . .' There were even interviews with retired detectives who had crossed Malone over the years. 'He's dangerous, ruthless and a killer. He'll stop at nothing. He was one of Dublin's most notorious criminals in the late seventies and eighties, but the Gardai thought he had faded from the criminal scene recently. He's been in and out of prison a lot, always complaining he was unlucky to get caught. Well his luck's run out again. This time everybody's looking for him, even the underworld. He won't get away with this one.'

'I dunno yet, Betty. I just dunno. Can ye put me up for a day or so till I get me wits about me?' Malone was counting on Betty, relying on her loyalty.

'Sure Tommy. But ye better think of somethin' soon.'

'Let's stick together, Betty.' Malone had been thinking about this ploy for hours and finally decided to sound Betty out. 'When the storm's blown over we could go away for a while. I've got a bit of money, not a lot, but a bit. We could go to England, I've a few relations on me uncle's side there. They might hide me for a while. Wadda ye think?'

'I'll think abou' it Tommy, I'll think abou' it. Just keep yer head down. Would ye like somethin' to eat? Ye havin' eaten all day. Keep yer strength up. Nuthin? Jesus, Tommy, ye can't just sit there smokin' them cigarettes all day. All right, I'll leave ye alone. I'm gonna make meself somethin' to eat. Suit yerself if ye want anythin'.'

But Tommy Malone wasn't hungry. He'd been in the game long enough to know this one had gone wrong, badly wrong, terribly wrong. Moonface was dead, Collins and Peggy were in the Bridewell holding centre, the baby was in a critical condition and the whole country was baying for his blood.

He lit up another cigarette and blew smoke rings at the naked light bulb in the ceiling.

They're not gonna get me. Fuckin' sure. They're not gonna get me.

They're not gonna crucify me.

I'll stay wan more day here and then move out tomorra night. That's what I'll do.

Wan more day here and then I'm off.

3.17 pm

'Wait till ye hear this.' Tony Dowling and the team met as arranged in Store Street Garda station. 'I called to his flat. His car was parked in the reserved spot, engine cold, frost all over it. It couldn't have been driven for hours at least. I spoke with a few of the residents but none of them had seen him all day. An oul fella, a retired college lecturer, has the flat underneath and gave out yards about him sayin' he'd had the television on all night, all mornin' and it was still goin'. So I called up and knocked on the door. No answer. I could hear the telly all right so I knocked again, real loud like. There was still nobody in or if he was in he wasn' takin' visitors.'

Hamilton and the team listened like it was the sermon on the mount.

'So I hammered and hammered for a good ten minutes or so, then walked around the outside lookin' for any sign of movement. I could see the lights were on and the fella underneath said he thought they'd been on all night.'

'He's skipped the nest.' John Doyle stated the obvious.

'That's what I think too. But let me tell ye somethin' else very interestin'. Ye know the way Kate found out about his fancy car alarms?'

Heads nodded. Hamilton felt that sense of foreboding return, that sense of impending doom.

'Well, I made a note of the alarm company who installed

his apartment system. It's on the outside box, Sensor Alarms in Clondalkin. I rang them. And waddye know?'

'Don't tell me, he works for them.' Doyle got a nervous laugh for that.

'He might as well be. He instructed them how to put in the alarm. Instructed *them*. Was a real expert, according to the boss man. He remembered the job clearly, just like the car alarm fella. He remembered Lynch like it was only yesterday. He said he couldn' believe he wanted such an expensive and sophisticated alarm system.'

'Why? Why shouldn't he?' Hamilton was trying to tie up the loose ends, there still wasn't a lot to be hanging a double murder charge on.

'Because there's nothin' at all in the flat. The man said that when he put the system in there was hardly anythin' in the flat. A few bits of furniture, TV, radio, cooker, fridge, bed, settee. I mean there was little else apart from one room where he had a wall-to-wall mirror and a lot of weights for workin' out on. Ye know, pumpin' iron stuff.'

'Maybe he was only starting up. Maybe he was gonna get some new things in later.'

Dowling smiled triumphantly. 'I thought of that one too, Kate, and that's what I said to him. But he came straight back at me. He told me that about eighteen months later there was a power cut in the area and the alarm malfunctioned. Lynch couldn't reset it when he wanted to go out, called up the company and gave out yards. Demanded someone come down immediately and put it right.'

'And did they?' someone asked.

'Dead right they did. He insisted they check the whole wirin' again and double check the fail safe mechanism. And what do ye think he'd got new in that big flat of his since then that made him so nervous about the alarm bein' off for five minutes?'

No one spoke, Dowling had the audience to himself.

'Nothin', not a goddammed thing. It was the same as the last time, as bare as the first time they put the system in.'

'Jesus,' said someone.

'Apart from one thing.' If Dowling had said he knew the third mystery of Fatima and was going to reveal it he would never have had a more attentive audience. 'He had two voice-activating microcassette recorders hidden. One on top and to the back of the fridge, the other behind a curtain rail in his work-out room, clamped and screwed in place. He had his own fail safe mechanism if the alarm packed in.'

'Let's go.' Hamilton checked her Smith & Wesson. 'If this is really *him*, for God's sake be careful. Check your hardware.'

They arrived in three unmarked Special Branch cars. Dowling drove the first with Hamilton in the passenger seat and John Doyle in the back. The other two cars had three detectives in each, all armed.

They pulled up in the car park and two went to the side, two to the back and the rest paused for the go-ahead outside the apartment entrance. Dowling, Hamilton and Doyle led the way up the stairs and along the corridor to flat twenty-three. One elderly lady, dressed for an hour's shopping in Grafton Street, almost fainted when she opened her apartment door and walked straight into the oncoming team. They shushed and ordered her back inside, identifying themselves.

Dowling tapped on the door, gently at first, then more loudly. The noise from the TV inside could be heard.

He shouted a warning: 'We have a search warrant. Open the door or we'll have to make a forcible entry.'

Which is what they did. Three thumps from Doyle's sledge hammer and the door gave way, setting off two piercing alarms, the noise swamping their thoughts, dulling their curses, and driving John Doyle to take the sledge hammer to one of the inside sound boxes. Mercifully this stopped it, only the outside alarm box continued its whoo-whooing with blue light flashing. But inside the flat, apart from a Sky early evening news programme, there was no sign of life.

*

Outside Dean Lynch watched and listened to his alarms from the shadows of a darkened telephone box, his hand on the receiver in the speaking mode, one foot pushing the door slightly open.

He slipped the bullets into the magazine. One, two, three, four, five, six, seven, then clipped the magazine into place. Metal slid over metal as he fed one round into the breech. He unclipped the magazine and slipped in another bullet. Seven in the magazine and one up the breech, just like London John had taught him.

He watched for almost ten minutes until she came out.

'Pull the place apart.' Hamilton followed the team as they opened the fridge, ripped the mattress, pulled out drawers, prised at floorboards. They discovered the secret compartment and old syringes, needles, sterile water ampoules and green bags with traces of white powder that Lynch had overlooked when he fled the nest.

They discovered everything but Dean Lynch. Who was slowly making his way towards them, sheltered by the shadows of the late evening, hidden by the trees that lined the road.

'Tony,' she motioned to Dowling, 'I'd like a word outside.' The others stopped for a moment. 'Keep looking, bring anything important into the middle of the kitchen and we'll bag it. I want to get a forensic team down here. Everyone put on gloves. I'll be back in a minute.'

She walked with Dowling back down to the car park where she shone a torch into Lynch's car. There was nothing visible, just seats, seat belts, steering wheel, gear stick, the usual, but nothing else. The alarm company logo was etched on all four windows.

'For Jaysus' sake, Kate, don't break inta the car. Me head's still ringin' from that other alarm. The bastard's flown. I bet there won't be a scrap in there tellin' us where he's got to.' Hamilton shone the torch back inside again, but she knew Dowling was right.

The shadowy figure came closer, now only about fifty yards from where the two were standing.

'We better put out an alert and notify all stations. There's road blocks all over the place looking for that kidnapper. We'll need to warn them.'

Hamilton suddenly felt the sense of foreboding again, the sense of impending doom. She looked up and peered at the surrounding gloom. Nothing. Nothing that was unusual.

The figure in black, with hood pulled up and gun held down at his side, came closer, checking all the time he wasn't being followed or watched. One or two cars drove past but no one inside saw or noticed anything amiss.

'I'm freezing, let's get into the squad car and ring HQ from there.'

'I'm all for that,' muttered Dowling, blowing against his cupped hands in a vain attempt to restore some feeling to his numbed fingers.

Lynch finally crossed the road, walking casually and directly. He looked neither left nor right, eyes firmly fixed on Hamilton, watching as she opened one of the car doors and climbed inside. He watched Dowling climb in the other side and smiled. He half-suppressed a fit of coughing that tore at his chest and spat a blob of phlegm onto the road, tasting blood in his mouth again.

'Flick on the light, Tony, would you? I'm going to ring the hospital and see if he's turned up there. I can't see a thing in the dark.'

Dowling flicked the light above the rear vision mirror, noticing a slight movement, like a dark shape that came out and went back behind some bushes. He squinted through the steamed up window, rubbing a circle clear with the back of his right hand. Nothing moved again. He turned towards Hamilton as she talked to switch at the hospital on her mobile phone.

'No, Dr Lynch hasn't been in all day. I'm afraid no one knows where he is. It's very strange, they had to cancel a theatre list because he didn't turn up.'

'Where is the bollox?' muttered Dowling as he turned the engine on.

Hamilton looked at him suddenly. 'Where are you going?'

'I'm not goin' anywhere. I'm freezin'. I just wanna get some heat in the car. Relax, we're not goin' anywhere.'

Lynch made his final move.

He walked out from behind the bushes, Walther held down by his side, firm, purposeful strides towards the car with the inside light on, where he could clearly make out Detectives Hamilton and Dowling. Hamilton was still speaking into her mobile phone, Dowling wondering whether he'd go fishing that weekend for a break.

'Who's that?' Dowling suddenly noticed the figure, now only twelve feet from the car and flicked on the car headlights, fiddling for full beam. 'Who the fuck's that?' This time he shouted.

With his left hand Lynch pulled back his hood, revealing his face. Just as quickly he raised the gun, clasped firmly in both hands, cup and saucer style. Don't forget to shout, Bobby boy, don't forget to shout. Don't go for a head shot, go for the body. Heads can be ducked out of the way.

Kate Hamilton looked up in time to see the face in the headlights. The mobile phone dropped from her hand and she started to scream.

'Ah Jesus . . .' were the last words Tony Dowling ever spoke, ever roared.

The image of Rory, screaming in his nightmare, flashed across Kate Hamilton's mind as the flashes from the Walther PPK opened up.

Shooting against the beam of the headlights Lynch was slightly dazzled, his target indistinct. But he kept the pad of his finger firm and squeezed gently, each recoil confirming a successful discharge. London John had been a good teacher.

The first bullet passed through the palm of Tony Dowling's right hand as he held both up in a futile attempt to ward it off. The second entered the side of his left cheek, shattering gums and teeth, spinning his head around so that he was splayed momentarily across Kate Hamilton as she tried to curl into a ball. The third bullet entered the back of his head, ending his life. Hamilton felt his blood spurt across her face, heard his gurgling and grunts.

Then a sharp sting hit her right chest.

Desperately trying to crouch deeper and at the same time pull her own handgun into action she had no chance as the next bullet shattered the side window, tearing open her scalp. Only the searing pain kept her thinking. I'm still alive, I'm still alive, Rory. The splintered side window was smashed in by an elbow and she looked up to see Dean Lynch's wild eyes, a half-smile on his face as he pointed the Walther straight at her head.

The scream wouldn't come out, her throat constricted. All she saw was the flash before darkness closed in.

'She's stable, she's stable. She's lost a lot of blood but she's stable.'

Three trauma surgeons and four nurses were working on Kate Hamilton. She had taken a direct hit on her right rib cage, her third thoracic rib shattering but directing the bullet away from a major artery and out of her body. The splintering bone had punctured her lung, the resulting pneumothorax collapsing almost two-thirds of that lung. A considerable amount of blood had entered her right chest cavity. A second bullet had shaved the left temporal scalp but did not penetrate the bony skull. There was heavy bleeding from the wound also. The third bullet had entered and exited her left upper arm, tearing a large skin flap from which she had bled heavily as well. The surgeons decided not to graft that wound, it was better left until she was in a more stable condition. A rough estimation suggested she had lost about three pints of blood. It was a lot, but not fatal, she would survive. At that moment she was heavily sedated and breathing on oxygen via a face mask, with an intercostal drain at the upper right chest to re-expand the collapsed lung. A second drain had been inserted at the base of the right lung to drain away the collection of blood. An IV line trickled a Crystalloid infusion while a second IV line in her other arm trickled antibiotics.

'Get a full blood count, immediate haemoglobin and

haematocrit. I want a repeat chest X-ray in two hours, basic obs recorded every fifteen minutes, pulse, blood pressure and respiratory rate.'

Nurses busied themselves preparing blood sample bottles, ringing the laboratory for urgent access to results.

'Give her the first two litres Crystalloid over an hour. Let the third litre drip in over the next two hours. Keep both IV lines open, though.' The senior trauma surgeon barked his orders. It was all routine to him but it was life and death for Kate Hamilton.

She would survive, thanks to the immediate attention. Unlike Tony Dowling, who did not.

He was lying in the hospital morgue, pronounced dead on arrival by one of the casualty officers.

'Take her up to ICU. Anyone know who did this?'

John Doyle stood outside the theatre, still shaking. He knew. He'd chased Lynch for almost a mile before losing him along Baggot Street. But he knew who did it and he equally knew he could just as easily be on that operating table himself, or, even worse, lying in the morgue, like Tony Dowling.

'It doesn't look good.'

In the radiology department of the Central Maternity Hospital Paddy Holland was looking at the viewing box along with Donal Collins, consultant radiologist. Flicked up on the screen were the latest AP and lateral chest X-rays of Gordon O'Brien. The pneumonia was not abating.

'No, it doesn't, Paddy. How does he look?'

'Terrible.'

'Do you think he'll make it?'

Holland looked at the screen closely again, the lung markings, the infective shadowings, the heart outline. He glanced down at the most recent blood results, taken in the past hour. The white cell count was still very high as was the ESR. The blood culture had finally been reported confirming a Group B Streptococcal septicaemia. Holland looked again at the observations: pyrexial, rapid tachycardia, and remembered how the baby looked fifteen minutes previously.

'No, I don't Donnie. I don't. I don't think he'll make morning.'

9.00 pm

The RTE nine o'clock news was extended as were bulletins on Sky, BBC, ITV, CNN, NBC and a number of other national and cable broadcasting organisations. The news out of Dublin was so hot camera crews were working overtime, dashing from one flash point to another. Images of the Elms apartment complex and the bullet riddled car partly hidden by police screens and yellow incident tapes were beamed across the country and the world. The word was out. The detective team investigating the murders at the Central Maternity Hospital had been attacked, almost certainly by the man responsible for the murders themselves. One female detective lay in a critical, but stable condition in the intensive care unit of the Merrion Hospital in Dublin. Another older and very experienced detective lay in the morgue of the same hospital. Lifeless. The news reader solemnly added that the detective's name could not be released until next of kin had been notified, but Garda sources had revealed he was only weeks away from retirement.

The cabinet was meeting in emergency session, Alice Martin and Commissioner Quinlan both attending to brief the government on developments.

Tommy Malone watched and listened, Betty sitting beside. They were nibbling on a Chinese takeaway.

'Jaysus, Tommy, ye're not even the main attraction tonigh'.' It was a forced attempt at humour. Then, like a bombshell, the screen showed a photograph of Dean Lynch followed by front and side views of Tommy Malone.

Lynch first, then Malone.

'The government has announced that a reward of half a

358

million pounds will be paid to anyone providing information leading to the successful arrest of either of these two men. They are Dean Patrick James Lynch, aged forty-five years, five foot six inches tall, grey-haired, of stocky build but said to be showing signs of recent weight loss. He was last seen in the Baggot Street area of Dublin wearing a black tracksuit top and bottom with hood pulled up over his head. The other is Thomas, also known as Tommy, Malone, aged fifty-eight years. He is five foot eight inches tall, usually well dressed and with steel-grey hair and has a thick moustache. Gardai have warned members of the public not to approach either of these men but to immediately notify their nearest Garda station or contact the Garda confidential telephone line if they are spotted. The number is on the bottom of your screens and will remain there for the rest of this extended news bulletin. Both men are considered highly dangerous and are almost certainly carrying fire arms.'

The newscaster shuffled papers and turned back to autocue. 'In other news,' he added, trying hard to lift even his own mood, 'Sister June Morrison, the nurse attacked and left unconscious when baby Gordon O'Brien was kidnapped, has made a full recovery. Doctors at Wicklow General Hospital expect her to be able to go home within the next day or two.'

Tommy Malone turned the volume down and stared at the screen. He couldn't have given a stuff about June Morrison's recovery, there was too much else worrying him. Betty's hands were shaking.

'We can't stay here, Tommy. Ye know they'll find ye here. Nothin' happens aroun' here without somebody noticin'. Ye just can't stay here for much longer. Sandra'll be up tomorra and she'll notice somewan's stayin' here, sure as God. She misses nuthin'.'

Malone ground out a cigarette and turned to Betty, looking her straight in the eyes. For a moment he didn't speak.

'Will ye come with me, Betty? I know how to get outa

here. I've done it before. I'll get away, no sweat. But will ye come with me?'

Betty put down her plate and reached across. For a moment they just held one another and she kissed him lightly on the cheek. The left cheek. 'Let me think abouta, Tommy. I need time. I've Sharon to think abou'. I can' just disappear withou' her knowin'.'

'Ye can ring her once we're outa the place.'

'Lemme think abouta, Tommy. Lemme sleep on it.'

'I wish to Jaysus I could sleep. I didn't close me eyes all last night.'

Betty went over to a cupboard, opened a drawer and rattled a small bottle. 'Here's a coupla Zimovane. Take them and ye'll ge' a nigh's sleep. Ye'll think better tomorra if ye've had a nigh's sleep.'

Tommy looked suspiciously at the two small oval-shaped tablets. 'They won't bomb me out? I need to keep me wits about me.'

'Take them, for Jaysus' sake, ge' a nigh's sleep. If I'm goin' with ye I'm not goin' with some sleepless zombie.' She smiled at him.

And there was something in her smile that worried Malone.

'Go on, take them.'

Malone popped the tablets in his mouth and made a great show of trying hard to swallow. He pushed both between his upper teeth and gums, holding them there with his tongue.

'I'll make a cup a tea.'

Malone nodded, and spat the tablets out into his hand when she left the room. He flicked the sound back on the TV. There was an interview with the new English soccer manager making great predictions for the match the next night, the one Moonface wouldn't be going to. 'Three nil, easy. It won't be a dirty match but it'll be a tough, hard contest between two competitive teams. Both have pride to restore after recent bad form. Both want badly to win. I hope it'll be a good, clean contest with no crowd trouble.'

The interviewer turned to the camera; in the background

revellers were already working themselves up outside city centre pubs. He wondered if it might in fact not turn out to be a repeat of the last encounter when there was a riot with pitched battles along the streets of Dublin between opposing fans. He confirmed that all Gardai leave had been cancelled and at least three hundred would be on duty for the match, two hundred inside the ground, backed up by another one hundred outside. All the main Dublin hospitals would be on full emergency alert. The Merrion Hospital in Sandymount, closest to the stadium, was bracing itself for a possible onslaught.

And an onslaught it would be.

But not the sort they were expecting, or planning for. Dean Lynch would see to that.

As he watched the news he bayed like a wounded animal, not loud, but deep.

The bitch! Critical, but stable.

He unclipped the magazine and squinted along the inside of the barrel. It was blocked. He ran his fingers along the length of the barrel and felt the slight bulge. It had jammed. London John's warning had come to pass. The Walther had jammed. In fact there were two bullets jammed in the barrel, the pressure of the second against the first causing it to swell slightly. The gun was now effectively useless. Lynch threw it violently against the wall.

That's why she's critical but stable. I didn't empty the full magazine into her.

On the TV screen a photograph of Kate Hamilton was flashed and he stared at it, mesmerised. He looked back down at the gun again, there was no way it would ever work again.

There's more than one way to skin a rabbit, he thought as he settled back on the sofa, smiling again, his rage abating. He set up a fix at the small kitchen table. Yeah, there's more than one way to skin a rabbit.

I'll get you, Kate Hamilton. Just you wait. I'm not finished yet, not by a long chalk.

Just you wait.

I'll make you suffer, like I suffered. You'll know what suffering really means, this time.

The heroin disappeared into a vein.

10.17 pm

'I'm going home for a few hours. Nurse Gallagher will stay with you until midnight and then she'll be relieved by the night duty sister. My senior registrar will be around all the time should anything change. I only live a five-minute-drive away so I can be here quickly if needed.'

Sandra and Harry O'Brien hung on Paddy Holland's every word, their faces taut and drawn, their eyes red and distraught, their hands wrung almost until blood was drawn. Beside them on a trolley lay undrunk cups of tea, plates of uneaten sandwiches and a wastepaper bin full of tear-filled crumpled paper tissues.

Lying in the incubator, their one and only child was still fighting for his life, IV lines dripping, heart pads stuck to his tiny chest leading to an ever-flickering monitor. The name tag hung loosely from his wasted wrist and his tiny chest heaved rapidly.

But even when Paddy Holland finally slumped into his bed, exhausted, trying desperately to sleep, sleep would not come. The images of the baby and the look on his parents' faces haunted him. There's nothing more I can do, it's in the hands of God now.

But what tormented him even more was the news about Kate Hamilton. Her face, too, kept forming in his exhausted brain, her pretty, vivacious, full-of-life face. The mother of the little four-year-old boy was now fighting for her life in the Merrion Hospital ICU. He turned onto one side and stared at the wall. Please God, don't let her die. Let her live.

He turned back onto his other side and stared at the

digital clock on his bedside table. He watched the numbers flick all night.

'Grandad, what time is Mummy coming home?'

'Shush, Rory, go to sleep. I don't know. It'll probably be late. Go to sleep. I'll mind you until she comes home.'

'Will she be here when I wake up in the morning?'

'Rory, will you go to sleep. I'm exhausted. I'll mind you until she comes home.'

'But when will she be home?'

Grandad had to turn away and stifle the pain.

'When will she be home, Grandad?'

'Tomorrow, Rory, hopefully she'll be home tomorrow.'

Rory put his thumb in his mouth and stroked Grandad's face with Ted. His eyes were heavy with sleep, he was drifting. 'Grandad?'

'Yes, Rory, what is it this time?'

'When Mummy comes home can we get a puppy?'

'Maybe, maybe.'

'Oh great.' Rory turned over and fell asleep.

11.57 pm

'Tommy, are ye asleep?'

'I would be if ye'd only shut up.'

'Good man. Try and ge' some sleep. Ye'll need yer strength for tomorra.' She turned her back to his in the bed and within minutes he sensed her heavy breathing. Minutes later she was snoring.

But Tommy Malone couldn't sleep. There was something about that kiss, that smile, that disturbed him. It reminded him of something. He'd been lying for an hour trying to think what exactly had disturbed him so much about Betty's simple affectionate gesture. It was only as he drifted into twilight sleep that the image entered his subconscious.

Judas. It was a Judas kiss.

Day 10

Tommy Malone knew there was something wrong, something seriously wrong.

He had slept fitfully all night, one arm wrapped around Betty's ample waist. At about one o'clock she'd mounted him, turned on him like a wild animal and put him through more sexual variations than he'd experienced for years. He lost count of time, his mind and body bounced in a sea of unrestrained pleasure. Exhausted and finished, they'd clung to each other before he felt her body slacken and give way to sleep. But his body wouldn't yield.

There was something wrong. He knew it. He sensed it.

It was all too much, just too much.

He felt her slide quietly and gently out from the bed, first one foot onto the floor and pause, listening to his breathing, watching for any movement. Then her body shifted to the edge and both feet rested on the floor. He felt the bed give ever so slightly as she lifted herself totally, her breathing rapid and shallow. Nervous. He sensed her stand at the side of the bed for maybe five minutes, watching and listening. Then came the slow and deliberate pad across the carpet and out the door. He sat up slowly and quietly, ears tuned to the slightest noise. A step creaked on the stairs, followed by another pause. Even from the bed he could hear the sound of strained breathing, not laboured but suppressed, rapid, shallow, nervous breathing. He heard two more steps and another pause. She was listening. He was listening.

Finally came the emboldened final seven steps and the sound of the kitchen door closing gently, closing ever so gently, ever so quietly.

Malone looked at his watch in the gloom. She's in the kitchen and it's only gone six.

Then he remembered. That's where the phone was.

'It's abou' tha' kidnapper ye're lookin' for. Yeah, Tommy Malone. Well I know where he is righ' this minute.' There was pandemonium at the other end of the confidential Garda telephone line. 'Wha' abou' the reward? How can I be sure I'll ge' the reward? Can it be paid anonymously? Can I be sure to ge' it withou' anywan knowin' who dobbed him in?'

All sorts of pleadings came down the other end of the line.

'Are ye sure?'

The Garda on telephone duty almost did cartwheels to satisfy her.

'Righ'. He's . . .'

Malone pulled the telephone cable from its socket.

Betty shook the dead handpiece, then turned to see him in the gloom from the street lights outside.

'Ah, Jaysus, not ye Betty. Not ye. Fuck it, not ye as well.' He started to wind the telephone cable into his hands, pulling the handset from her. Betty was paralysed with fear, frozen to the spot. She knew Tommy Malone from old, knew him only too well. She knew how he felt about traitors and in the gloom she could just about make out the telephone cable, taut between both his hands. And she remembered how strong those hands were.

'Fuck ye, Betty, fuck ye. Fuck ye, fuck ye, fuck ye.'

'Tommy I didn' . . .' Were her last words before the cable was suddenly pulled around her neck and twisted. And twisted. And twisted. And held in a tight twist for nearly twenty minutes, as Tommy Malone sobbed for the first time in years.

'Fuck ye, Betty, fuck ye. Fuck ye, fuck ye, fuck ye.' He let her body slide to the ground. 'Ye fuckin' Judas. Fuck ye.'

6.47 am

'Grandad, is Mummy home yet?'

Rory was standing at the side of his mother's bed where Grandad had spent the night, sleepless, tormented and crying.

'No, Rory, she's not back yet. I'm sure it won't be long. Go back to bed for a while. It's too early.'

'Grandad, can I come in beside you?'

He pulled back the clothes and the two snuggled up. Rory put his thumb in his mouth and started to run Ted across Grandad's face.

'When will she be home?'

'Maybe later this morning,' lied Grandad, 'I'm sure it won't be long. Try and go back to sleep, it's very early.'

Rory ran Ted across Grandad's face again and Grandad hadn't the heart, or the strength, to give out.

'Would you like to go to the zoo later on?'

Rory sat upright, and even in the dark Grandad could see the excitement on his face. 'Oh, great. The zoo. I just love the zoo. That's great, Grandad.'

'You'll have to be a good boy all day for me, though. No shouting or whinging. When I say it's time to go then it's time to go. I don't want any arguments. Okay? Understand?'

Rory, thumb back in mouth, nodded his agreement in the dark. 'Grandad?'

'What Rory? What is it this time?'

'Will Mummy be able to come to the zoo as well?'

Tommy Malone sat at the kitchen table, smoking his sixth cigarette and drinking his fourth mug of strong tea. He hadn't as much as looked at the body, lying where he left it, slumped at the side of the telephone. He was dressed, washed, and ready. He'd shaved his moustache off carefully with one of Betty's leg razors, almost cutting the face of himself as he did. Then he'd searched for Betty's car keys in her handbag and took them and everything else that was inside apart from her cosmetic bag. He looked out the window at the main estate road where one or two cars were already on the move, their headlights picking up other houses as their drivers sped to work before rush hour. Where can I go now? Where the fuck can I go now? It's all up.

He looked again at the front page of the newspaper stuck through the letter box only minutes before. There he was. Thomas, also known as Tommy, Malone. Ireland's most wanted man. Him and some other bollox called Dr Dean Lynch, both their mug shots splashed across the front page.

Dr Dean Lynch, he read again. *Dr* Dean Lynch. A fuckin' doctor. On the run and wanted by the police.

A fuckin' *doctor*.

Even Tommy Malone couldn't help but wonder what the country was coming to.

'I'm afraid there's been no real change in his condition.'

Paddy Holland, the night sister and his senior registrar were gathered in front of Sandra and Harry O'Brien. The medical team had scrutinised the night's observations, inspected the first X-rays taken thirty minutes earlier and noted the latest blood results.

Gordon O'Brien was not improving. He wasn't deteriorating, but he wasn't improving either.

The only other baby in ICU had rallied and rallied very successfully. She had been moved out and back to the recovery ward, closer to her mother. But as her incubator was trundled out there were none of the usual signs of glee, no whoops of joy, no punching the air. Success!

'I'll be back in a short while. I just have to check my other charges in the pre-term unit. I'll call back soon.' Sandra O'Brien's eyes never left her baby. Harry O'Brien's lifeless eyes looked up at him but didn't really register.

The medical team exchanged glances.

The night shift moved out and the day shift moved in.

There was no end to the battle for life in the Central Maternity Hospital in Dublin, day or night.

Tommy Malone checked his .38 Smith & Wesson revolver, flicked open the chamber and put in two extra bullets. He now had a full chamber. He took Betty's portable radio, her car keys, a red scarf and all the money he could find throughout the house. He'd taken her life, what difference would a few extras mean? All were stuffed inside a blue and grey tartan duffle bag. He closed the back door, locked it and slipped the key inside his coat pocket, having already made sure the front door was firmly locked and double bolted. Before he left he half pulled some blinds up and partly drew some curtains across.

Finally, and with suppressed tears brimming his eyes, he dragged the body of Betty Nolan across and behind the kitchen counter, covering her with a blanket. She wouldn't be easily seen through the window.

Outside he started up her car, a grey Datsun Almera, heaving a sigh of relief as he noticed the petrol tank was almost full. He pulled out of the estate, double checking in the rear-vision mirror no one had gone near the house. Satisfied, he slipped into third gear and drove out onto the main road, the tartan duffle bag on the passenger seat beside him.

The paper had warned motorists to expect delays on all major roads into and out of the city as Gardai manned roadblocks so Tommy Malone decided to head for the Dublin mountains to give him time to think and plan his next moves.

I've gotta get it right this time, gotta get it right this time. There's no goin' back to any old haunts. There's more than the Gardai gunnin' for me. If that bitch Betty was gonna turn me in there's no wan left to trust. Ye're on yer own now.

He lit up a cigarette, noticing he had only two left. Jaysus, everythin's runnin' out. Even me luck.

'How are you feeling?'

Kate Hamilton was only too glad to be alive. She managed a weak smile, a very weak smile. Her chest ached where the intercostal drains were positioned and every cough tore at her insides. She felt helpless, both arms restrained by IV lines. The right side of her chest was agony and restricted all movement. She had a dreadful headache. The trauma team had shaved half her head, half her long dark hair, to insert the twenty or so sutures that closed up the bullet wound. The gaping wound on her arm was dressed but hardly bothered at all.

The sedatives had worn off and the new painkillers weren't making her as groggy.

'How are you feeling?' Sean Mulligan, senior trauma surgeon, asked again. He was surrounded by his surgical team and four nurses.

'Fine.' She didn't actually speak, but mouthed the word.

'You're going to be real fine. Real fine.' The team were all beaming at her. 'You've lost a good deal of blood but you stabilised quite quickly. We're not going to give you a transfusion, a strong, healthy young woman like you should make up that loss soon.'

Hamilton attempted another smile.

'We've been in touch with your family.' Hamilton's eyes suddenly came to life. 'I spoke with your father myself and told him everything was fine and that you were in no danger. I don't think the media have quite got that message yet so we felt your family should hear the news direct from us and not through the papers.'

'What happened to Tony? What happened to Tony Dowling?' The words were barely audible, whispered through parched lips.

'Now you save your strength for getting better. The least you say the better.'

'What happened to Tony Dowling?'

The team exchanged embarrassed and guilty glances, as if they personally were responsible.

'He didn't make it. We couldn't save him.'

Hamilton turned away and stared into the distance. The lovely man from Cavan, just weeks away from retirement. The man who loved country dogs. 'Now they've gotta bit o' character, Kate. Not like that constipated lot o' city dogs that spend all day chasin' cars up and down the Stillorgan dual carriageway. D'ye think Rory'd like fishin'? Ye could bring him up sometime and I'd show him how to cast a line.'

'Did they catch Lynch?'

There were even more embarrassed glances from the surgical team.

'No, no, they didn't. I heard on the news this morning they think he's in England. Apparently he was on a late crossing last night on the Stena Line.'

But Hamilton shook her head. No, he's not in England. She said nothing.

'Don't you worry anyway about him. There's a twenty-four-hour armed guard on you. This floor is sealed off and there are armed Special Branch men all over the hospital. Forget about him, Mrs Hamilton, forget about him. He can't reach you here. He's gone.'

I'm not Mrs Hamilton. And he's not gone.

Grandad and Rory's journey across the city to the zoo was slowed by roadblocks and a heavy Gardai presence throughout the city centre. Gangs of English soccer supporters, many without tickets and more than a few from the National Front, were spoiling for a fight. Union Jacks were taunted provocatively at passers-by with lots of SAS shouts. 'We've got the SAS! We've got the SAS!' Then came a big cheer from a large section of this crowd as the official team bus carrying the English soccer squad made its way slowly through the city centre traffic. There were alternating boos and cheers from opposing fans. The match was due to kick off at seven, but already the atmosphere was tense, too much drink consumed, passions aroused. TV crews at the two port sites, Dublin docks and Dun Laoghaire, filmed as hundreds more English soccer fans arrived off the ferries, again taunting the locals with their Union Jacks and provocative slogans.

Grandad shook his head sadly, stuck in yet another traffic jam. Rory stared out at the scenes with a mixture of fascination and fear. He could sense danger on the streets. At last they were clear and heading towards the Phoenix Park and the zoo there.

'Grandad?'

'Yes, Rory?'

'When's Mummy coming home?'

11.00 am

Dean Lynch watched the Sky news bulletin, his photograph and that of Tommy Malone making the top stories. There were clips of Gardai manning roadblocks, snap interviews with the man or woman in the street about what should be done to both whenever they were caught.

Lynch smiled at that. *Whenever I'm caught.*

Nobody's going to catch me.

I have an appointment with Death.

I don't know when. I don't know how soon.

But I have an appointment with Death.

First I have some unfinished business to do.

A photograph of his unfinished business flashed on the screen as the report continued.

'Detective Sergeant Kate Hamilton is still in a critical but stable condition in the intensive care unit of Dublin's Merrion Hospital.' It was another 'piece-to-camera' report with the hospital in the background, one long lens showing two Special Branch detectives conferring just outside the main entrance, their UZI sub-machine-guns not easily concealed. The report made a big deal about the heavily armed guard surrounding Detective Hamilton. Then came the piece that made Lynch smile, even allowing him a short laugh.

'Reports suggest Dr Dean Lynch may already be out of the country.' There was a clip of the Stena Line boat and offices where a ticket in the name of Dean Lynch had been purchased for the last sailing out of Dun Laoghaire the previous night. Another piece of careful and cunning planning by Lynch had proved fruitful. The report continued with even better news. There had been sightings of him boarding a train to London with another sighting of him hiring a cab to Chester. No cab driver had yet come forward to confirm or refute this report. There had been a number of other sightings and police on mainland Britain were treating these reports seriously and all would be followed up. But they did warn that there could be hoax calls and they appealed to the public not to waste valuable police time. Dean Lynch was a very dangerous and desperate man. The public should be vigilant and alert and report any possible sightings.

Lynch flicked off the remote control, staring at the blip in the middle of the screen. He sighed deeply.

It's time to get ready. It's time for the final push.

He picked up the bottle of hair dye, read the instructions carefully, then inspected the moustache he was letting grow. There wasn't a lot, but enough.

For the next move he wasn't going to use the wig or false moustache, for the next move everything would be *au naturelle*.

Just before noon Tommy Malone climbed out of the car outside Lamb Doyle's pub in the Dublin hills, locked it carefully and walked to the opposite side of the road, gazing down at the city below. It was another cold but bright morning. Rain had been forecast for later in the week which would lift temperatures a degree or so, but that day, the day of the big match, the weather conditions were reasonably good. Despite the bitter cold there was a hint of sun through the dark grey clouds.

Malone lit up his last cigarette and picked out the land marks of the sprawling city and suburbs spread out as far as his eye could see, Howth Head, the chimney stacks at Ringsend, Ballymun Towers. Jaysus, what wouldn't I give to be able to go back and start all over again? Cars passed by, but Malone was oblivious to everything but the view beneath him.

This is me, Tommy Malone. This is where I grew up and fought my way out of the slums and squalor. I can't leave here. I can't leave this city. This is me, Thomas, also known as Tommy, Malone. He flicked the butt into the frost-covered field in front and returned to the car.

There was something Tommy Malone wanted to do. He started up the engine.

Now, how am I gonna get inta town without bein' seen?

The RTE radio one o'clock news carried reports on the continuing hunt for Malone and Lynch. There had been plenty of sightings with raids all over the city and suburbs, even at deserted farmhouses, holiday homes and mobile homes. Anywhere and everywhere. But no arrests had been made. The newscaster reported the government had ordered the army in to help local Gardai comb rural areas. 'These murderers must be caught and brought to justice,' Alice Martin was quoted as saying.

Tommy Malone and Dean Lynch both listened to the bulletin, Malone on the car radio, Lynch on his Sony Walkman as he made his way back to the Stillorgan shopping centre.

He smiled as he walked, laughing occasionally at the thought of the police and army breaking down farmshed doors, city centre shebeens, scouring the country.

For little ol' me.

How *simple* it all was to create such mayhem. I should have thought of this years ago.

Anyway, I sorted out Tom Morgan. And I'll beat Luke Conway too. And that bastard Armstrong.

He walked past a Garda checkpoint at the top of Booterstown Avenue with a tail back of traffic for five hundred yards, each driver cursing and swearing at the delay. Lynch noticed all this and just couldn't help smiling.

What fun.

He now had a full head of jet black hair, thin black moustache and looked quite bulky again inside his four thick sweaters underneath thick, black anorak with hood up. He was wearing his clear-lens glasses and didn't look at all like the man whose photograph was on every TV news bulletin and splashed across the front page of every newspaper.

Tommy Malone drove down Ballinteer Road, taking short cuts through various housing estates to avoid the main roads. He couldn't help but notice people going about their daily chores, putting out rubbish bins, collecting groceries, walking the dog. Life was going on all around him and people were living normal lives. The stark contrast between his day and theirs tore at his spirit. He came out along the Sandyford Industrial Estate in South Dublin where there were no road blocks and the traffic moved smoothly. He cut down towards Stillorgan, swerving sharply into the shopping centre overflow car park when he spotted a Garda car pulled across half of the road ahead, all faces in the slow moving queue being carefully scrutinised.

Don't draw attention to yerself. Don't draw attention to yerself.

He stuffed the duffle bag under the passenger seat, got out of the car and pulled up his coat collar. It looked natural enough, everyone was going around like that, shielding themselves against the cold. He walked around the Stillorgan Centre like any other shopper, accidentally bumping into a small, bulky looking man who seemed as preoccupied as himself. They grunted a 'sorry' to one another, each noticing the other had barely lifted his head, both sets of eyes fixed firmly on the ground. The smaller man paused only to adjust his glasses higher on his nose.

The small, bulky man with the hood pulled over his jet black hair and tied across the lower half of his face so that his thin, black moustache was also hidden, made his way into the Quinnsworth Life and Leisure store where there was a photo booth. He sat down, adjusting the seat to the right height, and checked no one was waiting before beginning.

The hood was quickly pulled down, the anorak slipped off, the glasses removed. All four jumpers were pulled over his head within a minute. Then he slipped on his old Central Maternity Hospital white doctor's coat over his new plain white shirt. He wore a grey, muted tie.

He inspected his reflection and smiled. You look the part of a doctor again.

He thrust a comb through his gelled hair, giving a neat parting, combed to the right. He inspected the result again and grunted his approval. He slipped the glasses back on, fed in the money and waited.

FLASH! FLASH! FLASH! FLASH!

As quickly as the flashes were over, he was back inside his sweaters, anorak with hood up again. He glanced past the curtains around the booth entrance, there was no one waiting. He counted the three minutes on his watch, noticing for the first time how loose it now hung off his wrist. I've lost a lot of weight. A lot. An awful lot. And I don't feel hungry. I couldn't be bothered to eat, the very thought of it makes me feel sick.

The strip of four photos which finally dropped out showed a thin-faced man with strong head of dark hair and moustache, wearing glasses.

He went across to the pharmacy opposite and bought four packets of Ensure Plus, high-protein, high-calorie complete feeds, to get some strength. I must get some nourishment into me, I need all the strength I can get.

For the final push.

Tommy Malone went back to the car and headed away from the Garda checkpoint, pulling into Mount Merrion and down Trees Road until he met the Stillorgan dual carriageway. He planned to head for the city centre that way but decided to cut into Merrion Avenue. He was only halfway down when he spotted another Garda checkpoint, only about fifty yards ahead. Now he was stuck in a queue, unable to get out of it without the people in the car behind wondering why. A young Garda ahead was checking up and down for anyone trying to sneak away. Out of the corner of his left eye Malone noticed a car pull out and over to the big off-licence on the left, McCabes. That's it!

He waited for a minute and followed.

People were streaming in and out, stocking up to watch the match at home, planning a few beers in front of the telly, fire on and a great night in watching their lads knock the stuffing out of England. Tommy Malone parked the car halfway up on the pavement, lifted out the duffle bag and strolled as casually as he could inside.

The place was packed, six-packs of beer flying off the shelves. A TV in the corner was tuned to Sky news. Malone started inspecting the rows of wine, keeping his eyes and head down towards the bottom shelves so no one would notice his face. The two o'clock news bulletin came on and everyone in the shop turned to watch.

The newscaster was reporting on Sam Collins and Peggy Ryan being taken from the Bridewell holding centre to be formally charged in court. The clip captured the ugly mood of the people gathered outside the courthouse, with lots of booing as Collins and Ryan were shoved inside for the three-minute hearing, blankets over their heads. They were then seen being dragged from the courthouse after the hearing to a waiting Garda van and then driven away at top speed to Mountjoy gaol. The newscaster reported that Gordon O'Brien was still dangerously ill in the intensive care unit of the Central Maternity Hospital. The mood in the off-licence became as ugly as that on the TV screen with lots of angry mutterings and warnings of what should be done to the bastards.

Tommy Malone listened and worried. He worried a lot. I knew it was bad, but this is woeful. Jaysus, there's nowhere to turn. He picked up a bottle and inspected the label. Château Mouton Rothschild 1983. That'll do. He waited until the crowd thinned, then placed the bottle on the counter, averting his eyes as if he was looking for something else. He gradually noticed the young, dark-haired assistant staring at the bottle.

'That's an expensive one, sir. That's one hundred and twenty-five pounds.'

There was no time to start arguing the cost. I gotta get out of here as fast as possible. 'I'm still takin' it. Gimme a couple of Monte Cristo cigars as well. Number one.' The wine and cigars were carefully wrapped in purple tissue and then gently laid inside a green carrier bag, the bottle wrapped separately inside six layers of mauve tissue paper. 'Gimme a bottle opener and a glass as well.'

'Glass?'

This time the assistant couldn't help but stare at the face that was trying so hard to avoid being seen.

'Yeah, gimme a bottle opener and glass as well.' Malone peeled off three fifty-pound notes and dropped them on the counter. 'Put the change in the poor box.'

'Certainly sir.'

But the young dark-haired assistant couldn't figure this out, there was something about the face that looked familiar. He almost asked Malone if he'd seen him on the telly recently. But Malone was out the door and someone else was pressing for attention wanting a six-pack of Budweiser and a packet of Pringles. In an instant Tommy Malone's face was forgotten.

Malone checked the scene outside and decided it was too risky to drive. Duffle bag in left hand, McCabes' carrier bag in the other, he turned the corner into Cross Avenue. I'll walk to the Dart in Booterstown, like old times.

'I'm sorry, but there's no fault on that line. I can't get a ringing tone either. Possibly the cable's been pulled out of the socket.'

The faults operator on Telecom Eireann was trying to explain to Sharon, Betty Nolan's one and only girl, the reason she couldn't get through to her mother on the phone

378

had nothing to do with a telephone fault. 'Have you been trying long?'

'All morning. She usually comes over at eleven on a Wednesday and minds the baby for me while I do the shopping.'

'Well, all I can tell you is that the line is perfect into the house and there's been no report of any faults on that line or any others in the area. Sorry I can't help more.'

'Thanks, anyway. I think I'll call over and make sure she's okay.'

'Well if you find the phone's working but not taking any in-coming calls please ring this number back and report it.'

'Will do. Thanks again.' Sharon hung up, nibbling at her nails thoughtfully.

Tommy Malone took the Dart into Westland Row, the McCabes' carrier bag now stuffed into the duffle bag. He stood outside the station for almost five minutes wondering what would be the best way to go. Then he sat in the small café beside the station, sipping on a mug of strong tea, deep in thought, trying to decide his next move. He knew which way his feet would eventually lead him, but his mind wanted to go elsewhere. He wanted to walk back along the Liffey, back towards the old Steevens Street flats complex. His mind wanted to feel again the smell of the sea, the rush of the traffic, the noise of sirens as police, ambulance and fire engines rushed along the city centre. His mind wanted to return to his old haunts, seek out a few buddies, maybe have a pint and a yarn. But his mind couldn't control his feet.

And he found himself drawn, dragged in the opposite direction.

At the exact time that Tommy Malone started his lonely journey, in the paediatric Intensive Care Unit of the Central Maternity Hospital Gordon O'Brien showed the first signs of rallying.

Sandra O'Brien was staring into the incubator, whispering to her baby. 'Come on Gordon, Mummy's here. Your Daddy's here too, Gordon. You're back with us again.

379

You're going to be all right. Mummy won't let you out of her sight again, don't you worry about that. You're home to stay, home to stay with me and your Daddy. But you'll have to get better, Gordon. You'll have to keep fighting and not give up. We're waiting for you.'

She'd been saying variations on that same theme ever since Paddy Holland had sat her and Big Harry down earlier. Harry O'Brien was holding his son's hand and stroking his head. Every now and then he would reach down and kiss the child's forehead. But as he watched his heart was silently breaking.

The first movement was no more than a stir, the kicking of a foot for the briefest of seconds. Neither Big Harry nor Sandra noticed it. But Liz Egan, the intensive care nurse on duty, most certainly did. She glanced at the monitors recording the baby's vital signs and felt a slight stir in her stomach. The too rapid pulse rate had slowed, the too rapid breathing had slowed, the oxygen level was improving. Trying very hard to look as cool as possible she checked Gordon O'Brien's temperature. Ignoring Sandra and Harry's intense stares, she recorded the reading in a chart at the bottom of the incubator. Then she checked the temperature again.

'Everything okay?' Sandra asked anxiously, hoping against desperate hope that the nurse wasn't recording the signs of a decline in Gordon's condition.

Liz Egan smiled slightly. 'Maybe a bit better. I'm just going to get Dr Holland. I'll be back in a moment.' She left ICU before she was interrogated any further.

Paddy Holland listened closely to the nurse's report, then followed her quickly back to the ICU. Sandra and Harry stood up slowly as they watched him come in. Neither wanted to ask a question in case the answer would devastate. Holland checked the same monitors Liz Egan had checked only minutes before, then pulled a chair up beside the incubator, opposite to where Big Harry and Sandra were sitting, and sat down himself. He stared down intently at the small baby, noting his chest movement as it rose and fell with each breath. He followed the breathing pattern to the child's sunken belly, then jerked his head quickly back up as he sensed movement. Gordon O'Brien's head had moved ever so slightly. The movement was barely perceptible but Holland and Nurse Egan both spotted it. Then Holland gently placed a paediatric stethoscope onto Gordon O'Brien's chest and listened. The bell of the stethoscope moved in half-inch steps along the front and side of the chest, pausing at each move.

Barely able to believe what his eyes and ears were registering, Holland straightened up and began pressing at buttons on the monitors. An ECG trace flickered across a screen, an oxygen-saturation level flashed up, the previous three minutes' pulse, respiration and blood pressure appeared and were read. Sandra and Harry O'Brien watched with an anguish and fear that was almost palpable. Is this the end?

Paddy Holland tore an ECG strip from its monitor and ran his finger along the tracing. Then he turned to the ashen faces opposite and smiled. 'He's getting better. He's getting better. He's turned the corner.'

Merrion Square was one of the jewels in Dublin's crown. It was an elegant square of fine architecture surrounded on each side by wide, well-kept roads lit at night by ornately carved street lamps. On three of its sides stood high Georgian buildings, once town homes for the Dublin aristocracy, now mainly used as offices and flats. In the middle was Merrion Square Park with its beautifully kept and carefully planned gardens. There was rarely a scrap of litter on the many meandering lanes where one was likely to suddenly come across a statue or piece of sculpture. There were magnificent heather beds and occasional natural wood carvings.

On the East side of the park was a children's playground and open spaces with wooden benches to rest on and admire the beauty of nature as it changed all year round. Spring bulbs, summer roses, winter pansies. The park was surrounded by wrought iron railings where amateur painters displayed their wares each Sunday. Then the square and park would be busy with families, children wanting to use the playground, parents wanting to look at the gardens or paintings.

The Irish National Art Gallery stood on Merrion Square West, set back from the road and behind high, black wrought iron railings. As a building its architecture blended well with its neighbours. There was a small, well-tended lawn in front of the entrance with a number of wooden benches beside a statue of George Bernard Shaw, one arm resting on the other as he stared thoughtfully into the distance.

Which was more or less what Tommy Malone was doing at three thirty on Wednesday, 19th February 1997. The day that came to be known later as Black Wednesday.

Tommy lit up one of his cigars and sat, huddled for warmth, on the wooden bench, watching the traffic and people. The duffle bag rested by his side on the bench.

It was decision time, big decision time.

As the cigar burned to the end, Malone ground it underfoot and reached inside the bag. With a quick furtive look around to make sure he wasn't being watched, he lifted the Smith & Wesson out and stuffed it inside his waistband. Then he stood up and made his way towards the front entrance of the building.

I'm gonna have one last look at that paintin' by yer man.

He checked the duffle bag into reception security and slowly made his way to room eighteen.

There it was. Caravaggio, 'The Taking of Christ'.

Malone sat down on the bench and stared.

There's Betty, with her Judas kiss, and there's me in the middle. I don't have the long hair, or the beard or the moustache, but that's me in the middle, with the snatch squad comin' to get me, to crucify me. Well, I'm fucked if they will.

The glint of light on the soldiers' armour, the expressions on the faces, the darkness of the painting was all too real and Malone reached inside his waistband to check his gun. I can't keep runnin' for ever. The whole country's agin' me now. They'll crucify me now, if they get me. And I'm fucked if they will.

Malone stood up slowly, gradually becoming aware of the attendant's open-mouthed stare. It was written all over his face. That's him! That's the fella they're all looking for. That's yer man, what's his name? Christ, what did they call him? It's him! Definitely. I better call the Gardai.

Malone sensed all this and sighed deeply, a deep sigh of resignation.

He looked again at the face of Jesus, meek and mild, subdued, hands clasped together, resigned to His fate. And He knew what was comin'. That's the bit I can't figger out, He knew what was comin'. And *still* He let them, without a fight, without as much as a struggle. Well, fuck ye, is all I can say. Fuck ye, but they're not gonna take me like that.

He collected his duffle bag, very much aware of the stares, knowing only too well the word was out. Out of the corner of his eye he noticed two security men approach. They weren't big men, but strong enough looking and he just knew they were trying to be heroes. He pulled his Smith & Wesson out and let off one round over their approaching heads, damaging the delicate plasterwork behind. Everyone ducked and ran for cover. Except Tommy Malone, who walked slowly and deliberately out the main entrance, across the road and into Merrion Square Park.

He found a quiet bench to sit on, noticing daffodil and tulip bulbs coming up with some in early flower. The snowdrops looked well past their best. He opened the duffle bag, took out the radio and turned it on. Then he uncorked the Château Mouton Rothschild 1983. It was a good year for Château Mouton, not that Tommy Malone knew. He cleaned the glass with a piece of the mauve paper so lovingly wrapped around it, poured himself a liberal measure and took a sip. Not bad, not bad at all. I'd prefer a pint meself, but it's not bad at all. He took a long deep slug, then laid the gun beside him, checking the chamber was ready for firing. In the distance he could hear sirens. Tommy Malone sat back and waited. They're comin'.

He poured another glass, knocking it back in one go, then poured one more, set it down on the bench, double-checked the gun, and had another sip. He lit up his last Monte Cristo, blowing smoke rings into the frosty air around him. A cold breeze wafted the smell of roasted malt from the Guinness brewery and Malone smiled briefly. Jaysus I could murder a pint right this minute.

On the square outside the park he could hear car doors

being slammed and shouting, loud angry shouting. Out of the corner of one eye he noticed a young mother with her toddler and baby in pushchair being dragged away by a dark suited man wearing a black peaked cap.

They're comin'. The soldiers are comin'. I can see the glint on their armour.

Jack McGrath briefed his team. They were all flak-jacketed, faces blackened and wore black woollen caps. He spread them out in a circle along the park while other uniformed Gardai ran like frightened rabbits around the rest of the paths rounding up any innocent bystanders who had come for a quiet walk and unwittingly wandered instead into a potential blood bath.

Office doors on all sides of the square were hammered on and the occupants told to keep away from the windows which only made them crowd at them, determined not to miss anything. From their vantage points they could make out a lonely looking man, sitting on a bench in the middle of the park, with what looked like a bag at his side. 'Do you know,' said one, 'I think he's drinking something. I can see a bottle and a glass, I'm sure of that. Who is he?'

McGrath had his men in position, he was ready. They nodded and acknowledged one another over their two-way radios.

Tommy Malone turned the volume up on the radio. He was coming to the end of his cigar, there was only a quarter left in the bottle, the rest inside, warming him on the bitterly cold day. He noticed movement in the bushes not far from him and picked up the gun.

McGrath watched his every movement and ordered the team to get ready. Safety catches were unslipped, fingers rested on triggers. Just give us an excuse, Tommy, just give us an excuse.

'We interrupt this programme to bring you a news flash.' Malone was only half-listening, more concerned with the dark shapes closing in. 'Reports are coming in from Garda headquarters that there has been an incident at Mountjoy

385

gaol involving Sam Collins, the man arrested yesterday for the kidnapping of baby Gordon O'Brien. While the initial reports are sketchy and unconfirmed it appears that Collins was set upon by a group of prisoners and badly beaten. He was transferred to the nearby Mater Hospital and is undergoing emergency surgery there for extensive head wounds. There will be a further update on this and other stories in our next bulletin on the hour.'

The report finally penetrated Malone's consciousness and he stared at the ground for a moment, then looked up. The dark shapes were closer again, moving in and around the bushes and trees. He could hear twigs break underfoot and the crunching of gravel.

They're comin' to crucify me. And crucify me they will if they get me.

If they get me.

He placed the gun barrel slowly and deliberately inside his mouth, tasting the metal for an instant.

Jack McGrath stood up. 'Holy Jesus!' For a fleeting moment his eyes met those of Tommy Malone, who now had two inches of the barrel inside his mouth.

McGrath started running towards him. 'Don't! Don't! Do . . .'

Tommy Malone's eyes fixed on McGrath's and the weariness and resignation was obvious. He shook his head slightly. It's no use, I'm goin' to sleep.

He pulled the trigger.

The Greystones Gardai broke down the door of number thirty-three Roselawn Heights just after five that afternoon. They arrived with Sharon after she checked the house from all angles and still couldn't make out what was going on. The doors were firmly locked, but the curtains and blinds were drawn in an unusual way, unusual for her mother anyway. She'd never leave the house like that, Sharon worried. But her car was gone. Sharon asked the neighbours and it was Nebby Nora, as usual, two doors down who spotted everything. Nothing much happened in Roselawn Heights without Nebby Nora, as Betty had called her, knowing. And it was Nebby Nora who had seen Tommy Malone get into and drive away with Betty's car earlier that morning.

'But why didn't you ring the police?'

'Because it's none of my business who comes in and out of your mother's house,' replied Nebby Nora, who wouldn't in a hundred years have known what the phrase 'not my business' meant.

Sharon called the local Garda station and within ten minutes two young uniformed Gardai cruised up in a squad car. It was one of them who noticed what he thought looked like a foot sticking out from behind the kitchen counter. It was Sharon who gave the nod for the door to be broken down, and it was Sharon's screams that echoed throughout the house and filtered all the way down to Nebby Nora who never had such a news break in her life.

The two uniformed Gardai notified base and rang Dr Noel Dunne, asking him to attend. As if he hadn't enough to do at that moment standing as he was beside Jack McGrath in the darkness of Merrion Square Park, over the body of Tommy Malone, the area sealed off, arc lights glaring. Dunne listened on his mobile phone to the request and initial crime scene findings, nodding gravely, muttering responses as his eyes scanned the darkness of the park from where he stood. He barked instructions and glanced quickly at his watch, then gave an approximate time of arrival. He turned to Jack McGrath, knowing how well he and Tony Dowling had got on together over the years, knowing how well they had worked as a team. But he had spent all morning in the mortuary of the Merrion Hospital, performing the postmortem on Dowling. It had been heartbreaking for a man whose heart didn't break easily. He couldn't let it get to him. He knew long ago he'd never get out of bed in the morning if he let it get to him. But Tony Dowling, lying on the mortuary slab, lifeless and bloodied, was very hard to take.

'Detective Inspector McGrath?' McGrath turned. 'I want to tell you how sorry I am about the loss of your colleague last night.'

McGrath said nothing, his eyes tried to respond but his heart wouldn't allow his mouth to speak.

'However there's something else, Detective Inspector.' This time McGrath looked straight into Dunne's eyes. 'I don't think Dr Lynch has fled the country.'

Without another word Dunne picked up his bag and started towards the Garda squad car waiting to take him to Greystones.

'Neither do I,' McGrath shouted after him.

Dunne struggled into the back of the car, pulling his bag in with him. He paused and wound down the window. 'He'll try and do it again, Detective Inspector. Believe me. He'll try and do it again.'

McGrath stroked his moustache as the car drew away.

Lesley Cairns from Southside Properties stared long and hard at the front page of the *Daily Post*. Then she looked at the *Irish Times*, then the *Star*, then the *Irish Independent*, the usual quota of papers left in reception for clients. Two photographs occupied almost half the front pages of the spreadsheets and all the front pages of the tabloids: Tommy Malone and Dr Dean Lynch. It wasn't Malone's photograph she was staring at. There was something about the other face and description that unsettled her.

The man who had called on her didn't look at all like what was described in any of the papers. But it was the eyes that disturbed Lesley Cairns. Those eyes, she thought as she studied the photograph intently, those eyes. I'm telling you you'd be hard pressed not to remember those eyes. She read the description again. Nah, this fella had glasses. But then, how could I have seen those eyes so clearly? I mean they were, like, dead clear. They'd frighten the life out of anyone if you asked me. Wasn't he supposed to be renting it for an English businessman? She picked up the phone and rang the rented apartment in Booterstown. It'll be easy, she thought nervously, her hands shaking slightly, if an English-sounding voice answers I'll just ask if everything's all right and hope the apartment suits and please call again if you need similar accommodation. The phone rang out. She redialled and it rang out again. She put the receiver down slowly and picked up the *Daily Post* again, staring at the photograph of Lynch. Nah, it's definitely not him. But secretly she knew she wasn't sure. Secretly she felt she didn't want it to be him. Secretly she knew the thought that it might be him frightened the life out of her. It was easier to ignore the possibility than get involved.

The coach carrying the England soccer team threaded its way through the milling crowds making their way towards Lansdowne Road Stadium. It was followed by boos and two-finger salutes from the fans, with only an occasional cheer and thumbs-up. A very occasional cheer and thumbs-up. Even though there would be a sizeable, usually sensible, Official English Soccer Fan presence, Gardai had strict instructions to keep the rival camps apart. So those pouring along the roads to the stadium off the buses, out of taxis and private cars, were mainly Irish fans wearing green shirts and scarves and heavy green sweaters to keep out the cold. They were chanting as they walked. 'You'll never beat the Oirish, you'll never beat the Oirish.'

The Irish team were already inside the stadium getting the pre-match hype, the psyche-up so intense one or two felt they'd be going over the trenches when the whistle blew. Let me at those bastards. Football match me arse, this is war. Just let me up and at them.

The coach outside inched closer to the stadium and twin doors opened to allow it inside. Tom Dalzell just couldn't resist. He'd waited too long for this night, dreaming of playing for England against Ireland in Dublin, the home of IRA terrorists, according to his ex-SAS father. 'When you kick a ball, think of it as the head of one of those IRA scum who nearly killed me,' he'd advised. Tom Dalzell had the strongest kick in the FA Premiership League and now he was on enemy territory. His kicking boots just ached to lash out. As the coach passed inside the safety of the stadium doors, Dalzell lifted up a Union Jack and waved it tauntingly at the crowds behind. SAS was clearly written on it in big letters. He two-fingered the crowd. A small group broke free and rushed the retreating bus, enraged and baying for blood. Fortunately for Dalzell enough stewards were on hand to restrain them, allowing the double doors to close.

The stadium terraces were full. Just before seven o'clock the stewards estimated there were about twenty-two thousand genuine Irish fans and about seven thousand genuine Official England Soccer fans. The rest, they decided and reported to the Gardai crowd control centre, were trouble-makers. Two hundred Gardai were positioned inside the stadium, all in riot gear, with shields and long batons, helmets and perspex visors.

Inside the media commentary boxes there was an unusually strong national and international presence. Because of other events in the city over the previous ten days, a large number of foreign commentators were on hand to explain to their viewers and listeners the complexities of the fixture. 'We're all looking forward to a great match with hopefully none of the dreadful scenes we've witnessed before,' commented the RTE soccer correspondent. Which wasn't really why there were so many foreign correspondents present. If they thought all they were going to see was a soccer match they'd have stayed in their hotel bedrooms and watched it on the telly.

6.53 pm

'Mummy? Is that you, Mummy?'

'Hi Rory, yes it's me. How are you?' Tears streamed down Kate Hamilton's face.

'Mummy, where are you? Grandad said you'd be home after we came back from the zoo.'

'Rory, I've had a little accident and I've had to go into hospital for a few days but I'll be home soon, really I will.' She could hear him crying down the other end of the line. Oh don't, Rory, don't. I'm in enough pain, don't, please Rory. 'Now Rory, don't start crying. The doctors said I'll be home tomorrow or the next day.'

'Can I come and see you?'

'Not tonight, darling, it's too late. I'm too tired. Let me get some sleep tonight and then Grandad'll bring you in tomorrow.'

Down the line she could hear more sobs, uncontrollable sobs, unconsolable sobs. In the background she could make out Grandad's desperate attempts to comfort the child, without much success.

'Rory, can you hear me? Rory, listen, stop crying. Can you hear me?' A feeble and weak 'yes' came back through all the sniffles and suppressed sobs. 'Rory, if you're a good boy and do exactly what Grandad says, when I come home we'll maybe get a puppy.'

The line went silent.

It was too easy. Rory was no fool, that puppy had been held back for a long time. There's something up. In his own little mind he sensed something was wrong, something was terribly wrong. 'Mummy, are you all right?'

'Of course I am.' I've got an intercostal drain in my upper chest, an intercostal drain in my lower chest, an IV line in both arms, I'm minus three pints of blood and a large chunk of flesh from my left arm. I've never felt better, she thought bitterly as the tears poured freely.

'Mummy, when are you coming home?'

'Tomorrow, Rory, I'll be home tomorrow.'

The Merrion Hospital was built in 1954 on a green field site and brought together a number of decaying inner-city hospitals that had served Dublin over the centuries. It was a centre of excellence where only the highest calibre of medical talent was appointed to consultant level. It was also a teaching hospital where medical students and young doctors trained and there was an associated school of nursing. It pioneered techniques in surgery, liver transplantation, oncology and diagnostic radiology. On Wednesday, 19th February 1997, the hospital was in the middle of a fund-raising campaign to build a new intensive care unit. On that day the ICU of the Merrion Hospital was located on the top of the five-floored building.

When you entered the main hospital entrance, the wards were to the right or left of a wide central dividing corridor with lifts to all floors located in the middle right of the bottom corridor. A stairwell connected to all levels from middle left. There were fire escapes at the back of the main building. The revamped Accident and Emergency department, a relatively recent addition, was located to the left and end of the main original building and connected to it via a narrow corridor. Off that same corridor were radiology services where X-rays and other forms of diagnostic imaging were carried out. Patients entering through Accident and Emergency could be evaluated radiologically, if necessary, before transferring to the wards, saving unnecessary time-wasting and making for an easier 'traffic' flow for those seriously ill or injured.

The ICU on Black Wednesday shouldn't really have been in use at all, it had originally been a storage level. Indeed, on that day, there actually were no formally structured intensive care facilities. The original ICU had been demolished and hospital plans included a new, high-tech, state-of-the-art ICU and recovery room incorporated into the wing currently being built. For a six-month period in 1997 the ICU of the Merrion Hospital was located in converted storage rooms and could only be reached by lift, the stairwell to that floor having been sealed off as part of the ongoing building works.

On the evening of Wednesday, 19th February 1997, a Special Branch officer armed with a Garda issue Smith & Wesson revolver and UZI sub-machine-gun sat a lonely vigil facing the lift. No one could get past and along the corridor behind without being seen. Not only seen, but stopped, identity checked and searched, these strict instructions coming directly from Commissioner Quinlan himself. Detective Sergeant Kate Hamilton was to be guarded at all times, he'd ordered.

Behind the armed officer stretched a thirty-yard corridor. At exactly halfway and to the left, overlooking the back of the building and with a view of the on-going building works, was the current intensive care unit, a twenty foot by twenty foot four-bedded room, each bed surrounded by medical technology. There were monitors for heart tracings, ventilators for artificially breathing those deemed too weak or unwell to breathe spontaneously, IV lines awaiting use and separate screens on which blood pressure levels or respiratory rates could be read immediately. There were tubes for every bodily function, tubes connecting oxygen, other tubes to drain body fluids, tubes running into bottle flasks to collect all body fluids. Whatever fluid drained, it was collected, measured and recorded.

Directly opposite the ICU was another, two-bedded room, the current recovery room. It had once been a store room for all the IV fluids used throughout the hospital: normal saline, glucose, Hartmans, Crystalloid, the like.

Once you entered ICU as a patient you either left via recovery or the mortuary. Further along the corridor, and again in a converted storage room to the right, was the nurses' station. This was a small room, no more than twelve feet square with a desk, telephone and alarm connections to all monitors in both ICU and recovery. A little further along again, towards the closed-off stairwell entrance, was a small room for making tea, coffee and light snacks. There was also a portable TV.

On Black Wednesday, as well as the armed Special Branch officer guarding the lift, there were two nurses on duty, a senior sister, trained in intensive care, and a staff nurse. There was one other girl wearing a nurse's uniform but who also carried an official Garda-issue loaded handgun. She was part of the Special Branch, one of its few female officers. The ICU and recovery room had been cleared of all other patients and only Kate Hamilton occupied a bed.

She was stable and out of danger. Her collapsed lung had re-expanded almost fully and the drains would be removed the next morning but her IV lines would remain up until then, doctor's orders. She was in pain but not as much as the previous evening, she was exhausted, sleeping fitfully, the image of Dean Lynch still haunting her. Those eyes, those hate filled eyes.

At seven o'clock exactly, as Tom Dalzell kicked off for England in the big soccer international only half a mile away, Dean Lynch sat in Donnie's 'wee gem' in the hospital car park. On his knees rested an A4 pad on which he had scribbled names, a list he was preparing. The names were in order of priority of how he would deal with them.

Dean Lynch was planning to settle all scores.

First there was Detective Sergeant Kate Hamilton.

'Her first, definitely,' he muttered in the dark. 'Then it'll be that little bitch on the check-out in the Centra supermarket on Baggot Street.' This unwitting girl had the misfortune to short change him one day and then call the manager when he complained. She'd made a show of him in front of the whole shop. 'Her definitely. Next.'

Then Breda Mullan. 'That bitch, she's another definite. She's annoyed me a few times. Well, she'll live to regret that. No, she'll *die* to regret that.' He smiled to himself at the thought of that little change in emphasis.

'Then that stupid bastard Donnie with his "wee gem". Yes, him too. I'll wrap that chain around his neck and pull on it till his eyes pop out.'

He stopped and thought for a minute, looking out at the lights of the hospital in front of him, noticing in particular those burning brightly on the fifth floor where his first potential victim lay.

'That's where I'm headed,' he whispered to himself. 'I'm just biding my time, waiting for the right moment. I know when to make my move. They'll know all about it, when it's too late and it's all over. I know all about hospitals, especially big hospitals like this one. I've worked in so many, I know them like the back of my hand.' Lynch had the Merrion hospital assessed to the last detail. He knew many of the staff there wouldn't know each other with doctors coming and going every six months as they changed specialities in training. Sometimes doctors left and locum doctors filled in for a few weeks or longer. The regular staff would just get to know somebody and next they were gone. A face might be recognised one day and the following day it could be a different face inside the same white coat. He knew all about hospitals, and he knew this one in particular, he had trained there. He'd performed his first operation there when he first considered wielding a scalpel, opening his first body in its theatre.

He looked up at the lights again. I'm coming back. They don't know it yet, but I'm coming back.

Only this time he was hoping the flesh wouldn't yield, he was hoping she'd put up a fight, sort of make his journey worthwhile.

I'm hoping to make a killing. Tonight. He laughed in the dark at that little gem.

I'm hoping to make a killing. Tonight.

He looked out the window again. Up there, on the fifth floor. See yah later, Detective Sergeant Hamilton.

He turned back to his notepad. Now, who else will I add?

In the dark he smiled his thin smile as he thought of a name and a face. Out of the corner of his eye he noticed a Garda squad car pull up outside the hospital entrance and a familiar-looking figure go inside. He couldn't make him out exactly, not that it mattered, he was well prepared, his plan rehearsed to the finest detail.

There's nothing like careful planning. Meticulous, exact, precise planning. I've never yet had a well-planned operation go wrong. Like the time I strangled the orphanage pet black labrador. Jet his name was, as in jet black. Oh, how she doted on that dog. That bitch who tormented me all my days there, and all my nights since, the tormentress of all my dreams. She terrorised me as a child and came back to haunt me as a man. But I sorted her out once, I got Jet. And I pinned the blame on somebody else and she bought it. In the darkness of the car he relived the memory, savouring again the moments.

He'd saved a few biscuits from the little bit of tea he used to get every night. But he was so hungry in those days, so hungry all the time that he couldn't hold back from nibbling and then finally eating them. Until one particular day.

He'd been put in the dark room again. Dragged, screaming and kicking, and locked inside again for hours despite all his pleadings and begging and crying. She had left him for hours, more hours than usual and more than he could cope with. When she finally let him out she stood watching and smiling, stroking Jet's neck.

So he had saved his biscuits. This time he didn't eat them, despite the hunger that gnawed at his empty belly every day. And a week later, when he'd been forgotten about, he struck.

He lured Jet into the garden shed at the back of the

orphanage and let him nibble on a few broken pieces first. He stroked Jet's neck, just the way she did, gently and caressingly. In the darkness and quiet of the car Lynch could almost hear Jet's breathing, could almost feel the warmth of his breath, the wetness of his tongue on his hand as he nibbled the biscuits. And then, slowly and casually, not so fast to frighten and scare him off, but slowly and deliberately he slipped his hands around Jet's neck. And choked him to death, holding tight until all struggles ceased.

Just like he'd done to Mary Dwyer.

Then he brushed Jet's coat with a pair of gloves and left the gloves back inside Danny Rogers' bedside locker. Danny Rogers used to torture him too. He was tall where Lynch was small, he was strong where Lynch was weak. But Lynch was smart, a lot smarter than Danny Rogers.

And when his black-haired bitch with the white face and long thin bony hands finally found the gloves, boy, did Danny Rogers suffer. In front of the whole orphanage. And all the time Lynch managed to keep a straight face and a surprised look, appearing unruffled, as he watched the blood run down Danny Rogers' legs from the thrashing. That was the beauty of careful planning. You could do something and pin it on somebody else. Like he'd done to Tom Morgan.

It'll be easy, easy to reach her. Careful planning, that's all it takes.

He watched as an ambulance pulled up outside the Accident and Emergency department. It was time to make his move, it was time to go. Hey ho, hey ho, it's off to work I go.

He looked up at the brightly lit fifth-floor area. I'm coming. Look out. I'm coming.

7.20 pm

'There's an armed officer on every floor patrolling constantly. The stairwell at the end of the corridor is sealed off at the next level down. It's been checked a hundred times. No one can get up that way, definitely.'

Jack McGrath was being briefed on the security surrounding Kate Hamilton. Noel Dunne's comments had worried him. He'd been worried enough before Dunne spoke, he was even more worried after. Dunne was rarely wrong. He didn't often offer advice but he hadn't been short with it on the hospital murder hunt, as if he knew the mind of Dean Lynch. But after doing three postmortems on his victims, Noel Dunne knew this was no ordinary murder investigation, he knew the Gardai were chasing a very dangerous and cunning foe, a will o' the wisp, a puff of smoke. Now you see me, now you don't. And right now they didn't.

And that worried Jack McGrath, who had been there from the beginning and had seen the first body, scalpel firmly embedded in the neck. Then he had lost his partner and best friend in the force.

'There's another fifteen plainclothes officers mingling among hospital visitors all the time. The lift and stairwell at each level is guarded. He'd need to be Houdini to try and get past all this.'

McGrath stroked his moustache and walked along the corridor to where Kate Hamilton lay. She tried a weak smile when he came in but he shushed her quiet. 'I'm just checking everything.' She nodded and let her head slip back on the pillow. McGrath walked up and down the corridor twice, checking that the spare doors were well and truly locked and the rooms inside well and truly empty. Finally satisfied he made his way back to Kate Hamilton and slipped something down between the sheets to her hand. 'That'll keep you warm during the night,' he whispered in her ear.

She reached down, felt and acknowledged with a tired nod. 'I'm exhausted, Jack. I'm going to try and get some sleep.' From further down the corridor the commentary on the big match reached her ears. 'Who's winning?'

'England, one nil. I just got a glimpse of it as I looked in.

The girls say it's a great match, they're kicking the lard out of one another already.'

Hamilton tried to smile, then lay back, sighing deeply. She didn't see McGrath's brow furrow. He was still uneasy.

He walked down the corridor. 'I'm going to watch the match down in the canteen. I'll stay in the hospital a while longer.'

The officer at the lift nodded.

7.45 pm

When the ball finally did hit the back of the Irish net a mini riot broke out on the terraces of East Stand. The Gardai on duty were under strict instructions: at the first sign of trouble, go in and go in hard, which is what they did. Riot shields and visors protecting, batons flailing, the rowdy element was first segregated, then cornered and finally bludgeoned into submission. All the TV crews caught the action and there was no disguising the delight of some of the riot squad as they lashed into the Union Jacks.

A fleet of ambulances waited outside to transfer casualties. The first were driven up to the doors of the Accident and Emergency department of the Merrion Hospital just as the teams went in for half-time. Sirens heralded their arrival. Dean Lynch made his way through the car park, waiting briefly until the first were unloaded, some on stretchers. No one paid any attention to the small, dark haired man with the thin, black moustache, bulky framed from the heavy sweaters underneath his new white shirt and tie. When the third ambulance arrived he was there on hand to open the doors and assist the still cursing and swearing and even fighting soccer fans. He chose one who had blood streaming from a head wound and directed him to the waiting room, sitting him down and rushing inside the casualty department for a wadge of cotton wool to stem the flow. Still no one paid the slightest attention to him.

The casualty department resembled a battle ground with

about twenty opposing fans in supporters' colours, in various states of concussion, bleeding and general disarray. Some were squaring up to each other and twelve hospital security men sweated under the lights as they struggled to keep the peace and allow the doctors and nurses to get on with their jobs.

There were sixteen screened-off cubicles occupied with casualties. Nurses ran from one to another with suturing material, cotton wool, bandages, syringes, needles, local anaesthetic, eye pads, the lot. Doctors moved briskly from cubicle to cubicle, assessing, ordering, laying on hands to assist the less experienced staff, trying to gauge time and resources versus the anticipated overall load.

'If this is only half-time what sort of a night are we in for?' one of them voiced out loud. No one dared guess. No one would know until it was all over.

By then it would be too late.

Dean Lynch moved coolly and casually, peering past curtains, pushing his glasses back up on his nose, looking as preoccupied as the rest of the white coated doctors. All anyone could remember later was the small, dark-haired man, with the thin moustache and the glasses. They all agreed he had seemed so pleasant.

It took almost twenty minutes before an opportunity arose. The noise and the lights and the crowds heated the department up quickly and it wasn't long before one of the doctors slipped his white coat off, wiped the sweat from his brow on a rolled up sleeve and went back inside a cubicle to stitch up a deep wound on a baton-scarred head. He never noticed until the next day that his identity badge was missing.

Dean Lynch quietly lifted it off and slipped it inside his own white coat pocket. Then he moved from cubicle to cubicle until he found exactly what he needed, an unattended patient beside a stainless steel trolley on which lay a small instrument tray, in which lay a scalpel handle. It disappeared into his white coat pocket. Lynch had discovered where the nurses went for fresh equipment and, in an unguarded moment, he slipped inside, emerging with a handful of scalpel blades. They were all size twenty-three, the widest and the strongest.

'What's the score?' he asked one of the doctors joining to help, noticing him stuff his Walkman earphones into his pocket.

'One all. Micko equalised just before half-time.'

'Brilliant,' enthused Lynch and he made his way along the corridor, out from the Accident and Emergency department towards the main hospital building. Closer to where Kate Hamilton lay.

8.00 pm

Lesley Cairns hated soccer, hated it. She was one of the few in the country not watching the big match that night. She had gone home to wash her hair and watch a bit of telly. Which is what she was doing at eight o'clock exactly, the Sky news bulletin carrying the latest from around the world, but especially from Ireland. Tommy Malone was dead by his own hand but there was still no sign of Dr Dean Lynch. Police on mainland Britain now did not believe he actually had taken the Stena Line crossing. All reported sightings had been checked carefully and nothing found to suggest he'd left Ireland. Gardai had issued a computer enhanced photo-fit of what Dr Dean Lynch might look like if he tried to disguise himself. And the third photo-fit nearly lifted Lesley Cairns out of her seat.

'That's him,' she almost screamed at the television. 'Oh my God, I'm sure that's him.'

She scrambled in her handbag, finally finding the business card stuck in between her own credit cards. Hands shaking, she dialled the Southampton number. It didn't ring out. She dialled the Hammersmith number. It didn't ring out either. She checked with the operator.

'Quick, please check this quickly. It's very important. Are you sure? Sorry, no I'm sorry, it's just that it's so important.

You're absolutely sure? God!' She hung up and began scanning the telephone book, her hands by now almost uncontrollable. Garda, Garda, Garda . . . here it is. Blackrock. Steadying her trembling fingers just enough, she punched in the numbers and waited for what seemed an eternity.

'Hello, Blackrock Garda station.'

'Look officer, I may be wrong, but . . .'

8.10 pm

The second half was underway with the commentators almost hoarse from trying to shout above the roar of the crowd. It was even Steven all the way with Tom Dalzell shadowed like a hawk by Dinno Regan, Ireland's veteran centre back. 'A man plagued by injuries, though none of them to himself,' as the BBC soccer pundit reported drily. There were plenty of early attempts at goal and some great saves at both ends. It was settling down to become a cracker of a match.

Inside a cubicle in a toilet beside radiology, Dean Lynch carefully cut open the back of the stolen identity badge, holding the plastic in both hands. He gently slid his recent photograph up against the one currently in place and cut the correct shape. He lifted it back and pared a little more away, then checked again. It was perfect. With the merest trace of super-glue he stuck his photo in place, waited until he felt it had dried, then placed the plastic inside its outer cover. It, too, was super-glued back into position. He waited again, this time for almost five minutes by his watch, before checking. It looked perfect. He then clipped the new identity badge onto his pen-stuffed top pocket, flushed the toilet, started humming and unlocked the cubicle door. He washed his hands at the basins, inspecting the result in the mirror. The toilet door unexpectedly opened and another white-coated doctor came in, barely acknowledging Lynch. He began washing his hands at the basins and glanced at Lynch, who was still checking himself.

'It's gonna be a rough night by the looks of things.'

Lynch smiled. 'Yes, it looks like it, doesn't it?'

When the door closed again, Dean Lynch knew he had successfully completed stage one. He emptied his pockets into a small plastic bag and stuffed it behind a radiator. He gently patted the side pocket of his white coat. Scalpel handle, scalpel blade, a few pens and doctor's pocket book, pen torch and patella hammer. He had everything to make his disguise look authentic. He was a careful, meticulous planner.

Unwrapping a size twenty-three scalpel blade from its foil, he admired the light glinting against its steel before snapping it into place on the scalpel handle. Finally he looked back at the mirror above the basins, not quite sure which he admired most. His disguise, or the scalpel.

Don't worry, Dean boyo, they're both important tonight. For stage two.

He cleared his throat and spat into the sink, taking deep breaths in and out. Then he walked over to the toilet door, paused and opened it.

At the official public enquiry chaired by Chief Justice Terence Kearney, Detective Sergeant Tom Delaney of Blackrock Garda Station explained how and why the delay occurred.

The call was logged at 8.12 pm and we immediately scrambled a patrol car and team of officers. There was a manpower shortage that night because so many uniformed Gardai were deployed at the international football match being held in Lansdowne Road Stadium. Also, because of traffic restrictions around the stadium, there was a lot of diverted traffic on the main Rock Road, along Booterstown Avenue, even as far as the Stillorgan dual carriageway. There were four Gardai in the patrol car, including myself. Three of us were armed with standard issue .38 Smith & Wesson handguns. They were loaded and ready for use. We met Lesley Cairns in the car park of the Stillorgan Park Hotel as arranged. It was about eight thirty by then. She was under strict instructions not to go near the flat herself. We proceeded to the apartment complex, arriving at eight forty-two exactly. Exactly, yes exactly. I remember checking the time on the car digital clock.'

8.42 pm

Tom Dalzell came down inside the penalty box and the whole England team appealed for a penalty. The French referee, after a thirty-second pause, pointed to the spot. There was an immediate scramble on the field. 'The fucker dived,' screamed Dinno Regan, but Monsieur Perdieux pretended not to understand. The Irish team, including goalkeeper, crowded around.

As they did, Dean Lynch was walking along the bottom corridor of the Merrion Hospital towards the lifts. In his right hand he held a large orange-coloured hardbacked envelope containing X-rays which he had stolen from the radiology waiting room. Written on the front in thick black felt-tip pen was the name Kate Hamilton. From inside the wards the turned-up TVs recorded the chaos at Lansdowne Road. Patients who were classified as too unwell to even go to the toilet sat up on their beds shouting obscenities at the referee. Those who couldn't shout mouthed while those who couldn't mouth rattled their drip sets.

'Fucking frog!' was the general opinion, followed by 'that bollox Dalzell!' and a number of carefully chosen suggestions as to what would happen to him if the viewers could only get hold of him.

It was unfortunate the excitement spilled out onto the corridors. Unfortunate for Kate Hamilton. Very fortunate for Dean Lynch.

The lower lift went unguarded for only a minute as the armed Special Branch officer had a quick peek at the nearest TV. And one minute was all Dean Lynch needed. He was inside the lift and had punched the button for level five within those few unguarded seconds.

LEVEL FIVE IS OUT OF ACCESS UNTIL FURTHER

NOTICE. The message, written in thick red felt-tip pen, was held firmly in place with sellotape. Lynch acknowledged with a smile, watching as lights lit up when each level was reached.

'We reached the front door of the flat at about 8.45, certainly within minutes. We could hear the TV on inside so we rang the bell three times in quick succession. I think we waited a minute, then we hammered loudly. Then Ms Cairns opened the door with her company keys. We were all inside within seconds. I remember exactly the time we finished searching because the match commentator on the TV was going on about the Irish team still protesting about the penalty award. It was Detective Sergeant Nolan who noticed the hair-dye material and scribbled diagram of the Merrion Hospital.'

'What did you do then?' asked the Chief Justice.

'I telephoned the Merrion Hospital immediately.'

8.47 pm

The penalty area had been cleared and the players restrained from taking further chunks out of one another. Another mêlée on the terraces settled as fans watched the unfolding drama on the field. Tom Dalzell was squaring up to take the penalty. In the commentary boxes reporters spoke in muted tones as the stadium hushed. Even the Irish supporters quietened with only an occasional voice from the terraces trying desperately to distract.

The lift to level five opened and out stepped Dean Lynch.

Protection duty in any police force is boring. Gardai Special Branch detectives on regular protection duty often complain about the boredom. 'It's ninety-nine per cent boredom, only very occasionally relieved by one per cent excitement.' The difficult part with protection duty is trying to decide when that one per cent of action is likely to arise.

It proved too difficult for the officer on duty at the lift on Black Wednesday at exactly 8.49 pm. He was listening to the match on a Walkman, ear plugs firmly in place, heart racing as he tried to imagine the scene and excitement on the pitch and in the stadium. The radio commentator had his listeners worked up to a frenzy. 'Dalzell definitely dived. It's an outrage, a disgrace, the most disgraceful piece of refereeing I've seen in years. We can see it here clearly on the action replay and it's obvious to anyone with two good eyes in his head that Dalzell dived. The referee was miles away and the linesman didn't lift his flag either. It's really quite disgraceful.'

'And you had difficulty getting through to the hospital?'
'Yes. It took nearly a minute for an operator to reply.'
'But that's not long really in a busy hospital.'
'I'm afraid it was, your Honour, on the night in question. I asked to be put through immediately to the ICU.'
'And?'
'The line was engaged.'
'Was there only one line to the whole of ICU?' The Chief Justice found this very hard to believe.
'On the night in question, yes.'
'How long did it stay engaged?'
'I believe, in total, it was almost seven minutes.'

It was eight. The sister in charge was discussing with the senior casualty surgeon on duty the possibility of allowing one serious head wound up to the ward from Accident and Emergency. She blocked the move. 'We have strict instructions to keep this floor clear until that detective is transferred. She's our main responsibility. If anything happens to her I may as well commit suicide.'

Lynch was given only a cursory inspection at the lift. He flashed the X-rays at the Special Branch man, pulling one out for effect.

'Have to check her chest drain,' he mouthed, noticing the

Walkman. His identity badge was noted, his pockets frisked. The scalpel handle and blade went unnoticed, stuck down the spine of one of the pocket books. He was nodded on. Lynch smiled acknowledgement and turned down the corridor. To his delight he discovered it empty, the only noise coming from a TV.

'What did you do then?'
'I immediately telephoned HQ in Harcourt Square and asked for the mobile phone number of the officers on duty at the hospital.'
'How long did that take to get.'
'About a minute, maybe two.'

8.51 pm

Dalzell's rocket penalty shook the cross bar and rebounded onto the back of Dinno Regan's neck who was standing with his back to goal, unable to watch. An English foot stabbed the ball back goal-wards and suddenly the penalty area was a mass of scrambling, seething, flashing boots and arms. The terraces erupted and TV cameras flashed from one area to another, the commentators unable to keep up with action on and off the field.

At that exact time, on level five of ICU, the sister was still on the phone and the nurse and female Special Branch officer were glued to the TV.

Dean Lynch was inside the intensive care unit.

For a moment he just stared at the figure in the bed, the only figure in the four-bedded ICU. The other three beds were empty. The head was heavily bandaged and there were two IV lines connected to arms that were covered by bedclothes. Two tubes reached to the chest level, one showing blood-red fluid draining. An oxygen mask was strapped to the face and the gentle hiss of the gas could be heard.

Dean Lynch smiled.

The figure didn't move as he entered and still didn't stir as he approached. A pity, he thought briefly, no fight. What a pity.

He reached inside his pocket and slipped out the pocket book, dropping the scalpel onto his free right hand. A glint of light danced briefly off the wide stainless steel blade. Gripping the handle firmly he edged closer, glancing quickly at the door to ensure he wouldn't be disturbed. He could see the mist on the face mask, the blood-red staining on the head bandage, the jet-black hair beneath the bandage.

With one vicious and decisive stroke, he slit the throat deeply.

The tailor's dummy head came off its body. It rolled off the pillow and bounced onto the floor, coming to a rest at Lynch's feet. He stood there, mesmerised, scalpel still in hand.

Then it hit him. *The bitch! She's outwitted me!*

Then he noticed the small receiver attached to the head, flashing red. As in red for danger.

The receiver had been primed to set off all alarms. Every officer on duty at the hospital had one and as each alarm pierced, for a split second those who heard it looked up in astonishment.

Then they ran.

From all corners of the hospital they ran, but particularly from in front of the lift and from the TV room on level five. Three entered the corridor in time to see the white coat tail of the small, bulky man with dark hair and thin, black moustache disappear into recovery.

Where the real Kate Hamilton lay. Expecting him. Her alarm had gone off too, she knew he was coming.

He was inside the room, and had slipped the lock. Outside he heard shouts and the sound of running feet along the corridor. A smile flickered across his lips.

Their eyes met.

And there she was again. Elizabeth Anne Duggan, with

her black hair pulled back severely, revealing her white face, one long thin bony hand resting on the bedclothes. Elizabeth Anne Duggan, his torturer, his tormentress.

The pounding on the doors only worked him up more, sounding so much like his own fists pounding against that door he knew so well in the orphanage, the under-stairs room. His dark room, his personal dungeon, his private hell.

It would end now, finally, with *her* death, no matter what happened to him. He didn't care if he died. He didn't care how he died, so long as she came with him.

He threw off his glasses to get a better look at his victim. And once again Kate Hamilton stared into the eyes of death. Eyes full of hate, full of rage. Full of evil. Full of intent. To kill.

As the first splintering of wood sounded on the locked door, he smiled slowly and lifted the scalpel above his head. 'Goodbye bitch.'

The pain in her chest from the two drains restricted her, but Kate Hamilton still managed to point Jack McGrath's personal revolver in Lynch's general direction and fire off one round. The bullet entered his right chest, tearing a hand's-breadth hole in the lung, and stopping him in mid-flight. He staggered back against the wall.

Outside the door was crashed against, the lock slowly giving. More wood splintered, the shouts became desperate.

Hamilton managed a second round but it drilled into the wall harmlessly. The pain in her chest seared and she struggled to sit up and get a better aim.

Lynch lay slumped, half on his knees, half on the floor, fighting desperately for air. Every strained breath only filled his lungs with blood, obstructing them more. He sensed the room becoming dark. He looked up again and there was Miss Duggan still. Sitting up on bed, smiling at him.

Kate Hamilton grabbed at the bars of the bed head with her left hand and pointed the gun weakly in his direction again. She could feel her strength ebb, the gun becoming like a dead weight. She felt it slip from her grasp and she looked desperately at the door. She could hear the voices, the pounding. The lock giving, but not given.

And Lynch was looking at her.

At his Miss Duggan. And she was smiling at him. 'You can sleep in hell now, Dean Lynch,' he heard her say. 'You can sleep in hell.'

With an animal howl he exhausted his dying strength and staggered to his feet, blood streaming from mouth and nose. The scalpel swung in an arc through the air as he lurched towards the bed.

'Biiitttcccchhhh!'

The scalpel cut through the thin cotton sheet and Dean Lynch's dying body propelled it further.

The gurglings and grunts were the only noises Jack McGrath heard when the door finally gave way. They came from the lungs of Dean Lynch, whose body lay across Kate Hamilton, the scalpel firmly embedded between her legs. In the blood stained mattress. Not in her body.

She had collapsed from the effort and pain. But she was alive.

Dean Lynch was dead. At last.

He had gone to whatever peace his tortured soul might claim, he had fled from every Miss Duggan who'd ever tormented him.

'Sweet Jesus!' was all Jack McGrath could remember saying.

Day 11

It was, by any standards, an extraordinary morning. As Noel Dunne and Jack McGrath discussed sometime later, it seemed unreal, unbelievable, fantastic. A media circus.

Every journalist and reporter and TV crew in the city was diverted to cover the transfer of the body of Dean Lynch from the mortuary of the Merrion Hospital to the city morgue. At one point there were five privately chartered helicopters in the air, cameramen hanging precariously out of their sides, recording every move. The event was beamed live and direct on CNN and Sky, with the morning television programmes on BBC and ITV interrupted repeatedly to 'go to the scene'. In an unprecedented move RTE decided to run the event live as well and the nation came to a standstill to watch. It was one of the most dramatic events ever recorded live on television, the transfer of the body of the most evil and mentally deranged man in modern Irish criminal history. It pushed reports on the drawn football match right off the agenda.

The decision to transfer the body to the city morgue was for operational reasons. Dr Noel Dunne already had two other 'patients' awaiting his investigation. 'I'm not going out to the Merrion Hospital in the full view of every photographer and TV crew in the country to perform that postmortem. It's crazy and I'm not doing it. Bring him in here.'

There was little stomach for discussion or argument. The

413

body would be transferred. The assistant state pathologist was on her way up from Cork. Noel Dunne didn't much fancy spending all day and all night working.

Lynch's body was wheeled out on a trolley inside a black zip-up body bag and transferred to a waiting unmarked Garda estate wagon. The transfer took place at the back of the hospital mortuary, well away from the lenses and eyes of the waiting photographers and journalists who were held back by a heavy uniformed Gardai cordon. Only the helicopter crews captured that moment.

With two squad cars at front and back and four motorcycle outriders, the estate made its way along Merrion Road, down Shelbourne Road, across the Liffey arriving outside the opened double gates of the city morgue at 10.17 am. There was a second heavy Gardai presence around the building, all journalists, reporters, photographers and cameramen kept well back and behind crash barriers. As the estate wagon pulled in there were flashes from cameras, shouts from reporters and general mayhem as they vied for the best angle, the best viewpoint. Above, the whirling of helicopter blades added to the drama, their cameramen recording the unloading of the body onto a different trolley and it disappearing inside the morgue itself. The crews were enraged when they discovered they couldn't record anything else, the opaque ripple glass on the roof impervious to their lenses.

Inside Noel Dunne oversaw the lifting of the body onto the last autopsy table. The other two were already occupied. Dan Harrison stood by, Nikon at the ready, face as expressionless as usual. Pat Relihan waited for the nod to fingerprint. There were seven white boiler-suited ballistics men leaning against benches. The rest of the room was crowded with Gardai, uniformed and Special Branch. They spread out to allow Dunne to move freely.

'Dan?'

Dan Harrison looked up, his thoughts suddenly disturbed.

'Dan, I'd like an overall shot of the three from a number of angles. Try and get in some of the background, uniforms and the like. I've a feeling we're going to need to record this little event for posterity.'

Harrison moved slowly around the room, looking for the best angles. Those watching shuffled to the side as he approached. Then the flashes began.

FLASH!

He moved to another corner.

FLASH!

And another.

FLASH!

'Take one of me in the middle, looking down at this fellow.' Dunne stood between tables two and three, making a show of inspecting the body.

FLASH!

In this way was the scene captured and later shown at the official public enquiry. A crowded city morgue with its three autopsy tables fully occupied.

On the first, with a plastic ID tag hanging around her right big toe, lay Betty Nolan, the telephone cable still tight around her neck. Her lifeless eyes stared up, as if straining to see the helicopters hovering above. On the second table lay Tommy Malone, his face and back of head totally disfigured, features distorted. Only the plastic name tag around his right big toe gave a clue as to his identity. And on the last table lay a black zip-up body bag.

'Okay, open it up,' ordered Dunne.

The zips came down in one movement, like the blade of a scalpel slicing. Three attendants, wearing plastic overalls and double surgical gloves, lifted the body up as Noel Dunne pulled the body bag away. They gently laid him back on the table.

There it was, finally. The body of Dean Lynch, still in his hospital whites. White coat, white shirt and muted tie. He was still dark haired with his thin black moustache, but no clear lens glasses perched on his nose. The whiteness was heavily stained by blood. And the wild eyes that had cast so much fear, that reflected so much evil and hate and anger and betrayal. The eyes of death that Kate Hamilton had stared into, not once, but twice, were lifeless.

The tortured soul had fled. Only the body remained as testimony to his living. The spirit that had moved him, that pushed him to such extremes, that urged on his revenge, that drove his tormented mind to drive his tormented body to such destruction had gone.

Noel Dunne looked down at him, gradually noticing Jack McGrath at his side. The two said nothing, their fleeting eye exchange was enough.

Dunne turned to the audience. 'The forensic postmortem always begins with an external inspection of the body,' he began for the benefit of the younger Gardai assembled. He paused and looked along the three autopsy tables. 'The only question is, which one to start on today?'

Jack McGrath almost managed a grin.

'Well,' continued Dunne robustly, 'let's start in the order they came in. We'll start with the female.'

And the audience turned to Betty. Leaving the lifeless eyes of Tommy Malone and Dean Lynch to stare at the ceiling.

The sound of Rory's feet on the corridor and his excited screams finally penetrated Kate Hamilton's consciousness just after four o'clock that afternoon. She had woken, briefly, three hours earlier but was so distressed and agitated it required ten milligrams of Valium by injection to settle her. She dreamed she was being chased by Dean Lynch along a dimly lit corridor. Each time she looked over her shoulder she saw his hate filled eyes, blood-streaked face and hands, the scalpel clutched and swinging at her retreating back. As fast as she tried to run her legs felt more and more leaden and she sensed him gain and close in. She could almost feel his breath on her neck. In the dream she rounded one corner, then another, finally coming up against a closed door. Her desperate hands pulled and dragged at the handle but they too seemed useless, powerless. Suddenly the handle gave and she pulled the door open. There stood

Dean Lynch, waiting, thin evil smile across blood-smeared face, scalpel in right hand held in the air. 'Goodbye, bitch.' The scalpel swung viciously down and pierced her right upper chest. The pain seared and she sat forward in the bed, screaming.

'It's all right, Kate, it's all right,' the nurses tried to comfort. The pain was real but came from the intercostal drains being removed. She had to be restrained in the bed and coaxed and consoled. But still her agitation wouldn't settle. As the injection took effect she relaxed enough to allow the doctors to remove the second drain and both IV lines. She relaxed enough to understand that the nightmare was over, that Dean Lynch was dead. That she really was alive. A nurse held her trembling body until sleep, mercifully, took over again.

Rory's feet, Rory's voice, Grandad's shushing pleas finally entered her consciousness, stirring her awake. She slowly became aware of the murmuring of voices. She felt, for the first time, a hand holding her own. It was a man's hand, she sensed that. It was a big hand, a strong hand, holding on to her own in handshake fashion. The grip wasn't firm but comforting. The hand felt strong, secure, rock steady. The thumb of the hand gently stroked the base of her own thumb. It was a comforting caress. The overwhelming feeling was one of control, care, reassurance. Affection. She opened her eyes slowly and found Paddy Holland.

'Hi,' he said.

'She's awake, Grandad, she's awake.' Rory was on the bed and allowed to hold her and kiss her and cuddle against her still-aching chest. Even though her tears would not stop this time they were tears of joy, of happiness, of relief. The nightmare was over. And even though Paddy Holland tried gently to remove his hand twice he found himself held tight. Don't let go of me. Ever.

'Mummy, Mr Holland has a puppy. He says he'll let me come to his house and play with it.'

Grandad watched from the foot of the bed. He watched

the hands that held each other and seemed not to want to release. He listened to the exchanges.

'I'm going to go down to the canteen to get a cup of tea.' He leaned down and kissed his only daughter on the forehead, his eyes telling her not to say anything, not to disturb this moment. As he slipped out the door he glanced back at the scene. Rory had cuddled up against his mother and with her left hand she was stroking his face, running her hands through his hair. He had his thumb in his mouth, Ted in his other hand. He was contented again. He had his mother. And Kate Hamilton was still holding tightly to the hand that held just as tightly to her right hand.

Three miles away in the ICU of the Central Maternity Hospital, Gordon O'Brien had his mother as well. He was content again, he could feel her caress, hear her heart beat, smell her body. In his own little way he too felt the nightmare was over.

Paddy Holland had allowed Sandra and Big Harry to lift their baby for short spells at a time. 'He's doing really well, fantastically well,' he'd said earlier. 'We just don't want to overtire him. He's got a lot of catching up to do and I don't want him rushed.' Sandra and Big Harry had nodded. They were barely able to contain the joy and relief at their child's remarkable recovery. They hardly dared believe the nightmare was over lest some other evil hands would come to snatch him away again.

The IV lines were still in place on his arms and he was still connected to the monitors but he was now alert, if very weak. He was even opening his eyes and looking around every now and then. Holland had inserted a naso-gastric tube, a line leading directly into the child's stomach, so that he could be fed. He was still too weak to suck but showing definite signs of hunger. The sunken eyes and shrunken belly had gone and his skin texture was looking much healthier. The small seven-pound baby that Sandra O'Brien had fed and winded and changed on the night Tommy Malone came to steal him was indeed recovering. His drowsy eyes showed signs of sparkle, his limbs felt stronger when they moved.

'I'll tell you this,' Holland had commented admiringly, 'he's a real battler. He started life fighting and he's continued life fighting.' He had smiled at Sandra and Big Harry as they listened. 'And he's only eleven days old. What a start to life. What a baby.'

It was almost as if the child had understood Holland's words for at that very moment he let out the first cry to be heard since he'd arrived in hospital. Sandra had rushed to him and kissed his cheek and forehead and hands. 'Shush my pet, shush. Mummy's here, everything's fine, Mummy's here.' Big Harry had gone over and stood beside the crouched figure of his wife and lain a hand on her shoulder. She reached one hand back and held him. Her other hand was rested on the side of the incubator, fingers gently stroking at her baby's cheek.

'Mr O'Brien?' Big Harry turned around to find the sister in charge of ICU standing with a tray of tea and sandwiches. 'Take a break the two of you,' she advised. 'You've hardly eaten a thing all day.' She set the tray down on a chair and began pouring. 'You'll have to keep your own strength up, you know. When that wee boy gets on his feet he'll be a handful, I'm telling you. Eat up.' She placed a cup of tea in one of Sandra's hands and stuck a toasted cheese sandwich in the other. 'There's more if you want some. Just give a nod, I'll be along the corridor.' Then she was gone.

Sandra and Big Harry wolfed the food down, surprised at how hungry they were. They looked at one another for a moment and allowed their eyes to rest. Then Big Harry took the cup from Sandra's hand and laid it down gently on the floor so as not to disturb his sleeping baby boy. He took Sandra in his arms and held her, feeling her sob gently against his chest. He kissed the tears from her eyes and lifted her face so that he could see her better.

'It's all right, Sandra,' he said. 'It's all over.' They both turned and stared down at their baby, now stirring awake again and beginning to whimper with hunger. Sandra took one of his small hands in her own and held it gently.

Looking through the ICU window, Theo Dempsey allowed himself a smile for the first time in what seemed like ages.

Epilogue

Tom Morgan resigned from the Central Maternity Hospital and left the country. The *Daily Post* tracked him down to a small country town in Western Australia and ran a tabloid style exclusive: STUD MORGAN'S PLACE IN THE SUN.

Luke Conway continued as Master of the great Central Maternity Hospital and did see it safely into its two hundredth birthday celebrations. He made sure the two vacant posts in the staff were filled by female consultants, breaking the male-dominated tradition for the first time.

Sam Collins recovered from his injuries in time to be sentenced, along with Peggy Ryan, to a twenty-year gaol stretch for their part in the kidnapping of Gordon O'Brien. As he handed down the sentence the trial judge saved most of his condemnation for Ryan. She barely heard a word he said, spending most of the time talking to herself.

Tommy Malone's funeral was attended by a small number of fellow criminals and he was buried in a little known graveyard in north county Dublin. No one erected a headstone.

The body of Dean Lynch lay unclaimed in the city morgue for almost two months before the state ordered its cremation. Noel Dunne scattered the ashes into the foaming seas off Howth Head one stormy April evening. He was watched by Jack McGrath and the two retired afterwards to a nearby pub where they drank the best part of a half bottle of Jamesons 1790 whiskey between them.

June Morrison returned to work in the Central Maternity Hospital in May and was appointed Matron six weeks later.

Kate Hamilton left the Garda Siochana after a series of relapses in her recovery. The *Daily Post* ran a story in July: MURDER COP'S ROMANCE, accompanied by two photographs. One showed Hamilton strolling arm in arm with Paddy Holland in Dublin's Herbert Park. The second caught Rory chasing after a small dog.

Gordon Henry Donal O'Brien was christened in September in the big church on Roundwood main street. June Morrison and Theo Dempsey were the godparents. It was a wonderfully warm and sunny day and the village looked at its best. Hanging baskets still carried late-flowering blooms and the tubs and troughs in the street were filled with plants and shrubs. At the family's request the media stayed outside the church railings and in return for their cooperation Big Harry promised a fifteen-minute photo-call after the ceremony.

As the cold water was poured along his brow, Gordon O'Brien's arms and legs threshed in protest and he cried forcefully. June Morrison listened and smiled.

Outside, in the sunshine, film crews from national and international networks waited patiently to record the occasion, while the newsprint photographers, as usual, fought with each other for the best shots. While they waited one or two shot off a roll of film catching the early browning of the surrounding trees, the first fall of leaves blowing gently in the breeze across the gravel in front of the church door.

Just before the congregation left in a fleet of limousines for the celebratory lunch in Beechill, Harry and Sandra O'Brien posed for the cameras. The image was flashed around the world that evening. It showed a big, grey curly haired man impeccably dressed in a dark navy pin-striped suit, white shirt and red tie with a white kerchief flowing from his breast pocket. He had one arm resting proudly on the shoulder of his beautiful young wife. She was wearing a cream-coloured Irish lace two-piece trouser suit set off with wide brimmed hat. In her right arm she cradled a baby, wrapped in a shawl with only a tiny wisp of hair showing above the lace. The baby was wide awake and smiling up at his mother.

'Show us the baby, Sandra, show us the baby,' one of the photographers shouted.

Big Harry pulled the lace shawl down from his son's face while Sandra moved him into both her arms and turned so that the lenses of the world could get a better view.

Gordon O'Brien stared at the cluster of cameras now trained on him, fascinated by the whirring of their shutters. As his head moved from side to side the photographers and cameramen captured a bonny looking baby with wispy dark hair, long dark eyelashes and deep blue eyes. His skin was healthy and pink, his eyes bright and alert.

He looked content.

He was in his mother's arms and he knew her touch, sensed her smell, heard her voice. All the shouting and roaring, all the curses and anger had ceased. All the pain and hunger and cold and misery had gone.

'Come on, Gordon,' a voice yelled. 'Give us a smile.'

FLASH!

FLASH!

FLASH!

Gordon O'Brien smiled to the world.

ALSO AVAILABLE IN PAPERBACK

Still Water	John Harvey	£5.99
Rogue Element	Terence Strong	£5.99
The Reluctant Investigator	Frank Lean	£5.99
The Last Don	Mario Puzo	£5.99
A Passion So Deadly	Hilary Bonner	£5.99
Truth or Dare	Sara Sheridan	£5.99
The Riddle of St Leonards	Candace Robb	£5.99
Silence of the Lambs	Thomas Harris	£5.99

ALL ARROW BOOKS ARE AVAILABLE THROUGH MAIL ORDER OR FROM YOUR LOCAL BOOKSHOP AND NEWSAGENT.

PLEASE SEND CHEQUE/EUROCHEQUE/POSTAL ORDER (STERLING ONLY) ACCESS, VISA, MASTERCARD, DINERS CARD, SWITCH OR AMEX.

☐☐☐☐☐☐☐☐☐☐☐☐☐☐☐☐

EXPIRY DATE .... SIGNATURE ....

PLEASE ALLOW 75 PENCE PER BOOK FOR POST AND PACKING U.K.

OVERSEAS CUSTOMERS PLEASE ALLOW £1.00 PER COPY FOR POST AND PACKING.

ALL ORDERS TO:
ARROW BOOKS, BOOKS BY POST, TBS LIMITED, THE BOOK SERVICE, COLCHESTER ROAD, FRATING GREEN, COLCHESTER, ESSEX CO7 7DW.

NAME ....

ADDRESS ....

....

Please allow 28 days for delivery. Please tick box if you do not wish to receive any additional information ☐

Prices and availability subject to change without notice.